DARK DAWN

II

THE EXLIAN SYNDROME SERIES

BOOKS BY SETH RING

THE EXLIAN SYNDROME SERIES

Advent

Dark Dawn

Apex (coming in 2025)

Evolution (coming in 2025)

Shattered Glory (coming in 2026)

Light's Ascension (coming in 2026)

THE IRON TYRANT SERIES

Chain of Feathers

Crow's Fortune

Healing Skies

THE SOUL CALLER SERIES

Soul Caller 1

Soul Caller 2

THE DREAMER'S THRONE SERIES

Dreamer's Throne 1

Dreamer's Throne 2

Dreamer's Throne 3

Dreamer's Throne 4

THE NOVA TERRA SERIES

Mad Master Alchemist

THE TOWER SERIES

Forgemaster

Reforged

Arcanist

Ignition

Bloodline

Avatar

Challenger

THE BATTLE MAGE FARMER SERIES

Domestication

Germination

Cultivation

Fermentation

Transformation

Preservation

Separation

Conservation

Culmination

THE TITAN SERIES

Nova Terra: Titan

Nova Terra: Greymane

Nova Terra: Kingbreaker

Nova Terra: Guardian

Nova Terra: Liberator

Nova Terra: Earthshaper

Nova Terra: Stormbringer

Nova Terra: Stone King

Nova Terra: Catalyst

Nova Terra: Worldbearer

DARK DAWN

THE EXLIAN SYNDROME SERIES

II

DETECTED

SETH RING

TESS | 0000002

BLACKSTONE PUBLISHING

Published in 2025 by Blackstone Publishing
Cover and book design by Larissa Ezell

Printed in the United States of America
Originally published in hardcover by Blackstone Publishing in 2025

First paperback edition: 2025
ISBN 979-8-8746-9485-2
Fiction / LitRPG (Literary Role-Playing Game)

Version 1

Blackstone Publishing
31 Mistletoe Rd.
Ashland, OR 97520

www.BlackstonePublishing.com

DARK DAWN

II

THE EXLIAN SYNDROME SERIES

1

"Its heart is three inches deeper than you would expect because of the expanded chest cavity."

With a squelch, Mark's fingers pierced through the skin of the half-frozen alien corpse stretched out on the table as his mentor, Abrams, directed him from the side. It was a brutish-looking thing, eight feet tall and packed with muscles. It appeared humanoid, though with four massive arms that now hung loosely over the edges of the table. It was so big that Mark had been forced to climb up onto the table to access its chest, and he was currently perched with one leg on a stool and his knee next to the hulk's ribs as he made his incisions.

"Unlike the hunters, which are the more common type of ghoul, hulks are focused entirely on strength. They'll rip apart solid steel with their bare hands. That doesn't mean they're slow, however, so be careful if you ever run into them."

Carefully peeling back the skin he had sliced open, Mark's fingers danced across the corpse's chest, neatly severing the muscle from bone. Ever since he had picked up the bone blade genetic memory from the Exlian mantis, Mark's efficiency when practicing alchemical butchering had risen drastically, and he barely felt any resistance as he dug into the monster's body.

Exlian were a weird type of organism, and while most of them were insectile in their biology, many had both internal skeletons and exoskeletons. The Exlian that Mark was currently butchering was made of flesh like a human, though its skin was quite a bit thicker, which provided a level of natural armor. As he located the heart, set deep in the chest cavity, Mark memorized its position, using other organs and the creature's skeleton as reference points.

Once he had a good grasp of its position, Mark cut it free, his fingers acting like scalpels as he worked his way around the heart. The last things to separate were the main veins that fed into the heart, and as he pulled it out, a thick drop of black blood dripped out and slid off his hand. Hopping down from the table, he placed the heart on a tray and wiped his hands off with a cloth.

"Are these the only two variants of this kind of Exlian?" he asked, gesturing to the smaller hunter variant that was hung by a hook at the side of the workshop.

"No, there are others too. Specifically, a screamer and what's called a brain," Abrams said, examining the heart Mark had just retrieved. "The Exlian in this category are called ghouls, after the mythical undead creatures, and we've identified four separate mutations, though there could well be more. Your deployment is heading north, which is where they're most commonly seen, so be on the lookout. Their sense of smell is rather extreme, and they are absolutely relentless—I once had a ghoul track me across close to three hundred miles of wilderness. Really, the only saving grace is that they don't move in waves, though they have been known to gather in large packs."

Pleased with the quality of the heart, he gave Mark a nod. "This is good. Next time, be a little bit more careful when you're cutting around the valves to try and make sure you keep all the heart blood. You can go ahead and get cleaned up."

Abrams carried the tray with the Exlian hulk's heart on it to the cold storage while Mark set a hook in the massive corpse and winched it up into the air. Steadying the swaying body, he pulled it over to where the hunter was hanging and grabbed the smaller Exlian ghoul's leg. After taking the hunter's and hulk's carcasses back to their places in the warehouse, he returned to the workshop.

He wiped the table and all the nearby surfaces, cleaned the clamps he had used to hold the monster's body in place, and then turned off the heat lamps, causing the temperature to fall immediately. As the cold rushed in around him, Mark headed for the alchemy lab to check on the potions he had in progress. It had been two weeks since he had gotten his assignment to the Engineering Corps, and Mark had spent almost every minute of his free time training his alchemy and martial arts. Of course, he still had his work with Abrams, and it had ramped up as well as his master tried to stuff his head full of knowledge about the Exlian who lived in the mountains north of the city.

After examining a couple of fermenting potions, Mark went over to the assessment machine to check on a potion he had finished the evening before. The potion should have been a dark-yellow color, but instead it was bright yellow, almost neon. Trying to read over the report the assessment machine spat out, Mark sighed. His mind simply wasn't in it. He was supposed to be reporting to the headquarters of the Black Mountain Battalion the following day for his first introduction to his new squad, and he found himself surprisingly nervous.

A buzz jerked him from his thoughts, and accepting the incoming call, Mark saw Noah's handsome face pop up on the virtual screen that hovered above his watch.

"You deploy tomorrow, right?"

"Nice to see you too," Mark said, cracking a smile. "But yes,

I'll go meet with the members of the battalion for the first time tomorrow, and then we leave a day or two after. Why, what's up?"

"Now that you finally got your assignment, we should celebrate," Noah said. "I've rented out a club for us—not one my family owns, don't worry, but a private place in the city center. The entire team will be there, and I've invited Sky too."

Surprised but pleased, Mark shook his head. "Hey, you didn't have to do that."

"It's not just for you. We've all got things to celebrate, or things to distract ourselves from. It'd be good to catch up before you leave."

Nodding, Mark swiped a finger, opening up his calendar and quickly entering the event into it. For a moment, he was distracted by the large block of red that stretched indefinitely into the future. It still hadn't sunk in fully that he would be leaving the city for an indeterminate amount of time. Never in a hundred years had Mark imagined he would be deployed into the wilderness with the Engineering Corps . . . but that was what fate had in store for him, and he wasn't ready to give up his dreams of the military quite yet.

Realizing that Noah was saying something to him, Mark refocused on the conversation just in time to see Noah nod and sign off. Hopefully, it hadn't been important. Glancing down at the readout in his hand, Mark sighed again and put it down on the table. Alchemy, like the alchemical butchering he was learning from Abrams, required absolute focus, something Mark simply didn't have at the moment.

Half an hour later, when Mark stepped out of the warehouse, the last glimmers of the day's sun dyed the horizon red and orange. The sky was clear, and the moon was already high in the sky, a giant silver coin that filled the world with an air of mystery. As he walked up to the train station, Mark chuckled. It hadn't been that long ago that paying for a train ride had been a dicey thing. Now, he could afford as many train rides as he wanted.

In the last year, his life had been upended at least a dozen times. He had reached his lifelong goal of becoming naturally empowered, joining the ranks of those who wielded supernatural abilities. He had made it into one of the military camps and graduated with honors. He had also gained a master in an incredibly valuable trade and was becoming proficient as an alchemical butcher. Leveraging the abilities his empowerment had given him, he had begun to learn alchemy, completely erasing the money problems that had plagued him for so long.

Not everything had been wonderful, however, and Mark couldn't help but frown as his brother, Joe, intruded on his thoughts. The doors to the train opened with a hiss. Mark stepped on, looking around for a seat. The train car was crowded with workers returning home after their shifts, so he opted to stand, planting himself by a window. A faint chime sounded as the doors closed and the train began to move. Glancing down at his wrist, Mark triggered his activator and saw his status sheet pop up.

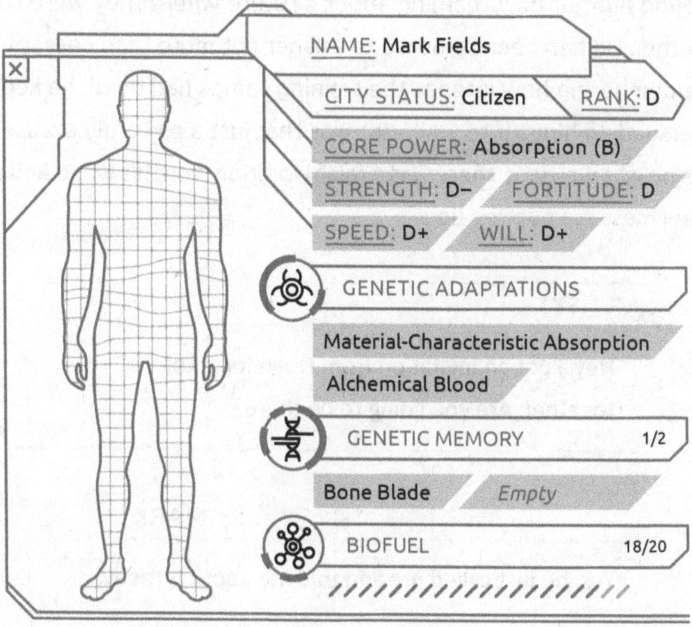

His status hadn't improved since his days in the training camp, though Mark could feel himself continually growing. But even as he stared at his status, trying to distract himself, thoughts of his brother continually returned to his mind. There had been no contact since Joe had fled with the other members of the so-called Green Line terrorist group, and Mark couldn't help but worry. Joe's deployments as a Ranger, facing down the Exlian threat outside the city, had been dangerous, but being at odds with the city itself, on the run and forced to hide in his own hometown, was another level of danger entirely.

Feeling a faint pang in his chest, Mark opened his watch to distract himself, scrolling through his last messages with Sky. It had been a few days since he had seen her, as she was exceptionally busy with her training. She had almost finished the first training camp and was getting better at controlling her power every day, which made him happy and even a little proud. After all, her flight ability had come from him. Though he didn't see her as often these days, Mark felt like he and Sky were growing closer, and he occasionally found himself daydreaming about a future where they were together. He had been tempted to ask her out more than once, but remembering how intense the training camps had been, he kept persuading himself to wait. But was that just a cowardly excuse? As he was waffling, there was a faint vibration from his wrist, and a new message popped up.

SKY

Hey, I got an invitation from Noah for a get-together. Are you going to be there?

MARK

Yes, he just called me and told me about it today.

SKY

Great, then I'll see you there. I've missed hanging out!

Suddenly feeling a lot more cheerful, Mark turned his attention to the city flashing by outside the windows. When the train arrived at his stop, he exited with the other passengers and walked the few blocks to his house. The sun had vanished below the horizon, taking its last vestiges of daytime with it, and darkness shrouded the streets.

Though few of the streetlamps worked, Mark didn't mind the darkness. There was something comforting about the deep shadows, something that called to him. Spotting a poster on a nearby wall, Mark stopped to read it. It was a warning about Exlian sightings. Many of the areas on the outskirts of the city had been seeing increased Exlian activity, and the poster and many others like it had been put up to warn residents to stay inside at nighttime.

Though he was well aware of just how dangerous the Exlian were, Mark was confident that he'd be able to deal with any Exlian that managed to make it through the city's defenses. A fifteen-minute walk took him to the home where he had grown up. After not one but two break-ins, he'd been staying with Abrams at the warehouse, but since he was about to leave the city with the Black Mountain Battalion, he'd wanted to come back home to pack up a few things. Punching in his code, he heard the whir of the lock and a smooth click as it opened. Like the rest of the house, the front door had been badly damaged in the fight that led to Joe fleeing, so Mark had had it replaced when the house was repaired. As the door swung open and he stepped inside, he caught sight of a dark shape hopping up onto the back of the couch.

"There you are, Mime. I've been wondering where you've been."

Mark's strange black cat let out a yawn and licked her lips. Of late, she had been going out a lot, but Mark never really worried about her, as Mime had proved time and again she was smart enough to take care of herself. Kicking the door shut behind him, Mark scratched her behind the ears and then headed upstairs to his room. When he had had the house repaired, he had also had a safe installed in his closet, and after fiddling with the combination, he opened the door, revealing three stacked trays of glittering blue vials.

This was Mark's safety net, a stack of millions of credits' worth of elixirs, and after a considerable amount of thought, he took the top tray out, leaving the other two in the safe. Placing them on the desk, he opened up Blackstar, the empowered forums and auction site. For a time, he had made good money selling elixir shards, but the market had dried up after he had flooded it, and since Mark had made enough, he had stopped selling them.

Now, however, since he was about to leave the city, he wanted to ensure he had the necessary gear, which meant he needed more disposable income. After browsing some of the elixir offers, Mark sent one of the sellers a direct message offering elixirs in bulk. Within minutes, he had received his reply, and soon after, a deal was struck, leaving Mark a cool 750,000 credits richer.

It pained him a bit to sell the elixirs at a discount, but considering that he had made them with a few drops of blood, he could always make more later. After arranging for the courier service to pick up the elixirs, Mark packed up everything he would need and left his room. Before walking down the stairs, he paused in front of Joe's room for a long moment, tempted to go inside and see if anything had changed. Ultimately, he didn't, not wanting to disturb anything. As he walked out the front door, Mime joined him, hopping up onto his shoulder, where she perched, her tail lashing back and forth.

Making sure the door was locked behind him, Mark paused

for a moment and then walked around the house to the backyard, where he hopped the fence and double-checked the windows. Before they had repaired the front door, he had always left one window cracked open slightly, to ensure he could get inside. Now, however, he wanted to make sure everything was sealed up before he left the city. The windows were all shut tight, which made it a mystery as to how Mime had managed to get inside the house. Of course, there was a very real chance that she had used the keypad at the front door, letting herself in that way, an idea that amused Mark considerably. Carrying his bag over one shoulder, Mark hopped the fence again and began the trek back to Abrams's warehouse, his mind filled with thoughts of the future.

2

Bright and early the next morning, Mark hailed a taxi from the warehouse and directed the driver to take him downtown. The Black Mountain Battalion had established its headquarters in the sprawling underground complex where the Engineering Corps was located. Mark had only seen a fraction of it when he had reported to get more information about his assignment, and he was beginning to suspect that the complex was even larger than he had originally thought.

Catching the elevator down to the main hub, he took one of the underground trains for nearly twenty minutes before arriving at the subterranean tower where the Black Mountain Battalion had its headquarters. The doors hissed open and Mark stepped off the train, his smile faltering as he took in the shabby surroundings.

The offices of the Black Mountain Battalion were neat but also old and badly in need of an update. There was a thick carpet with a well-worn path running down its center where, over the years, feet had stripped it of life. A few cracked frames hung on the wall, vintage motivational posters sitting crookedly inside them. The furniture looked like it might fall over with a touch, and Mark was genuinely unsure whether he should sit down.

Mime, still perched on his shoulder, was just as skeptical. Jumping down, she prodded one of the chairs with her paw, causing it to wobble alarmingly. There was a desk where a secretary should have sat, but its top was completely clean, and no chair was behind it, a clear indication that nobody actually used it. Since he had arrived a few minutes early, Mark stood awkwardly in the waiting room, occasionally glancing up at the corner, where the beady lens of a camera peered down at him. After a few minutes, the door to the waiting room opened, and a middle-aged woman wearing thick glasses walked in. She held a large folder in her arms, clutched to her chest as if it were a shield. She clearly hadn't been expecting to see anybody else, because when she caught sight of Mark, she let out a faint shriek and nearly dropped all her papers.

She barely managed to keep them from sliding down by pinning them to her stomach, and mumbling something that Mark didn't catch, she ran past him to one of the doors down the hall. Hand half outstretched, Mark watched her run away, his offer of help dying on his lips. When she got to the door, she realized that she couldn't let go of her papers to turn the handle. After considering her predicament for a moment, she stepped back, lifted her foot, and used the sole of her shoe with such practiced ease that Mark realized she must have done this before.

As she vanished into the room, the door to the waiting room opened again, and a heavily built man in uniform with sergeant stripes on his shoulder stalked in. His reaction to seeing Mark wasn't nearly as pronounced, and walking over, he eyed Mark up and down. "Welcome to Black Mountain Battalion headquarters. How can I help you?"

"The name's Mark Field, sir," Mark said, straightening up and saluting. "I'm here to report for duty."

"Oh, you're the new recruit. Welcome, I'm Staff Sergeant Fletcher." He returned Mark's salute.

The sergeant then offered one of his meaty hands, which Mark shook. If he had to guess, Sergeant Fletcher had a strength power, though he wasn't nearly as tall as the other brutes Mark had run into. The sergeant's hands were covered in a fine network of scars, and a few small scars dotted his thick jaw and neck. A chunk was missing from one of the sergeant's ears, and the longer Mark looked, the more old wounds he saw. It was clear that the staff sergeant was anything but a paper pusher, and he carried himself with the calm assurance of somebody who had stared death in the face countless times.

"Well, come on in. We have a meeting in half an hour, and everybody else should be here by then. You can come to my office for the moment."

Leading the way down the hall, the staff sergeant opened the door to his office and flicked on the lights, which blinked for a moment, as if deciding whether they wanted to come on. Clearly used to it, Sergeant Fletcher walked to his desk, put down his bag, and gestured to a rickety chair set against the wall. "Have a seat. I've got a couple of things to take care of, and then we'll get the meeting going."

Nodding, Mark sat down as the sergeant began to pull papers out and read over them laboriously. The room was silent, and though Mark felt a bit awkward, he managed to occupy himself with looking around. Sergeant Fletcher's office was spartan, with a single desk in the center of the room and four nondescript filing cabinets sitting against the wall behind him. There was a terminal on the desk, but the sergeant seemed to prefer paper, and the silence was occasionally broken by the whir of the printer that sat next to the desk. The only thing on the walls was a certificate identifying the staff sergeant's rank.

The minutes ticked by until the sergeant's watch gave a soft chime. Putting down the papers he had been reading, Sergeant Fletcher rubbed his forehead, took a deep breath, and stared into the distance, as if about to face a great challenge.

"Come along," he said as he got up and headed for the door.

He led Mark to a room farther down the hall, where there was a large table with close to twenty seats. Four people were currently in the room: the middle-aged woman Mark had seen earlier and three men who sat next to each other across from her.

"This is Mark Fields, private first class," Sergeant Fletcher said.

Two of the men immediately bounced up, grinning from ear to ear, as they headed around the table to shake Mark's hand.

"Welcome to the Black Mountain Battalion," the older of the two said, grabbing Mark's hand and shaking it vigorously. "The name is James, James Price. This is my brother, Cody."

"Hello, I'm Cody."

Taken aback by the enthusiastic introduction, Mark said hello and allowed the two brothers to pull him to the table. The third man didn't introduce himself, and from the cold look on his face, Mark got the feeling that he wasn't going to. The Price brothers sat on either side of Mark, their eyes sparkling as the middle-aged woman, after blinking at Mark through her thick glasses, lifted her hand in greeting.

"Lieutenant Kami," she said.

Surprised, Mark jumped up and quickly saluted. She wasn't wearing a lieutenant's insignia, and now that he looked closer, he realized it was because the jacket she wore didn't match her pants. She clearly didn't care about his salute and waved for him to sit down. As he started to take his seat, the door opened, and a man in his early thirties walked in. Broad across the shoulders and narrow at the waist, he had the classic good looks Mark had come to recognize in most of Noah's friends. Based on that, his sleek haircut, and the expensive-looking watch on his wrist, it was clear that he was from one of the upper-class families. Sergeant Fletcher and the others all jumped to their feet, quickly saluting, so Mark followed suit.

"Good morning, Captain Calder," Sergeant Fletcher said.

Dismissing the greeting with a nod, the captain looked around, his eyes narrowing slightly as he spotted Mark.

"You're the one they just assigned to us, right?"

"Yes, sir. My name . . ."

"I don't care about your name," the captain interrupted. "I'm sure I'll read it in the files later. Let's get on with this blasted meeting."

With an impatient scowl, he sat at the head of the table and swiveled his chair so that he was facing the large screen up on the wall. Giving Mark an apologetic smile, Sergeant Fletcher coughed and began to speak as the screen clicked on, showing a topographical map for the mission the Black Mountain Battalion had been assigned.

"This is the location of Felwer Mine, named for Abraham Felwer, the prospector who first discovered it. It was in operation for about fifty years, but around twenty years ago, there was a collapse in one of the main shafts, and it's been closed since. There's still a base on-site that has been occupied by the occasional Ranger squad, but for the most part it's been abandoned. Our job is to get that base operational again. We are the first part of a multistage plan to bring the mine back online and begin extracting ore once more."

"Where is this mine located?" Captain Calder asked, his forehead deeply furrowed as he stared at the map.

"About five hundred miles north of here," Sergeant Fletcher said, eliciting a groan from Lieutenant Kami.

"Five hundred miles? That's going to take forever. How am I supposed to finish my research if I'm five hundred miles away?"

Turning in his chair, Captain Calder stared at Sergeant Fletcher, his gaze stormy. "You said we're the first wave. Who else is in the first wave?"

It was clear that the staff sergeant had been expecting this question, and his face was carefully blank as he replied. "It would appear that it's just us, sir. We have a Ranger escort to get us to the mountains, and our mission is to secure the mining facility, reestablish the defenses, and wait for the main force to arrive."

"You're joking."

"No, sir. That's what our orders say."

Mark genuinely thought that Captain Calder was about to go ballistic from the way he slammed his hand down on the table hard enough to dent it. There was a faint crimson gleam in his eyes as he rose to his feet, and Mark could feel Mime tensing as mana started to gather around the captain.

"I didn't join this battalion to get shoved off to some remote corner of the wilderness," Captain Calder snarled. "Wait till my father hears of this."

Turning, he kicked his chair away, causing one of the legs to snap, and then stormed out of the room, slamming the door behind him so hard the hinges rattled. The cold-faced man who hadn't introduced himself jumped up and quickly exited after the captain, and Mark heard some shouting in the hall. The room fell into silence until the sound could no longer be heard, and James gave the staff sergeant a thumbs-up.

"That went much better than I thought," James said. "Well done, sir."

"Indeed," Lieutenant Kami added, taking off her glasses and using a handkerchief to clean them off. "Much better than the last time."

"What do you think? Is this order going to go through?" Cody asked, leaning forward.

Mark was quickly realizing that he was missing some key context. Thankfully, Sergeant Fletcher caught sight of his confusion and filled him in. "Captain Calder is not the most enthusiastic about missions that take place outside of the city. The last order we were issued would have taken us to the east, out toward the ocean. But he protested, and the order was rescinded. He's likely on his way to see if he can have this rescinded as well."

"His dad's a big shot. A general, in fact," James said. "Which on the one hand is nice, because it makes life pretty easy around here."

"On the other hand," Cody interjected, "it makes him insufferable."

Coughing into his hand to interrupt the conversation, Sergeant Fletcher rose to his feet and began passing out papers he had printed earlier. "Unfortunately, I don't think this order is going to be rescinded. I want everybody to read over the details."

Taking the paper, Mark quickly scanned it. Next to him, Cody shook his head. "You're kidding me, right? They're sending us out into the wilderness alone?"

"Not . . . technically. As I said, we'll have a Ranger escort as far as the mountains."

"But after that, they're leaving us on our own," Sergeant Kami said, shaking the page. "That is what the paper says, but there has to be some mistake. Why would they send a battalion that only has six members into the wilderness alone?"

"I mean, technically, we have seven members," James said, jerking a thumb at Mark. "Eight if you count his cat."

"Does the cat count?" Cody asked, peering at Mime.

"It's part of his power, so no," Sergeant Fletcher said, earning himself an arch look from Mime, which he ignored.

As he read over the order, Mark couldn't help but rub his forehead. "I don't mean to be impertinent, sir, but it seems a little bit unorthodox for them to be sending us out, especially considering I haven't been through boot camp."

"Whoa, are you serious? You're completely fresh?" James turned in his seat to get a better look at Mark. "You're going to have a lot of learning to do."

"And what better way to learn than on the job," Sergeant Fletcher said. "Regardless of how we feel about these orders, these are the orders we've been given."

"That doesn't mean they're not stupid," Lieutenant Kami chimed in. "Hopefully, the captain will be able to get them changed or at least get us some more help. But if there's nothing else, I've got some experiments going. So I'll see you all later."

Standing up, she hurried out of the room, clutching the paper Sergeant Fletcher had given her tightly to her chest.

Closing his eyes and rubbing his temples, Sergeant Fletcher sighed and then pushed his chair back. "James, Cody, show our new recruit around. Mark, they'll give you the lay of the land. In the meantime, I'll start organizing everything we'll need. We'll be leaving at some point in the next few days, so be ready for immediate deployment."

Standing up, the sergeant leaned heavily on the table, giving Mark a rather pitying look. "Welcome to the Black Mountain Battalion."

3

After the sergeant had left, James patted Mark on the shoulder. "It's really not so bad, though we could certainly use a few more people."

"That's an understatement," Cody muttered under his breath.

Ignoring his brother, James got up and gestured for Mark to follow. "We'll show you around. This place is pretty big, so you'll have plenty of space."

Once again, James's words were a tremendous understatement. The Black Mountain Battalion had an entire inverted tower that sank deep into the earth. It comprised ten floors, most of which were barely used. There were barracks with enough beds to house a thousand people, a massive mess hall that clearly hadn't seen use in years, and training rooms filled with state-of-the-art equipment, some still wrapped in the original plastic.

One of the floors housed a giant garage packed to the brim with all sorts of equipment, from excavators and tractors to armored vehicles and a crane. There was an armory, a full hospital, and a communications center whose lights didn't even work. Along with the office, these facilities took up the first five floors. Unlike the top five floors, the bottom five were all fully active research labs where various experiments were being run.

Far from the bustling halls Mark would have expected, the labs were eerily quiet. James and Cody were quite hesitant about entering the research floors and opted to take Mark to an observation window instead. It overlooked the highest of the five research floors, and after spending a few minutes there, staring down at the machines that appeared to be operating by themselves, they gestured for him to follow them back out, obviously not wanting to stay a moment longer.

"It looked like there were a bunch of experiments going on down there," Mark said, jerking a thumb at the window behind them as they entered the elevator to take them back up to the first floor.

"That's Lieutenant Kami's domain," James said, punching the button in the elevator.

The doors closed with a soft ding, and Mark caught sight of Cody's uneasy expression in the polished metal. Turning to face the two brothers, Mark crossed his arms over his chest. "Does she have help? I mean, are there really only six people in the battalion?"

"Seven now, including you. Eight with the cat."

Rolling his eyes at his brother's repeated joke, James nodded. "Lieutenant Kami has an interesting power that makes her particularly suited to running experiments."

The two brothers shared a glance, and then James continued. "She can be in more than one place at once, but only if nobody's looking at her. I don't understand it. You'll have to ask her if you want a better explanation. But essentially, as long as no one is paying attention, she can actually split herself up into different copies. It's just that when you look at her, all of the copies except for one vanish. She gets pretty mad if you wander around the lower floors, since it keeps her from splitting up, but otherwise she's really good at multitasking."

This was the first time Mark had ever heard of such a power, which made him curious. "What about everybody else? I mean, everybody else has powers too, right?"

"Oh yeah, the entire battalion is empowered. Maybe that's one of the reasons there are so few of us."

Patting his brother on the shoulder, Cody nodded. "James and I have some minor strength and speed powers. Plus, our bodies are abnormally tough."

"That's right," James said with a grin, slapping his chest. "We can take a lot of punishment. Sergeant Fletcher is the same. He's got superhuman endurance, and his body heals much faster than normal. I'm sure you've seen all the scars. Even if you were to cut his stomach open, he'd be back to normal in a day or two at most."

"And the captain?"

Taking a breath, Cody mimed an explosion with his hands.

"Fire powers. He can create bombs by snapping his fingers. That's actually how he ended up stuck here with us," James said, lowering his voice conspiratorially. "He used to be in one of the Ranger units. But there was an incident, and so he got shuffled off to this dead end, and he's really mad about it. Sergeant Rogers, who followed the captain out of the meeting, has a barrier ability, but he got stuck with us because he has to babysit the captain."

That assessment didn't bode well for Mark, but before he could ask for more information, they arrived at their floor. Stepping out into the hall, Cody looked back at Mark with considerable curiosity. "What about you?"

"Nothing so cool as the rest of you," Mark said with a shrug. "I can turn my arms into metal, or really any substance that I touch."

"Is that right? I can see how that would be useful," Cody said. "Does it make you stronger?"

"Not as such, though I can exert more force if my fingers are metal."

Exchanging glances, the two brothers appeared to communicate silently, and then, scratching his head, James turned back to Mark. "So how'd you end up in this battalion?"

"A great question," Mark said, keeping his face straight. "I'm still not one hundred percent sure myself. It might be because I've been training as an alchemical butcher, you know, taking apart Exlian corpses."

"Oh, that would make sense. We often have to hire in processors to get Lieutenant Kami the material she needs," James said as he led the way back to the front hall. "Well, anyway, welcome. You can stay here if you want, and you're welcome to use any of the facilities. We typically eat up here in the conference room because we don't have enough staff for the kitchen."

"And if you do end up taking one of the bunks, you'll have to clean everything yourself, which is a total pain," Cody added, "and that's why most of us live outside of the headquarters. We'll set you up with a desk in our office. But really, there's not a whole lot to do around here."

"And by 'not a lot to do,' he means there's nothing," James said with a laugh. "Though that might not be the case for you."

"Might not be the case for all of us soon," his brother grumbled, "especially if they cart us off to the wilderness."

"Oh, come on. They're not going to do that," James said. "They've been threatening to do that for years. And every single time, Captain Calder pulls some strings and we don't have to go. Well, let's hope that's the case again. Come on, Mark. I've got to do a maintenance sweep of the suits. You can give me a hand."

It was just after six when Mark left the battalion headquarters, taking the underground train back to the hub and exiting to the surface. His mind was full, mostly of confusion, as he reflected on the strange day he had just had. James and Cody Price were both talkative, though Mark's confusion only deepened with every statement they made. He had clearly stepped into an extremely abnormal situation, and as he headed back to the warehouse, he couldn't help but continually replay the odd conversations.

After lunch, which had been ordered in, Lieutenant Kami had found him, and he'd spent the next four hours taking apart Exlian corpses under her supervision. As he worked, he began to realize why the Price brothers were so unnerved about being down on the research floors. It wasn't so bad when he was looking directly at Lieutenant Kami, but every time he turned his head away or focused on something else, he would catch glimpses of her from the corners of his eyes, as if she were standing on both sides of him simultaneously. Of course, when he looked up, she wasn't in either spot and instead was standing in front of him, carefully observing what he was doing. If she noticed his discomfort, she didn't mention it.

By the end of the four hours, she had been quite pleased with everything Mark had done, and informed him that the following morning he should report to the third research floor at seven, where she'd have a list of ingredients for him to pull. On his way out, Sergeant Fletcher asked him to come in a bit early for a physical assessment, which Mark had agreed to, and after making plans to meet in the training center at five a.m., Mark was dismissed.

In truth, he had no idea what military life was supposed to be like, but whatever preconceptions he'd had certainly hadn't been like this. Reaching up, he absentmindedly scratched under Mime's chin, which helped him calm down. Mime had been with him all day, and nobody had said anything, apart from the few comments about his cat being part of his power. Mark could only assume that they had read that information in his profile, which was fine with him, because he quite liked having her tag along.

Abrams wasn't around when he got back, so Mark busied himself working on some of his potions while he waited. He heard

Abrams arrive, and putting down the vial he was working on, he washed his hands and walked out into the freezing warehouse. Abrams was in his office, and he looked up as Mark walked in.

"How was the first day?"

"Honestly, rather strange," Mark said, taking a seat across from his master. "I'm not sure what I expected, but it certainly wasn't what I found."

"I've heard that the Black Mountain Battalion has some interesting characters," Abrams said with a ghost of a smile. "That battalion has a long and storied history, though none of the people who were in it when I was active are still around."

"What happened to them?" Mark asked, a bad feeling springing up in his heart.

"All dead," Abrams replied with a shrug. "Most out in the wilderness, but some in the city. The Black Mountain Battalion has a pretty rough history, but I'm sure things are better now."

Mark thought he could hear sarcasm in his master's voice, but it was just subtle enough that he couldn't be sure. "How did they die in the city?"

Shooting a glance at Mark, Abrams picked up a piece of paper from his desk and began to read over it as he spoke. "This was some time ago, but one of the officers in the battalion was murdered, and most of the battalion turned out to be involved. They were rounded up by the Defense Force and sent to Gray Rock Prison, where they were executed."

Though Mark was familiar with the city's prison for empowered, he had never heard about anyone being executed.

Placing the paper down, Abrams gave him a mirthless smile. "The city doesn't take kindly to people who step out of line or disobey orders."

Biting his lip, Mark considered whether he should mention the mission. Ultimately, he didn't. The orders were not something to be shared outside the battalion, and if word got out that Mark had leaked them, he could only imagine how much trouble he'd be in.

After talking to Abrams for a little while, Mark went back to work on his potions, then headed to bed. The next morning, he was back at the Black Mountain headquarters at five o'clock. Sergeant Fletcher and both Price brothers were already there, down in the training room, getting everything set up.

"Good morning," James said, bounding over to Mark. "You ready for the tests?"

"Not sure," Mark said, glancing over at the machines Sergeant Fletcher was wheeling out. "What kind of tests are we talking about?"

"Just to figure out where your abilities are," Cody said, walking up and giving Mark a nod. "If we're going to be deploying, we need to know how strong and fast you are and how good you are at combat."

Walking over after he finished activating a large workout machine, Sergeant Fletcher greeted Mark, who gave him a quick salute. "Cody's right. Normally, the battalion would have recruited you after extensive observation during basic training. Unfortunately, the next round of basic training is going to be happening while we're out, so I thought it'd be a good idea to at least get a sense of where you'd be most useful. Lieutenant Kami was singing your praises last night, saying that you were exceptionally good at processing Exlian corpses."

"Yes, sir. It's thanks to my ability to transform my hands."

"Does it translate to being able to kill Exlian?"

Hesitating for the barest second, Mark nodded. "Yes, sir. During the training camp, I fought my share of Exlian in the dead zone."

"Exlian in the dead zone practically don't count," Cody said, laughing. "That's like comparing a house cat to a lion."

"It's not that bad," James said, "but it's true that the Exlian allowed in the dead zone tend to be less dangerous than those out in the wilds."

Mark didn't quite know what to say in response, and Sergeant Fletcher saved him from the awkwardness by gesturing for him to step forward. "We're going to start with the basic strength and speed tests to see where you're ranked. Go ahead and take the test without your powers, and then with your powers activated."

Nodding, Mark took off his jacket and stepped up to the machine. He had used a device like this when he had first assessed his abilities after his empowerment, and he was excited to see how he had grown. His status had him in the D rank, and after he'd punched and kicked a number of targets, both with and without his transformation, the machine confirmed it, showing a large *D* on the screen.

"All right, time to spar," James said, quite excited.

Sergeant Fletcher must have seen the hesitation on Mark's face, because he held up his hand. "Your file says that you use the Cutting Palm technique, is that correct?"

"Yes, sir."

"In that case, I'd like you to demonstrate with me. We can go at it for real, and you don't have to worry about harming me." As he spoke, Sergeant Fletcher pulled off his shirt, revealing a body covered in thick muscle. "I should be able to heal any damage you cause."

Feeling slightly nervous, Mark joined him in the training ring, and the two of them faced off. The nervousness vanished as soon as he turned to face the sergeant. He could feel his heartbeat slowing and his mind entering its cold, calculating combat mode. Slowly breathing in and out, Mark felt as if he saw Sergeant Fletcher's move before the sergeant made it, allowing him to react instantly as the sergeant took an extra-long step forward and then pivoted, launching a heavy sweeping kick. Rather than try to block it, Mark stepped forward as well, ducking low under the kick as his hands jabbed, punching a series of holes in Sergeant Fletcher's leg. The sergeant's skin was harder than it had any right to be, but it was no match for Mark's titanium fingers.

With a hiss, Sergeant Fletcher jumped back, drops of blood splashing onto the mat. The scent nearly caused Mark to leap forward, but with considerable effort, he forced himself to back up, allowing some distance between them. Sergeant Fletcher laughed and slapped his leg. The wounds had already closed, testament to the sergeant's tremendous regeneration ability.

"I told you, you won't be able to actually hurt me," he said, clenching his fists tightly and lifting them to face Mark. "Let's keep going."

Swallowing, Mark nodded. Dashing forward, he feinted an attack on the right and launched a flurry of finger strikes from the staff sergeant's left. Mark's hands were a blur, and every single time they touched Sergeant Fletcher's body, his skin would erupt and blood would begin to drip down from the wounds. Soon, his arms and legs were almost completely covered, and they were forced to stop when the floor began to get sticky with blood. More than once, Mark was forced to pull back to avoid going in for a killing strike, and when they stepped away from each other, Sergeant Fletcher had an appreciative look in his eyes.

"You're better than your profile suggests," he said, "a lot better."

Turning to James, who had been observing from the side, Sergeant Fletcher gestured toward Mark. "Do you want to have a go?"

"Me? No way." James shook his head. "Fighting somebody with knives for hands would be insane. I thought you guys would just punch each other, not cut each other to ribbons."

"That was some pretty one-sided cutting," Cody remarked. "Do your attacks work just as well on Exlian?"

"Yes," Mark said, brushing some of the blood from his fingers.

"My hands are about as effective as a mana blade, sometimes more."

Letting out a low whistle, James walked over to examine Mark's silver hands. Mark was close to reaching mastery of the second stage of the Cutting Palm technique, Fingers as Knives, and if he had used the bone blade genetic memory, his attacks would have been even more effective. Considering they were just sparring, though, he didn't want to accidentally hurt the sergeant, so he'd opted for titanium instead.

4

It was just about seven in the morning, and after grabbing a quick shower, Mark headed down to meet with Lieutenant Kami, who, true to her word, had a giant stack of Exlian corpses waiting for him to deconstruct. It took him the better part of the day to get through all of them, and when he finally finished, he was informed that the battalion was having another meeting. Taking his second shower for the day, he headed up to the top floor, where he found everyone else was already gathered. Captain Calder had an absolutely furious expression, and from the way he gritted his teeth, Mark could only assume he was too angry to speak. The mysterious Sergeant Rogers had elected to stand behind the captain's chair, and a couple of times, Mark caught the sergeant staring at him. As usual, Sergeant Fletcher was the one to take the floor.

"Our orders have been confirmed," he said, "and accelerated. We'll meet by the northern gate at oh six hundred and leave by fifteen after. I've collected all the gear we'll need, and we're planning on being gone for three months. As I mentioned, we'll be escorted by a Ranger unit, but we're hoping to travel light, avoid the larger swarms, and stay clear of the Exlian."

Noticing Cody's wide grin, Mark couldn't help but glance over. James, who was sitting next to his brother, had a wide grin as well, and Mark found himself slightly unnerved. Everything about this battalion and the mission was giving him an unsettled feeling, and Mark couldn't help but feel that he was being pulled into a strange morass, as if there were an unseen force manipulating everything. As Sergeant Fletcher finished explaining what they would need to bring, Captain Calder stood up and stormed out, Rogers trailing behind. He hadn't said a single word the entire time, and once he was gone, the mood lightened considerably.

James leaned forward, rubbing his hands together. "It's about time we got an actual deployment," he said.

Across the table, Lieutenant Kami frowned. "Do you know how hard it's going to be to keep my experiments going with my main body heading out into the wilderness? And what if something happens to me? Hundreds of research projects will all grind to a halt."

It was clear that Sergeant Fletcher had heard this line of argument before, because he simply shrugged. "I'm sorry, Lieutenant. That's out of my control."

"Yes, well, you can believe me when I say I'll be complaining to your superiors. This is completely unacceptable."

Cody cleared his throat. "Um, Lieutenant, you're his superior."

For a moment, Lieutenant Kami stared at Cody blankly, and then, taking off her glasses and cleaning them, she nodded. "Yes, well, I guess I'll be reading a lot of memos then."

After the sergeant had finished his brief, Mark left the battalion headquarters and caught a taxi back to the warehouse, where Sky was waiting for him.

"You're looking good," Mark said, admiring Sky's outfit. She was dressed in her uniform and smiled shyly at Mark's words. Her days in the training camp had caused her to gain some muscle, and the food they had been packing into her put some weight on her thin frame.

"I'll be right down," Mark said. "I'm just gonna change."

It didn't take him long, and a few minutes later, they were on their way. The club Noah had rented was on the outskirts of the central district and much less fancy than the last place they had met, at least on the surface. As soon as he walked in, Mark's senses started jumping, and it didn't take him long to spot the numerous security guards hidden throughout the establishment. Most of them seemed to work for the club, and based on the ease with which Noah spoke to the staff, this was one of his usual haunts.

He had rented a large room up at the top of the six-story building, with fantastic views of the downtown sprawl, whose bright lights painted a dazzling, colorful picture across the horizon. Mark and Sky were the first to arrive, with Phoenix appearing not long after. Glenn, Harper, and Danny all came together, and the discussion soon began in earnest.

Since Mark had just been assigned to a battalion and Sky was still in training, they mostly stayed quiet as the others described what they had been up to. Noah's unit had already been deployed once and was about to be deployed again, while Phoenix and Harper were preparing for their first deployments. Glenn had joined the Engineering Corps and was busy working on maintaining the defensive systems scattered across the city walls, while Danny had been patrolling those same walls for the last few months.

As nervous as he was about everything going on with the Black Mountain Battalion, Mark couldn't help but relax as he hung out with his friends. He had been a little bit worried that Sky would feel out of place but was gratified to see Phoenix and Harper both chatting with her happily. As the night wore on, Mark caught a look from Noah, and the two of them casually stood up and walked over to the window that stretched from floor to ceiling, providing a clear view of the cube at the center of the city.

"What is it with being rich and having the best views?" Mark asked.

With a chuckle, Noah shrugged. "It is nice, isn't it?"

Taking a sip of his wine, he crossed his arms and leaned against the window, turning to look at Mark. "You're in trouble. Deep trouble."

Lifting his glass to his lips, Mark was quiet, waiting for Noah to continue.

"The Black Mountain Battalion has always been a bit odd, but that's not the issue. You're odd enough that you'll fit right in. But according to one of my informants, the mission you're on was supposed to have three Ranger teams and another engineering battalion."

Lowering the glass, Mark licked his lips. "I heard it was just us and one Ranger team."

Nodding, Noah straightened up and glanced out the window. "And that's why I say you're in trouble. Just before the orders were passed down, the other two Ranger battalions were pulled off by orders that came directly from the city council, leaving you with only one battalion to escort the team. The other engineering battalion was reassigned as well. There was a note attached mentioning that they were looking for a replacement, but then the timetable was shortened and your deployment order went through. Additionally, all the requests to fill out the Black Mountain Battalion were denied. You should have been one of fifty people to be assigned to the battalion, but everyone else was diverted last minute. Supposedly, there will be teams following in your wake to make sure that the base has enough staffing . . ."

In the mirror, Mark could see Noah shaking his head subtly, and the sinking feeling in his chest grew. He couldn't help but imagine that this had something to do with his brother. He knew that the city was still on the lookout for the Green Line terrorists and that his brother was one of the prime suspects. Wondering if he was being used as bait, Mark couldn't help feeling bitter.

"Hey, Noah, come over here. You've got to tell Phoenix that story you told me the other day."

Hearing Glenn calling him, Noah turned around and patted Mark on the shoulder before walking over to where Glenn and Phoenix were sitting with the others. Feeling the need to clear his head, Mark headed for the door.

"Where are you going?" Glenn asked.

"Bathroom. I'll be right back. You don't have to wait for me. I've already heard the story."

Stepping out of the room, Mark closed the door softly behind him and walked to the end of the hall. As soon as he stepped through the bathroom door, he felt something was off, and in a flash, his hands transformed, taking on the ivory appearance of the Exlian bone blade. A figure loomed through the darkness next to him, and Mark's hand shot out, slamming into the figure's chest. To Mark, it felt as if he had struck a metal plate, but that didn't deter him, and with a twist of his wrist, his fingers sliced down, cutting a gouge through the abnormally tough skin.

There was a faint groan, and then a force locked itself around Mark's wrist. Before Mark could react, the floor underneath them melted, and Mark and his opponent dropped straight through to the floor below. They landed in a small storage room, both staggering. The room was pitch black, but that didn't bother Mark one bit as he launched himself toward the large figure half collapsed in front of him. He could dimly make out his opponent's neck, and as his hand shot toward it, about to cut through his opponent's jugular, the light in the room flicked on, and a heavy force slammed into Mark's body, pinning his arm to his side as he was driven back into the wall.

"Kev?" Mark managed to gasp out, staring in shock at the large man who had just tackled him.

A few feet away, Marv, Kevin's twin brother, surged to his feet, a wild look in his eyes. His chest was bleeding badly, a testament to just how dangerous Mark's slashing fingers were. Kevin released Mark and stepped back, hurrying to his brother, who had a hand pressed to his chest, trying to stanch the bleeding. Both brothers had incredible defenses, but Mark's Cutting Palm had punched through them like they were nothing, leaving Marv in shock.

"Everyone calm down. We're not enemies."

When he saw Perry step into view, Mark's breath hitched and he looked around before spotting Joe standing behind Perry. Pushing himself off the wall, he took a step forward before halting, unsure how he should treat his brother.

"Hello, Mark. You're looking good. And your reaction time is improving."

Unable to find the right words, Mark just nodded. He hadn't realized until this moment just how much his brother's absence had bothered him, but seeing Joe again awoke an intense wave of feelings that threatened to drown him. Perry quickly stepped back, clearly not wanting to be in the middle of the brothers' tense staring match.

"I heard you were being deployed with the Black Mountain Battalion."

"That's right."

"Deployments are always dangerous, but this one . . . You realize it's a trap, right? Someone has it out for you if they are sending you out into the wilderness with such a small team. You shouldn't go."

Hearing Joe confirm what Noah had said brought both a weight and a sense of relief to Mark. He knew that Joe was right, had known all along. There was something freeing about having the words out in the open, but Mark stubbornly shook his head. "An order is an order, Joe."

"Don't be an idiot, Mark. Just because you've been assigned to a battalion doesn't mean you should stop thinking for yourself. Not everyone cares about protecting New Emery, and a lot of orders only exist to serve the person issuing them."

Mark's jaw clenched as he stared at his brother, the roiling feelings in his chest threatening to burst out. Joe had long been Mark's biggest hero, and he remembered well all those evenings he'd spent watching the rankings to see if Joe had climbed any higher. It was painful to see his brother, once such a staunch defender of humanity and an integral part of New Emery's defenses, blatantly disparaging the military.

"Just because you abandoned this city doesn't mean I'm going to."

As soon as the words slipped out of his mouth, Mark wished he had kept his mouth shut. His brother's expression hardened, and the air between them solidified. It would have been better if Joe had reacted with an intensity that matched Mark's, but instead, he simply nodded. Swallowing the lump in his throat, Mark stretched out his hand . . . but his brother was already turning away.

"Joe . . ."

Pausing, Joe glanced back at Mark. His voice was as calm as always, his gaze clear and without any discernible emotion.

"Good luck on your deployment, Mark. Perry, let's go."

Perry looked between the two brothers, clearly wanting to interject, but ultimately, he didn't. With a sigh, he lifted his hands, mana tracing arcane symbols around his forearms. There was a shimmer, the air warped, and stepping into the twisting space, Joe disappeared, Kev following after him. Marv, whose hand was pressed tightly against the bleeding wound on his chest, patted Mark on the shoulder and, without a word, entered the portal after the others.

"See you around, buddy. Stay safe."

Perry's words lingered in the air even after he had vanished into the portal, and standing alone in the storage closet, Mark felt awful. The room was in complete disarray after their tussle, and to help himself calm down, he spent a couple of minutes picking up some of the things the altercation had knocked from the shelves. Once everything was roughly back in place, he left the storage closet and went to find the stairs that would take him back up to the VIP floor, where he found his friends laughing together. Standing in the doorway, Mark paused, his thoughts a mess.

"There you are," Phoenix called out, waving to him. If she noticed the turmoil Mark was experiencing, she didn't say anything, and doing his best to put on an easy smile, Mark walked over to join his friends. Bit by bit, as he chatted and laughed with them, the discomfort he was feeling faded, and soon his encounter with Joe had been tucked away in the back of his mind. As the night wound down, the conversation turned to Mark's upcoming deployment.

"Isn't it going to be dangerous to send out a small team like that?" Glenn asked after Mark had explained the situation with the battalion.

"Yes and no," Noah said, handing Mark another drink. "There are a lot of cases in which a small team is actually much more efficient and safer. The more people you have moving together, the easier it is to attract attention from the Exlian and the more likely that you'll inadvertently end up starting a wave."

"That's because of their psychic network, right?" Danny asked.

"Yes, once you start to encounter Exlian, and more importantly, once you start to kill them, they gather more of their kind. One of the greatest dangers in the wilderness is attracting the attention of a terror level or a nest, both of which are much more likely if you are moving with a very large group. Battalions often split into small squads, sending only a handful of people out to complete an objective. This is one of those situations where a small squad might be a better option."

"That doesn't mean it's not dangerous," Phoenix retorted, her forehead furrowing.

"Sure," Mark said, putting his drink down, "but I'm sure that all of this was taken into account when they were coming up with the plan."

Ignoring the skeptical look Noah sent his direction, Mark grabbed a slice of cheese from the snack platter on the table.

"I'm sure it'll be fine," he said with an unconvincing smile.

5

It was getting close to midnight when the party finally broke up, and after saying goodbye to everyone and thanking Noah for hosting the get-together, Mark and Sky caught a taxi back to the warehouse. Their ride was quiet, each of them occupied with their own thoughts, but Mark caught the occasional glances Sky was sending his way. He could sense that she was nervous about his deployment, and as they entered the warehouse, he stopped and grabbed her hand.

"It's really going to be okay," he said firmly. "I'm only going to be gone for a couple months, and we're heading to an already established base. I'll be back before you know it."

Looking like she might cry, Sky nodded and gave him a sudden hug. She squeezed tight, and Mark returned the hug, and for a few minutes they just stood there quietly.

Despite the optimism he projected, Mark didn't feel nearly as confident as he made it seem, and it was with considerable nerves that he gathered his things the next morning to join up with the battalion. He had said goodbye to his master and Mime back at the warehouse—despite the jokes, he did not want to bring her on the deployment—and as he arrived at the battalion headquarters, the reality of his situation started to set in. When he arrived, Sergeant Fletcher was already suited up, and he directed Mark to head down to the equipment room, where James and Cody were getting into their suits.

"Hey, Mark, excited for your first time out of the city?" Cody asked when Mark walked into the large garage.

Nodding absently, Mark examined the suit he had been assigned. The first thing he noticed was that it wasn't the same as the others. The twins wore streamlined power suits that were built for speed, nothing like the bulky suit that Mark was staring at or the typical suits used by the Engineering Corps. Covered in heavy armor, his suit had two servo arms attached to the back, one of which carried a massive slab of metal that could be used as a shield or as a tool for excavating. The other arm ended in a claw for manipulating objects. Curious about the difference between the suits, Mark glanced at James, who was already in his armor and was making some adjustments to a large metal crate. Noticing Mark's glance, James grinned at him.

"Once you've been in the corps for a while, you'll have the chance to customize your armor as well," he said. "But everybody starts with the basic suit. This is the NG-73. It's a basic engineering model that gives you everything you'll need. Go ahead and get suited up, and I'll explain how it works."

Mark crawled into the suit and felt it tighten around him. As the suit activated and the systems came online, he heard a hum, and then James's voice came through the speakers.

"The NG is an incredibly versatile suit. It's got heavy plating that will protect you from most drone attacks, and dispersive weave, which will mean basic energy attacks will splash. You won't have quite the speed that you're probably used to in the scout model, but that's to be expected considering your left servo arm is carrying a one-and-a-half-ton shield. You'll want to keep it positioned behind you when not in use to avoid losing your balance. Go ahead and try moving around."

Taking a tentative step forward, Mark nearly fell over sideways. As soon as he shifted his weight, the shield on his left side pulled him toward the ground, and he could feel the suit straining to balance it out. He was unsure how to control the servo arms, but then, as if reading his mind, the large shield swung to the right side, restoring his balance and allowing his foot to land securely.

"Don't worry about that. Happens to everybody," James said. "Try it again."

This time, Mark didn't immediately move. Instead, he closed his eyes and tried to control the two servo arms on his back. He quickly got the hang of it, as all he had to do was think about their positioning, and with a whir, they would shift. He wasn't quite sure how the suit was able to track his intentions, but it was awfully convenient. Positioning the two servo arms behind him, Mark walked forward. This time, his footsteps were stable, if a bit slower than he wanted.

"Your top speed is about forty miles an hour, which isn't nearly enough to keep up with the lighter scout models, and you'll need to be careful about managing your momentum, as once the suit gets going, it can't just stop." As he spoke, Cody tapped his chest armor, producing a sharp tinging sound. "Speed won't be an issue, as we're going to be moving pretty slow so as not to alert the Exlian. Believe me when I say that if you have to run, we're probably in trouble."

Shooting an annoyed look at his brother, James pointed toward the wall, where there was a rack with dozens of weapons. "Go ahead and pick whatever you're comfortable with. Just remember, you're going to have to carry the weight. The heavier your suit, the more strength and endurance it'll require to move in."

The rack contained just about any weapon Mark could have wanted, and after some consideration, he settled for two melee weapons: a short, wide mana sword like the one he had used in the training camp and a long lance. He considered picking up a projectile weapon, but without the ability to charge the arrows or bolts with mana, they would be practically useless against the Exlian.

Once he had selected his weapons, it was time to get underway, and he followed James and Cody out through a special exit into a massive service elevator that rose to the surface with a rumble. Lieutenant Kami and Sergeant Fletcher were already waiting outside, standing next to a large vehicle with heavy wheels that were as tall as Mark. They waved Mark and the brothers over.

"This is the command vehicle," Sergeant Fletcher said, gesturing to the massive truck. "It's part comms center and part supply truck and will be taking us to the base. We're just waiting for Captain Calder and Sergeant Rogers."

As he finished speaking, the two men arrived, walking with a third person that Mark recognized right away. Despite being much smaller than the suited soldiers around him and in civilian clothes, Andre Javesi still managed to look calm and imposing. Looking around, he caught sight of Mark and walked over. "Good to see you again, Mark. Noah mentioned you were deploying this morning."

"Hello, Councilman."

"No need to be so formal. You're my son's friend; just call me Andre."

Though Andre's tone was light, Mark couldn't help but feel a chill beginning to crawl up his spine. From how Noah and his other friends had described the councilman, his intimate behavior seemed entirely out of character, but Mark couldn't detect anything but calm friendliness in his tone.

"Though I don't like it, the council is going to have to rely on the Black Mountain Battalion this time. We desperately need to get that mine back up and running. Don't worry, though—I've asked Sergeant Rogers to take especially good care of you."

As he spoke, Andre gestured to the sergeant who stood behind Captain Calder. Rogers wore a gleaming silver-and-blue suit that Mark recognized as the Knight III, a sword-and-shield suit made popular by its knight helm. Meeting Mark's gaze, Sergeant Rogers flashed an unpleasant smile.

Realizing that Andre was waiting for him to respond, Mark quickly saluted. "Thank you, sir."

"The least I could do for my son's friend," Andre said, patting Mark's metal-clad arm. "Captain, I won't delay you any longer. Just don't forget what we talked about."

"I won't, Councilman."

The captain was dressed in a sleek black mana suit with red flame markings decorating the arms and chest, and from the tone of his voice, he was in high spirits. Though Mark didn't get more than a glance at the captain's mana suit, it looked state of the art to him, as did the long, thin mana blades the captain carried in sheaths on his back. Captain Calder tapped Sergeant Fletcher's shoulder and then climbed into the vehicle, Rogers clambering in after him.

Sergeant Fletcher was the only one wearing a suit similar to Mark's, though his was even more heavily armored. Rather than the large shield, he carried a blade in one servo arm and what looked to be some sort of launcher in the other. Lieutenant Kami's suit didn't look like a military suit at all, and it had next to no armor plating. The faceplate of the suit was completely clear and revealed her whole face, giving her an excellent field of view. She wore a backpack with six delicate servo arms extending from it. There was a considerable amount of gear next to her, and under Sergeant Fletcher's direction, Mark, James, and Cody loaded it up into the back of the vehicle. Once all the gear had been loaded, the rest of them climbed into the vehicle. Sergeant Fletcher and Lieutenant Kami joined the captain and Rogers in the front of the command vehicle, while James, Cody, and Mark piled in the back. The vehicle came to life, and with a rumble they were on their way.

The closer they got to the gate, the more excited James and Cody seemed to be, and their excitement was infectious. Soon, they passed through the large gate, entering the dead zone outside the city. Mark had never been north of the city, so it was with considerable interest that he peeked out of the vehicle's windows, watching as the empty buildings rolled by.

"This entire area was cleared yesterday, so we shouldn't have any trouble. Still, it's a good idea to stay on your toes," Sergeant Fletcher said, speaking through their comms.

Closing his eyes, Mark concentrated, doing his best to expand his attention and tap into the strange network the Exlian used to locate one another. As their car drove through the streets of the dead zone, he occasionally felt the slight tingle that marked an Exlian drone. However, they were always far enough away from the road that they weren't a threat, and he didn't detect anything bigger or more dangerous.

It took forty-five minutes for them to arrive at the outskirts of the dead zone, where they stopped at a fortified building. Jumping out of the car, Mark saw dozens of Rangers, arrayed in their powerful-looking stealth armor, decorated in grays and dark greens. Captain Calder didn't bother getting out of the car, but Sergeant Fletcher hopped down and greeted the Ranger lieutenant who was waiting for them. "Staff Sergeant Fletcher reporting."

"At ease, Staff Sergeant. I'm expecting Captain Calder," the lieutenant said, his eyes sweeping over Mark and the others.

Sergeant Fletcher jerked a thumb toward the car, and with a grimace, the lieutenant nodded. "Very well. If you're all ready to go, we can get on the road. We're sending three squads with you.

They'll get you to the mountains and make sure you're settled in before they come back."

"Thank you, Lieutenant," Sergeant Fletcher said as fifteen Rangers decked out in their battle gear filed out of the building to join them.

The Rangers were all ready to go, and within a few minutes, they were underway again, passing beyond the outer wall into the true wilderness. The wilds north of the city were mainly hills, with patches of thick forest dotting them. Despite the roughness of the terrain, they moved quickly. Mark wasn't sure if the Rangers were familiar with the path they were on or just incredibly adept at navigating terrain, but they picked the easiest paths, leading the command vehicle Mark and the others were in through gaps in the hills and around the thick stands of trees, maintaining a constant pace of nearly twenty miles an hour.

The heavy-duty vehicle had no issue with the route they had picked, despite the rockiness of the terrain, and by nightfall, they had made great progress, traveling over a third of the distance to the mine. When they finally stopped, Mark, Cody, and James jumped out. Unsure what to do, Mark paid close attention as James and Cody began lifting some of the large crates from the back of the vehicle.

"Are we setting up camp?" Mark asked, curious about what they were doing.

"There's no camp," Cody replied with a laugh, slapping Mark on the shoulder. "I mean, you're currently standing in your tent. We'll be in armor for three days, maybe longer, so you better get used to it."

Looking around, Mark saw that the Rangers, still in their armor, were gathering in small groups and appeared to be sharing food between them.

"Here, give me a hand with this," Cody said, grabbing one side of the box he had gotten down from the truck.

Helping him open it up, Mark saw the box was full of long spikes.

"We'll set up a fence around the truck," Cody said, "and we've got a second for the Rangers to use if they want it."

"What is this?" Mark asked.

"Early-warning system," James said. "It should keep the Exlian off of us while we rest."

"Should?" Mark asked, his eyebrows rising.

Flashing a grin, James shrugged.

Setting up the early-warning system wasn't particularly hard. The stakes were inserted into the ground, forming a rough circle around the vehicle, and the crate was attached to one of the stakes using a series of cables. The crate had a small keypad on it, and after Cody punched in the code and it activated, the stakes began to hum with mana.

Almost immediately, Mark felt a sense of discomfort, as if his stomach had just turned. He could faintly feel a prickling pain in his mind and had to suppress the impulse to retreat. Glancing at Cody and James from the corner of his eye, he didn't see any discomfort on either of their faces, so he took a deep breath and tried to ignore the feelings.

Anytime he got close to the stakes, however, the prickling feeling in his mind would grow, becoming more painful. Mark wasn't sure if it was because he had access to the Exlian network, but regardless, it was quite uncomfortable. He ended up spending the night in the back of the truck, hunkered down in his armor, doing his best to ignore the nibbling at the edge of his mind.

Thankfully, he managed to fall asleep, immediately finding himself sinking into his usual dream. Glad to be spared the prickling feeling, he spent the night fighting against Exlian. By this point, it had become so routine that Mark didn't even have to think twice about it. His martial arts were continuing to improve as he ground out fight after fight, and though it was a slow process, he could feel that he had reached a basic level of mastery in the second stage of the Cutting Palm.

Of course, a basic mastery of Fingers as Knives didn't mean he couldn't continue to polish his technique, searching for the elusive feeling that Abrams had said would precede the third level. Unlike the first two, which Mark had learned from manuals that illustrated specific movements, the final level of the Cutting Palm technique had no illustrations to follow.

In one of the brief moments between fights, Mark reflected on what Master Abrams had said. According to his master, the third and final stage of the Cutting Palm technique was one that transcended martial arts, transforming the entire body into a weapon. Curiously, it didn't even have a name, with each practitioner of the technique creating their own version of the ultimate level.

Abrams called his version of the third level Body as the Sword, and when he had demonstrated it, Mark was left dumbfounded. Even now, he could clearly recall the shiver that had run down his spine when Abrams flicked a finger, cutting through a chunk of steel from across the room. Faintly, Mark had been able to sense the force his master's finger had projected, but the attack had been all but invisible, and Mark could only imagine how terrifying it would be to fight against someone who could cut you up from such a distance. Master Abrams hadn't given any clear details on how to achieve it, however, and instead had instructed Mark to immerse himself in the second level, polishing his skill until every movement was second nature.

When Mark's dream ended, his eyes snapped open, the familiar prickling shocking him awake. Reaching up, he detached his helmet and grabbed a high-calorie nutrient pouch that he had placed beside him before going to sleep. Cody and James were both sound asleep, curled up in the back of the truck, so Mark got up, moving as quietly as he could, and hopped over the invisible fence, enduring the burning pain that caused.

The Rangers had set up around the vehicle, protecting it on all sides, and as Mark left the fence, he saw a few heads swiveling toward him. Lifting his hand to wave, he walked to the edge of the bluff where they were parked and looked out over the wide-open wilderness. As far as the eye could see were rolling hills with thick stands of woods. Far in the distance ahead of them, their destination, a heavy black line of tall mountains, decorated the horizon. Hearing a crunch, Mark glanced over his shoulder and saw a Ranger in a power suit behind him. The Ranger carried a massive composite bow in one hand and had a sword clipped onto his back.

"First time out in the wilderness?"

"Yes, sir," Mark said, shifting to face the Ranger and lifting his hand in a salute.

"No need to do that, kid," the Ranger said, and Mark caught sight of the flash of a smile through his helmet. "You only have to salute captains or higher."

Nodding, Mark turned and gestured toward the mountains in the distance. "Have you been out there?" he asked. "To Felwer Mine, I mean."

"Yes. Twice, in fact. We were one of the units that helped evacuate after the last wave. It's been years, though, so we'll want to be careful, as things will have changed."

His curiosity piqued, Mark glanced back at the Ranger. "Do you know why the base was abandoned?"

"Same reason everything's abandoned," the Ranger replied, shrugging. "Exlian. The base got caught in a war between nests. There were successive waves that clashed in the mountains north of the base. When those clashes began moving south, the order was given to evacuate. Hopefully, the fight's done now, and the base has been left clear. And if it's not, then you're in for a rough deployment."

With a wave, he continued on his patrol, leaving Mark alone in the early-morning darkness.

Mark knew that this deployment was dangerous. Any deployment, really. The Exlian were an ever-present threat, but when he was tucked safely behind the walls of New Emery, it was easy to forget just how dangerous they actually were.

Now that he was out in the open, the sky spread above him, a dark dome that covered the wilds, stretching to the horizon in every direction, Mark felt that threat in a new way. He had seen the videos of the Exlian swarms, massive seas of monsters, and now as he imagined them sweeping over the horizon toward him, he grew unsettled. Taking a deep breath, Mark focused, doing his best to sense if there were any Exlian nearby. The psychic network was quiet, and he was far enough away from the early-warning system that he could no longer feel the faint prickles it produced. For the moment, they were safe, but how long that moment would last, he had no idea.

6

The trip to the mine was only slated to take three days, but on the second day, they came across a deep gorge. The path that should have wound down it was gone, covered by massive boulders from a rockslide. Calling a halt, the Ranger scouts conferred with Sergeant Fletcher. Since the trip had started, Captain Calder hadn't appeared even once, and Mark was starting to wonder if he was even in the car at all. While he waited for orders, Mark got down from the back of the vehicle and looked over the path ahead.

The road wound down into this ravine along six switchbacks, and three of them were currently buried under tons of rubble. The rockslide, likely caused by a large storm and years of erosion, had dumped boulders the size of houses down the mountain. Even if the top part of the path could be cleared, there were sections lower down where the road was simply missing, obliterated by the falling stones.

"Ooh, Sarge looks mad," Cody said.

Looking up, Mark saw the sergeant walking toward them, a scowl on his face.

"There are two other routes," Sergeant Fletcher said, "and both of them will add time to the trip. One, we can manually lower the vehicle down the side of the mountain, skipping past a lot of the rockfall. We've got the winches to do it, but I've got some concerns about the integrity of the slope. The other option is to cut our way through a nearby forest and cross the river lower down."

Glancing down the steep hillside that dropped away into the ravine, Mark casually tossed a stone down the hill. It bounced once, causing a small smattering of loose dirt and rocks to tumble down after it. Almost immediately there was a rumble, and an entire section of the slope came loose, bounding down the steep hillside after the rock Mark had thrown. The slight rumble transformed into a loud roar as more and more stone separated from the side of the hill and plunged down into the ravine.

The Rangers gathered around, and everyone watched with ugly expressions as an entire section of the hill gave way, revealing fresh dirt and stone underneath. Stricken, Mark slowly stood up and put his hands behind his back. As the echo of the roar faded, Sergeant Fletcher coughed. "Looks like we'll be cutting wood for the next few days."

"Yeah, sounds smart to me," James replied with a gulp.

After seeing just how unstable the side of the hill was, everybody was in agreement, and they turned the car off the road, taking a slow, circuitous route down the length of the ravine. As they picked their way along the ridge, the elevation began to drop, the landscape eventually turning back into rolling hills. Just as Sergeant Fletcher had said, there was a large forest at the bottom of the ravine, filled with thick old trees, the shortest of which were thirty-five feet tall. By that time, evening was approaching, and they stopped to make camp once again.

Walking over to one of the trees, Mark tapped on it, his metal-clad knuckles striking with a dull thud against the hard wood. Turning to James, who had followed him over, Mark jerked a thumb at the trees. "How are we going to take these down?"

"The old-fashioned way, most likely," James said, peeling a bit of bark from one of the trees. "We've got some axes in the truck. Or you can use a mana blade."

When they settled down for the night, everything was quiet and still, though Mark did hear some muffled shouting from the large truck's cab. He couldn't make out the exact words, but from the hard set of Sergeant Fletcher's jaw after he came back out, it was clear that Captain Calder wasn't happy with the way the trip was going.

Early the next morning, armed with tools they had brought in the back of the truck, Sergeant Fletcher, the Price brothers, and Mark got to work.

As they slowly inched through the forest, Mark felt a faint prickle and paused. He currently had his hands wrapped around a stump, but he quickly straightened as the prickle grew stronger. The Rangers were spread out all around them, keeping watch in case the ruckus attracted any of the native wildlife, but none of them seemed to have noticed the incoming Exlian. Seeing Mark staring into the distance, Cody tossed aside the log James had just chopped and brushed a bit of bark from his hands.

"Everything okay, Mark?"

Mark waited a moment more before replying, wanting to make sure that he wasn't imagining things. As he focused his mind, the sensation became clearer. At least a dozen Exlian heading toward them from the southwest. They were moving quickly, and from the weight of their mental signatures, they clearly weren't drones.

"We've got incoming," Mark said quietly. "Warriors, and they are moving quickly."

Immediately, James and Sergeant Fletcher drew back, looking at Mark and then staring out at the forest that surrounded them. Everything was silent.

"What—?"

Sergeant Fletcher never got to finish his question. The radio crackled to life, and one of the Rangers reported contact with a sharp yell. "We've got a dozen devil hounds coming in fast from the southwest. Rangers, fall back."

In the brief moments before the Exlian burst from the trees, Mark's mind went back to one of his training classes. Devil hounds were Exlian who had adopted the frames of dogs, their bodies long and lean. They looked almost exactly like the wild dogs once found outside the city, except for the chitinous armor plates on their shoulders, chests, and rumps, and the mandible-like pincers that extended from what would have been their snouts.

Devil hounds were known for their sharp sense of smell, which allowed them to track their prey across great distances. Lean in body, they were incredibly quick, and their long legs gave them a considerable amount of agility. Mark couldn't help but marvel at how easily they swerved through the dense underbrush as they closed in. The most unnerving thing about them was that they moved in almost absolute silence—only a light patter as their feet hit the spongy forest floor indicated that they were there at all.

Thankfully, it was afternoon, and the sunbeams that pierced the thick canopy overhead gave just enough light to see the large dark forms hurtling toward them. Taking a deep breath, Mark readied himself, his gaze fixed firmly on the first devil hound. Before it could get close, however, another figure blurred into view, moving so quickly Mark felt his breath catch. A white-hot line rose from the ground as a Ranger stepped into the charging Exlian's path and slashed upward with his mana blade. His appearance was so sudden it caught the devil hound off balance, and a moment later its head tumbled to the ground as its body bounced a few times across the loamy ground.

The attack seemed to shock the devil hounds as much as it shocked Mark, and one of them opened its mouth, issuing a sharp shriek that made the hairs on Mark's arms stand up. The eleven remaining devil hounds reacted instantly, spreading out as they continued charging forward. They weren't quick enough, though, and three more fell to glowing arrows that punched holes straight through them. The Rangers were incredibly efficient, moving with ruthless ease through the pack of devil hounds. Most of the Rangers favored fighting from a distance, but a couple wielded their long, thin mana blades to deadly effect, ensuring that the devil hounds never reached their companions. Within less than a minute, all twelve of the devil hounds were dead, but the Rangers didn't relax their guard.

Wetting his lips with his tongue, Mark looked around, observing each of his companions. Captain Calder, Lieutenant Kami, and Sergeant Rogers were still in the vehicle, hidden from view, but Sergeant Fletcher was standing at the ready, holding his broadsword loosely at his side. The two Price brothers looked a little bit more nervous, but they had each drawn their own blades and seemed ready for a fight.

As each of the Exlian died, Mark had felt their psychic wail, and it wasn't long before he spotted the reason everyone was so nervous. The original attack had come from the southwest, but now at least three more groups were closing in from different directions. Each of the Ranger squads held five people, and they were arrayed around the truck in three directions, southwest, northwest, and east. At some unheard command, they suddenly rotated, shifting their positions to block off the devil hounds racing toward the truck.

Flexing his fingers inside his mana suit, Mark kept a close watch on the attacks, continually scanning the Exlian mental network for signs of more. For a tense few seconds, as each of the Ranger teams engaged, the charging devil hounds looked as if they had the upper hand. That perception only lasted for a moment, as the Rangers put down their adversaries with brutal efficiency, quickly clearing the forest.

Sergeant Fletcher sighed with relief as the last of the devil hounds was killed and gestured to the path in front of them. "Let's speed it up. I want everybody clearing."

"Yes, sir."

7

Grabbing an axe, Mark raced forward and set to work as the Rangers kept watch. Cody and James were beside him, with Sergeant Fletcher a bit farther ahead. Before, two people had been chopping the trees down while the other two cleared them from the path and removed the stumps. But now, they all felled trees, kicking them roughly to the side after they crashed to the ground. They still had to pause for a moment to rip the stumps clear of the earth, ensuring that the truck could pass through, but with all four of them at work, it went much quicker.

Twice more, as they carved a path through the forest, Exlian attacked, and each time they were repelled by the Rangers. Mark and the others didn't stop working, even while the fights were going on, and Mark found himself surprisingly calm, considering the situation. By evening, they had crossed to the other side of the forest, and Mark was starving. Glancing down at his wrist, he checked his biofuel meter and saw that it was starting to get a bit low.

One of the things that worried him the most about being out in the wilderness was the inability to eat as much food as he wanted. Back in New Emery, it wasn't an issue for him to fill up on his calorie-dense nutrient paste, but they had brought limited supplies out into the wilderness, supplies that needed to last them until they were relieved. Foraging in the wilderness was fraught with danger, as almost everything was poisonous to humans, including the Exlian themselves. Though many of them had plenty of meat on their bones, eating it was a sure way to commit suicide. The truck was carrying close to three months' worth of food, but given how much Mark ate, he was pretty sure that he could consume it all in one month by himself. Which was exactly why he had stuffed his bag full of extra nutrient paste and energy bars. His brother's warning about how the most important thing in the wilderness was energy management rang loudly in Mark's head as he accepted the two nutrient pouches that would serve as his evening meal. James sat down next to him.

"I'll never get used to this stuff," James said, shaking his head in disgust.

Sucking down the last little bit from his first pouch, Mark opened his second. "I'll eat it if you don't want it."

"As tempting as that offer is, I know I need the calories."

Fortifying himself, James started to eat as Mark polished off his second pouch. After packing the trash away, he took a moment to look around. Sergeant Fletcher and Cody sat by the back of the truck, while he and James were a dozen feet away, resting on a stack of logs. The captain, the lieutenant, and Sergeant Rogers were still out of sight, presumably in the mobile command center.

As if reading his mind, James grimaced and gestured to the large vehicle. "You'd better get used to it. Both Calder and Rogers will only step outside that thing once we get to the base."

"Have you deployed with them before?" Mark asked.

James nodded and squeezed the last bit of nutrient paste into his mouth. "Yuck. This stuff is disgusting. Yeah, I've deployed with them twice. Both times, it was the same thing. Calder hates being out of the city and probably won't let Rogers leave his side."

"Is he a bodyguard or something?"

With a conspiratorial smile, James tapped the side of his nose and then tossed his second nutrient pouch to Mark. "I can't stomach any more of this stuff. Rogers was assigned to the captain by his father and follows him everywhere like a leech. You can pretty much guarantee that neither of them will help at all. So anything we have to do is up to us."

"Cut the chatter, you two. Let's get our camp set up."

Jumping to his feet, still holding James's nutrient pouch in his hand, Mark saluted. "Yes, sir."

James was a bit slower, letting out a tired sigh as he pushed himself back to his feet.

"Are we expecting an attack tonight, sir?" Mark asked.

Sergeant Fletcher frowned and turned to gaze out into the dark forest. They were on the edge of the woods, with a narrow valley in front of them, only a few miles from the foothills.

"I'm not sure," the sergeant said with a shrug. "There's always the chance we'll be attacked while we're out in the wilderness, so better to be safe than sorry."

Though he wasn't looking forward to spending the night inside the fence, Mark kept his expression neutral as he set up the stakes with Cody. Once they had all been pounded in, creating a perimeter around the vehicle, James activated the system, and Mark felt the prickling sensation return. The best way to deal with it seemed to be sleeping, so he quickly turned in, passing a fitful night in the back of the truck.

The next morning, he was up before anybody, and unable to

stand it, he clicked off the fence and then packed it up. This would be his fourth day in his mana suit, and it was starting to get a little bit uncomfortable, but with a distance still to travel before they arrived at the mine, he had to bear with it.

Free of the forest, the vehicle made much better time, and by lunch they were cresting the foothills and beginning their ascent into the mountain range itself. Felwer Mine was located close to the center of the mountain range, forcing them to wind their way through a barely maintained road that snaked between the tall peaks.

Everything seemed calm, and Mark spent the majority of the drive admiring the beautiful views. As dangerous as the wilderness was, it contained a breathtaking sort of beauty. Unfortunately, that beauty hid terrifying danger, and more than once, that danger found them.

The first time, a swarm of insects, each as big as a baseball, descended on them from a pile of loose rocks where they made their nest. The bugs weren't particularly strong, and their sharp stingers couldn't pierce the armor of the mana suits. That didn't stop them from trying, however, and Cody nearly went crazy when the insects began crawling all over him, trying to pry up the armor plating on his suit to get to his flesh underneath.

There seemed to be no end to the annoying things, and rather than stay and fight, Sergeant Fletcher urged everyone to speed up. After they'd raced a mile down the road, the insects finally turned around and returned to their territory, though Mark wasn't sure if he should be happy or worried that they had given up their chase. He had a faint nagging feeling that something was observing them, something he couldn't quite see. He hesitated to mention it, however, as his abilities were already hard to explain.

The second incident happened as they were climbing up into a small pass. According to their guides, Felwer Mine was only a dozen miles farther on, and Mark was quite looking forward to arriving. It wasn't that the march was hard. In fact, even when clearing the trees, he hadn't felt tired once on the trip so far. Rather, his body was starting to itch from being in the suit, and he was looking forward to taking it off once they were out of the wilderness.

Halfway up into the pass, James, who was walking alongside the truck with Cody, had just turned to say something to his brother when there was a loud rumble and a massive slab of stone detached from the hillside above him. Mark, who was riding in the back of the truck, saw it happen, but it was so quick there was nothing he could do.

The stone that started the slide must have weighed at least two tons, and it carried an avalanche of dirt with it that engulfed Cody and half of the truck within seconds. Springing out of the back, Mark saw Cody's suit being swallowed by the wall of dirt, and then the boulder slammed down on the vehicle, crushing its side.

"Cody!"

"Get clear! There's more coming!"

James's panicked shout mixed with Sergeant Fletcher's roar, and looking up, Mark saw even more dirt and stone rumbling down the hill toward them. He had no idea what had started the rockfall, but it seemed to be bringing half of the mountain down on them. James, completely disregarding the sergeant, was lunging toward where his brother was buried, and after the briefest moment of hesitation, Mark turned and tackled him around the waist. James's suit, quite a bit lighter than Mark's, didn't stand much of a chance, and Mark felt his strength being amplified as he pushed James back.

At the same time, the massive metal shield on his suit rose over their heads, blocking a boulder that crashed down on them. There was a loud clang as the boulder was deflected, but the force of it still nearly drove Mark to his knees. More and more dirt engulfed them, and by this time, the vehicle was almost completely buried. With a heave, Mark threw James back, even as the wall of dirt engulfed his legs, trapping him in place. Rather than struggle against it, Mark pulled up his shield, angling it to ensure none of the falling stones would hit him in the head, and crouched, letting the dirt build up around him. A moment later, his vision went dark as his mask was covered, plunged into absolute black.

Mark could still hear the rumbling roar of soil and stone vibrating through his body. After what seemed like an eternity but was likely only a dozen seconds, everything subsided, and a great stillness surrounded him. The dirt around him wasn't particularly dense, but Mark didn't move, afraid he might accidentally pack it down, making it impossible for him to escape. Instead, he closed his eyes and focused on the psychic network, trying to pick up any sign of the others. Almost immediately, he could sense the large vehicle behind him, with three people inside. From the frantic way they moved about, they didn't seem to be hurt, so Mark stretched his mind farther.

There, on the other side of the vehicle, he sensed a dull-gray mind, just as frantic as the others, and realized that it was Cody. Mark had discovered that people showed up on the Exlian network back when he and Noah raided the mercenaries' base, though their minds didn't flare like the Exlian's did, but he wasn't sure why he could sense Cody's mental state. Mark turned his attention outward, and it wasn't long before he saw a small group of people working their way toward him. They were moving slowly, no doubt digging through the earth, so Mark waited patiently. About ten minutes later, he felt the earth around him loosen, and light flooded into his eyes. In the next second, Sergeant Fletcher's hands wrapped around Mark's arms, and he was yanked free from the giant pile of dirt.

Blinking in the sudden light, Mark took stock and realized that his first impression had been correct. A full half of the mountain had collapsed, completely burying the road in hundreds of thousands of tons of rock and debris. Thankfully, the avalanche had been widespread, stretching over a two-mile radius, and only a small fraction of it had covered the road. Now that he was free of the crushing dirt, Mark got to work with the others, using the large shield as a shovel to dig out great scoops of dirt. None of the Rangers had been caught in the avalanche, and while five of them kept watch, the other ten pitched in to help as best they could.

Only Sergeant Fletcher and Mark had suits that were suited for this sort of mass excavation, but between them, they made good progress. Mark focused on carving out a path around the back of the truck to get to Cody, while everyone else focused on clearing the ground ahead of the truck to allow it to pull free once they had cleared enough of the dirt.

It took almost forty-five minutes for Mark to dig through to Cody, in large part because of how deep the dirt was. Had he not had a clear sense of where Cody was located, it would have taken at least three times as long to find him, but thanks to the psychic network, Mark was able to dig straight to him. Once close, he switched from the shovel to his hands to avoid damaging Cody's suit. After freeing one of Cody's arms, Mark grabbed his wrist and yanked him free, pulling him out into the open trench he had just dug.

"'Bout time you got to me," Cody said, a wide grin on his face, despite the harrowing experience he had just been through.

Since Cody didn't seem any worse for wear, Mark sent him to Sergeant Fletcher to help clear around the truck, while Mark worked to clear its tires. For almost six hours they moved dirt, until finally the truck was able to get its wheels moving. With a loud roar, its engine came to life, and Sergeant Rogers gunned it, bursting forth from the large pile of dirt like a whale breaching the surface of the sea.

Once free, he pulled to a stop, and the door opened. Lieutenant Kami came out first, followed by Captain Calder, who looked irate. Mark didn't blame him. The avalanche had come out of nowhere and completely buried the road they had just taken under hundreds of thousands of tons of debris. It would be impossible to cross without serious effort, and there was no way the truck would make it through. Even worse, this would undoubtedly delay the reinforcements that were supposed to be following a week behind them. Positively seething, Calder stared at the fallen dirt for a long while, then turned to Sergeant Fletcher as Rogers stepped out of the vehicle.

"We keep going, as much as I'd love to turn around. We need to make it to the base and set up. Take stock of what damage we have, and let's get a move on."

Not bothering to give any of the others so much as a look, the captain headed back into the command vehicle, Rogers hurrying in behind him.

"If there's anything you need help with . . ." Lieutenant Kami looked around, her voice trailing off.

"Thank you, Lieutenant. I think we're okay," Sergeant Fletcher said with a salute. "Cody, James, I want a quick inventory to make sure that we're not missing anything. Mark, get those boulders out of the road. We're pushing forward."

8

Nodding, Mark headed to the front of the vehicle. Though it was free from the grip of the earth, there were still dozens of boulders in the path ahead that would block them from moving the truck across the loose earth that now covered the road. Mark's feet sank into the dirt as he headed for the first boulder. It was roughly the size of a dog, and without much trouble, he picked it up and tossed it away.

The next boulder was even smaller, and Mark was able to push it to the side with his foot. For the boulders that were too big to simply shove aside, Mark used his massive metal shield to tamp down the dirt next to the boulder, forming a small channel into which he could roll it. His suit amplified his strength considerably, especially for pushing and lifting, and it didn't take him long to get the path clear.

Rogers was driving the vehicle, and glancing over his shoulder, Mark could see him through the windshield, which still had clumps of dirt sticking to it. Carefully, Mark led the way forward, and though a couple of times the truck got stuck in the loose dirt, between Sergeant Fletcher, James, Cody, and Mark, they were able to push it free.

It took another two hours to pass through the debris field, and night had settled around them by the time they made it to the top of the pass, which was mercifully free of fallen rock and earth. Pausing for a moment in the pass, Mark could see a road winding down the side of the mountain. Approximately two miles away, shrouded by the darkness, he could see a small group of buildings.

"The base is just ahead," Sergeant Fletcher said. "Let's get a move on."

Piling into the back of the truck with the others, Mark took the opportunity to practice his active recovery as they rumbled down the mountain. Though his biofuel meter was getting low, the effect of the mana suit really helped mitigate much of the energy cost he would otherwise have been suffering. Given the extra labor they had done, Lieutenant Kami had handed out more food, and they ate in silence as the truck neared the base.

When they pulled up to the gate, everyone piled out, weapons in hand, and began to scan for Exlian. Anytime a human building was abandoned in the wilderness, there was a decent chance that Exlian would set up inside. But Mark wasn't too worried, as he couldn't sense anything through the psychic network. It wasn't long before the Rangers reported back, confirming Mark's suspicions.

"No active Exlian," the Ranger commander said. "The base should be good to go."

"Not sure about that," Cody called out.

He was trying to open the gate, to no avail.

"Power is probably cut to the whole place," Sergeant Fletcher said, pointing up at one of the dark floodlights. "We'll have to see if we can get it kicked back on."

With no way to open the gate, it wasn't possible to bring the truck inside, so Sergeant Fletcher, Mark, and Cody joined the Rangers in climbing over the wall. Roughly fifteen feet high and made from solid concrete, the wall was an imposing affair, with heavy barbed wire at the top. Grimacing as he heard the barbed wire scraping against his suit, Mark dropped to the ground on the other side with a heavy thud. Inside the base, everything was absolutely still. And as the sergeant checked the gate to see if it could be operated manually, Mark and Cody headed for one of the nearby buildings.

"Mark, come help me with this."

Hearing Sergeant Fletcher's shout just as he was about to check one of the doors, Mark turned and jogged back to where Sergeant Fletcher was standing next to the gate. With a glance, he saw that the heavy latches had been disengaged, allowing the gate to slide freely. It was kept in place by two large pins, and Mark lifted one as Sergeant Fletcher lifted the other. With heavy steps, they shifted the gate to the side, their suits straining against the weight. Once the gate was open, the command vehicle rumbled through, and the rest of the Rangers came in after them. After the vehicle was inside, Mark and Sergeant Fletcher shut the gate back up and reengaged the locks.

"Let's do an assessment," Sergeant Fletcher said. "We're looking for the generators. See if we can get the power restored."

Splitting up, the team began combing through the abandoned base. Mark had no idea what any of the buildings were, so picking one, he checked the door, only to find it locked. The lack of power meant all the doors were locked, which was likely why the Exlian hadn't been able to set up shop while the human defenders were gone. Though Mark likely could have bashed his way in, their goal was to live here, so breaking the locks simply wasn't an option. After half an hour of futilely trying doors and windows, they gathered with Sergeant Fletcher at the command vehicle again.

"No luck."

"Me neither."

"I didn't have any luck either. Everything is locked up tight."

Looking rather frustrated, Sergeant Fletcher knocked on the

door of the command center and spoke quietly to Lieutenant Kami when she poked her head out. After a few moments, Lieutenant Kami disappeared back inside and reemerged a moment later, carrying a small tool bag.

"Mark, grab the case marked 'B-14' from the back of the truck and follow the lieutenant," Sergeant Fletcher said.

"Yes, sir."

Hurrying to the back of the truck, Mark climbed up, clicking on his suit's light to check the numbers on the crates. Everything was meticulously organized, and it didn't take him long to find the proper crate. Opening it up, he saw a case inside and brought it out. It was heavy, weighing close to sixty pounds, but between his natural strength and the suit's empowering effect, he didn't have any trouble lifting it out of the back of the truck. Lieutenant Kami was waiting for him, and with a nod, she turned and led the way into the darkness. As she walked, she looked this way and that, until she spotted a box set high on the side of one of the buildings.

"There we go," she said. "Get me up there."

At first, Mark wasn't sure what to do and began to look around for something she could stand on. Feeling a tap on his shoulder, he looked over and saw Lieutenant Kami gesturing to the metal shield he carried on his back.

"You'll use this as a platform. Hold it horizontally and lift it above your head. I'll stand on it, which will give me access to the box."

Feeling enlightened, Mark nodded. After she climbed onto the shield, he lifted her up into the air, handing the case he had retrieved up to her when she asked for it. Because he was underneath her with the shield in between them, he couldn't see what she was doing, but he could hear the clank of metal as she messed around with the box. There was a whir and a bright hum, and suddenly, lights began to flicker on, dim at first but growing stronger, as mana surged through the system.

"That should hold for at least a couple of days. In the meantime, we'll need to fix the generators. You can go ahead and put me down."

Mark took a step away from the wall and lowered Lieutenant Kami to the ground, holding the shield still as she stepped off it. Whoever had built these suits had clearly thought deeply about their design, and Mark was finding that the shield was incredibly useful, even though he had yet to actually fight with it.

By the time they got back to where the command vehicle was parked, the others had already begun to split up, heading into the buildings to assess them. Mark was assigned the buildings on the southern side of the base, where he found a canteen, a barracks, and a storage room. The base also held a command center, two control rooms for the mine, an ore-processing station, more storage rooms, an armory, and a rec hall.

The mine itself was set on the northern side of the base, a large, gated cavern with a set of rail tracks extending from it. The door was sealed shut, and Sergeant Fletcher told everyone to ignore it for the moment. Once the base had been explored, everyone gathered in the rec hall, where Captain Calder was pacing nervously. The Ranger lieutenant came as well, though only to say goodbye.

"We're a bit behind schedule, sir," the lieutenant said, saluting Captain Calder. "And since we're going to have to detour pretty significantly, we'd like to get a move on."

Returning a rather shaky salute, Captain Calder swallowed. "You don't think you could stay, do you? Even for a couple of days? We're supposed to have our reinforcements, but they'll no doubt be delayed."

Impassive, the lieutenant shook his head. "I'm sorry, sir, we already have our next assignment, and we can't delay it."

"But what about the Exlian?" Captain Calder snapped. "There are only seven of us. If the Exlian show up, we're as good as dead."

"You've got a secure base here, Captain. As long as you can get the defenses back online, you should be able to survive against all but the largest waves. I'm sorry."

"No, you can't leave," Captain Calder said. "I outrank you, and I'm ordering you to stay."

"Afraid I can't do that, sir," the lieutenant replied, his expression hard. "I only came to say goodbye as a courtesy. My men have already moved out, and I have to join them. Best of luck to all of you."

With another sharp salute, the lieutenant turned on his heel and left the building, leaving Captain Calder staring after him. The room was quiet for a long moment as the reality of the situation sank in. They were a three-day journey from New Emery, alone, in the middle of the wilderness, and the reinforcements that should have arrived within the week would undoubtedly be delayed, forced to find a new path to the mine or shift half a mountain to get through the existing one.

Captain Calder, white faced and trembling, finally tore his eyes from the door the lieutenant had disappeared through and looked around the room, only to find everyone was staring back at him. Flinching slightly, the captain did his best to straighten his shoulders and puff out his chest, though to Mark, it only highlighted how terrified he was. "I am retiring to my room. Lieutenant Kami, take charge. Rogers, with me."

With hurried steps, the captain fled, Sergeant Rogers following closely behind, leaving Lieutenant Kami, Sergeant Fletcher, the Price brothers, and Mark behind.

With a sigh, Lieutenant Kami rubbed her forehead. "Fletcher?"

"Yes, ma'am."

"You know I'm no good at any of this. Our orders are to open the mine, which we will attempt to do once we have the generators back up and running. In the meantime, please do what you need to do to organize the base."

"Yes, ma'am," Sergeant Fletcher said, snapping a salute.

"I'm going to go and see if I can get my head around the mine controls," Lieutenant Kami said. "There's supposedly an operations manual somewhere around here, so I'll be reading all night."

Looking tired already, she waved to the others and left the rec hall.

"Well, seems like we're off to a good start," Cody said, flashing a wide grin.

With a wry smile, Sergeant Fletcher nodded. "Could be worse. You could still be buried under a mile of dirt. All right, since we're probably the only ones able to do any practical good, we better get to it. James, Cody, I want all of the supplies moved out of the truck and into the main shed. Take stock of what's already there and report back to me. Mark, I need an assessment of the base's defenses. I need to know what there is, what still works, what's broken, and what might be able to be salvaged. Additionally, you're on patrol as well, so keep an eye out for any enemies."

"Yes, sir," Mark said, snapping a salute.

He left the rec hall, heading for the front gate. The control room for the base's defenses was in the guard post he had seen right next to it. Though the doors were a little bit slow to respond, they drew power from the emergency generator, so Mark didn't have any trouble getting into the guard post. Inside, he found a simple desk and an inactive terminal. The console was off, and there was nothing else of interest in the room, so Mark left the guard post and headed along the wall to a short tower that stuck up from the fifteen-foot wall. It had a small mana cannon in it, one of six scattered around the perimeter. But like the console, it was powered down. Still, Mark checked it thoroughly, looking for any damage that it might have suffered. He didn't find anything, which was in keeping with what he knew about the evacuation of this base. The humans had abandoned it preemptively, not wanting to get caught in the fierce wave that had threatened to engulf them.

Only one of the six small mana cannons showed any sign of damage, and it didn't look significant enough to keep the weapon from working. Each tower had enough space for a single individual to climb into it and use the mana cannon. After checking all of them out, Mark headed back to meet with Sergeant Fletcher and explain everything he had found.

After making his report, he returned to patrolling, looping around the outside wall, paying careful attention to the psychic network. By midnight, all the supplies had been put away, and the existing supplies had been inventoried, and Sergeant Fletcher came out to meet Mark.

"I'll take the second shift," the sergeant said, patting Mark on the shoulder. "You're doing well, Fields. Very well indeed. Go ahead and grab something to eat and then turn in."

"Thank you, sir."

Normally, a battalion would have a cook who would have food ready at all hours to serve the needs of the soldiers. But given the size of the Black Mountain Battalion, Mark and the others had to fend for themselves. Grabbing one of the prepped meals and heating it up, Mark scarfed it down and then joined the Price brothers at the barracks. Both of them were sound asleep. He parked his suit at the foot of the bed he chose and climbed out of it, breathing a sigh of relief as he stretched his body. The suits were designed for maximum comfort and to be worn over a long period of time, but after days in the thing, Mark was happy to be free of it. After a quick shower and changing his clothes, Mark tumbled into bed and was asleep as soon as his head hit the pillow.

9

It felt like only seconds had passed when he heard a sound and his eyes snapped open, his heart beating loudly as he looked around. He spotted one of the brothers getting into his suit, though he couldn't tell who it was in the dark, and a quick glance at his watch told him that it was 3:30 a.m. Since he wasn't on shift, Mark turned over and went back to sleep.

He woke again when the sun was just peeking over the horizon at six thirty. Getting up, he did his morning stretches and climbed back into his suit. The sleep had done him good, and he was full of energy as he headed out to get some breakfast, James coming with him. While they were eating, Sergeant Fletcher and Lieutenant Kami arrived and joined them at their long table. Seeing James jumping up, Mark started to rise as well, but Lieutenant Kami waved for both of them to sit down.

"Given how few of us there are, there's no point in following protocol," she said. "It's unlikely the captain will be joining us for meals, and Sergeant Rogers probably won't either. With that in mind, I think it's okay for us to relax some of the standards."

"Thank you, Lieutenant," Sergeant Fletcher said, speaking for James and Mark.

As everyone ate, the sergeant ran through everything they would need to do that day.

"So far, we haven't found the power station. I have a sneaking suspicion that it's in the mine itself. What that means is we're going to need to get the mine doors open, get to the power station, figure out what sort of fuel it takes, and kick it back up. Mark, you're going to be working with the lieutenant here to see if you can do that. James, you, Cody, and I will be continuing to patrol and working on getting the rest of the base organized and ready to function."

"Yes, sir."

After breakfast was over, Mark followed the lieutenant to the command center, which she had claimed as her makeshift laboratory. Before they went to try to restart the generators, she had him help bring in gear from the command vehicle, allowing Mark to get a peek inside for the first time. The vehicle seemed to be composed of three main sections: the cab, which was large enough to seat six, each in their own individual chair; the laboratory, which took up the main body of the large vehicle and consisted of half a dozen workstations of various sorts; and the back storage area, where all the extra equipment and supplies had been stored.

"We're going to be moving these tables out into the main command center," Lieutenant Kami said. "Normally, stuff like this isn't mobile, but these are special versions. Just be careful with them, please. There's no way we're going to be able to fix them if they get broken."

As carefully as he could, Mark carried each of the workstations out of the command vehicle and deposited them where Lieutenant Kami instructed in the command center. Most of the stations held machines that he didn't recognize, but one of them was clearly an alchemist's workstation. Lieutenant Kami must have noticed

Mark's curious looks, because after he had put it down, she smiled and patted the machine. "This is an alchemist's station. Have you ever seen one before?"

"I have," Mark said, nodding. "In fact, I've used one quite a few times."

"Ha, that's what I guessed," Lieutenant Kami said. "Most people don't know how to arrange the items on the top, so when I saw you putting everything in order, I guessed you had some familiarity."

"The master I study under has been teaching me alchemy," Mark said, brushing a bit of dirt from the top of the table.

"Well, good. Maybe you can help me out sometime. This table's going to be awfully important if we're going to survive the wait before our reinforcements get here, but we'll have time for that later. Right now, we need to go and deal with this generator issue. I'm afraid my temporary generator isn't going to last more than another twelve hours. The draw on this base is significantly higher than normal."

Falling in beside the lieutenant, Mark peeked at her curiously. "Do we know where that power is going?" he asked.

"Nope. That's one of the mysteries we have to solve. Let's get the door open and check out the mine. Maybe the power is being pulled there."

The entrance to the mine was a twenty-foot-wide hole that sank deep into the side of the mountain. It was covered with a massive metal gate, completely sealing it away from the outside air. Though the rest of the doors in the compound were working, the gate to the mine wasn't. And considering that like the front gate, it was controlled through one of the dead control consoles, they would have to figure out a way to open it without power. That proved to be both easier and harder than Mark had anticipated. It didn't take Lieutenant Kami long to identify how the door worked, and when she did, she turned to Mark and shrugged.

"You're going to have to rip it open," she said, tapping a spot on the door. "Right behind here is where the main latch is. We need that open, which means we need a hole. See if you can crack it."

Thinking for a moment, Mark nodded and unclipped one of his gloves, freeing his hand. There was a shimmer of mana as his hand transformed, and with a shout, he lunged forward, thrusting two fingers into the heavy metal door. It was hard, much harder than anything he had ever tried to cut before, but his fingers still sank almost two inches into the door, leaving a neat little hole.

Withdrawing his hand, he shook his fingers, then thrust again, targeting the same exact spot. This time, his fingers broke through, piercing all the way through the two and a half inches of metal that made up the heavy door. From there, it was a relatively simple matter to shift the latch inside the door, and with a click, the entire thing swung open.

"Normally, even if you destroy the latch, doors like this won't open," Lieutenant Kami said, "but that's if they have mana flowing through them. This one doesn't, which means that it's relatively simple to open. We're lucky in that regard. Come on, let's see where this generator room is."

The entrance to the mine was up a small hill, and inside, the tunnel sloped down, heading deep into the mountain. Around sixty feet from the entrance was a series of rooms carved into the rock, none of which had doors. One was an office, another was a supply room, and the third was the room that Lieutenant Kami and Mark were looking for.

Through a short passage was a cavern close to sixty feet long and thirty feet wide, with a roof that soared to twenty-five feet. Inside were six massive machines, each one currently dormant. They looked completely unremarkable to Mark, but from the way Lieutenant Kami's eyes lit up when she saw them, it was clear they weren't.

"Wow, this is incredible," she said, rushing over to one of the machines. "Look at this. This is an Emberline Super 28. These things are insanely expensive, and the power output on them is astronomical." Even as she spoke, she seemed to realize how strange her words were. Turning, she stared at Mark in confusion. "Why on earth would they need six? One of these things is enough to power a mining operation."

Mark had no answer and could only shrug. Turning back to the generator, Lieutenant Kami began to check over it, her fingers flying over the control panel while the arms on her suit poked around.

"We're going to need to jump-start this one," she said, "but they're all linked, so we should be able to use this one to start the others in turn. It's a pretty ingenious configuration, actually, because having six allows the power to be cycled, providing an opportunity to do maintenance on the generators. This was the one problem with the Emberline series. Because of how much power they put out, generators have to be taken offline once a week in order to reset them. Otherwise, they run the risk of burning out."

"Do you know how to do the maintenance on them?" Mark asked.

"Oh yeah, it's pretty easy. Actually, I can show you while we're here." Gesturing for Mark to come closer, Lieutenant Kami began introducing the structure of the generators to him.

Her words flew fast, and Mark found himself barely able to keep up. Her explanation was a mixture of practical engineering knowledge and completely esoteric theory that went right over Mark's head. Thankfully, the Emberline Super 28 generators weren't particularly hard to run. Many of the maintenance tasks were automated by the generator itself and simply needed to be triggered by an operator. The maintenance of each generator only took half an hour. After double-checking that all six generators were in good working order, Lieutenant Kami had Mark connect one of her smaller, temporary generators to the first Emberline.

"All right, let's get this ready," Lieutenant Kami said. "We're gonna kick it off in three, two, one."

Flipping the switch on the first generator, Mark held his breath. For a moment, nothing happened, and then, with a hum, the generator sprang to life. An almost oppressive wave of mana spread from it, causing Mark to cough as it washed through him.

"Ah, I love that feeling," Lieutenant Kami said, taking a deep breath. "Let's get the other generators going and make sure that all the connections are good. By the time we get out to the base, everything should be powered up."

Following Lieutenant Kami's directions, Mark switched each of the other five generators on, adding to the heavy hum that filled the room. Once everything was working and they had monitored it for a few minutes, they headed back out and traced the heavy cables that now carried the mana out and into the base. When they got to the door, Lieutenant Kami gestured to the hole Mark had created.

"There should be a welder and some scrap plate in the shed. You'll want to patch that up to prevent any problems."

"Yes, ma'am," Mark said, saluting.

The base had come alive, with all the doors, lights, and consoles now operating at full power. The weapon emplacements were operating as well, and as Mark stepped out of the mine, he saw a mana cannon he hadn't noticed before sitting on top of the command post, swiveling to face him. Freezing in place, he saw it stop as well, facing the entrance to the mine. Nervousness rose unbidden in his chest, and he took a small step to the side, watching as the tip of the mana cannon shifted to follow him. "Um, Lieutenant?"

Lieutenant Kami had already walked some distance away but now stopped and looked back. "Yes? Something wrong?"

Moving his hands slowly, so as to hopefully not trigger the

mana cannon, Mark pointed at it. "I don't think it's supposed to be doing that."

"Doing what?"

Taking a deep breath, Mark took another careful step to the side, and the cannon once again shifted to follow him.

"Oh yeah, it's not supposed to be doing that at all. Don't move." Lieutenant Kami's voice held considerable urgency, and Mark remained absolutely still as she rushed off to the command center.

The base's defenses were largely automated, much like the massive mana cannons that sat on top of the walls of New Emery. A few minutes after Lieutenant Kami disappeared, Mark heard her voice through his comm.

"The profile on this thing is all mixed up, and it's tagging you as a suspicious individual, a potential threat. Hold on, I'm putting in a manual override."

No more than thirty seconds later, the mana cannon wiggled slightly, and the mana it had been building up dispersed. Breathing a sigh of relief, Mark took a small step backward, but it didn't continue to track him and instead began to slowly rotate, scanning the yard for any potential threat. When he got to the command center, Lieutenant Kami came out of the door, shaking her head.

"That was weird," she said. "I put your suit in as a friendly, because it kept tagging you otherwise. Thankfully, the system hadn't quite decided what to do with you and had submitted for validation, so it didn't just open fire. I've checked everybody else's profiles and made sure that we're all good. You seem to be the only one with any issue, but that's fixed now. You shouldn't have any trouble."

"Thank you, ma'am," Mark said, his appreciation genuine. He had no idea if he'd be able to survive a blast from a mana cannon and frankly had no interest in finding out.

With the power fully restored, Lieutenant Kami kept Mark busy, setting up the various workstations she had brought with her.

"You know, originally, I was just going to keep them in the command vehicle," she said. "But since we're likely going to be here for a while and we may need to find and process extra food sources, they'll be better in here. And besides, I don't really want to hang out in the command vehicle any more than I have to."

Glancing out the window of the command center at the massive vehicle parked outside, Mark didn't blame her. Captain Calder had spent practically every moment since they arrived squirreled away in the large vehicle. Mark could only imagine how difficult it would be to work with him moping around nearby.

That night, to celebrate getting the power back on and the base set up, Sergeant Fletcher cooked up a meal. Though it wasn't much better than the ready-made meals that they normally ate, the sergeant was generous with the portions, giving everybody almost three times as much food as usual. Lieutenant Kami ate her normal amount and then gave the rest to the others. For the first time in almost a week, Mark felt like he was actually full.

"We've gotten everything set up," the sergeant said. "Our supplies will last us for a month and a half, and the base is in surprisingly good shape. There's some maintenance to do here and there, a couple of things to fix, and it's probably a good idea to start exploring the mine a bit, at least to make sure that the carts are still working. Additionally, we'll continue patrolling and even set up some observation points around the base. Otherwise, we're hunkering down, trying to cause as few disturbances as possible, and waiting it out. Any questions?"

Glancing at each other, James, Cody, and Mark each shook their heads. The actual mission they had been deployed on had turned out to be rather easy, as the base really was in great shape. Mark had expected to come and find considerable damage, but to him, it looked as if the Exlian swarm that had caused the miners to abandon the mine in the first place had never arrived. There was almost no sign of Exlian presence, apart from a bit of damage here or there where a door had been tested. But since the base had been sealed up tight, the Exlian hadn't gotten inside any of the buildings. And since there was no accessible food, any Exlian who had wandered in hadn't stayed. In truth, Mark had been anticipating a much more difficult mission, and as he settled down that night, he couldn't quite figure out if he was pleased or disappointed.

10

Over the next few days, they settled into a regular routine. Mark, James, and Cody were responsible for patrols and assisting Lieutenant Kami whenever she needed help. Sergeant Fletcher was in charge of security and spent most of his time patrolling the base or watching the sensors that they had set up on the mountainside outside the wall. Occasionally, Mark would spend time with him, learning how to read the sensors and how to distinguish regular animals from Exlian.

The days slowly trickled by, and Mark found himself spending more and more time with Lieutenant Kami, delving into how the machines that ran the mine worked. In Mark's imagination, the mine had been operated by an army of men and women with pick-axes who would chip out pieces of ore and toss them into carts, which they'd push up to the surface. In reality, the mine had been operated by a number of autonomous machines, with humans working alongside them to ensure that they operated properly.

All these machines now sat dormant, but with the power restored, they could be brought back online. Unfortunately, the machines hadn't fared as well as the sealed buildings, and many of them needed significant repairs. This was what Lieutenant Kami and Mark, as her assistant, spent their time doing.

Though Lieutenant Kami wasn't a naturally gifted teacher, she was incredibly adept with the machines themselves, and Mark quickly learned how to both diagnose and repair over a dozen different pieces of mining equipment. That included the rail line, which used a magnetic rail system to pull carts in and out of the mine, depositing their contents at the smelter. Mark could just imagine how efficient the system would be once they turned it on. They didn't have enough people to begin the operation, but he was hopeful.

Two weeks passed like this, and news finally came from New Emery. Unfortunately, it was the worst possible news they could have received. The damage from the rockslide was extensive, much bigger than they had realized. Even worse, the rockslide had triggered the collapse of two bridges, further delaying the battalions that were supposed to come and reinforce them.

James was the one monitoring the comms channel when the message arrived, and not wanting to be the one to face Captain Calder's wrath, he went to find Sergeant Fletcher. The sergeant accepted the message with a stoic sigh and then, like a prisoner walking to the gallows, went to discuss the news with the captain.

Mark was all the way up in the mine when he heard the screaming. Captain Calder was unloading on the sergeant, and not wanting to get caught in the cross fire, Mark decided that it was an opportune time to check a few of the machines down below. When he emerged an hour and a half later, after triple-checking every machine, things were quiet once again, but from the way James and Cody were tiptoeing around, it was clear that the tension had yet to fade. Sergeant Fletcher had a particularly hard set to his jaw at dinner that night, and when he had finished eating, he tapped the table to get everyone's attention.

"Given the unfortunate news we received this afternoon, we're going to be shifting our timeline. It's going to take them at least three months, and that's a conservative estimate, to clear a path so they can get the equipment here. In the meantime, they're dispatching another Ranger team with supplies. We've also been ordered to do our best to start the operation of the mine."

His brow furrowed, Mark leaned forward. "Sir, we don't have enough people to do that."

"I'm fully aware, Fields, but those are the orders we've gotten. So to the best of our ability, we'll be operating the mine. We're on a bit of a time crunch, it seems, and they want to be able to make the first ore delivery as soon as the path is reconnected. Tomorrow, you and Lieutenant Kami will work on that. Even if we're only operating at a hundredth of our capacity, we need to be operating."

"Sir, why don't they just deploy personnel without the equipment?" Cody asked, and for a long moment, the table was silent.

Shaking his head slightly, Sergeant Fletcher put his large hands on the table and pushed himself to his feet. "I don't presume to know the intricacies of how the higher-ups think," he said heavily. "We've gotten our orders. We'll do our best to carry them out." With a heavy nod, he left the mess hall, and James, Cody, and Mark just stared at each other.

"I knew this whole thing stank," James said, poking glumly at the food on his plate with his fork.

"Stinky or not, it's our swamp to wade through," Cody said, patting his brother on the shoulder. "And besides, all we're doing is kicking the mine back on and then hanging out. We just have to slip under the radar for a couple more months, and then we'll be back in New Emery, our feet up, with a drink in hand. What could go wrong?"

As it turned out, a lot could go wrong. It started when Mark was out on patrol. He was up on the slope of the mountain when he heard a hum and saw the lights dim on the base below. Concerned, he returned as quickly as possible, and by the time he got to the base, the power had gone out completely. The gate no longer worked, so he was forced to scramble over the wall. When he landed in the yard, he saw Lieutenant Kami sticking her head out of the command center. "Mark, we've completely lost power. Go check the generators."

Thankfully, the door to the mine hadn't been shut, so Mark didn't have to punch his way through it again. As soon as he stepped into the mine, he felt a faint prickle. There were Exlian present. Facing a dark mine with unknown monsters, Mark should have been frightened. Instead, he felt a cold anger that drove him forward.

It didn't take long to spot the culprit, a strange, floppy creature that looked quite like a slug, if one didn't pay any attention to the large claws extending from the front of its body. As soon as it saw Mark, it let out a faint shriek, and its body bunched up. Though Mark had never faced an Exlian drone like this before, he instinctively dodged to the side just before it sent a jet of acid that burned through the wall as it landed.

Shifting power into his legs, Mark lunged forward, his foot lashing out to bat aside one of the claws. At the same time, he drew the mana blade from his back, hacking down on the slug-like Exlian's body. There was a faint sizzle as the mana blade cut into its flesh, then a popping sound as the disgusting creature exploded in a fountain of gore and acid.

Thankfully, Mark's reactions were quick, and he was able to step back and lift his shield, blocking the deluge of acid and ichor that splattered down on him. As the creature's death shriek echoed in his mind, Mark scanned the environment, looking for another monster. The Exlian had chewed into one of the main cables and had been draining the power from the generators. It didn't seem to have any companions around, so Mark set about repairing the connection, first turning off the generators, then soldering the wires back together, rewrapping them, and finally kicking the generators back on.

By the time he got out and reported what had happened to Sergeant Fletcher and Lieutenant Kami, the power was back on, and everything seemed normal. It turned out that the creature Mark fought was called a power slug, an annoying type of Exlian that not only ate mana but stored it. It was concerning, of course, that the Exlian had entered the mine, but considering how well Exlian drones could dig, there really wasn't much that could be done apart from paying more attention in the future. Over the next few days, things seemed to settle down, but Mark couldn't shake the bad feeling that was growing in the back of his mind.

On the fifth day, when Cody came back from his patrol, his face was paler than it should have been. Though he wanted to ask what was wrong, Mark just followed quietly behind him as Cody went to find Sergeant Fletcher. "Sir, I saw some Exlian movement."

"What are we talking about?" Sergeant Fletcher asked, his eyes narrowing as he took in Cody's expression.

"Nearly a hundred, sir. Hunters."

Sergeant Fletcher took in a sharp breath. "A hundred? Are you sure?"

"Yes, sir."

By this time, Lieutenant Kami and James had both joined them.

"I thought hunters were mainly solo," James said.

"They are, unless there's a higher-ranked ghoul with them," Lieutenant Kami said quietly.

"That's right," Sergeant Fletcher agreed. "Cody, did you see any of them that stood out, either much larger than the others or with a strange frill-like thing around their head?"

When he saw how quickly Cody nodded, Mark's heart fell.

"Yes, there were at least three or four who were a lot bigger. They looked like ogres. And then I saw at least one with a frill around its head."

"The ones with the frills are screamers. They can let out a blast of sound that'll kill you outright if it hits you at close range. And worse"—Sergeant Fletcher tapped his chest, producing a ringing sound—"the suits do nothing against them. Screamers are tremendously dangerous, and if you face one, make sure you don't stand in front of its mouth."

"They're not the worst of them, though," Lieutenant Kami said, causing everyone to turn to her. "The ghoul line has a third, more dangerous adaptation. They're called brains, and they have the ability to wield mana directly, sort of like an energy controller."

"Where did you see them?" Sergeant Fletcher asked, pulling up a map of the surrounding area and projecting it onto the table with his watch.

Taking a moment to orient himself, Cody pointed.

"I saw them through the scope," he said, referring to the built-in magnification his helmet carried. "They were about six miles east of us, working their way through a ravine."

"Were they heading our direction?"

Swallowing, Cody nodded, and Sergeant Fletcher swore under his breath.

"Apologies, ma'am," he said, turning to Lieutenant Kami.

"No need to apologize," she replied. "I feel quite like saying some of those words myself. Sergeant, the captain will have to be apprised of this, but I don't think that it would be expedient to mention anything to him at this juncture. There's a fair chance that the Exlian swarm Private Price spotted will pass us by. I think the best thing we can do is reduce our footprint and hope for the best. We'll alert the captain once it becomes necessary."

Mark could swear he heard a sigh of relief from the sergeant as Fletcher quickly nodded his head in agreement. "I think that's wise, Lieutenant. What about Sergeant Rogers?"

"As far as I'm concerned, Sergeant Rogers is in the same position as the captain," the lieutenant said, her lip curling disdainfully. "He's on a need-to-know basis. In the meantime, what do you suggest is the best way to handle this situation?"

"We need to stay inside," Sergeant Fletcher said, "and reduce the noise and mana output of our camp as much as possible."

"That will be difficult, as we're scheduled to start bringing the mine online in the next couple of days," Lieutenant Kami said with a frown. "Of course . . . it's a good idea to double-check all of the equipment before we try operating it. Private Fields?"

"Yes, ma'am."

"Weren't you just saying the other day that the equipment in the mine needs to be double-checked?"

Saluting smartly, Mark nodded. "Yes, ma'am. Given the recent presence of that slug, I think it's important that we do a triple check on all the equipment to make sure that we didn't miss anything."

Of course, Mark had already checked all the equipment many times. The machines were in perfect working order, and the power slug had done no damage to any of them, as it was only interested in sucking the mana from the generators. Still, Mark was smart enough to understand the hint Lieutenant Kami was giving, and from how pleased she was with his answer, it was obvious he had guessed her intent correctly.

"We'll continue to monitor the Exlian swarm as best we can without alerting them," Lieutenant Kami said. "Otherwise, everybody needs to stay inside. Continue as normal."

Though they did their best, it was quite difficult for Mark and the others to continue operating as if everything were normal.

Having spent a good few hours tearing apart ghoul bodies, Mark couldn't imagine what it would be like to face one hundred of them. Hunters were D-ranked Exlian that pushed into the D+ rank, while the hulks, screamers, and brains were all in the C rank. Though their team had multiple B-ranked empowered, Mark, James, and Cody were not nearly so strong, and facing off against a horde of ghouls was dangerous no matter what rank you were.

The next few days in the camp were tense, and the tension only continued to grow as the enemy slowly made its way closer. Even worse, the ghouls' numbers seemed to be swelling, and though they weren't moving very quickly, in large part thanks to the massive hulk trudging slowly along behind them, Mark could feel the pressure mounting.

On the fourth day, it became obvious to everyone that the ghouls were heading in their direction, and Lieutenant Kami finally broke the news to Captain Calder. He didn't respond with yells the way Mark thought he would. Instead, his face went white, and his lips set in a sharp line. He nodded and stalked out of the room, Sergeant Rogers trailing after him. He was gone for half an hour, then came back, his eyes bright.

"Get ready for a fight," he said, leaving Mark and the others stunned.

11

James, Cody, and Mark had been talking about it quietly, out of earshot of the officers, and they had all reached the conclusion that Captain Calder would flee at the first sign of trouble. Instead, he seemed to have found his courage somewhere. Sergeant Fletcher, clearly just as skeptical as everybody else, quickly snapped to attention, and the others followed suit.

"How are the defenses looking?" Captain Calder asked, scanning the wall.

"They're stable," Sergeant Fletcher said. "As long as we can keep the mana flow from the generators to the control center uninterrupted, we've got a total of seven mana cannons: six of them on the wall, one on the command center itself. They can be set for autotargeting or can be targeted manually."

"And they'll kill a C ranked?"

"It might take a couple shots, but yes, sir."

"Good, then we should be fine. Between my power and the cannons, there shouldn't be any issues. Sergeant Fletcher, you know the team the best. I'll leave the deployment of our troops to you."

"Yes, sir."

Turning to the others, Sergeant Fletcher laid out the situation. "We have a few hours before they make it to us, at least at their current pace. However, it's likely that the hunters will separate from the hulks, who are the ones slowing them down, and will launch their attack sooner. With that in mind, we'll start our active defense now. Mark, you're going to be in charge of keeping those generators running. If the Exlian manage to cut them out, we'll be in trouble, so protect them with your life. James, Cody, and I will man the walls with Captain Calder and Sergeant Rogers. Lieutenant Kami will assist anybody who gets wounded."

Having reached the end of the list of people to assign, Sergeant Fletcher licked his lips and took a deep breath. "Thankfully, the automated systems are working, so we'll have at least some protection. That's it. You're all dismissed."

Saluting, Mark walked out of the building with James and Cody. Looking at the two brothers in turn, Mark found he didn't have anything to say. They were about to face their first, and potentially last, fight as a battalion. Cody suddenly broke into a wide grin and patted Mark on the shoulder.

"Don't look so stressed," Cody said. "I'm sure it's going to work out fine. Besides, I've always wanted to shoot a mana cannon."

"Yeah, me too," James said, giving Mark a thumbs-up. "As long as you keep the juice flowing, we'll blast those scum into oblivion."

"You got it," Mark said, and reaching out, he bumped fists with the two brothers.

He was on his way up to the mine when a thought struck him, and he took a quick detour to the supply room to grab a small crate packed to the brim with nutrient pouches. They still had over a month's supply of nutrient pouches stacked on the shelves, so he took the crate with him to the generator room just in case everyone needed to retreat into the mine. He was hoping it wouldn't come to that, but if it did, it would be good to have some food on hand.

Heading back to the mine's entrance, Mark double-checked to make sure that the mana flow was unimpeded. He had just finished when he heard a loud hum, and one of the mana cannons let out a sharp crack. From where he stood, Mark had a good vantage of the entire compound, and he could see that the easternmost tower had just unleashed a blast.

Almost immediately, there was an answering roar, and then the other towers began to light up. Though it was hard to see beyond the wall, Mark could imagine what was coming. In fact, he didn't even need to, because he could feel it. A fierce wave of brilliant energy rushed toward him, filling his mind. He had never seen Exlian in this number, and as they closed in on the base, he realized that he had taken a step forward, nearly leaving the entrance to the mine. It was with effort that he held himself back, grabbing the doorframe tightly.

There was something alluring about that luminescent wave that made him want to rush forward and join it. Thankfully, the feeling passed quickly, as the crack of the mana cannons erupted into a steady tattoo. Each explosive blast was met with a shriek, and each time light in Mark's mind dimmed slightly. Yet the horde rushed forward, and soon the first of the hunters reached the wall.

With a massive leap, it rose into the air, its forearms waving wildly, as if to claw its way over the wall. Before it could make it, there was a shout, and Sergeant Fletcher leaped up, his suit propelling him high into the air. His sword lashed out and met the Exlian hunter, bisecting it neatly. But he didn't stop there. Rather than retreating behind the wall, he landed on the other side, disappearing from Mark's view. Occasionally, Mark could see the flash of his blade rising into the air above the wall.

Then the rest of the Exlian hit, and the scene dissolved into chaos. Captain Calder was standing on the roof of the command center, and lifting his hands, he began to unleash his power. This was the first time Mark had seen him use it, and almost immediately he could sense the similarities between Calder and his brother, Joe. While Joe wielded fire absolutely, Calder unleashed explosive blasts with snaps of his fingers. He seemed to be able to position them anywhere he could see, and as the Exlian tried to breach the wall, they were met with explosions that sent them hurtling backward.

Sergeant Rogers wasn't nearly so flashy, but his power was just as effective in keeping the Exlian out of the compound. Thrusting out his palms, he created barriers that he hurled into the leaping hunters' paths, halting their momentum completely. Often, the two coordinated, with Sergeant Rogers hurling out a barrier to set up a group of Exlian, giving the captain perfect targets. The two Price brothers soon waded into the fight as well, hacking and slashing with their blades as they fought the Exlian warriors.

Forced to just watch, Mark found himself growing tense, his grip on the doorframe tightening. No longer was the bright light in his mind enticing him to join in. Instead, a desperate hunger awoke in his chest, pressing against his self-control as it drove him to throw himself into the fray. With a growl, he forced himself to look away, and as he did, a faint presence tickled his mind. It was slight, almost impossible to detect, and every time Mark tried to lock onto it, it slipped like a fish from his grasp.

Something didn't want to be found, and Mark couldn't afford to ignore it. Pushing the battle from his mind, he stepped back into the darkness of the mine, trying to calm his senses as he slowly homed in on the elusive feeling. It took him almost a minute of absolute concentration to find it, a faint, lilting melody that drifted through the mana around him. It sounded like no music he had ever heard, whispering that it had something to share.

But before he could learn what it was, another presence

appeared in Mark's mind, this one sharp and piercing—and heading straight for him. It was coming from outside the mine, and immediately any thought of finding the elusive song was gone. Spinning around, Mark darted for the door. Like a small sun burning in the psychic network, it closed in on the base and then stopped some distance away, not participating in the fight. Yet he could tell from the way it inched closer that its attention was fixed on what was happening inside the base.

Standing just inside the door, he scanned the darkness beyond the lights, trying to identify the monster that was coming. At the same time, he heard a loud roar, and three massive hulks lumbered closer to the wall. Each was at least ten feet tall, and their bodies were packed with muscle. Their hands were huge and hung all the way to their knees.

"Don't let them get near the wall," Sergeant Fletcher yelled, and launched himself toward the first of the hulks.

Almost immediately, he was surrounded, and the hunters began to tear at his armor, but the heavy plates of his engineering suit stayed strong. The arms on the back of his suit began to spin, rotating so quickly they pulverized everything that came close.

Hacking and slashing with his blades, Sergeant Fletcher cut a swath through the Exlian to the first hulk, which let out a roar and lunged for him. Though he had been rushing forward, he took a neat step back, causing its grab to barely miss, and then brought his blades down on the monster's reaching arms. With a twist, he forced them aside, at the same time pulling the hulk in toward him. His foot lashed out, the metal tip of his boot driving up through the hulk's exposed throat with such force that its neck snapped. As the creature's head lolled to the side, one of his blades flicked out, decapitating it and sending its head tumbling.

Even as he eliminated the first hulk, James and Cody slammed into the second. Their assault wasn't nearly as precise as Sergeant

Fletcher's, but it was no less effective. James and Cody were like madmen, their teeth bared in wide grins as they threw themselves at the enemy with no regard for their own safety. One of the hulk's long arms smashed into Cody's chest, threatening to hurl him backward. But at the last moment, he hung on to the arm, his body flailing as the force of the blow rattled through him. Yet even as his bones were being shaken, his mana sword was thrusting through the hulk's ribs half a dozen times.

On the other side, James was tearing apart the hulk's legs, and the monster quickly collapsed. James and Cody both pounced, trying to kill it as fast as possible, even as dozens of hunters piled on top of them. A moment later, with a loud roar, the brothers broke free. Both of their suits were badly damaged, but they didn't seem to care one bit as they tore across the battlefield, looking for the other hulk.

Sergeant Fletcher had no chance to keep an eye on them, as he had spotted one of the screamers in the midst of the enemy forces. Letting out a loud roar, he crouched and charged, the whirling arms on his back taking care of any hunters who tried to leap toward him.

Back in the compound, Captain Calder and Sergeant Rogers were continuing to keep the enemy off the wall to the best of their ability, but occasionally, one or two of the hunters would slip through. When they did, Lieutenant Kami was always there to meet them, and though she looked exceedingly nervous every time she faced off against a hunter, her method of fighting was no less lethal than the captain's.

The arms on her suit each wielded a short mana spear, and they struck like a swarm of wasps, riddling her opponents with holes and slowing them down. She would then dispatch them with the sword she carried, always targeting their heads or hearts to cut them down as fast as possible. Though things looked stable, the fight was only just beginning, and the entire time Mark could feel the powerful Exlian lurking in the darkness. Even worse, he could tell that it could sense him as well. Just as he had been able to sense the panic in Cody's mind when Cody had been buried under the landslide, he could feel the curiosity and hunger of the creature as it regarded him.

Mark imagined that just as the Exlian sensed each other in the network, it could sense him as well. After all, he had never encountered any other human who could use the Exlian psychic network the way he could. The creature appeared to have locked onto him, and Mark got the distinct impression that if he shifted his attention for even a moment, the monster would strike. As the rest of the battalion engaged in a fierce struggle, Mark was locked in a struggle of his own, a tense standoff that left him overwhelmed. As his nervousness grew, the battle changed once again, but this time not in the defenders' favor.

It started with the powerful Exlian lurking in the shadows. Mark felt its attention flicker and then vanish. Suddenly that Exlian was speeding backward, retreating from the battlefield. While that relieved some pressure on Mark, what he noticed entering the scope of the psychic network did not. A new group was heading toward them. But rather than appearing as a bright light as the first assault force had, this group of Exlian created a strange dampening effect, as if a great shadow were being cast over everything.

Though he couldn't directly sense them in the network, Mark could see a group of hunters sweeping toward the front gate. Thankfully, whatever was shrouding them from psychic view didn't work against the mana cannons, which suddenly lit up, blasting away at the hunters as they charged. Fumbling to activate his radio, Mark sent a message.

"There are more enemies coming from the west!"

Mark saw Captain Calder, who was still on the roof of the command center, spin around, his expression ugly. Another force of at least seventy-five Exlian was just about to assault the gate, and Sergeant Fletcher and the two privates were still outside, battling fiercely against the first Exlian horde. After gritting his teeth, Captain Calder ordered Sergeant Rogers and Lieutenant Kami to intercept the new enemy. Sergeant Rogers moved immediately, and though much more hesitant, Lieutenant Kami was right behind him. Rushing over to the gate, they arrived just in time to hear a terrifying crunch. Mark caught a flash of movement and felt an intense surge of mana that left the gate torn into two pieces that were thrown to either side. The first Exlian to pass through was a screamer. It landed on all six of its limbs, its mandibles peeling back as its mouth widened into a gaping maw, and let out a blast of sound that caused Mark to wince. The force of the sound wave blasted Lieutenant Kami backward into the wall with such force she fainted and the wall shattered. When Mark managed to refocus his gaze, he saw the lieutenant crumpled in a heap and Sergeant Rogers locked in battle with the screamer.

12

With no time to waste, Mark sprinted for the front gate. He was under strict orders to keep the generators running and ensure power continued to feed into the mana cannons on the walls, but he couldn't abandon his comrades to the Exlian horde. Sergeant Rogers was engaged in a fierce fight against the screamer, but he appeared to be holding his own. Mark headed for Lieutenant Kami, hoping to intercept the Exlian hunters swarming toward her position.

Feeling the pull of the heavy suit slowing him down, Mark let out a low growl and put more power into his legs, leaping the last fifteen feet just as one of the hunters stretched out its arms to tear at Lieutenant Kami's armor. He slammed into the creature with a heavy bang, sending it reeling backward. Crouching as his feet hit the ground to absorb some of the shock, Mark spun his heavy shield around him, battering back another of the hunters. At the same time, he lifted his blade with two hands and brought it chopping down on a third.

Hunters were wiry creatures, roughly humanoid in appearance but with four long arms that ended in razor-sharp claws. They had bits of armor plating here and there but were clearly built for speed and agility. This was evidenced when the hunter he had targeted dodged backward, nearly escaping his strike. The tip of his mana sword hacked through the monster's shoulder, and it let out a sharp shriek as one of its arms drooped. Not wanting to give it a chance to recover, Mark twisted his blade and lunged, piercing through its chest. As his foot landed, he tore his blade upward and felt the sharp mana edge cleaving the Exlian's sternum.

There was no time to confirm the kill, as more hunters leaped toward him. Mark pulled back, using the shield to ward off the hunters on his right as he slashed to the left, claiming an outstretched arm. With the unconscious lieutenant behind him, Mark was forced to stay in place, doing his best to ward off the Exlian attacking from the right and left, while keeping half an eye on the fight between Sergeant Rogers and the screamer.

Despite the fact that this was his first real-life fight in these sorts of conditions, Mark found himself moving with calm certainty. He had never battled hunters before, but the countless nights he had spent fighting warrior Exlian in his dreams stood him in good stead. He shifted smoothly from one defensive position to another and was able to instinctively stay out of reach.

He was helped, of course, by the nearly one-ton slab of metal he wielded, and he soon made that his primary defense. While it was excellent for blocking, it could do a lot more than that; when swung swiftly enough, its blunt edge could cleave through flesh and bone alike. Which made it even more effective when brought crashing down on a charging Exlian, reducing it to pulp, and it wasn't long before bodies were scattered around Mark's feet.

Near the gate, Sergeant Rogers was still battling the screamer. The sergeant used energy barriers that he projected from his hands, constantly pushing the screamer and keeping it off balance as he dodged the piercing waves of sound it unleashed. As

Mark watched, he saw Sergeant Rogers dart to the side, slipping past the screamer's head. It reacted swiftly, turning on its six legs as its mouth opened to unleash a blast.

Without panicking, Sergeant Rogers ducked, flinging his hand up and sending out a glimmering wave of air that slammed into the bottom of the screamer's head, causing it to bounce upward, deflecting the wave of sound. At the same time, the sergeant lunged forward, drawing his mana sword. As the blade crackled to life, the screamer realized its vulnerability and reared back, only to find another barrier had appeared behind it, locking it in place.

Prevented from retreating, there was nothing the screamer could do as Sergeant Rogers's blade slashed across its throat, cutting through its heavy neck. Rogers didn't slow down, and as soon as his blade cleared, he pressed forward, stabbing the screamer in the chest a half-dozen times. With each stab, his blade punched a hole deep into the screamer's body, causing green blood to splatter. With his last strike, the creature shivered and fell, and Sergeant Rogers jumped back.

Mark, who had watched the fight with appreciation, was still battling the swarming Exlian, doing his best to keep them off the lieutenant. By this point, he had been forced to retreat until he was almost on top of her. With a leap, Sergeant Rogers easily cleared Mark's head, landing on the edge of the building above him. He thrust out his hands, forming a thick barrier that blocked the hunters momentarily.

"Get the lieutenant to safety," he barked, and Mark, glad for the respite, complied.

Slipping his sword back into his sheath, he reached for Lieutenant Kami, grabbed one of her limp arms, and hauled her up onto his shoulder. He was just deciding where he should take her when there was a sharp crack behind him, and a tremendous force slammed into his side, causing him to stagger and nearly drop the lieutenant. Steadying himself against the wall, Mark turned and saw the barrier Sergeant Rogers had erected had shattered, and the remnant force of the blow that had broken it had been what hit him.

Striding through the ruined gate was a tall, thin Exlian, boasting six arms and an abnormally large skull. Mark felt his breath catch, and cold fingers of fear gripped his heart as he recognized the dreaded brain that Lieutenant Kami had warned about. The brain's presence in his mind was strangely muted, and in the thick swarm of Exlian mental signatures, he hadn't noticed the powerful creature coming. The air around its head began to tremble, warping as mana gathered in a dense field around its heavy skull.

Realizing it was going to unleash another blast, Mark lifted his shield and jumped away. He heard a loud whomp and felt a beam of pure mana slam into his shield. It hit with such force he was knocked from his feet, and as he scrambled to regain his balance, he was horrified to see his heavy shield had a hole the size of his head burned straight through it.

Since his shield was only slowing him down at this point, Mark abandoned it, hurling it desperately toward the brain as he fled around the corner, hoping to gain some distance from the creature. As it disappeared from view behind him, Mark heard a blast, which he hoped was Captain Calder attacking the brain.

Unfortunately, before he could figure it out, a wave of psychic power rolled through the network, and shrieking, the hunters turned their attention to the captain, swarming from all over the base toward the command center, on whose roof he stood. At the same time, Mark could feel the brain's attention locked on him. He had no idea why the creature was fixated on him, but it didn't matter. It was coming to kill him, and Lieutenant Kami as well, and he needed to find a safe place.

More explosions rocked the air as Captain Calder fought against the ever-increasing swarms of hunters darting toward him, and Mark ran for all he was worth. Retreating to the command center had been his original plan, but now there was no time, and doing so would put him in the heart of the fight. Without his shield, he didn't think it was very likely he'd be able to keep Lieutenant Kami safe.

So he ran for his next best option: the entrance to the mine. Sprinting up the small slope toward the door, he paid careful attention to the psychic network, trying to anticipate the brain's next attack. He had no idea what rank the Exlian was, though he imagined it was at least B. Mark felt another blast charging up behind him. He dove to the ground, tossing Lieutenant Kami out in front of him into the mine's passageway. A moment later, a powerful blast burned through the air above his head, slamming into the side of the mountain with a massive explosion of stone and dust.

Scrambling on all fours, Mark made it through the mine's entrance, pushing Lieutenant Kami's body past him and slamming the door shut as fast as he could. As the heavy lock engaged, Mark couldn't help but feel slightly worried. The force of the blasts the Exlian brain unleashed was enough to melt straight through his shield. His only hope was that the mana-reinforced door would be enough to ward off the strikes. Grabbing Lieutenant Kami, Mark pulled her farther down the passage, peering through her faceplate to try to assess the damage she had suffered. He could see a hint of blood that had trickled from her nose, and he was worried that the sound blast had caused internal bleeding.

Placing her down in the passage that led to the generators, Mark grabbed the medical kit she carried. It had been cracked when she slammed into the wall, and half of its contents had been scattered across the base during Mark's mad sprint toward the mine, but he found one of the emergency-treatment syringes and an uncracked healing potion. With careful fingers, he lifted off her helmet, trying not to disturb her head too much. He was worried that her neck might have been broken from the way her head lolled uncontrollably from side to side.

Hearing a muffled whomp and feeling the earth shaking around him, Mark glanced toward the door, his heart pounding in his chest. There was no sign of damage on the inside, which meant that the door had held. With its power gone, Mark had had no trouble cutting through it, and the same would go for the Exlian, but now that the generators were back on, the door was reinforced with mana, increasing its toughness drastically.

Slightly calmer now that he knew the brain wouldn't simply be able to burn its way through the door, Mark focused on the lieutenant. The vital signs her suit was putting out were bad, and it was clear that the damage she had suffered was severe. So after injecting the first healing potion, Mark quickly administered a second. After a tense sixty seconds, Lieutenant Kami suddenly gasped and sat up. "Mark, where are we?"

The last thing she probably remembered was facing off against the screamer, so to wake up in a dark cave, her body in pain, with Mark looming over her must have been disorienting.

"We're in the mine, and we've got enemies banging on our door. The others are still fighting outside."

"The screamer?" Lieutenant Kami asked, grabbing her helmet from the ground beside her and buckling it on. "What happened to the screamer?"

"Sergeant Rogers killed it, but a brain came in right after. It's the one directing this attack. It sent all of the hunters after Captain Calder at the command center. And then it came after us."

Letting out a shaky breath, Lieutenant Kami tried to push herself to her feet, only to wince and sag against the wall.

"I'm still badly hurt," she said, reading over the biometric data her suit was displaying for her. "Internal bleeding, broken ribs, pierced lung. Oof, I'm in rough shape."

"There's one more potion," Mark said. "Do you want it?"

"No. The damage will heal over time, and another potion won't make it go faster. Plus, potions heal the body by drawing on its natural energy. They only work if you have nutrients to burn. I'm completely out."

Without a word, Mark darted down the passage into the generator room, ripped open the box with all the nutrient pouches, and grabbed a handful. He returned to Lieutenant Kami, holding them out to her.

"I grabbed some just before the fight," he said, "in case we got into this situation."

For a few seconds, she stared at them, then looked up at Mark, as if trying to decide whether she should say something or not. Ultimately, she didn't, unclipping her helmet again and forcing the nutrient gel from one of the packs down her throat. "Ugh, this stuff is disgusting."

Before Mark could reply, there was another muffled whomp, and the earth shook again. Turning to look at the door, Mark closed his eyes and concentrated, searching for the presence of the Exlian brain. It was just outside the mine, focusing on charging another blast.

In the distance, the hunters were still swarming Captain Calder and Sergeant Rogers, who had retreated from the top of the command center back to the command vehicle that had brought them to the base. Mark could sense the cannons still firing, but their attacks were haphazard at best, and two of them had been broken, including the one on top of the command center. The others were designed to fight enemies outside the wall and so were of no help against the horde of Exlian hunters.

Sergeant Fletcher and one of the Price brothers were still fighting just outside the eastern wall of the base, and with a sinking heart, Mark realized he couldn't find Cody's presence anywhere on the battlefield. Lieutenant Kami slowly limped out from the passage, supporting herself with the wall and gripping her ribs tightly. She was in no shape to fight, and Mark genuinely was at a loss. He wanted to rush out and help the others, but opening the door would be a death sentence.

Lieutenant Kami was clearly just as conflicted, and the troubled look that she gave Mark wasn't reassuring. The smart thing to do would be to keep the door closed, hoping that it would protect them from the swarm long enough that the Exlian would lose interest. At the same time, Mark knew that if they really wanted to get into the mine, he wouldn't be able to stop them, as they could simply dig around the massive door, eventually breaching the passage from the side. While the blast door was keeping them safe for the moment, in another sense, rushing into the mine had left them trapped like fish in a barrel.

"We may need to retreat," Lieutenant Kami said, pointing down the passage.

"Wouldn't that just delay the inevitable?" Mark asked, his brow furrowing as he glanced down into the darkness.

Lieutenant Kami hesitated as if weighing what she would say next. Before she could say anything, however, the situation shifted again. Mark was the first to sense it. Emanating from the brain outside, a wave of strange energy began rushing through the door toward Mark and Lieutenant Kami.

13

Previously, Mark had found it difficult to detect the brain in the midst of the other Exlian. He had assumed it was just because the brains' psychic signatures covered them. But now he realized that there was something else at play. As the wave of strange energy spread out from the brain, Mark felt the mana faltering in the conduits under his feet. Wherever the energy spread, mana stopped flowing and quickly faded away. It was a bizarre sensation, one that left Mark and Lieutenant Kami gasping. Her voice filled with horror, Lieutenant Kami stared toward the door. "Oh no. No!"

She took a step back, her hand still supporting her as she leaned against the wall.

"What is it? What's wrong?"

"Null field."

No sooner had the words escaped her lips than they heard the tremendous screech of metal being sheared, and a pair of claws punched through the door that had sealed the mine shut. At the same time, Mark felt his suit powering down as the mana that fed into it was rapidly drained. Before, every one of his movements had been magnified, made easier by the mana-powered suit, but now, as the mana flowing through it bled away, it transformed into a heavy and cumbersome metal cage.

His mind whirling, Mark could only watch in stunned silence as the brain's claws ripped the blast door apart, tearing through it with ease. Casting the scraps of metal to the side, the brain stooped and poked its head through the door, its large eyes locking onto Mark. Instinctively, he tried to step back, only to find his suit unresponsive. The Exlian brain stepped into the mine, and Mark willed his suit into motion. He took a lunging step forward, covering Lieutenant Kami as the brain leaped. Its claws raked against the armor of his suit, tearing a thick gash in the plates on his arm. He felt the monster's fingers brushing against his forearm, but thankfully, he had had the presence of mind to transform his arms already.

He could feel the null field all around pressing against him, suppressing the mana outside his body. His suit felt more like a tin can than a magically empowered piece of armor. With a sense of fierce desperation, he slammed his fist against the brain's bony body. The blow sent the brain stumbling backward, but a moment later, it returned, its arms slashing toward Mark from multiple directions. He did his best to block the strikes, but the monster's sharp claws ripped through his armor like paper.

Waves of strange power continually pulsed from its large skull, suppressing all the mana in the area, including the mana that should have been running from the generator through the wires out to the base outside. Mark barely had room to pay attention, as he was embroiled in a fight with a monster at least two ranks above him. It was all he could do to protect his own life. Every single strike of the Exlian brain's claws sent him staggering, but Mark gritted his teeth and held on.

By this time, his armor had become more of a hindrance than a help. After rushing forward to push the Exlian brain off balance, he disengaged with a leap backward and climbed out of his suit as fast as he could. Behind him, Lieutenant Kami was still recovering, and in front of him, the brain let out an angry roar. Thankfully, the null field it expressed prevented it from using its mana blast ability. Though its claws were sharp, its close-combat ability was relatively weak considering its rank, barely allowing Mark to keep up.

Still, Mark was continually forced back and needed to burn through his energy reserves at a tremendous rate as he pushed his body to the absolute limit. He could barely see the brain's strikes, and more than once he suffered nasty gashes as he failed to dodge the hits. As his biofuel meter dipped toward zero, Mark knew that he couldn't keep this up. He was racking his brain for something, anything, that might help when there was a loud roar and the door to the mine practically exploded, sending shards of shrapnel through the air.

Distracted, the brain spun around, and a moment later, Sergeant Fletcher's heavy fist slammed into its chest, sending it tumbling down the passageway. The sergeant was in rough shape, chunks of his armor missing and his helmet badly dented. Yet even as he took a step forward to give chase, the mana drained from his suit because of the null field, and his speed slowed drastically.

Scrambling to his feet, Mark saw the sergeant quickly shed his armor, and as the brain let out a sharp scream and jumped forward, Sergeant Fletcher met it in melee combat. He didn't have bone blade hands like Mark, and every time the brain slashed, bloody streaks were left across the sergeant's body. But with his face set like flint, Sergeant Fletcher ignored the wounds and pounded away at the brain, doing his best to deal as much damage as possible.

Mark, his energy bottomed out, knew he would be of no help in the fight. In a stumbling run, he headed for the crate of nutrient pouches and grabbed one. Ripping it open, he gulped it down as fast as he possibly could and then grabbed another. Though Sergeant Fletcher was completely unarmored and every single one of the brain's claw strikes tore his skin to shreds, the sergeant's body healed almost as fast as it was damaged. As Mark felt energy starting to trickle back into his body, the sergeant slammed a fist into the side of the brain's head, causing it to wail in pain, even as its claws scored his arm deeply. The damage was so bad that his next blow faltered as his arm completely lost strength. But a moment later, his skin knit itself back together, and he lifted that arm to block one of the brain's blows.

It was a battle of attrition, and the sergeant, who only had his fists to rely on, could hardly deal any damage to the brain. His suit had been discarded, and his mana blades didn't work, completely negating any offensive advantage that he had. Lieutenant Kami was in even worse shape. She was still in her armor, which, being lighter than Sergeant Fletcher's and Mark's, had not restricted her movement quite as much. But she had no way to contribute to the fight and could only hunker by the wall, watching as Sergeant Fletcher and the brain hammered at each other.

Mark's energy levels were starting to return, and shoving another nutrient pouch in his mouth, he launched himself into the fight. Unlike the sergeant's, Mark's weapons were built in, and as he landed his first strike on one of the brain's arms, it let out a sharp shriek and leaped backward. Much slower than Sergeant Fletcher's healing, the wound Mark had caused began to close up, but the fact that they had broken the creature's defenses gave both of them considerable hope.

"I'll hold it down," Sergeant Fletcher yelled, and rushed forward.

In that moment, Mark's heart lurched, his instincts screaming at him. What happened next was too fast for Mark to react. The brain, with a cunning that sent a spike of despair through Mark, withdrew the null field, pulling the suppressive energy back into its body. As mana flooded through the space, the air around the brain's head warped. The generators, which had been pumping out mana this entire time, filled the air with a wave of power, causing the brain's ability to charge almost instantly.

Too late, Sergeant Fletcher caught sight of the disturbance around the brain, and then piercing light filled the space as the brain unleashed an attack at point-blank range. Superheated mana cut through Sergeant Fletcher's unprotected chest, punching a hole through him like a hot rock dropped on snow. At the very last moment, Sergeant Fletcher had managed to turn away just enough that the attack had missed his spine, but a massive chunk of his side was now missing, and as his body started to drop, the brain let out a roar of triumph and leaped forward, intending to finish the job.

There was a shout, and just before the brain slashed down at Sergeant Fletcher's neck, Lieutenant Kami hit it from the side. The power in her suit had been restored with the null field's withdrawal, and the six arms on the back of her suit tore into the monster's side. She lifted her sword, trying to stab it through the chest, but it spun, slapping the blade from her grip. Mark sprinted for Sergeant Fletcher, grabbing him and pulling him back. They were only a dozen steps from the entrance to the mine, and as he dragged the sergeant toward the opening, he saw the brain turn on Lieutenant Kami, tearing into her with all its claws.

Grabbing one of the arms on her suit, it yanked her free and threw her against the wall before shrieking and lunging toward Mark and Sergeant Fletcher. The fight outside seemed to have ended, and Mark could sense Captain Calder and Sergeant Rogers right outside. With the entrance only a few feet away, he put all his power into moving as quickly as he could, and the monster was a few steps behind him when Mark reached the entrance of the mine. Outside, on the slope leading down toward the base, he could see Captain Calder and Sergeant Rogers. Behind them, the entire base was filled with wreckage. The buildings were smashed and destroyed, and most of the wall that had once surrounded it was torn down. Signs of the battle were everywhere. What gave Mark pause, however, was the strange expression on Captain Calder's face.

Dragging Sergeant Fletcher, Mark saw Captain Calder raising his hands. He tried to dive through the door, intending to get out of the way to let Captain Calder attack the brain. Yet even as his body fell forward, he came up short, slamming into something invisible in the air. That was when he saw Sergeant Rogers's cold smile.

The barrier Sergeant Rogers had created sealed the mine's entrance, preventing Mark from leaving, and as the brain arrived behind him, Captain Calder's explosive power rocked the mine entrance. Mark had seen Captain Calder at work and knew that the explosions were powerful. This was the first time he had ever been close to one, however, let alone experienced it in an enclosed space.

There was a moment of silence, as if the world were pausing in anticipation of the sound, and then everything transformed into an inferno. Blistering heat scorched his flesh, and explosive force shattered his bones. Mark's entire world went white, then black, and he must have been screaming, though he couldn't hear the sound of it over the roar of stone crashing down around him.

The moment of pain passed quickly, as did the sound, fading into blessed silence. When Mark gathered himself, he realized he must have fallen unconscious. For the second time since he had left New Emery, Mark felt earth packed all around him. This time, however, he wasn't wearing a suit, and he sincerely doubted anyone was coming to save him. Taking stock of his situation, he tried to wiggle his fingers and found, to his surprise, that he could.

One of the last things he remembered was his body being shattered, his bones broken by the reverberating waves of force and then further crushed by falling stone. Yet not only could he move his body, but he seemed to be able to do so with no pain. He had no idea how much time had passed, but since he could move his arms and legs, he carefully tried to shimmy his body back out of the dirt. It was slow going and took almost half an hour of careful work, but he eventually managed to get himself extracted. By chance, a few rocks had fallen around his legs, forming a small gap that gave him space to move. When he was finally free, he sat, trying to make sense of his circumstances.

The last moments before the explosion were burned into his memory, and it was disorienting to suddenly find himself in a completely different situation. After a moment, he checked his watch, only to find it had been shattered in the collapse of the cave entrance. Next, he checked his status and felt mana crackling along his arm, producing a glow that cast a bit of light around him. At least he wasn't currently in a null field.

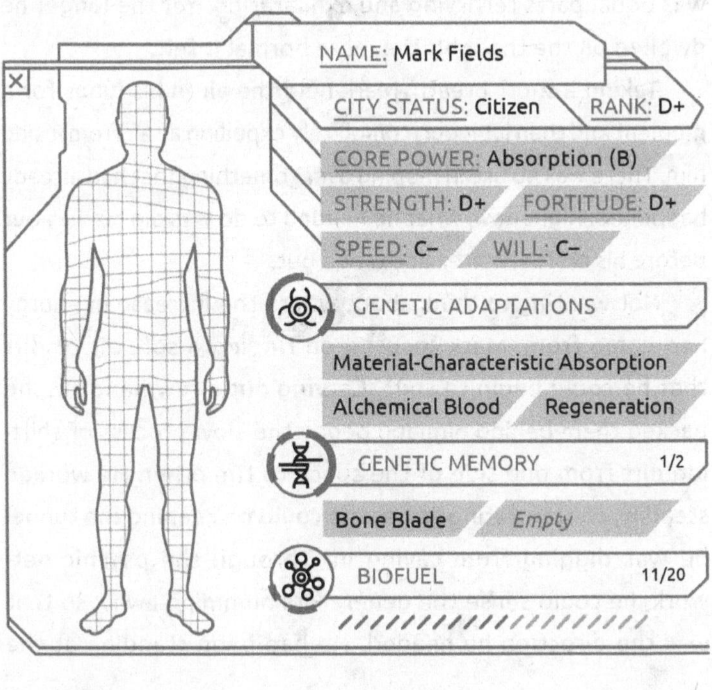

Staring at the words uncomprehendingly, Mark tried to make sense of what he was seeing. All his stats had gone up by one or two minor grades, which seemed like the opposite of what should have happened. Additionally, where had he gotten a regeneration power from? When he shifted to the side, Mark's hand brushed up against something, and using the light from his status, he tried to see what it was.

As the dim light revealed a desiccated hand attached to an arm crushed under tons of stone, Mark's breath caught. Visions of watching Sergeant Fletcher's body heal raced through his mind, and as the light of his status faded away, Mark sat in darkness. He should have felt sick, or at least remorseful, but instead, he felt nothing. Mark once again had the strange experience of knowing how he should be reacting but finding he reacted completely differently. The thought that he had somehow absorbed the power from Sergeant Fletcher's body was equal parts terrifying and exhilarating. Yet the longer he dwelled on the thought, the more normal it felt.

Taking a short breath, Mark held the air in his lungs for a moment and then let it out, completely expelling all air from inside him. There was no use in moping over something that had already happened. Right now, what he needed to do was dig his way out before his biofuel meter bottomed out.

Not wanting to think about where the increase in energy had come from, Mark focused on finding a soft bit of dirt that he could begin to shift. Carving out a few handfuls, he packed them behind him and began the slow process of shifting dirt from one side of the space to the other. He worked steadily, concentrating as best he could on keeping the tunnel he was digging from caving in. Through the psychic network, he could sense the generators humming away, so that was the direction he headed. He had been standing at the entrance when the blast went off and was originally a good distance from them, but the explosion must have thrown him back into the mine, even as it caused the mine's entrance to cave in.

14

Time slowly ticked past, and Mark maintained his slow pace. Coming to a large stone, he dug around it with his fingers, gripped it tightly, and carefully pulled it back through his hole until it was behind him. As he turned around, he suddenly saw a large claw and froze. It took him a moment to realize that it wasn't moving, and with his heart pounding, he inched closer and reached out to touch it. The flesh was cold, and Mark couldn't sense any life in it. As his fingers brushed over the claw, an incredible hunger suddenly erupted in him, and it was all he could do to keep from lunging forward and biting down on the dead Exlian's flesh.

With a deep breath and ironclad control, he shifted his direction, doing his best to dig around the body of the brain, half afraid that it might spring back to life at any moment. It took him another half an hour before he was finally free of the earth, breaking out into the interior of the mine. As he pulled himself from the dirt and collapsed to the ground, he found he had never been so grateful for breaths of air.

The first thing he did once he was recovered was look for Lieutenant Kami, and his stomach dropped. She lay crumpled against the wall, completely unmoving, and when he walked over, he realized that she had been dead for at least a day. Reaching up with careful fingers, he removed her helmet, the inside of which was splattered with dried blood. It seemed that she hadn't fully recovered from her injuries before attacking the brain, and when it had thrown her aside, those injuries had worsened, killing her.

Not knowing what to do, Mark slowly stood up and tried to take stock of the situation. The cave-in had buried the first twenty-five feet of the mine's entrance and scattered large rocks everywhere. One of those stones had crushed the crate of nutrient paste, destroying the majority of the packs, leaving only a few, dirty but otherwise unscathed. Sitting in the darkness, Mark ate all of them to replenish his energy as he tried to figure out his next move. The psychic network was quiet, and Mark imagined a few days must have gone by, as there was no sign in his awareness of Captain Calder or Sergeant Rogers outside in the ruins of the base. The Price brothers were nowhere to be found either, and it suddenly struck Mark that he was alone. Alone in the wilderness, isolated from New Emery, and surrounded by enemies. Hurrying over, he checked Lieutenant Kami's watch. It still worked.

According to the watch, he had been buried for almost two days, which meant that if the captain and Sergeant Rogers had survived, they were long gone. That tracked, as Mark couldn't sense the presence of the command vehicle either. The thought of Calder and Rogers caused fury to fill Mark's mind, but he pushed it aside. He would deal with them and their betrayal at some point, but right now, survival was most important. Finishing the last of the nutrient pouches, Mark checked his biofuel meter.

Biofuel 17/20

He had spent six biofuel units digging through the earth and replenished four, but the strange, gnawing hunger hadn't gone away. Occasionally, he found his eyes darting toward the pile of earth that blocked the mine's exit, and Mark knew that the body of the brain was calling to him. Ignoring the hunger as much as he could, he sat down and began his meditation, trying to come up with a plan.

Food and shelter were his two pressing concerns. Shelter was taken care of at the moment, as any Exlian still roaming around outside would have to dig through a mountain to get at him. That left food as the primary concern. Assuming the Exlian hadn't completely ransacked the base, there was food in the storage rooms, but Mark had a sneaking suspicion that he wouldn't find much left untouched. From what he had seen, the base had been empty of Exlian even before Calder brought the mountain down, and if that was true, the captain had likely taken most of the supplies with him as he and Sergeant Rogers headed back to New Emery.

Exlian meat was poisonous, and though Mark knew that there were ways to neutralize the poison, he wanted to avoid having to try them out. Of course, he also knew full well that it might not be an option. Before that, there was something he wanted to try. Getting up, he walked over to where Lieutenant Kami's body lay and crouched down beside her. For a long moment, he looked at her still, cold face. Part of him, though only a small part, was screaming at him that this was a bad idea, but Mark felt like he had no choice. He had to know.

Reaching out, he touched the corpse's exposed cheek and closed his eyes. As he activated his absorption power, Mark didn't see his growing shadow. Like dark water, it rippled and stretched, joining with the corpse's. Multiple crimson eyes opened on the shadow, blinking at Mark and then at the corpse. The lieutenant's body began to visibly wither as vital energy was sucked out of it.

Mark felt his biofuel meter shoot up, and it soon topped out, leaving him feeling stuffed. Despite the disquiet that caused, Mark didn't stop his absorption, and suddenly he felt something break free from Lieutenant Kami's body and rush into him. An electric shiver ran up his spine, and he rocked back on his heels, staring at the notification that had just popped up on his status.

> Sufficiently advanced genetic material acquired. You have unlocked the A-ranked ability Quantum Clones.

Blinking, Mark didn't move for a long time as he felt his body shifting to accommodate the new energy he had just taken from Kami's corpse. It took a few minutes for it to settle down, and once it did, he opened up the new ability that had just been added to his status.

> Quantum Clones: Your consciousness can be split, forming Quantum Clones that can perform different actions simultaneously. Quantum Clones can continue to exist indefinitely, so long as your concentration is maintained and they are not observed. Maintaining a Quantum Clone will drain your biofuel.

Blinking, Mark stood up.

Almost immediately he could feel the drain as he looked down at himself. He was still crouched by Kami's body, staring up at himself. It was an incredibly odd feeling, to have his thoughts split into two different tracks that both felt completely real.

Taking a few steps back, he saw his other self stand up and walk around to the other side of Kami and crouch down to grab her shoulders. Taking the corpse's legs, the two Marks carried the body toward the generator room. Halfway there, his foot caught on a rock that he hadn't seen, and he stumbled. As soon as his concentration broke, the other Mark vanished, and the body dropped to the ground.

"Wow, this is weird."

He had only had the clone active for a few minutes, but already he could tell that his stored biofuel was being depleted. After moving Kami's body to the hallway leading into the generator room, Mark created another clone and set it to digging through the cave-in while he watched. He dug fast, moving a tremendous amount of earth, and Mark quickly found that once the task had been set, it didn't take that much concentration to keep it going. Of course, if it had been a more complex task like alchemy or hand-to-hand combat, it likely would have been harder, but digging was mindless enough that he could do it on autopilot.

Eventually, he grew tired of watching and joined in the effort to dig through the collapsed passage. He carefully avoided the body of the brain, leaving only one arm exposed so he knew where it was located. However, he spent extra time digging out Sergeant Fletcher's body. Just like Lieutenant Kami's corpse, Sergeant Fletcher was withered, a vital piece of his physical form missing. As carefully as he could, Mark gathered the badly damaged corpse and carried it to lie next to Lieutenant Kami. He planned to bury both of them once he made it out of the cave, but for the moment, they would have to remain by the generators.

Once he had taken care of Sergeant Fletcher's corpse, he returned to his work. As the hours flew by, he made slow but steady progress. The repetitive work gave him plenty of time to think, and what occupied his thoughts most of all was his strange power.

Mark had no idea how he had been able to acquire two additional powers from the corpses. He was becoming increasingly aware that his body was incredibly mutable and worked nothing like a normal empowered body. After all, he had managed to transform his blood into an alchemical substance on top of unlocking the ability to absorb specific genetic codes.

What he wasn't sure about, however, was the difference between the two powers he had just absorbed and the bronze skin ability he'd had the option of absorbing from the brute who had kidnapped Sky and then chased him out into the dead zone. His two new powers hadn't been added to his genetic memory but instead had been granted to him as if they had been with him from the beginning. Mark also couldn't take powers from skill gems the way a normal person could. So why then was he able to absorb Kami's and Sergeant Fletcher's powers?

There seemed to be no readily apparent answer, and until he had more bodies to test it on, Mark didn't anticipate getting one. As he dug through the dirt, he ran into Sergeant Fletcher's mana armor, which the sergeant had pulled off when he'd encountered the null field. Though there was considerable battle damage, the main functions seemed intact, so Mark hauled it out of the earth and dragged it into the generator room, where he had placed Sergeant Fletcher's corpse. Even as he set it against the wall, he was still back in the passage, continuing to dig his way out.

"This sure is convenient."

After a solid twelve hours of work, he still hadn't made it all the way through the dirt, but he was starting to get quite hungry. He had figured out that having a clone around for an hour cost one biofuel unit, which wasn't bad at all, considering he had just gotten another hour's worth of work done. Wondering how Lieutenant Kami had been able to fill an entire multifloor laboratory by herself, Mark tried summoning another copy but quickly found that while he could do so, his concentration wasn't strong enough to maintain both clones if he wanted to work as well.

Additionally, the draw on his energy levels close to tripled with a second clone, and Mark could see how summoning a large number of clones would get very expensive very quickly. Still, his twelve hours of digging had put him close to the entrance, and when he paused to take stock of his situation, he realized he only had a few more feet to go. At the same time, Mark's hunger was nearly overwhelming, making it very hard to concentrate on even simple things. Licking his lips, he dismissed his clone with a wave, glancing back at the clawed hand sticking out of the dirt. Every fiber of his being was screaming at him to walk over and bite down on it, but the thought was still too unsettling.

"I can't go out there hungry. I mean, what if I open up the rest of the tunnel and there are Exlian waiting to ambush me?" Mark said out loud.

As he reasoned with himself, Mark took a step toward the brain's corpse.

"But Exlian are poisonous if you don't prepare their meat properly."

Mark stopped in place.

"Maybe I could just absorb a little bit. After all, when I absorbed the lieutenant's ability, it filled up my biofuel."

He took another step forward.

"This is ridiculous. Who's ever heard of a person eating Exlian? Isn't this supposed to be the other way around?"

For some reason, at that moment, Mark imagined Mime rolling her eyes. The thought distracted him from his hunger, and with a sigh, he rubbed his forehead.

"I wonder how Mime is doing. Hopefully she's getting enough to eat. Ugh, this is so gross."

Despite knowing that what he was about to do was objectively disgusting, Mark felt nothing but anticipation as he walked over to where the brain's arm extended from the wall. Rather than just grabbing it and beginning to devour the meat, he dug out the monster, moving carefully, always on guard in case it was just playing dead. When he worked his way up to its shoulders, he realized that wasn't possible, as its head had been detached from its torso by the sharp edge of a large boulder. Feeling a bit better, Mark quickly uncovered the rest of its body. As much as he wanted to tear the flesh off the thing and shove it in his mouth, he restrained himself and placed his hands flat on the Exlian brain's back. This time, he didn't close his eyes as he started to absorb. But after a solid minute, nothing had happened. Straightening, he frowned and stared down at the corpse. "Huh. That should have worked. With Lieutenant Kami, I just tried to absorb her power. Why isn't it working now?"

Biting his lip, Mark looked at the brain's head. Still unsure, he reached over and picked it up, trying to absorb its energy once again. Again, it didn't work. Ignoring the hunger that was practically burning a hole in him, Mark thought about the problem and soon realized a key difference in his body's reaction to the two corpses.

"With Lieutenant Kami, I just wanted to take over her power," he said. "But my body seems to be telling me something different this time."

While he had been attracted by Kami's body, it hadn't been hunger but instead a more esoteric feeling resembling greed. Holding the head in one hand and reaching out to touch the corpse with his other, Mark shifted his line of thinking. Rather than activating his ability and trying to absorb the power from the Exlian body, he focused on his desire to devour it. Almost immediately, his shadow grew large, jagged teeth along its edge as it lunged forward like a black wave. This time, Mark was watching, and the sight was so shocking he fumbled the head, dropping it to the ground. It bounced off his foot and started to roll away, but suddenly a tendril of his shadow stretched out, wrapping itself around the head before it could get far. At the same time, it seemed to wave at him, and Mark got the distinct impression that his shadow disapproved of him wasting food. The sheer absurdity of the situation and the idea that his shadow could communicate with him left him bemused.

"I'm sorry?"

What answered him was a faint crunching sound as the corpse rapidly vanished into the shadow, chewed up in big bites until nothing was left. With a burping motion, his shadow spat out a gleaming marble that rolled to a stop against Mark's foot. He stared at it blankly for a moment and then reached down to pick it up, still trying to wrap his head around what had just happened. Taking a deep breath, Mark pushed aside his conflicted feelings and shoved the Exlian core into his pocket. There was no time to get mopey about his situation, and if he wanted to ensure his survival, he couldn't waste a single thing. His biofuel surged, rapidly reaching peak levels as he processed the tremendously powerful flesh of the B-ranked Exlian. Mark, however, was distracted by the window that had popped up.

> Sufficient specialized genetic material acquired. Would you like to remember Null Field?

15

Swallowing, Mark slowly nodded, and as the notification window vanished, he saw a blinking light on his status, indicating that the second slot of his genetic memory ability had been used up.

The bloody corpse was gone, and as his shadow retreated into its normal form, Mark realized that the earth upon which the Exlian had lain had been completely cleaned.

"So that's what happened."

His words were quiet, but they still rang loud in the empty mine. A lot of mysteries were beginning to be revealed, but for every question that was answered, two more took its place. One thing Mark knew for certain, however, was that his power wasn't absorption in the way that it had been assessed.

He had thought that the ability to transform his arms into any substance he touched was a relatively strong one, but it turned out it very well might be his weakest. He would need further study to understand why, by devouring an Exlian corpse, he could unlock genetic mutations to transform his body, and why that was different from the way he absorbed powers from the bodies of empowered humans. But right now, with no other corpses to test with, Mark turned his attention to the new power he had just gotten.

Closing his eyes, he activated it and felt the back of his neck squirm. The sensation only lasted a moment, and then a wave of strange energy spread out around him, causing the mana that flooded the entrance of the mine to stagnate and begin to disperse. Soon, there wasn't a hint of mana anywhere within a dozen feet. Even the mana from the generators had been dispersed, though Mark could feel it threatening to overpower his null field as it filled the area outside the field's range. After taking a breath, Mark realized that it wasn't precisely true that all the mana had dispersed. All of it outside his body had fled, chased away by the strange energy field he now produced. At the same time, the mana inside his body was untouched. Mark flexed his fingers, transforming them into bone blades, and found they conducted mana perfectly fine.

"Well, that's cool."

Canceling his hand transformation, he touched the back of his neck but was unable to find anything out of the ordinary. Still, that was where the null field originated from, so Mark could only assume that his body had changed in some way.

"As long as I didn't grow a third eye or something, I'll probably be fine."

Canceling the null field, Mark headed for the tunnel, and half an hour later, he broke through to the outside. Rather than the light he was expecting, everything was dark. The stars and moon were covered by thick clouds that made the ruins of the base appear even more eerie. The generators were still running, of course, and a few flickering lights blinked in the darkness, casting pools of yellow amid the gloom.

Taking a deep breath of the fresh night air, Mark closed his eyes, letting his senses roam freely as he checked for any Exlian. Nothing. Flexing his hands, he transformed them into bone blades and headed down the slope. The command vehicle was gone, no doubt driven off by Captain Calder and Sergeant Rogers, and almost every building he saw was badly damaged. The mana cannons hung limply, and a few of them were missing altogether. Considering there was still power, it was clear that all of them had been broken. As Mark walked through the ruins of the base, a hint of nostalgia washed over him. The atmosphere was almost exactly the same as in the dead zone. There was no hint of life, no Exlian corpses. They'd likely been dragged off by the survivors, to be reprocessed in a nest somewhere to produce more of their brethren.

The first thing Mark did was head toward the eastern wall, where Sergeant Fletcher and the two Price brothers had been fighting. Mark climbed through a gap in the wall and found himself in the midst of a scarred battlefield. The devastation outside the wall was at least a dozen times worse, and Mark could only imagine how fierce a fight it had been. Just like inside the wall, however, there were no corpses. When Mark caught sight of a smashed faceplate, sadness welled up inside him. He knew how silly it was, but he had been holding out a hint of hope that one of the Price brothers might have survived. Instead, all he found was the ruined remains of their suits.

Exlian didn't take prisoners, as they had no interest in the minds that inhabited the bodies of their prey. So the likelihood of either brother being alive was zero. Swallowing the lump in his throat, Mark turned and headed back into the base. His first stop was the storage buildings. There, he found that just as he had suspected, everything had been ransacked. Whoever had taken the goods, likely Sergeant Rogers and the captain, considering they had carried everything out in the crates instead of breaking them open, had only done a quick sweep, but they had taken all the food. The things that remained behind were parts and equipment intended to help bring the mine back online.

Still, Mark searched thoroughly, moving everything salvageable from the storage units back up and into the mine. Next, he headed for the barracks and mess hall, then the infirmary and armory. It appeared that both of those last buildings had been missed, and Mark found a small box of emergency rations, the type normally distributed to soldiers during combat. There were also a number of vials of medicine, along with some pieces of equipment that looked interesting and a first aid cart, all of which Mark packed up and carried to the mine.

His last stop was the command center, where, to his dismay, things were worse than he had expected. The primary computer system had taken a direct blast, completely obliterating it, and much of the other equipment in the room had been caught by the shrapnel. Still, carefully recalling how to disconnect everything, Mark salvaged what he could, carrying everything he could get his hands on back to his temporary base.

Of course, he didn't like the idea of not having a door he could close. So after breaking out the plasma torch, he spent the early hours of the morning cutting a door from one of the guardhouses and salvaging some steel beams. He drove them into place with a makeshift sledgehammer, burying them deep into the fallen stone that now covered the mine's entrance. Each beam was nearly twenty feet long, and the sun was already above the horizon when he finished hammering the last one in.

Part of the reason it had taken him so long was that he stopped every few blows to scan for enemies, as the loud clang of his hammer on the metal beams echoed through the mountains. Thankfully, he didn't sense anything, so after taking a short rest, he set up the doorframe he had swiped and then welded it in place, creating a fortified entrance. To further secure the doorway, he added a powerful magnetic latch that he scavenged from one of the other buildings. When mana was run through it, the latch might as well have been welded to the frame, but once the flow of mana was cut off, it popped open with a simple tug.

Of course, it wouldn't stop any powerful Exlian, as it wasn't mana enhanced like the previous mine door had been, but it would serve to separate him from the outside, which would hopefully be enough. Once he was finished, it was lunchtime, and Mark, who had chewed through a couple of biofuel units setting up the new doorway, grabbed one of the energy bars. As he swallowed it down, he couldn't help but crack a smile, remembering days when these energy bars were just about all he could afford to eat.

"And here I thought I was going up in the world," Mark said with a chuckle.

Looking around, though he stood in the middle of the ruins of a base, most of his battalion dead around him, Mark couldn't help but appreciate just how beautiful the world was. Unfortunately, that reminded him of just how strange his new mentality had become, and with a sigh, Mark put his tools down and headed back down into the base, intending to do another sweep.

Apart from a bit of maintenance equipment he found stuffed in some lockers, there didn't seem to be much else of value, so Mark headed for his new base of operations. Most everything he had brought in was just piled up at the moment, but he didn't bother organizing it and instead headed straight for the two corpses that lay in the generator room.

First, he stripped off Lieutenant Kami's suit. Though it had suffered some damage, Lieutenant Kami had been killed by blunt trauma rather than with piercing attacks, so her suit was largely in one piece. Of course, it was too small for Mark to fit into, but he still arranged it neatly next to Sergeant Fletcher's mana suit, then collected their watches. The screen of the sergeant's watch was broken, but otherwise it seemed to be in working order, and after placing them with the suits, Mark began carrying the corpses out of the mine.

He didn't take them far, finding a spot at the edge of the base where he dug a deep hole for each of them. It was already night by the time he finished burying the bodies, and when he was done and the last bit of earth had been tamped down, he stuck his shovel into the earth and sat down beside it. The feelings he had been pushing aside rushed back like a tsunami as he stared out at the star-covered sky, and he could feel tears starting to well up at the corners of his eyes. Mark hadn't known the members of the battalion all that well, but they had accepted him immediately and worked hard to ensure he felt like he belonged. The cool night breeze dried the tears that slipped down his cheeks, not giving them a chance to fall, but Mark didn't bother to wipe at them as he recalled his interactions with each of the members of the battalion.

"Sorry I couldn't give you something better, and I hope you don't mind me taking your powers. I'll do my best to put them to good use, and if I can ever get out of here, if I ever make it back to New Emery, I'll avenge both of you. You have my word."

As Mark's voice faded in the starlight, he turned his gaze to the west, in the direction of New Emery. Somewhere between the base and New Emery were Captain Calder and Sergeant Rogers. Their betrayal had gotten Fletcher and Kami killed and nearly killed Mark as well. Even thinking of them sent spikes of anger through Mark's mind, and though it might be some time before they met once again, Mark swore to himself that when they did meet he would make them pay.

Of course, first he had to make it back to the city in one piece, a task easier said than done. Rather than attempt a solo trip across the hundreds of miles between the mine and New Emery, Mark figured it would be better to wait for the battalions already on their way. It would be easier to survive hiding out in the mine than it would be in the wilderness. As his mind turned to survival, Mark began to grapple with his newfound abilities.

Since he had a place to stay in the mine, his next biggest concern was food. That had been solved by his ability to devour corpses. Even the thought of it made him shiver, but what was even scarier was that a growing part of his mind assured him it was fine. After all, they were already dead, and consuming them would ensure Mark was able to stay alive. He was simultaneously revolted by what he could do and pragmatically pleased with it, leaving his mind in turmoil.

What he couldn't deny, however, was the potential of his ability to integrate both Exlian and human powers. In a sense, it was like an extension of his trait selection, but it wasn't limited to his arms. Feeling conflicted, Mark stood up and brushed the dirt from his hands. Grabbing his shovel, he headed back to his new, and hopefully temporary, home.

For the rest of the day Mark worked inside, taking the occasional trip back out into the ruined base when he needed something. There was much to organize, and Mark occupied himself with digging out the rooms that had caved in, using them to house all the equipment he had pulled from the base. Thankfully, the cave-in had been largely contained to the mine's entrance, and he was able to pull the dirt and rocks farther down into the mine to avoid having to dump it outside. He worked slowly, trying to make sure that his limited supply of energy bars stretched as far as possible. Unfortunately, no matter how he scrimped on biofuel usage during the day, he was forced to expend it at night.

When he fell asleep that night, nothing in the dreamscape looked like it normally did. Instead of standing in a jungle, Mark found himself in the midst of a ruined base just like the one outside Felwer Mine. Surrounded by badly damaged buildings overgrown with grass and vines, Mark looked around cautiously, fully expecting a drone to jump out at him. Instead, he was faced with a deep silence. He could see a broken-down wall in the distance, and slowly scanning the buildings around him, Mark took a few hesitant steps toward it.

Unlike the jungle dream, Mark had no trouble walking away from where he initially appeared, and he had almost made it to the wall when he heard a faint noise from a nearby building. A moment later a hunter, its four arms outstretched, lunged toward Mark, forcing him to take a step back. Eyes narrowing, Mark dropped into his stance and leaned back to avoid the first slash. Before the second could follow it up, he stepped inside the hunter's range, his hands shooting out.

A slice of his fingers tore apart the Exlian's attacking arm while his other hand jabbed forward, cutting through the front of the hunter's face. Such an attack would have killed a drone instantly, but the hunter reacted with a scream and wild flailing. Barely warding off the dying creature's frantic strikes, Mark kicked it away but suffered a slash on his leg. Falling back, he glanced down at his leg to assess how bad the wound was, but apart from the blood on his pants, he didn't see any wound. It took a moment for him to realize that just as he had been able to manifest his bone blades in the dream, his other abilities were working as well.

Spinning around as the hunter breathed its last, Mark looked for another attacker, but once again, all that he faced was a deep quiet. It was unnerving, as he had been deeply conditioned that a new wave would always follow the previous, but there were no enemies nearby, and as he took tentative steps toward the wall, he felt himself starting to relax. The tall concrete wall was exactly the same as the one around Felwer Mine, though this wall looked as if it had been hit by a couple of dozen bulldozers. Wide gaps filled with rubble appeared every dozen feet, and more of the wall was scattered across the ground than was standing.

Stepping into one of the gaps, Mark saw a valley of scattered trees and rolling hills stretching ahead of him. About half a mile farther down the valley was a large hill covered in massive boulders and scraggly trees. It stood out to Mark, as it had next to no grass on it. He was just about to step out of the base and go take a closer look when he heard a sound behind him and turned around. There, half inside one of the broken windows of a nearby building, its mouth already open, was a six-limbed screamer.

"Oh, come on!"

With a screech, the Exlian screamer clambered out and raced toward Mark. He could see its throat moving, and remembering the effect the sound attack had on Lieutenant Kami, he dove to the side. A deafening shriek rang out, and Mark's body, caught by the edge of the blast, went tumbling through the air. Hearing the sound from a distance was deafening, but experiencing the destructive noise with his body was completely different. Mark's bones rattled, cracks running through them, and the skin on his back was flayed open. Though he could feel himself starting to heal immediately, that did nothing to stop the searing pain. It was so painful that Mark's body spasmed as he tried to get to his feet, causing him to miss a block when the screamer pounced on him. Feeling a claw pierce his eye and tear out of his eye socket was even more painful than having his back flayed, but even as Mark collapsed to the ground, he could feel an intense heat gathering in the wound.

Rolling to the side to avoid the screamer's stomping leg, Mark lurched upright, his hands trying to ward off another attack. As he weaved in place, he caught sight of the monster's throat moving again and realized he had no time to dodge. The sound wave coming out of the screamer's mouth was so loud Mark didn't hear it. His eardrums had already popped. The sound hit him like a pounding wave, and he felt his bones shattering even as his flesh melted away.

16

Mark's ears were still ringing when he rose the next morning. His encounters with the screamers in his dream had proved disastrous, as every time Mark had spawned in, he was quickly assaulted with sound waves that battered his body and shredded his organs. The regeneration ability he had acquired only made it worse, as it meant that he occasionally survived the sonic attack and had to suffer through the pain it brought. Often, he recovered just in time to be hit by another blast, ending his miserable experience and giving him a few seconds of rest before another screamer crawled out of the abandoned buildings to attack him again.

For a long moment, Mark sat on his makeshift bed in the darkness, just staring at the wall as he tried to calm his body down. He had grabbed one of the mattresses off a bed in the bunkhouse and dragged it into the mine, setting up a small encampment near the generators. They were humming along nicely, though one had started to blink, indicating it would soon be shutting down for its maintenance routines. Thankfully, they weren't complicated, and Lieutenant Kami had taught him everything he needed to know to keep them running.

Rubbing his face, Mark got up and left the generator room. At first, he had been a bit concerned about having to head out into the base every day for water, so it had been a pleasant surprise to find a tap in one of the rooms he had uncovered. After washing his face, he began his daily exercises, using the motions as a way to calm himself down and plan for the coming day. The list of things he wanted to do was tremendously long, and since he was feeling spry and full of energy, he got to work right away.

Most of the supplies had already been organized, but the workstations Lieutenant Kami had brought and Mark had moved into the mine weren't operable. All of them required power, and while that wasn't a problem in the command center, which had a computer, nothing like that existed in the mine. So Mark had to build it.

The main challenge was that the systems that drew power from the generators were all closed loops, and he was wary of what would happen if he tried to bootleg something and it didn't work. Heading for his supply room, he pulled out a few lengths of cable and the tools he thought he might need. Since the Black Mountain Battalion's goal had been to get the mine working, they had brought a lot of equipment and replacement parts, just what Mark needed to make his adjustments.

Picking a spot along the wall where the thick power cables ran, Mark activated his null field and waited a few minutes until all the mana running through the cables had dispersed. Shifting his hand into its bone blade form, he carefully cut the exterior of the cable, peeling back the thick rubber that insulated it and revealing the crystalline structure of the conduit inside. He was unsure exactly how to go about tying the new cables into the old ones but figured all he could do was try.

Cutting back the casing on one of the new cables, he exposed the glimmering interior and did his best to position the two pieces of exposed cable together. Using the rubber he had stripped away and some heavy-duty tape, Mark wrapped everything up, then double-checked his work to ensure that there were no gaps. The last thing he wanted was for heavy streams of mana to be pumped into the mine's enclosed space.

After he had finished wrapping everything and reexamined it for the third time, he took a deep breath and stepped back, cautiously deactivating the null field. Immediately, mana surged back through the conduit, refilling it in an instant. Just as he had anticipated, mana surged along the offshoot wire he had attached, and the end of the wire, which he was holding in his hand, began sparking and spraying mana. With a surprised yell, he jerked his face away, though not quite in time. A few sparks of mana fell on his skin, burning coin-size holes in his face and neck.

Hissing in pain, Mark reactivated his null field, and the mana quickly bled away. As he had no mirror to look in, Mark could only imagine just how much damage had been done. With careful fingers, he reached up and touched his exposed jawbone. Everything the mana had touched had simply melted, reinforcing Mark's fear of working with raw mana. Of course, mana only had such a destructive effect in incredibly concentrated doses. But still, it just underscored how dangerous this task would have been without the null field.

Mark's skin felt itchy as his regeneration kicked in, and a few moments later, the holes in his flesh were gone. Running his fingers over his restored cheek, Mark could only shake his head, wondering how powerful an A-ranked regeneration was. Since he had confirmed that his cable was working, Mark added a plug box to the end, then began setting up each of the machines.

He had just finished wiring the last of the machines when a thought struck him. The flow coming through the cord, having been pulled from the main power conduit, was tremendously powerful, and channeling it directly into the workstations was probably a bad idea. Unplugging each station, Mark put the power conduit in a place where it would be out of the way if it erupted, and hurried to the storeroom.

As soon as he left the area, he could hear the hum of mana coursing through the cables once more, as well as the snap and crackle as sparks filled the air. In the storeroom, he searched through all the equipment, looking for a regulator, what Lieutenant Kami had called a bleed box. He found one buried in a crate of miscellaneous equipment, and bringing it back, he connected it to the end of the cable before attaching the plug box to it.

The regulator would ensure that only the necessary amount of mana was allowed through to the plugs so that each workstation could pull the power it needed without worry of being overloaded. Once everything was hooked back up, Mark said a quiet prayer in his heart and deactivated his null field, taking a large step back just in case anything exploded.

There was a soft hum, and one by one, the workstation began to come to life. Mark had moved four benches into the mine: two that were used for alchemy, one designed for electronics, and the fourth meant for medical examination and creating medicines. When all four of them booted successfully, he was ecstatic. Unfortunately, they began to throw errors almost immediately, leaving him scratching his head.

Taking a look at one of the alchemy tables first, he poked around it for a few minutes and quickly realized the problem. All the workstations were designed with a network in mind, and had the base's network still been functioning, they would have operated just fine. As it was, none of the equipment could communicate, leaving the workstation struggling.

Opening up the console, Mark hunted through it, looking for a manual mode, but unfortunately, there didn't seem to be such a thing. In New Emery and at any base the human forces established, having access to a virtual network was a given. In fact, it was such a ubiquitous part of life that Mark hadn't even considered it.

Curious, he retrieved the two watches to see if they'd be helpful. Though both watches worked, Mark quickly realized that he couldn't use anything beyond the basic functionality of the watches, as they weren't connected to a network either. This got Mark thinking. If the network was down, communicating with New Emery was an impossibility. In New Emery's eyes, Felwer Mine had gone dark almost immediately after reporting an Exlian attack.

The battalions that were supposed to be on their way to reinforce and run the mine had no way of knowing if the base had survived. Considering that the network was down, they would probably assume that everyone had been killed. Of course, Captain Calder and Sergeant Rogers were currently on their way back. Mark could only assume that if they made it, which was a big if, they would assure command that no one else had survived the attack. This cast Mark's plans in a new light, as there was a genuine possibility that the battalions would simply abandon the mine.

Still, Mark was hoping that, at the very least, a squad of Rangers would be assigned to come and check out what had happened, giving him some protection on his way back to New Emery. The power problem in the mine had been solved, and since he had water and a supply of food, albeit a limited one, Mark was in pretty good shape as far as basic needs went.

"I guess the next thing is to take a crack at getting the network back up."

He wasn't 100 percent sure why he found so much comfort in speaking out loud, and he could imagine that if he was stuck here long, it might soon become a habit. With a wry smile, he grabbed his tool bag and headed for the base to see what he could hack together to get the communication network back online. Pausing at the door to scan the psychic network, he didn't notice anything concerning. Unlatching his makeshift metal door, he slipped outside. The sun was bright overhead in the cloudless blue sky, but there was a slight chill. Taking a deep breath of the crisp mountain air, Mark stood by the door for a moment, looking out over the vast mountain range. Everything looked so calm, so peaceful, but he knew that hidden among the peaks was a vast and terrifyingly dangerous host of the enemy.

Though Mark was rather strong in his own right, his dream fight against a screamer the night before kept him grounded in reality. At best, the screamer was C rank, barely above Mark. Yet he had been helpless against the creature, illustrating to him just how dangerous the Exlian could be. As he walked down into the base, heading for the command center, Mark mulled over how he might be able to beat a screamer. He had tried everything he had at his disposal, including his null field, but to his surprise, the screamer's sound waves were not produced through mana the way that a brain's blasts were. Instead, the sounds originated from the screamer's body, creating a cone of amplified vibration that was strong enough to melt metal at close range and had a devastating impact on biological bodies.

The door to the command center, though badly broken, was wedged shut, which was exactly how Mark had left it. Carefully opening the door, Mark propped it up against the wall, to be put back when he was done poking around. Unfortunately, he had no idea what he was doing, and after staring at the ruined computer and scratching his head, he sighed, "What I really need is a manual. Wait, didn't Lieutenant Kami say she had a bunch of manuals?"

Leaving the command center, Mark didn't bother putting the door back, as there really wasn't anything there that could be broken any more than it already was. Lieutenant Kami had stayed in one of the officers' rooms, and though Mark had swept through them previously, he hadn't been looking for books. He did, however, remember a short shelf with a few books stacked on it and was pleased to see they were still there when he entered her room.

Most of the books looked as if they were manuals for the mining equipment, but Mark collected all of them and retreated back to the mine once more. There were twelve volumes in total, and after a cursory search through them, Mark was able to put eight of the thick tomes aside, confident they had nothing he needed. The other four, though they didn't deal directly with establishing a network, had tangential information about troubleshooting the computers themselves.

For the rest of the afternoon, Mark read carefully, making notes on things he thought might be useful. Once he had compiled everything, he went through it all again, line by line, trying to get his head around how the communication network actually worked. That evening, after grabbing a quick bite to eat, he went back to the command center and began the painstaking process of taking the destroyed computer apart.

To Mark's untrained eye, it looked as if Captain Calder had unleashed a blast from directly in front of it, melting through the outer casing and destroying a number of the components inside. Thankfully, not everything was completely ruined, and after about two hours of careful work, Mark struck gold, noticing a heavy panel toward the back of the computer that was badly melted. Mark carefully cut it free. With a clang, the plate fell away, revealing a dim blue crystal.

It was long and thin, shaped like a carrot, and as Mark pulled it free, he could see something moving inside it. This was the communication crystal, engineered to enable the instant passing of information. Each of the machines that connected to a network, from watches to alchemical equipment to the massive mining machines, held a small blue crystal like this one that allowed it to tap into the network. But what Mark held in his hands was called a nexus crystal, and it served as the backbone for establishing a network.

Placing the crystal at his side, Mark turned his attention to the hardware in the computer, continuing to salvage as much as he could. As far as he could tell, the blast hadn't actually damaged the nexus crystal and instead had simply fried all the components around it, cutting off power to it and thereby bringing down the network. If he was correct, then all Mark had to do in order to get the network back up and running was replace the damaged components.

Though little in the destroyed console was usable, there were plenty of other machines around, and Mark was confident that he'd be able to scavenge what he needed from them. It was starting to get late, however, and Mark was starting to get hungry, so he carefully packed up everything he had retrieved, including the nexus crystal, and headed back to the mine.

He had just stepped out of the command center when he felt the hairs on the back of his neck stand up, and he realized that he had been so enthralled with what he had been doing that he hadn't checked the psychic network in hours. Remaining absolutely still, Mark closed his eyes and focused his mind, almost immediately spotting the blazing mental signature of a powerful Exlian.

17

Much calmer than he had any right to be, Mark slowly opened his eyes and turned to look toward the front gate. Though it was dark, the moon was bright, casting a soft silvery light across the mountainous landscape. That light illuminated the creature perched atop the ruined gate. It was unlike any Exlian Mark had ever seen, with a humanoid body and a long tail that curled about its feet, hands that ended in sharp talons hanging at its sides, and a head that looked at first like some sort of helmet.

There was an almost human look to its neck and chin, though its mouth was filled with needlelike teeth that gleamed in the moonlight. Where its nose should have been, a chitinous plate stretched up over the creature's forehead, spreading out like a fan and curling into sharp horns at the sides. The creature regarded Mark with a sort of predatory curiosity, as if trying to identify what sort of being he was.

Mark, on the other hand, felt no curiosity, only dread. He recognized the mental signature of the Exlian immediately. This was the same creature that had watched the fight before and retreated when the brain arrived. Mark wasn't sure where it had been since the attack, but the fact that it was back and it had spotted him didn't bode well for his quiet life out in the countryside.

Mark shifted slightly, his arms shimmering as they transformed. He was preparing to unleash his null field when the Exlian stood up with languid grace. Mark froze, watching the creature's every movement. The Exlian reached over and grabbed the barrel of the mana cannon hanging limply above the gate and casually tore it free, the metal bolts holding it to the cement wall groaning in protest before snapping under the pressure. Swinging it back and forth, the Exlian held it by the barrel like a club.

For a moment, Mark genuinely thought the creature was going to hurl it at him, and he prepared to dive to the side. Then something seemed to catch the monster's attention, and its head turned.

Sitting on top of the mess hall, her tail lashing lightly against the roof, Mime looked down on the monster on the gate through narrowed eyes. There was no tension in the cat's form, but the same couldn't be said for the humanoid Exlian atop the gate. Though it was subtle, Mark could sense the creature's body tensing as it slowly stopped swinging the ruined mana cannon.

For a long moment, the three figures remained still, forming a triangle. Though Mark was shocked to see Mime out in the wilderness, he was even more surprised by the powerful Exlian's reaction. He wasn't sure if the creature's hesitation was because it had never seen a cat before or because of something else, but he sincerely hoped that it would turn around and leave.

As if granting his wish, the Exlian dropped the mana cannon and shifted backward. Before it left, it turned its head, looking sightlessly at Mark. A wave of mental pressure assaulted him, causing his head to pound. It was as if thousands of voices were speaking to him simultaneously, forming an unintelligible murmur that echoed through his mind, disorienting him. He heard a quiet hiss, and the sound suddenly cut off. When Mark blinked, the humanoid monster had vanished over the gate.

Through the psychic network, Mark watched it go, his teeth clenching as he realized just how fast it was. Had it attacked him, he likely wouldn't have been able to react quickly enough to block, and its sharp claws would have torn him to shreds. As it retreated beyond the range of his psychic network, Mark felt his shoulders relaxing, a tremendous tension bleeding out of him. "Well, that was terrifying."

Mime yawned, padded down the roof of the mess hall, and then jumped to the ground. As she trotted over, Mark bent down to greet her. "What are you doing out here? Not that I mind, of course, but shouldn't you be staying in New Emery, where everything is safe?"

Part of Mark was anticipating an eye roll, but instead, he got a very serious look as Mime shook her head. Lifting a paw, she pointed at Mark, pointed up at the gate, where the humanoid Exlian had been a moment earlier, and then pointed at Mark again. He wasn't quite sure what she was trying to communicate until a sharp claw popped out of her paw and she made a slicing motion across her neck.

"You came here so creatures like that wouldn't kill me?" Mark asked, scratching his head.

With an emphatic nod, Mime jumped up onto his shoulder and patted his cheek with her paw. Feeling surprisingly warm and fuzzy inside and not thinking about how she could travel that distance, Mark laughed and reached up to scratch her fur and then, after gathering up the things he had dropped, headed for the mine. There was a part of him screaming in the back of his mind that he should flee, run as far away from this place as possible, because now that the creature knew he was here, it would undoubtedly be back. The more reasonable part of Mark was fully aware that the creature he had just faced off against would likely be able to track him wherever he went.

Though it had no visible nostrils or eyes, Mark got the sense that the humanoid Exlian was a consummate hunter and that even if he were to run as far and fast as he could, it wouldn't help him avoid being hunted. Instead, it was best to take advantage of the creature's retreat. The only thing that puzzled him was that he genuinely wasn't sure how strong the creature was. Based on the speed with which it moved, it was at least C ranked. But if that was the case, then why it hadn't just come to kill him, Mark wasn't sure. It looked like it had retreated because of Mime, but Mark thought that he must have missed something that had scared it away. After all, an Exlian being scared of a cat would be ridiculous.

After entering the mine, Mark put the computer components down near the electronics workstation and went to get Mime some food. Of course, all he had to eat was energy bars, and after she turned her nose up at them, Mark scarfed them down himself. He was loath to go back out into the base after the strange encounter, so Mark locked the door and settled down to an evening of trying to rebuild the network equipment around the nexus crystal.

Though most of the equipment on the workstation wouldn't function since it didn't have an active network to connect to, the soldering iron worked fine, and Mark spent the next few hours building his makeshift transmission system. It took a considerable amount of trial and error, and for the next few days it was all Mark worked on.

Mime occasionally vanished, heading deeper into the mine to explore things, and after a few hours, she would return, often licking her lips. She spent the rest of the time lounging around on Mark's shoulder or occasionally draping herself over a nearby workstation. After Mark's fourth attempt, he finally managed to build something that would feed mana into the nexus crystal.

While this was an important step, it was only the first, as he still needed some sort of control system that would allow him to tune the crystal's wavelengths to create the network.

After some thought, he opted to scavenge Lieutenant Kami's watch. Carefully taking it apart, he began to connect the components, soldering wires directly into the small circuit board the watch ran on. If his theory was right, he would essentially be replacing the watch's small communication crystal with the larger nexus crystal, allowing it to establish a network of its own while also giving him access to the controls he would need to tune the crystal.

Unfortunately, he had no idea what sort of frequency the crystal had used before, meaning even if he was able to restart the nexus crystal, he wouldn't necessarily be able to connect to New Emery's network. That was frustrating, but at least he was able to set up a local network, one that would allow his workstations to communicate.

After three solid days, Mark finally succeeded. When he saw the nexus crystal light up, he couldn't help but do a little jig, incredibly happy at his success. From there, it was simply a matter of tuning the equipment to the right frequency, which, thankfully, the machines were able to do automatically.

There was a practically endless number of frequencies that could be used, and it could have taken a lifetime of tuning to try to get them connected. But as soon as the nexus crystal came to life, the other devices nearby with crystals of their own began to vibrate in harmony. Mark couldn't directly sense the crystal network he had just set up, but as the machines each came online, he grinned.

"What do you think of that?" he asked, poking Mime in the side.

She was currently stretched out on top of the electronics workstation, and she batted half-heartedly at Mark's finger.

Grinning, Mark connected Sergeant Fletcher's watch to the network and then slid it on his wrist.

"All right, that's step one. Network is back up and running. Step two is to get these suits working."

The entire time he'd been working on the network, Mark hadn't forgotten the powerful Exlian. Though he wasn't sure how much help one of the mana suits would be, he figured it was better than nothing, so repairing Sergeant Fletcher's mana suit moved to the top of his priorities. Grabbing the suit from where he had laid it in the generator room, Mark brought it out and began to assess the damage. A number of armor plates had been torn from the suit, and a few more looked as if they had been melted. Overall, however, the basic integrity of the suit was uncompromised.

Of course, Sergeant Fletcher had been considerably larger than Mark, which meant the suit was almost two sizes too big. This was particularly problematic in that the frame upon which the suit was built was almost impossible to resize. This left Mark stumped, and after scratching his head, unsure what to do about it, he decided to try to make do.

Retrieving Lieutenant Kami's suit, which was decidedly too small, Mark began searching for a way to combine the two, meeting somewhere in the middle. This led Mark down a rabbit hole as he examined the two suits in detail, learning how the joint mechanisms worked. Rather than being purely mechanical, the joints were made with a variety of different materials that acted sort of like tendons. The armored plates were laid on top of these, but this interior layer of synthetic muscle gave the suits the ability to amplify the wearer's strength, speed, and agility.

Figuring that the frame itself could be rebuilt, Mark set his mind to understanding exactly how the synthetic muscles worked, as all of them connected to a stable power pack set on the suit's back. While not in use, the power pack absorbed mana from the air, storing it for when the suit was activated. This absorption increased when the suit was in use, offsetting the mana usage to ensure that the suits could run almost indefinitely.

The larger the suit, the more mana it required to move, as there were more synthetic muscles to animate, but the larger in turn the power pack could be. While Sergeant Fletcher's engineering suit carried one large power pack on its back, Mark was surprised to find that Lieutenant Kami's much slimmer suit, built for finer and more technical tasks, had smaller batteries attached to each leg, each arm, and the front chest plate instead.

Though the total battery capacity wasn't even close to that of the heavy engineering suit's massive battery, the localized batteries explained why Lieutenant Kami's suit had been so much more agile and reactive. Truth be told, Mark was quite nervous to start working on the suits, because he only had two and an extremely limited number of replacement parts. To distract himself, he spent time with the alchemy workstation, focusing his efforts on producing base, the liquid that served as the foundation for potions.

The workstation came with a considerable amount of salt, and the only other ingredient he needed was water. Rather than just mix the two, however, Mark took the time to try to purify the water as much as possible, even going so far as to rig up a filter with crushed charcoal and a couple of spare air filters designed for one of the mining machines.

Eventually, however, he realized that he was just delaying, and with a sigh, he put aside the base he had created and turned his attention back to the suits. Every day, he had been going to the door of the mine and scanning to see if the humanoid Exlian had come back. So far, he hadn't seen anything, which was both reassuring and disquieting.

As Mark got ready to take the plunge and start stripping down the two suits, he took a moment to pause and reassess his situation. He had plenty of water, and the mine was turning out to be more than adequate as a shelter. His food situation, however, was rather abysmal, and he was going to have to go out and try to find something to eat soon.

Having a suit would certainly help with that, so, his priorities set, Mark got to work.

18

He started by carefully removing all the pieces of armor plating and putting them aside. Next, after isolating the suits with his null field, Mark carefully peeled each individual synthetic muscle from the suits, taking care to label them so as to not get them all mixed up.

18As he deconstructed the suit, he made sure to take copious notes and draw diagrams of how everything had fit together to ensure he'd be able to reassemble them. His goal was to use the various lengths of synthetic muscle to create a suit that would work for him. He wanted something that would give him speed over strength, a suit that would leave his hands free while also protecting the other parts of his body. Though Mark had the regeneration ability, he preferred not to get hurt in the first place, as every time it kicked in, he was guaranteed burning waves of pain.

It took almost two days to completely strip down the two suits, but by the time he was done, Mark was more than confident that he'd be able to build something that suited him. He started by creating the thin alloy frame that would sit close to his body, providing the structure for the muscles to cover. Thankfully, he didn't have to make the frame completely from scratch but was able to cut down the engineering suit so that it fit him a bit better.

Next, he took the battery system from the lieutenant's suit and welded it into place. As he had taken apart the engineering suit, he had discovered that the large battery pack on its back was actually made of three panels, so he took one of the panels and attached it across the small of his suit's back, further reinforcing the battery system of his new suit.

The muscle layer was next, and it was the most time-intensive part of the process by far, as it required Mark to check and double-check every single muscle he added. Thankfully, the muscles were self-adhering, and as soon as mana was introduced to them, they would bind themselves together, forming a cohesive whole.

Of course, this meant that when he placed a muscle incorrectly, he was forced to strip it back off. Starting from the ground, since mobility was his primary concern, Mark obsessed over every single piece, testing the suit's lower legs and thighs obsessively. He wanted to ensure that he could execute his martial arts in this new suit, so his focus was on keeping freedom of movement.

Ultimately, this meant that he couldn't add as many synthetic muscles as he'd originally wanted, which in turn reduced both the power and the speed the suit could produce. Furthermore, because the suit was being hacked together, he had concerns about how robust it was. There wasn't anything he could do about that, though, so he just did his best, focusing on making everything as perfect as possible given his limited equipment.

By the time he reached the suit's waist, Mime had taken an interest in what he was doing, and she began wandering around the suit, observing it with great curiosity. She was particularly entranced by the synthetic muscles, and more than once, Mark caught her pilfering one of the long strips and taking it back to the workstations to chew on and bat around. Since he had extra,

Mark let her do what she wanted, and occasionally he paused in his work to watch as she played. All told, it took Mark a full week to construct the skeleton and attach all the muscles.

The day he placed the last muscle was the same day he ran out of food. Thankfully, his biofuel was still full, which meant that he had at least three days before it started to run low, assuming he didn't get into any fierce fights. But that put him on a clock, so without taking any time to rest, Mark turned his attention to the armor.

As he'd been building the suit, he had spent a lot of time thinking about how he wanted to armor it. He ultimately decided to use Lieutenant Kami's armor, along with some small pieces he crafted himself out of the engineering suit's armor. The plates from the lieutenant's suit were a soft white color, which Mark wasn't a huge fan of, as it would stand out sharply. After fixing everything in place, he found a can of nonconductive paint and brushed it onto the white metal plates. Though the result was rather ugly, it suited Mark just fine. The best way to hide was with a patchwork of different colors, and that was exactly what his suit now had.

When he had finished installing and repainting the armor, Mark stepped into it. He had already tested it numerous times and had no concerns about whether it would work or not. Yet as it sealed around him, he couldn't help but feel a hint of trepidation. He had built the suit light, maintaining a slim profile while still providing some strength enhancement. Jumping up and down, Mark put the suit through its paces and was quite pleased.

The suit's musculature ended at his elbows, and the forearms were covered by a light set of flexible plates that Mark could draw back over his upper arms, providing more protection while freeing up his forearms and hands. Considering his bone blade was even harder than the suit's metal armor plates, Mark had genuinely wondered if building a suit from such material would be possible.

Of course, a better option would be to figure out how to turn his entire body into the substance. Then he wouldn't need a suit at all.

Because bone blade could conduct mana so well, it made his fingers and hands considerably more powerful than they would otherwise be. Forming an entire body of bone blade would allow Mark to channel mana into every part of himself, mimicking the effect he was currently getting with his mana suit. Of course, simply wishing to convert his body didn't help him at all. For the moment, he had settled on a combination of the two, empowering his arms while he was wearing the suit. Mark had also added one of the comm crystals to the suit's helmet, allowing him to project information from his watch onto his visor, including a topographical map of the area.

"Well, better get to it before I get any hungrier."

Mime jumped up and stretched her body before hopping onto Mark's shoulder. Though he couldn't even feel her weight thanks to the strength enhancement of the suit, Mark felt a wave of comfort roll through him. Pausing at the door, he scanned for threats, then stepped outside when he didn't find anything. His goal today was to see if he could hunt a wild animal or, failing that, find an Exlian.

The trick, of course, would be finding an Exlian by itself, rather than one that was part of a wave. Exlian, especially drones, tended to group together, and while Mark was more than confident in his ability to kill drones, he didn't fancy his chances against a swarm of hunters or other warrior-level Exlian. He chose to head south from the base, down the mountain, and into the small valley, figuring that it would be easier to find prey in the forest below the mountain than on the bare slope above.

As he walked down the mountain, Mark marveled at the natural beauty around him. Though the terrain was rocky, there were trees and shrubs everywhere in a million shades of green. Many of them had beautiful flowers, and Mark occasionally paused to admire them. Spotting a particularly large purple flower, Mark had stopped to take a second look at it when he felt Mime stiffen, and a vine lashed out of the undergrowth, wrapping itself around his foot.

Caught off guard, he was nearly pulled off balance, but at the last moment, he anchored himself against the tugging vine and slashed out with his hand, severing it from his foot. The purple flower shook violently, and a dozen more just like it burst open. The entire shrub Mark was standing in front of began to shake, and half a dozen more vines lurched out toward Mark, unfurling like whips.

The vines had tiny suction cups covering their surface and exuded a sticky, glue-like substance, allowing them to stick to anything they touched. Mark retreated swiftly, but as fast as he was, he couldn't outrun danger. In this case, that danger came from a swarm of insects that burst up out of the ground behind him. With angry buzzes, they engulfed him, their stingers bouncing futilely off his armor.

One of the vines, still swinging wildly as it tried to locate Mark, slapped against an insect and instinctively curled up, carrying the struggling insect with it. Mark, seeing an opportunity, rapidly batted the insects toward the swinging vines, and two more were wrapped up. Drawn by their companions' frantic struggles, the insects abandoned their attack on Mark and headed for the vines, pincers bared. Mark retreated as quickly as he could, keeping an eye on the situation as it developed.

The insects, determined to free their friends, began to bite the vines, seeking to tear them apart. Yet in order to do so, they had to touch them, and the insects ended up stuck, bound to the vines, even as they attempted to chew through them. Wanting no piece of either threat, Mark turned and hurried away, keeping a closer eye on the world around him as he continued down into the valley.

As he went, he also kept tabs on the psychic network, and slowly but surely, he began to understand how to recognize things other than Exlian and humans. In the network, Exlian looked like small balls of fire that burned with different intensity depending on how powerful they were. Humans, on the other hand, looked like dull marbles, indicating their lack of connection to the network.

Though they were faint, Mark soon realized that the insects and plants he encountered also had their own special signals. Predatory plants typically looked like a faint green spark, while insects looked like a white mist that shimmered as they moved. Once he understood what to look for, it wasn't particularly hard to avoid the carnivorous plants, though occasionally, Mark would pause when he found a new one and toss a rock or a stick toward it to see how it reacted. The majority of these plant creatures used vines to entrap their prey, though one emitted a heady scent and then slowly began to crawl toward Mark, its roots leaving furrows in the ground.

After traveling a few miles, Mark finally spotted something that would be suitable prey, an Exlian drone trundling along through the forest, carrying what looked like a chunk of mashed-up bark in its mandibles. The drone looked a bit like a spider, with six long legs and a hard-shelled back. The thought of consuming it was off-putting enough that Mark waited for it to pass by before he continued. In truth, he was hoping to run across some devil hounds, or anything that looked a bit more like a mammal and less like an insect.

Over the next couple of hours, Mark saw dozens of drones, all of them carrying some sort of material farther into the valley. He was just about to give up and hunt one of the drones when he felt a faint prickle at the edge of his mind, and a moment later, a small pack of devil hounds entered his range. As soon as Mark detected them, they detected him as well and shifted direction, spreading out as they ran toward him. Taking a deep breath, Mark put his back to a tree and got ready. This was the moment of truth, when he would find out if this suit he had hacked together was actually going to work or if it was going to leave him high and dry, and most likely dead.

It didn't take long for the devil hounds to come into view, but when they did, they actually hung back for a moment, clearly confused by what they were seeing. Mark could feel their ravenous hunger through the psychic network, and it wasn't long before that hunger overcame their reason and survival instincts. The first to arrive lunged forward, only to pull up short as two other devil hounds shot toward Mark from the sides, one targeting his left leg and the other his right arm.

Mark met them calmly. Though he hadn't fought devil hounds in his dreams, hunters were even more dangerous and more cunning. The devil hounds relied on their agility and speed, but their attacks were straightforward, and Mark, taking advantage of the tree at his back, stepped around it, focusing on the devil hound attacking his right shoulder. His hand shot out, knocking aside one of the monster's claws. As he ducked under its belly, his other hand tore through its stomach and intestines with ease.

He could feel his suit hum as mana surged through it, increasing his speed and agility. The eviscerated devil hound slammed into the other attacker, tangling it up. Before either could recover, Mark had stepped back around the tree and brought his palm down, severing the unwounded devil hound's spine. With two of the creatures down, Mark didn't hesitate and drove forward, catching the largest of the devil hounds mid-leap.

Though Mark had had some misgivings about how his suit would perform in a combat situation, he was pleasantly surprised by how smoothly it moved. There were a few times when he found himself oddly hampered, but he quickly adjusted and tore through the remaining devil hounds. With the death of each one, a sharp wail echoed through the psychic network, and Mark had no doubt that more would be on the way.

Sure enough, he had just finished putting down the last of the dogs when another group arrived. This one was larger, thirteen in total, and rather than face them head-on, Mark began to retreat, luring them back toward the mountain. Thanks to his mana suit, he could keep pace with the devil hounds, but rather than outrun them for real, he slowed slightly, letting the ones in front catch up.

Three of them, faster than the rest, reached him first, and just before they pounced, he spun around and met them in combat. Hands blurring, he tore the first two apart, but the third managed to land a bite on his thigh. The armor plates creaked ominously, and flecks of paint came off where the monster's mandibles landed, but Mark was glad to see that they ultimately held.

It was easy enough to dispatch the third monster, as it was locked around his leg, but as it fell, the other ten devil hounds burst from the underbrush. This time, Mark didn't get away unscathed, and despite his valiant efforts, a claw to his waist slipped in between the armor plates and tore one of the synthetic muscles and his skin beneath. Almost immediately, he felt heat rushing to his stomach, and the wound began to close, but the damage to the suit made his movements awkward, and he was rapidly buried under a swarm of enemies.

19

Rolling on the ground, he did his best to protect his neck and head while striking back when he could. There was a flash of silver above him, and one of the devil hounds, which had been about to try to bite its way through his faceplate, suddenly vanished, or at least its head did. Blood spurted from its cleanly severed neck, and Mark jerked his head to the side to avoid having his faceplate drenched.

There was a shriek, and another of the devil hounds fell apart, cut in half at the waist. No longer pinned down, Mark rolled over and lunged to his feet, his hand tearing through one of the devil hounds' chests in the process. Spinning, he caught another devil hound leaping for him, his hand closing around its throat and tearing it open. At the same time, his foot lashed out, struck the creature in the chest, and sent it tumbling backward.

The last two devil hounds both closed in, but even as Mark dispatched the first one with a crushing blow to its skull, the silver flash appeared once more, and the other devil hound froze in place. Then, with a squelch, it split in two, its body bisected cleanly at an angle that ran from one shoulder across its chest to just behind one of its forelegs.

As its head and front leg tumbled to one side and the rest of its body flopped to the other, Mark caught sight of a dark shadow scurrying along the ground. A moment later, Mime hopped up onto Mark's shoulder, and he stood as frozen as the devil hound, trying to make sense of what he had just seen. As he calmed his surging emotions, he reached up and attempted to wipe some of the blood from the front of his visor, though his attempts simply smeared the blood further. After doing a quick scan of the psychic network, Mark unclipped his helmet and pulled it off. Mime was sitting on his shoulder, casually licking her paw, and as Mark glanced over, she gave him an arch look, then gestured to the corpses all around, as if to ask him why he wasn't eating them.

"Uh, thanks for the assist."

As if it were the most natural thing in the world, Mime nodded, then leaped from Mark's shoulder to a nearby tree. She crouched on the branch, her tail hanging over the side, and settled down to watch Mark, her eyes glittering. Rather weirded out by the fact that his cat had just executed as many Exlian as he had and with considerably more ease, Mark crouched and reached out to touch the corpse of one of the devil hounds. While he had originally considered bringing his game back to the mine to cook it, he was starting to realize that he'd be a fool not to take advantage of his ability to consume the Exlian corpses directly. It would save considerable time, and Mark was also curious as to whether devouring all the devil hounds would unlock a new ability for him.

Concentrating on the feeling of hunger that had been plaguing him ever since he had slain the first devil hound, Mark saw his shadow begin to ripple. What he didn't see was how Mime's eyes flashed red in the tree above him, her fur mirroring the shifting shadow below. As if awoken from a slumber, it took a moment for his shadow to move, and then, as if starving, it rapidly spread out, engulfing all the slain devil hounds. Mark could feel the crunching as bone and flesh alike were rapidly devoured, leaving nothing behind.

To his disappointment, Mark didn't get a notification that he had unlocked a new ability. But when he stood up after his shadow receded, he suddenly felt slightly lighter. It was an incredibly faint thing, the barest hint of difference, but the more he focused on it, the more apparent it became. It was as if he had spent the last week training. A slight increase in his speed, a millimeter more precision in his movement. The implication was terrifying.

In truth, if Mark had to decide between gaining a new ability and gaining an increase in his stats every time he consumed an Exlian corpse, he would take the stats increase any day of the week. When he had been assessed, they had told him that the highest he would ever go in any of his stats was D, despite having a presumably B-ranked absorption ability. Though Mark's current situation was grim, what he had learned through it was that everything about his assessment was wrong. Not only had they gotten his absorption power completely wrong, but he was rapidly approaching the C rank, and now, having consumed a dozen devil hounds, Mark had felt his speed increase.

With his biofuel meter full, Mark and Mime headed back to the mine. Along the way, he couldn't help but think about just how life changing his new discovery was. Mark was improving beyond anything he had thought possible, and the rate of his improvement was terrifying. Though he had no idea how many devil hounds he would have to eat in order for his stat to actually go up a rank, the fact that he had any increase at all was a clear indication that his body could accommodate power beyond D rank.

Trying his best not to be distracted as he traveled, Mark stayed low and moved slowly to avoid attracting any attention. He would be hunting in the valley from now on, and now that he had a better idea of where the Exlian were, it wouldn't take him so long the next time. His biofuel would last him a few days, meaning he wouldn't have to go out and hunt constantly. Since he had resigned himself to consuming the Exlian directly, he could even target drones, making his hunting even easier still.

Arriving at the mine, Mark locked the door behind him and headed for the workstations. His suit had suffered some damage, and he wanted to repair it and also add a few more plates to help prevent further damage. As he worked, he often glanced over at Mime, who had resumed lounging on the medical desk.

It was very hard for Mark to reconcile the cute cat currently lounging on the bench with the fierce attacker that had instantly slain the devil hounds. But the more he thought about it, the more he realized just how oblivious he had been to Mime's powers. Of course, he had thought it strange that she could perfectly replicate the sound of Sky's voice, and the way she seemed to appear and disappear at will had always puzzled him. Additionally, it was clear even from the very beginning that she was much smarter than any cat had the right to be. And now many of the events over the last year or so that had puzzled him became clear. Pausing his work, he walked over and scratched her belly.

"You were the one who saved me those times, weren't you? I mean, with the woman in the alleyway, and then again when those two men were chasing me. Huh, that was also in an alleyway. Weird how many times I've almost died in an alleyway, but thank you. I mean, it's even weirder that I'm talking to a cat, but then again, I guess most cats aren't empowered, are they? I didn't even know animals could be empowered. I thought only humans could be. But then, I guess, what are Exlian except empowered animals? Terrifying, hive-mind, empowered animals . . ."

Realizing he was babbling, Mark scratched his cheek and fell into an embarrassed silence. The more he thought about it, the more he realized how similar to a powerful Exlian Mime was. The thought should have been terrifying, but she had never showed even an inkling of aggression toward Mark or the people around him. Besides, if she was, what did that make Mark, who had somehow gained the ability to absorb Exlian genetic codes? Not daring to think about it further, Mark patted Mime's side. "Anyway, I guess I just want to say thanks."

Mime had been watching him with a curious expression as he spoke, and now she opened her mouth as if to meow, though no sound came out, and rested her paw on his hand. Mark could have sworn that she mouthed *you're welcome*, but he was pretty sure cat mouths didn't move that way, and when he blinked, she had closed her eyes and rolled onto her back, enjoying his belly scratches.

After getting his fill of petting her, Mark returned to work on his suit, adding a few more armored plates and shifting the location of some of the others that had been impeding his movements. One of the things he was finding hardest about building a suit was testing the full range of motion, as there were many ways he would never move unless put into an awkward combat situation.

Mark's combat style, driven by his relentless dreams, favored unpredictable movements with a solid center of gravity, ensuring he could react to almost any situation without ending up off balance. This meant his body twisted in all sorts of unusual ways, which often caused the armor plates to rub against one another. That friction, though mostly minor, slightly impeded his ability to move, and when it came to life-and-death situations, that could prove disastrous.

Frustratingly, shifting the plates often caused new problems, impeding different movements. After a few hours of tinkering, Mark realized that if he was going to move freely, he would have to sacrifice some of the armor itself. He didn't like that idea, but without any other solution, he could only put it aside to ponder.

Since his biofuel was full and he had reached an impasse on

his suit, Mark turned his attention to the alchemy desk. He had already created a whole batch of base, which he could use to construct his potions. The question was, What sort of potions did he actually want to make? He had already mastered health potions and successfully created the false-death potion, but he had something else in mind.

Getting out the core the brain had left behind, Mark examined it closely. According to what he had learned from Abrams, skill gems were an incredibly rare specialized core, appearing in one out of every thousand. Considering that only one in every thousand Exlian had a core, finding a skill gem was like winning the lottery.

While skill gems could be used to absorb a particular skill, a normal core's only use was elixir, which was exactly what Mark intended to try to create. Given his ability to upgrade elixir, Mark had studied elixir creation in detail, and as he examined the core in his hand, he recalled what he knew about preparing it. A B-ranked core like the one he held should be able to produce a hundred vials of B-ranked elixir if processed properly.

Mark had no illusion he'd be able to process it properly, let alone succeed in mixing the elixir, and was simply hoping for a single success. Considering that the small marble he held in his hand was worth a minimum of half a million credits, he could understand why people said alchemical training was terrifying. Still, he was excited to see if he could produce his own elixirs. He had a feeling he was going to need a job after getting back to New Emery, and becoming an alchemist seemed like his best bet.

The first step in preparing a core was to crush it into dust that could then be mixed into the base, along with a number of other materials, to try to produce elixir. Of course, crushing it was easier said than done, but thankfully, Mark had some alchemical devices that could help him, including a press designed to crush ingredients.

Hunting through a drawer in the workstation, Mark found a small bowl that could be attached to the press, holding the core in place. The bowl was made from specially treated ceramic, which Mark hoped would keep the materials untainted. Mark clicked it into place, tightened down the screws to hold it in position, and placed the core inside. He had picked a bowl that fit the core almost perfectly, though there was a little bit of wiggle room around the edges.

Firing up the machine, he moved the tempered glass barrier into place to guard against any flying shards and used the control rod to begin slowly lowering the press. According to one of the old books he had read, alchemists used to do this by hand, using their own strength to crush the cores. But Mark would have to have A-ranked strength in order to even crack a B-ranked core.

The machine could exert significantly more force than he could, and as it pressed down on the core, Mark held his breath. For a moment it didn't seem to be moving at all, and then the core, unable to withstand the incredible pressure, cracked, a spiderweb of fissures running through it. Then, with unstoppable momentum, the press pushed farther, and the core shattered, crumbling into pieces.

The majority of them stayed in the bowl, and as the press continued its descent, the pieces were broken up smaller and smaller. Reversing the lever, Mark watched as the press opened a few inches, giving him just enough room to drop the shards that had escaped back into the bowl. There was no need for the tempered glass enclosure anymore, so he slid it to the side and then continued to crush the core into dust.

The hardest part of the core was the external shell, and now that it had been cracked open and the largest pieces had been broken down, Mark began working the core by hand, using a pestle to pound away at it, making the shards smaller and smaller. After half an hour of steady work, he put the dust in a small box that had a filter in the middle. With gentle taps, he sifted the fine dust down into the bottom of the container, leaving the larger shards that he hadn't been able to break down behind.

The dust stayed in that container while he poured the larger shards back into the mortar and pestle and began a second round of grinding. He repeated these steps four more times before he had finally gotten everything reduced to that very fine powder, filling the bottom of his container. The next step, though easier than crushing the core, was much more technical, and Mark reviewed everything he needed to do as he readied his equipment.

20

The next step in creating elixir was to mix a pinch of the powdered core with the base, which was easy enough. Then the mixture had to be heated to a specific temperature based on the salinity, and three different additives had to be mixed in at precise timings and heats.

First was esper, used for mana amplification. When mixed with the core powder, it would ensure the liquid remained stable and active, as long as it wasn't exposed to oxygen. The second substance Mark had to mix in was zirban, a mana-activated sedative and muscle relaxant. Without it, anyone who consumed elixir would find their muscles seizing up, making it much harder for them to receive the benefits.

The final ingredient was something called factor X. Mark had no idea what it was or what sort of effect it had, but it was vital to the success of the potion. Factor X was present in almost every potion, but no matter how Mark had searched, he had never seen a description of what it actually was. He had even asked Abrams, who gave him a long look and then shrugged, clearly not wanting to answer. Regardless, factor X seemed to be the key piece, allowing the other substances to meld together.

Though the recipe was very simple, making elixir successfully was not. Absolute precision was needed to ensure not only the correct amounts of each substance but also the shifting temperatures required to allow for proper mixing. Esper needed less heat, while zirban needed more, and the entire mixture had to be cooled before factor X could be added. The problem was, as soon as the cooling process began, the esper in the mixture would start to break down, and there was a window of less than a second to add the factor X.

Mark, calming himself as much as possible, retrieved the three secondary substances from the workstation's storage and set them up on the counter. He was hesitant to begin, worried about wasting resources. Even though the workstation was well stocked, he had a limited amount of everything. While he had enough core powder for approximately fifty attempts, there were only twenty-one units of factor X, meaning his number of attempts had been cut in half. Picking up one of the vials, he held up the blackish-red liquid to the light, watching the traces of crimson.

"Well, I guess it's now or never."

Suppressing his nervousness, Mark put the vial back down, rubbed his sweaty palms on his shirt, and got to work. His first attempt was rather clumsy and, as expected, ended in abject failure. The main problem wasn't his timing but rather his unfamiliarity with the machines. The entire process required three separate machines, all of which had to be manipulated using a set of controls that consisted of a small joystick, a series of buttons, and a dial. Mark could switch between the different machines by pressing the buttons, but there was a microsecond's delay. Furthermore, Mark simply wasn't very good at using the controls, as this was the first time he had worked on a potion that could not be exposed to air.

Punching the unlocking code into the control panel, he heard the chamber with his failed potion hiss as air filled the vacuum it had created. There was a click, and the casing opened, allowing Mark to take the failed potion out. It was a muddy gray, and the powerful mana that should have filled it was nowhere to be found.

Putting the inert liquid aside, Mark considered for a moment, and then, instead of trying again, he filled a vial with base and clipped it into the chamber. He figured it was a better use of his time to get more familiar with the controls than to continue to attempt to make the potions. With his practice vial in place, he closed the casing and entered the command to lock it. This time, there was a whoosh as all the air was pulled out of the chamber. Mentally reviewing the steps in his head, Mark began to execute them. He had control of two small robotic arms, as well as a syringe that could rotate between different substances, and for the next few hours, he immersed himself in dry run after dry run.

He started by going through the process normally and noting down every single movement he made. Once he had everything broken out into a complete list of detailed steps that included where his hands should be when, Mark began to practice in earnest, focusing on completing the motions in a step-by-step process until they began to happen naturally, burned into his muscle memory.

After a couple of hours of practice, his hands were starting to feel fatigued, so he stopped and took a break to meditate. After his meditation, he exercised, keeping his workout light to avoid burning through his biofuel. By that time, it was pretty late, so Mark headed to bed, falling into a dream where he fought swarms of devil hounds.

He had just finished putting down a pack of three of them when a thought struck him, and even as the bushes started rustling, Mark closed his eyes and concentrated. In truth, he hadn't expected it to work, but he was pleasantly surprised when, a moment later, a group of three hunters emerged from the underbrush. Rather than eliminate them, Mark let himself be killed, complaining the entire time because of how long it took and how painful it was, thanks to his regeneration. A few times, he even thought about ending his own life in the dream, but something in him simply wouldn't allow him to do it.

After he fell, the world warped and he reappeared, and he once again closed his eyes and concentrated. Instead of the three hunters that should have appeared, nine devil hounds sprang from the undergrowth to attack him, surrounding him on all sides.

This was the first time Mark had tried to shift his enemy in the dream, and after the devil hounds had fallen, he attempted to summon some mantises. A few seconds later, five of the large warrior-level Exlian charged out of the ruins, attempting to skewer him with their bone arms. Such a fight would have been completely impossible for Mark before, but his new regeneration ability allowed him to take devastating wounds and still survive.

It was impossible to escape the attacks of all five of the mantises, so Mark was forced to trade hits for hits, allowing himself to be wounded in exchange for landing killing blows. It was a long and grueling fight, and by the time Mark was done, he was more than ready to wake up. Unfortunately, that was not to be, and as the last of the mantises fell, Mark knew he was in for a long night.

His attempts to summon drones to fight failed, and Mark groaned when a screamer poked its head out and stared down at him from the roof of a ruined building. Mark spent the rest of the dream being badly abused by the screamer, though he did manage to land a few hits of his own.

Despite the fact that Mark was alone in the wilderness, his days were busy. To a degree, this was out of necessity, as he didn't want to give himself time to think about his situation. While he was making the best of it, Mark could feel a faint creeping anxiety in the back of his mind, and in the occasional free moments between tasks, he found himself wondering if anyone was coming for him.

He knew that dwelling on such things simply wasn't helpful, so he pushed on, burying himself in practicing alchemy. Mark's days soon fell into a simple rhythm: exercise in the morning, then an alchemy session, followed by a break for meditation at lunch, then more alchemy, and finally martial arts practice or tinkering with his mana suit in the evening.

Mark spent two days in the mine, and on the third day, he ventured out once again, heading down into the valley to hunt for food. He moved slowly, avoiding the carnivorous plants and insects, and as he reached the valley floor, he spotted a drone in the distance. Rather than pass it by, as he had the last time, Mark sprang into action, racing toward the drone with his mana-empowered steps. As he arrived in front of it, he lashed out with his fist, striking it on the top of its head, even as it tried to drop the bundle of grass it held in its mandibles. With a crack, its shell shattered, and Mark's fingers pulverized its brain, killing it instantly.

As its death shriek rattled through the psychic network, Mark grabbed the corpse and, on a whim, scooped up the grass it had been carrying as well. As quickly as he had arrived, he retreated, wanting to get out of the area in case the drone's death cry attracted any attention. Retreating almost a mile, he hunkered down among some rocks on the slope of the mountain.

With one hand on the drone's shell, Mark willed his shadow into action, and a moment later, the drone was gone, completely devoured. He could feel the drone's energy replenishing his, and as he meditated there, his biofuel meter rose by three. This meant that in order to fill up the meter completely, Mark would need seven drones. That tracked with his experience absorbing the warrior-level devil hounds, as each of them had given him approximately six biofuel units.

At the same time, Mark was slightly disappointed, as he didn't feel any improvement at all in his stats from devouring the drone's corpse. If drones really didn't add to his stats, they might not be worth consuming at all, but it could also be that he just needed significantly more of them before he would notice an effect.

Heading back down into the valley, Mark continued to target the drones as he found them. Many of them seemed to be tracing roughly the same path, and by ranging along it, he was able to claim another four kills. Since his biofuel hadn't been empty before he started the hunt, those four kills completely filled his meter.

He was just deciding whether he wanted to retreat to the mine when he felt a tickle through the psychic network and spotted another drone. This one was coming toward him, and on a whim, Mark decided to kill it as well. Not bothering to hide, he darted straight for it. It was holding a lump of earth in its mandibles, and when it saw Mark rushing toward it, it reared back, lifting its legs to try to ward him off.

A moment later, it fell dead to the ground, and Mark stretched out his hand to engulf it. As the crunching rang out, Mark caught sight of a slight glimmer in the chunk of earth that had fallen from the drone's grasp as it died. As his shadow finished devouring the drone's body, Mark picked up the clump of dirt and squeezed lightly, breaking off much of the excess.

There was a stone inside that glimmered as it caught the light, and Mark could sense a dense mana inside it. Turning it over, he continued to brush off the loose dirt until he was holding a rough stone approximately the size of his fist. A piece of the stone had been chipped away, and the chipped spot shone brightly every time Mark shifted the stone.

Though he had never seen a raw manastone before, Mark had no trouble identifying it. Manastones were one of the staples of life in New Emery, and Mark could only imagine what one of this size would go for. It was likely the drone had been bringing the manastone back to its nest, and from how moist the dirt was, it looked as if the stone had been pulled from the earth recently, which got Mark wondering if there were more.

Putting it in the pouch with the grasses he had shoved in there earlier, Mark tried to retrace the drone's path, but he didn't know anything about tracking and was quickly lost. Mark thought about getting Mime, but she was back at the base, having elected not to come with him on his hunt.

He was just turning back when the psychic network lit up, and he saw a dozen Exlian moving through the underbrush some distance away. They didn't seem fast enough to be devil hounds, and Mark really didn't want the attention that fighting them would bring, so he carefully retreated. Unfortunately, they spotted him and shifted direction, heading straight for him.

This was the one downside to being connected to the psychic network. Though Mark could use it to see Exlian, they seemed to be able to use it to see him as well. Noticing that they were speeding up, Mark gritted his teeth and got ready for a fight.

When the first four-armed hunter emerged from the trees, Mark's hand was already there, slicing through its neck with ease. The second hunter met a similar fate as Mark drove forward, his suit allowing him to move too fast for the hunter to react. The other hunters let out roars and raced toward him, each eager to be the first to taste his blood.

What met them was a newly reinforced suit of armor and two deadly bone blade arms. Mark danced through their attacks, his fingers flicking this way and that as he laid open their bodies. Though his attacks didn't always manage to kill, he had only to touch the hunter's skin to split it open, and after a furious few minutes of fighting, all the hunters lay dead or dying around him.

He quickly eliminated those he had failed to kill, his fingers piercing through their skulls to destroy their brains. Even as he did so, Mark was already activating his shadow. The devil hounds had given him a slight increase in his speed, and he was curious about what the warrior-level Exlian hunters would give him.

In the course of the fight, Mark had burned through three biofuel units, and the first of the hunters he absorbed went to replacing them. As the shadow devoured the second hunter, Mark felt a trickle of energy racing down his spine and paused, clarity setting in. When he lacked energy, the Exlian he consumed went straight to his biofuel, filling it back up. It seemed that it was only after he had reached his maximum biofuel that the devoured Exlian's power would be added to his stats.

Just like the devil hounds, the hunters appeared to be adding to Mark's speed, causing a slow but steady improvement in how quickly he could move his body. When he got to the last corpse, Mark hesitated and then elected not to devour it. Instead, he brought it with him as he retreated back up the mountain to Felwer Mine.

21

There were a few things Mark was curious about and wanted to test. The first was whether he'd be able to find any usable parts. Though he had been working with Abrams for over a year, there were still many parts of Exlian bodies Mark wasn't familiar with. Since he had significant time on his hands, he thought adding alchemical butchering back onto his training schedule would be a good way to both advance in the field and pass the time.

Additionally, he was curious as to whether, after removing some of the more important organs, he'd still benefit from devouring the rest. If he did, it'd be like killing two birds with one stone, as he'd be able to harvest the most important alchemical ingredients while also improving his stats. A third, very real, though minor benefit would be not having to deal with the corpses afterward. Mark didn't have a freezer warehouse and didn't really fancy having chunks of Exlian flesh rotting in the mine. He also didn't have a butchering workstation, so after dropping the hunter's corpse outside the mine, Mark set to work scavenging parts from the base to build himself a sturdy table.

He started by grabbing one of the large tables from the mess hall. It had a wooden top, which would help avoid contamination of the alchemical ingredients. However, he was concerned that it wouldn't be heavy duty enough to support the weight of some of the larger Exlian. There was a metal table in the kitchen, and after looking it over, Mark began to carve it up, his fingers slicing through the metal with ease. He separated the four legs and carried them, along with the top, out to where the wooden table stood.

After flipping that table over, Mark cut the metal one down to size so that it would fit underneath the wooden tabletop and between the wooden legs. Using the extra metal he had cut off, he fashioned supports and then welded the metal legs back into place. Finally he banded the metal and wooden legs together with metal strips.

When he was done, he had two tables stacked together, a metal one on the inside supporting a wooden one on top of it. It wasn't pretty to look at, but Mark didn't need pretty; he needed functional. It took some doing to get the table out of the mess hall, and when he arrived at the mine, he stopped, his expression ugly. He hadn't actually considered how he was going to get his large table through the small door, and it was clear that there was no way it was going to fit as it was.

With a groan, Mark carefully took the entire thing back apart, unscrewing the legs of the wooden table, and carried everything in piece by piece before reassembling it inside the mine. It took him a full two hours longer than he had intended, but when he finished, Mark was quite pleased. The table was ten feet long and four feet wide, big enough to place two Exlian corpses on without trouble.

Mark headed back outside to where he had dumped the hunter's corpse, grabbed it, and brought it in. He had none of the fancy equipment Abrams's butchering station had, but he didn't let that stop him, and soon, the hunter had been laid open. Mark's primary goal was to become more familiar with hunters' corpses, trying to understand the creatures' strengths and weaknesses as best he could.

He had a growing suspicion that he was going to be out in the wilderness for a long while, and if he wanted to survive, he felt he needed to understand the world around him better than he did. Exlian were an ever-changing species, and the amount of variation between Exlian of the same type was astounding. So the more Mark knew about them, the easier it would be to deal with surprises.

By the time he had finished his detailed examination, the corpse had been reduced to a bloody mess, and the organs that could be used for alchemy were spoiled. Deciding he'd harvest from the next one, Mark placed his hand in the wide-open chest cavity, and his shadow surged, crawling up the table and enveloping the ragged corpse eagerly.

He was gratified to learn that his shadow didn't mind the state of the corpse, and a moment later, all signs of the Exlian were gone, including the blood that had covered his hands. Looking at the spotless table, he smirked. "Well, that's convenient."

His energy full, Mark considered heading back out to hunt for more Exlian, but he was wary of alerting them to his presence, so he stayed inside for the next two days. He was getting better and better at controlling the robotic arms and faster at executing the motions he needed.

Toward the end of the second day, he decided to give mixing an elixir another shot, and rather than using a vial of base by itself, he added a pinch of the powdered core to it. After shaking the vial up, he stuck it into the vacuum chamber and began the process. He was surprisingly nervous as he engaged the lock and set the vacuum, but he had practiced the motions enough times that they had become familiar, and soon his muscle memory kicked in, and his shaky motions smoothed out.

The secondary ingredients were ready to deploy, and as Mark

monitored the heat carefully, he added each in turn. Though he felt good about his performance, he still ended up with a tube of inert gray sludge, and with a frown, he pulled the failed elixir out of the machine and shook it. The mana it should have contained had dissipated as soon as he had added the factor X, and though he wasn't exactly sure why, he thought it might have something to do with how quickly the potion had cooled. Creating elixir required a frustratingly precise control of the mixture's temperature at all stages, and while Mark's control of the machines had improved considerably, he hadn't been practicing with active temperature changes. With a new goal, Mark took some time to redesign his practice regime and then went to bed.

The next day he crept down the mountain, moving slowly to avoid disturbing any of the insect swarms that were buzzing around in the predawn air. Mark's goal for his hunt was threefold. First, he needed to refill his biofuel. Second, he wanted to collect a variety of corpses to study. And third, he was interested to see if he could discover where the raw manastone had come from.

Felwer Mine was an ore mine, not a manastone mine, though according to the reports he had read, manastones had been found tucked among the veins of ore. While it was possible that the one he had retrieved was singular, judging from the size of it, it was more likely that it had come from a vein, and if Mark could find that vein, he would probably find other stones as well.

Manastones could be processed in much the same way that cores could and would drastically improve the effects of most potions. Mark was also interested in making sure that he had power sources for equipment like his watch, so having more stones would always be better.

Unfortunately, he had no luck and didn't see a drone carrying a manastone all day. Instead, what he found was trouble, or more accurately, trouble found him. It started with a small group of hunters that combed quietly through the brush. Mark ambushed them, successfully killing all three before devouring their corpses.

He had been paying careful attention, and he had a feeling that after another twenty-five warrior-level Exlian, he'd see an improvement in his speed. As a result, it was with some eagerness that he ambushed another group of hunters, six this time, and devoured them as well. Eager to improve his speed, Mark began to hunt in earnest, killing every Exlian he came across. He only noticed something strange when he spotted two groups of hunters, both small. One was north of him, the other east, and after picking one of the groups and starting to rush over, Mark was surprised to see the group he was chasing after retreating.

This was wildly unusual behavior, as Exlian simply didn't retreat as a matter of principle. Warning bells went off in Mark's head, and he slowed. When he checked the psychic network again, a frown flashed across his face. The two groups of Exlian were approximately the same distance away from him as they had been before, meaning that as he'd moved, the other group of hunters had followed after him without closing in. Taking a few steps back, as if he were turning to chase the group to the east, Mark saw it retreat as well. At the same time, the hunters he had originally been chasing retraced their steps, still maintaining distance.

"Well, this isn't good."

He was too far away to see them directly because of the thick forest. So he abandoned his hunt, retreating to the west. Yet he had only gone a hundred feet when he saw a group of hunters appearing in front of him. *They were surrounding him*. The only direction that seemed open was east, but Mark didn't need to head that direction to know it was likely closed off as well. By this time, close to sixteen hunters were showing up in the psychic network, and Mark realized he had been baited into a trap.

Rather than wait for them to spring it, Mark took a deep

breath and charged forward, no longer worrying about avoiding attention. As he crashed through the woods, branches whipped at his suit, snapping as he barreled straight through them. The hunters in his path started to retreat, and when they did, Mark shifted his direction, heading northwest to slip between the two groups. At the same time, he sped up, sprinting at maximum speed. He could feel the heat in the synthetic muscles of his suit as they worked overtime to carry him through the forest.

The hunters, sensing his imminent escape, tried to close in, but Mark was moving too fast for them, and a moment later he slipped out of their net. Just as he was starting to celebrate, he noticed the presence of Exlian only a thousand feet ahead. He was moving so quickly that he had trouble shifting directions, and within moments he barreled straight into a large group of hunters led by a hulk. Drawing his sword, Mark hacked at the closest hunter, and his blade tore the creature in half. Two other hunters launched themselves at him, and he managed to dodge past one and kill the other with a stab. That slowed him down, however, and hearing a roar from beside him, he brought his blade up to block.

The hulk's fist slammed into him, and Mark felt the shock deep in his bones as he was hurled sideways. His body slammed into a tree with enough force that the trunk splintered, and he felt his armor crack. He had no time to assess the damage, though, because the hulk was still after him. Pushing himself from the trunk with a groan, Mark threw himself backward, rolling on the ground as the hulk's claws tore through the tree like it was paper. He had managed to keep a grip on his sword, but so many hunters were swarming him that there was no space to use it.

Trying to get to his feet as he warded off the hunter's claws, Mark felt the earth shake and realized that the hulk was charging him. Though not as immediately deadly as a screamer, the hulk was just as dangerous thanks to its size and strength. If one of its attacks caught him squarely, Mark was positive it would be game over, so he tried to retreat out of its path, cutting his way through the swarming hunters.

It had been less than a minute since the fight started, but already Mark's suit was in shreds. The damage to the underlying structure wasn't too bad, but the armor plates had nearly all been pulled off or pierced through, and Mark knew that if he didn't get free soon, he would be in tremendous trouble. Barely avoiding the hulk's charge, Mark cut down a hunter and saw the forest in front of him. Without hesitation he fled for his life, desperately running up the side of the mountain.

There was a loud roar behind him, then an answering howl that sent a shiver down Mark's spine. During his trip to hunt in the valley, Mark had realized that the Exlian all had their own hunting grounds. The devil hounds tended to range in the mountains, while the hunters spent more time down in the deep valley. The large fight must have attracted the devil hounds' attention, because a pack of thirteen was now sweeping toward him. Mark's legs burned as he forced himself to speed up once more, and his lungs felt like they were going to burst as he desperately tried to suck in air. Thanks to the empowerment of his suit, he barely managed to outpace the hunters, but that still left the devil hounds in his way.

Mark slammed into them at full speed and heard something in his suit snap as he lowered his shoulder and rammed a leaping devil hound. He was moving so quickly the Exlian's body popped, showering him in blood. Barely slowing down, Mark continued through the pack, suffering multiple attacks that left him covered in bloody wounds. Then the hunters arrived, with the hulk trailing behind them, and they set upon the devil hounds. Though Exlian were all categorized as the same species, those who came from different nests were mortal enemies, and that was exactly what Mark was counting on.

As the fight erupted behind him, Mark retreated to the mine as quickly as he could. He was afraid that the hulk would follow, but by the time he made it to the outer wall, it had long been left behind. Mark's wounds had healed during his frantic run, but his biofuel had been mostly spent, and his suit was a complete wreck. Though he would eventually have to go out again, Mark was wary about getting spotted, so he decided that he would wait as long as possible. He had to repair his suit, so keeping busy wasn't a problem, and he hunkered down, immersing himself in fixing the broken armor and studying alchemy.

The next day, however, he was checking the psychic network when he spotted some faint movement at the edge of his perception of the base outside. Mark's awareness covered the majority of the base, though when he was in the mine, a few spots at the edge of the southern wall were outside his range. He was picking up movement at the very edge of his range, but rather than stepping out of the mine, Mark remained where he was, watching quietly.

After close to half an hour, just as he was becoming impatient, he sensed two Exlian presences creeping into the base from the south. They moved slowly, as if searching for something, and as soon as they sensed Mark, they froze and then retreated rapidly. Worried, Mark, who wasn't wearing his suit, threw open the door and hurried outside. As fast as he could, he raced to the southern wall and climbed on top of it, staring down the mountain.

In the far distance, he could see two Exlian retreating, scampering through the rocks as they headed down into the valley. Though it was hard to make out from a distance what they were, Mark thought they looked like hunters, which didn't bode well for him. He knew that hunters were consummate trackers, and it was likely that after seeing their brethren hunted in the valley below, they had tracked him back to the mine.

22

Mark stood on the southern wall in silence, even long after the two Exlian hunters had vanished from view. It would be impossible to catch up with them, and even if he could, killing them would likely just draw others. His only hope was that their packs were mostly thinned, as when they returned, it would undoubtedly be in force.

What was strange to Mark was that the hunters, who were typically solitary creatures, seemed to be moving in groups. That spoke to more powerful Exlian leading them, and Mark was rather worried that those Exlian would come with the hunters the next time they arrived.

As much as he wanted to retreat into the mine, shut the door, and distract himself with his alchemy, Mark knew the Exlian would come for him, so he needed to make sure he was ready. Heading back to the mine, Mark got his suit on. As he buckled his helmet, he mentally reviewed his options.

The base's defenses were shot, which left him with himself, his weapons, and Mime. If, that was, he could get the cat to co-operate. Mime had been venturing into the depths of the mine with increasing frequency, to do who knew what. And it wasn't like you could control a cat. But hopefully, she'd be around when the attack came.

After considering his options for defenses, Mark settled on a relatively simple, if risky, plan. Rather than wait for the hunters to come find him, he decided to go find them. While fighting the enemy out in the open was dangerous, Mark was confident he'd be able to make a strategic retreat, fighting as he went. That would hopefully keep him from being surrounded while allowing him to eliminate the enemy without worrying about damage to his base.

Of course, if Mark was right and the hunters were being organized by a more powerful Exlian, then he was playing with fire, as engaging with a powerful Exlian on its home turf was doubly dangerous. Mark didn't feel like he had a choice, however, and preferred action to waiting around like a fish in a barrel. Mime was nowhere to be seen, so Mark headed for the door. He had just stepped outside when he felt a weight on his shoulder, and glancing over, he saw Mime sitting there. She was staring at him with a severe look, as if she knew what he was about to do. With a sheepish grin, Mark locked the door behind him and gestured to the south. "Want to go hunting? I could really use your help, especially if you could track those two hunters who were scouting us."

Mime considered him for a long time, then nodded. She leaped from his shoulder, and he gave chase as she bounded through the base. Even with his mana-empowered suit, he could hardly keep up with her, and more than once, he completely lost sight of her, only for her to pop up a few hundred feet ahead, waiting for him to catch up.

When she reached the southern wall, she paused for just a moment, her head low to the ground as she sniffed out the scent, and then she took off, heading down the mountain. Mark followed behind her, trying to move as quietly as he could while still keeping up with her quick trot. Oddly, Mime made no special effort to avoid the carnivorous plants that dotted the landscape. Instead, as she moved past, the plants would curl up tightly, withdrawing as far as they could from her path. The air was strangely silent as well, and the normal hum of insects was nowhere to be found.

Mark was too focused on the coming battle to pay attention to these things. When they reached the bottom of the mountain forty-five minutes later, he had entered an almost trancelike state. His mind was blank, carrying no thoughts as he calmly observed his surroundings. Though he couldn't track the hunters, he moved quietly behind Mime, ready to explode into action at a moment's notice. When she slowed down, so did he. When she sped up, he matched her pace.

Slipping through the trees, she soon brought him to a hill in the center of the valley, where she paused behind a bush. Mark crouched behind her, his eyes fixed on the cave entrance in front of them. He had been scanning the psychic network, and as they had approached the hill, he had begun to feel a mass of creatures up ahead. Suddenly struck by a sense of déjà vu, Mark took a second look at the hill, observing the large boulders, scattered bushes, and sparse grass that covered it. He had seen this hill almost every night in his dreams. Unable to believe his eyes, Mark peered past the hill and saw the faint outline of a broken-down wall and the tops of buildings poking up above it.

Mime, who had lowered her body to the ground, glanced back, her eyes flashing with a hint of red. Mark's attention had been firmly fixed on the hill, but suddenly, he felt his connection with the Exlian network grow hazy. Jerked from his single-minded focus, he glanced down and saw Mime creeping forward on quiet paws. He followed behind her as quietly as he could, fully expecting the Exlian swarming in the cave to spot him at any moment.

Yet even as he arrived at the entrance, they seemed completely oblivious to his presence. Peeking at Mime, who was peering into the cave, it suddenly struck Mark that she had never appeared to him in the psychic network. It was as if she simply didn't exist. Mark would have expected her to show up like humans and other creatures who didn't have access to the network, as a dull-gray mass. Instead, there was nothing.

Even more curiously, when Mark tried to examine his own position, he could barely find a hint of his own presence. Normally, he appeared to himself as a bright spark, but now that spark had become a faint flicker, only visible when he concentrated on it. Feeling something smack his foot, Mark realized that Mime was glaring at him. With a jerk of her head, she gestured for him to enter the cave. Pushing his curiosity about Mime and her abilities to the back of his mind, Mark complied.

There were dozens of Exlian in the cave system, but though their combined presence lit up the psychic network like a city at night, Mark was relieved to see no particularly powerful signatures. This reassured him that he wouldn't suddenly come face-to-face with an enemy he had no hope of beating. Creeping along the wall of the cave, Mark peered into the darkness, spotting an Exlian hunter up ahead. The hunter was moving about the passage sporadically, occasionally stopping to stare this way and that. As Mark drew closer, the hunter suddenly froze and then whipped around, its large eyes frantically searching.

At the last second before the monster had looked up, Mark had ducked down behind a stone. But as the hunter took two steps toward him, he knew that he had been made. Hunters had a fantastic sense of smell, and it was likely that that had alerted the creature to Mark's presence. Vaulting over the rock, Mark reached the surprised hunter in three quick steps. His hand split the creature down the middle, slicing through its skull, neck, and chest until he had reached its stomach. Dead instantly, the hunter gave a death cry that echoed through the psychic network, alerting all the other Exlian that an enemy had appeared.

Immediately, the cave system transformed into a frenzy of activity, and Mark could sense all the Exlian starting to rush toward his position. He felt more than saw a shadow brush past him. But before he had time to worry about what Mime was doing, the hunters arrived, throwing themselves at him with abandon.

Roughly five feet wide, the passage was too small for Mark to swing his sword, but that suited him just fine, as it meant no more than two of the hunters could reach him simultaneously. As the first two arrived, Mark took a quick step to the left, his hands piercing through a hunter's chest to strike its heart.

As the creature flopped to the ground, Mark took a step back, dodging a slash from his right, and then pressed forward, slamming an elbow into the other hunter's shoulder, knocking it off balance. His foot crushed one of its legs, and as it screeched in pain and fell to the ground, one of its companions trampled over it, arms flailing as it slashed at Mark.

Sometimes advancing, sometimes retreating, Mark blocked and attacked, each of his strikes doing devastating damage. The Cutting Palm technique was incredibly efficient, and every strike was designed to be lethal. Empowered by his mana suit and burning through his biofuel with wild abandon, Mark pushed his body to the absolute limit, cutting down the hunters as quickly as they could come.

As he fought, he kept a thread of attention on the psychic network and saw Exlian at the back of the swarm vanishing one after another. Mime had gone to work, and after a dozen minutes of fierce fighting, the last of the hunters fell. In those brief few minutes, Mark had burned through nearly all his biofuel. But it didn't bother him, as there was plenty more lying around. He was just about to say something to Mime, who had appeared at the end of the passage in front of him, when he realized her hackles were up and she was staring past him.

Anything that could cause such a reaction in Mime was likely terrifying, and Mark didn't hesitate, diving to the ground and scrambling through the bloody corpses as a tremendous blast of sound echoed through the tunnels, shaking stones loose and popping one of Mark's eardrums.

With a groan of pain, Mark reached out, grabbing one of the corpses, and activated his devouring ability. He could feel his ear healing even as the sound faded from the tunnel around him. Mark had no idea where it had come from, as he couldn't detect any enemies nearby.

As the corpses around him vanished and his biofuel began to rocket upward, Mark suddenly saw it. His fight had taken him far enough from the entrance to the cave that the psychic network didn't cover it, but as he struggled to his feet, he saw a burning sun advancing toward him.

It had unleashed its roar into the cave, and the sound had ricocheted from the walls, drastically increasing the range and intensity of its sound blast. Realizing that getting caught by one of the screamer's sound blasts in such a narrow space would be a death sentence, Mark quickly retreated.

Mime had vanished, and as Mark sprinted down the passage, he had no time to pay attention to the notification that had popped up.

> Your speed has increased from C– to C.

There was another loud scream behind him, and Mark felt the wave of force slamming into his back a moment later. Unable to keep his balance, he tumbled forward, nearly sliding off a ledge as the tunnel opened up into a large cavern at the center of the hill.

His fingers scrabbled in the dirt, managing to catch a rock before he fell into the yawning pit at the center of the cavern. Though he thought he would survive the forty-foot drop, Mark would prefer not to risk it, and he hung on as the screamer's echoing cry faded. Unfortunately, he realized he could see no way down except for dropping, and the small landing at the tunnel's entrance was too small for Mark to hide on. Gritting his teeth, he let go of the rock.

As he fell, he thrust his hands into the dirt wall, carving a furrow down it that filled the air with dust. Thankfully, it slowed his fall enough that he was able to land stably. He could sense the screamer rushing down the passage toward him. He looked around for a place to hide but found nothing. The floor of the cavern had a small pool of water that glowed with a faint light, but it was otherwise bare. Part of him had anticipated finding a nest, but there was nothing except a few small rocks.

Taking two steps toward the pool to check its depth, Mark pulled up short as the screamer hurled itself out of the tunnel and over his head. It turned in midair, landing on the opposite wall of the cavern, where it clung with its six clawed limbs. The cavern was almost completely dark, apart from a few faintly glowing mushrooms and the silvery light produced by the pool of water. Despite the dim conditions, the screamer had no trouble locating Mark. It let out a sharp hiss, then rushed down the wall toward him.

Quelling the nervousness in his heart, Mark realized he was out of options. He had no idea where Mime was and didn't have the luxury of looking for her. Sensing the screamer was about to unleash another attack, Mark dove to the right, landing belly first on the ground. As soon as his chest touched the earth, he bounced straight up into the air, using his hands and legs to propel him. Empowered by his suit, he rose close to fifteen feet in an instant, at the same time that the screamer, having shifted its head in his direction, unleashed a blast of sound.

The majority of the sound was absorbed by the earth, but Mark was still caught by the edge of the cone. His body tumbled through the air and landed with a hard thud. Knowing he didn't have time to wait, Mark threw himself at the screamer, hoping to catch it before its scream reset.

As dangerous as the fight was, Mark had spent hours upon hours in the dream world every night, desperately looking for ways to defeat screamers. Though he had managed to wound them a few times, Mark had never survived the encounters. Now, however, he didn't have a choice. Unlike in his dreams, there was no reset in the real world, no coming back to life once you were killed.

You won, or it was game over.

As he dashed toward the screamer, Mark drew his sword, activating the mana edge. He was three steps away when he realized he wouldn't make it in time. And as the screamer's mouth opened, Mark abruptly changed direction, moving to the left. He knew the screamer would be able to track him. It could shift the trajectory of its attack with unbelievable speed. So he hurled his sword straight toward its open mouth.

Busy adjusting its aim to accommodate his abrupt change of direction, the screamer didn't have a chance to avoid the blade, and with a sharp thwack, the tip of the mana sword sank deep into the side of the screamer's cheek and into its mouth, piercing through its flesh and releasing a spray of blood. The screamer's head jerked to the side, and its sound blast mixed with a cry of pain. The mana sword, which had been stuck in its mouth, melted under the fierce vibration that erupted from the screamer's throat, and Mark's heart clenched.

23

As the creature thrashed in pain, shaking its head back and forth to try to dislodge the half-melted blade stuck in its cheek, Mark lunged close. As distracted as it was, the screamer still lashed out with one of its six limbs, attempting to rend Mark in half. Knowing that he didn't have the strength to contend directly, Mark shifted to the side, using his palm to deflect the limb, and then launched attacks of his own, his hands flying in a flurry of blows that targeted its joint.

Within moments, the limb was a bloody mess, and the screamer jerked back. It was large, nearly ten feet in length, and had a bulbous body. Though stronger than Mark, it wasn't built for close combat, so it tried to distance itself, pulling back to get its sound blast lined up. Desperate not to let it, Mark stayed close, sticking to its side and attacking as fiercely as he could.

Unfortunately, while his attacks were strong and pierced through the monster's skin easily, he couldn't deal enough damage to keep it from pulling away. With a powerful leap, the monster launched itself into the air, escaping from Mark's range and landing on the wall of the cavern. One of its legs hung loose, useless after Mark's barrage of attacks, but it still managed to grip the wall as it glared murderously at Mark.

Though the mana sword hadn't been dislodged, its sound blast was ready to deploy, and as it aimed its opening mouth toward Mark, he retreated as fast as he could. His only hope was that the cavern was large enough that the sound would dissipate before it reached him. Unfortunately, he strongly suspected that that wouldn't be the case. His other option, of course, was to try to hide under the water, but in reality, that would simply hasten his demise, as the pool wouldn't stop the vibration from the attack.

Not wanting to be boiled alive, Mark retreated to the other side of the cavern, racking his mind for options. Though the screamer was only a C-ranked Exlian warrior, Mark honestly would rather have faced a B-ranked brain. At least then his null field ability would work, protecting him from the blasts. As it was, the null field didn't do anything against the screamer's roars.

When the sound came, it filled the cavern, shaking Mark's bones and rupturing both of his eardrums. Intense pain filled him, and he nearly collapsed to the ground, barely managing to keep himself on his feet with a hand against the wall. The sound grew dull, though he could still feel it reverberating through his body. With a groan, he staggered to the side, losing his grip on the wall and stumbling to the ground.

The screamer, taking advantage of his weakness, rushed closer, its throat working as it began to recharge its sound blast. Mark's body was already healing, his regeneration sucking up his biofuel to knit his wounds back together, but he knew full well he wouldn't recover in time. Skittering across the wall, the screamer arrived above Mark, its mouth opening wide as it stared down at him.

Mark felt as if he should be afraid of his impending death, as if it should have somehow bothered him. Instead, he felt a fierce surge in his heart, and struggling to his feet, he glared up at the screamer defiantly. As if mocking him, the monster opened its mouth all the wider, its chest vibrating as the blast of sound began to emerge.

Yet just before the ability truly activated, there was a flash of silver, and three of the monster's five remaining legs were cut free from its body, causing it to lose its grip on the wall. Hanging face down above Mark, it suddenly plunged toward the ground, slamming headfirst into the dirt. The sound blast drove straight into the ground, superheating the soil and causing it to melt into a fiery slurry that burned the screamer's mouth and head.

Dumbfounded by the sudden development, Mark stared up at the wall, where he saw Mime perched like a gecko, one paw extended. A gleaming silver claw slowly retracted into the paw as she gave him a decidedly sentient grin. The screamer was flailing on the ground in front of Mark, its head and shoulders badly burned by the intense heat of its blast.

The shock of the sudden reversal was immense, but Mark wasn't going to let this opportunity slip away. With a shout of his own, he lunged forward, driving his hand into the base of the screamer's neck. It pierced through, his fingers meeting the monster's spine. As its large body began to flail underneath him, he brought down his other hand, chopping deep into the bone. It took two more strikes before the screamer's spine was severed. As soon as he felt the bones parting, Mark jumped to safety.

Though dead, the screamer's body continued to spasm, jerking this way and that. Mark stayed well clear of its flailing claws until finally, with one last mighty shudder, it fell still. Still perched on the wall, Mime looked down at the corpse, licking her lips. Mark collapsed to the ground, flat on his back as he tried to catch his breath. With shaking hands, he reached up and unclipped his helmet, letting it roll to the side as he stared up at the dark ceiling.

Mark heard the soft patter of paws, and then Mime climbed onto his chest and stared down at him.

"Thanks."

Mark's voice was rough. Even though his regeneration had healed all the wounds he had suffered during the fight, he could feel a gaping emptiness in his chest, the result of his total mental and emotional exhaustion, to say nothing of his nearly empty biofuel. Mime nudged his chin with her nose and then pointed toward the body of the screamer, as if urging him to hurry up.

With a groan, Mark pushed himself into a seated position and reached out, touching one of the screamer's fallen limbs. Mime had slid down to his lap when he sat up, and now she turned to stare at the corpse, her eyes burning crimson. Mark's shadow shifted, rising up in a wave to engulf the massive corpse. For a long time, the cavern was filled with a faint crunching sound. The screamer's flesh was filled with energy, and Mark's exhaustion quickly dissipated.

By the time he had gotten through a fourth of the body, his biofuel was already full. As he continued to consume it, Mark felt the energy filling him. It seemed to carry a faint vibration, stimulating Mark's flesh and bones. Uncomfortable at first, the vibration produced a heat that sank into every corner of Mark's body, making him feel like he had just received a massage.

By the time he had finished devouring the corpse, Mark knew with certainty that something had changed. Glancing down at his wrist, he saw multiple notifications blinking up at him.

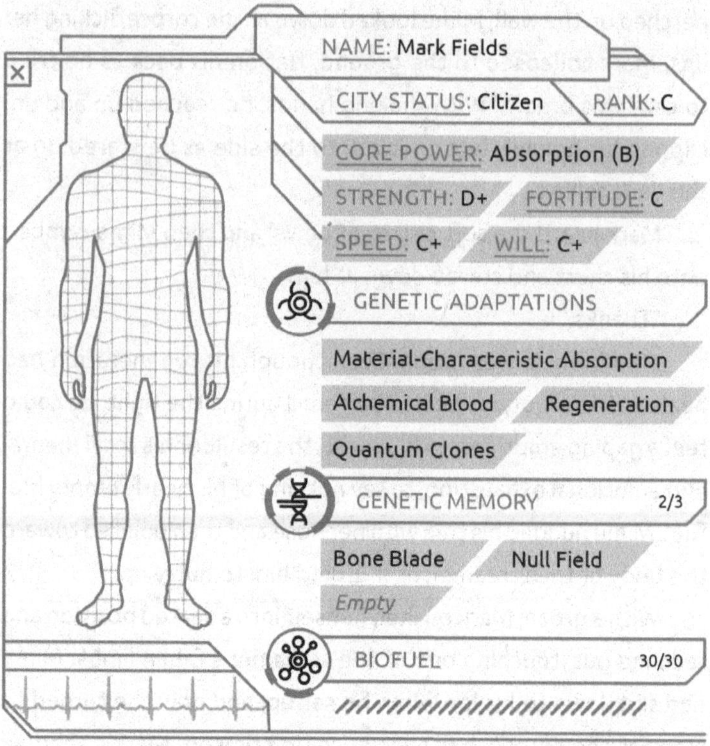

Mark's absorption of the C-ranked screamer had been enough to push him over the edge, causing his stats to jump. The only one that hadn't shifted was his strength, likely because of the attributes that the screamer prioritized. It made him wonder what would happen if he devoured a hulk or another Exlian who focused on strength.

Though the rank-up only took him from D+ to C, Mark could feel the powerful difference having a C-ranked fortitude made. His body was clearly tougher and would be able to withstand damage easier. But more than that, Mark realized as he stood up that fortitude affected his own movements as well. His speed had grown to the C rank first, yet he hadn't truly been able to take advantage of that, as his body simply couldn't keep up. Moving too quickly would have caused him to damage himself, so his body had naturally capped how much of his speed it unleashed. The same was likely true for strength, though Mark's strength seemed to be lagging behind his other stats. Now that his fortitude was C ranked, Mark could use his increased speed to its full effect.

Sufficient specialized genetic material acquired. Would you like to remember Sound Blast?

Realizing he now had an extra slot for genetic memory because of his upgrade to C rank, Mark opened up that ability.

Genetic Memory (2/3):
Slot 1: Bone Blade
Slot 2: Null Field
Slot 3: Empty

For a few minutes, he debated taking the screamer's sound blast ability, but remembering how the null field had done something to his body, Mark ultimately decided it just wasn't worth it. He imagined that to use the sound blast ability, he would have to modify his throat and mouth, and he could only imagine what he might end up looking like. Besides, there would likely be other, better abilities in the future, and he still didn't know if he could discard an ability he had claimed or if they were permanent.

Though the experience of fighting the screamer had been harrowing and Mark had only survived thanks to Mime's sneak attack, Mark was in high spirits as he climbed out of the pit and wound his way through the cave to leave the tunnel system. As he advanced, he continually scanned the psychic network, looking for threats, and was pleased to see that his range had grown slightly.

It appeared that as he ranked up, it would continue to expand, allowing him to sense others at a greater distance.

There were no enemies nearby, so Mark headed for the mine. Physically, he was in peak shape, his body completely recovered from the damage he had suffered and filled to bursting with energy. Mentally, however, he was exhausted and badly in need of rest. When he arrived at the mine, everything was quiet, so after locking the door, he crawled into bed and quickly fell into a deep sleep.

Though he still found himself in the dream world, all his mental exhaustion had been wiped away, and Mark spent the time getting used to his new stats. The major improvement in both his speed and his fortitude, as well as the minor improvement in his strength, made it even easier to eliminate the D-ranked Exlian warriors, and Mark had a rather relaxed training session. He focused on keeping at least one of his enemies alive as long as possible, practicing controlling the fight as he explored the limits of his new physical abilities.

The next morning, he arose bright eyed, and after stretching and moving through a light workout, he wandered outside. The sun had yet to fully peek over the horizon, and the sky was cast in blues and pinks. Climbing up the mountain a little ways, Mark sat on a rock overlooking the base and spent a few moments just appreciating the view. During his contemplation, Mime appeared and joined him. She seemed quite curious as to what he was doing, and for some reason, Mark felt the need to explain it to her.

"Isn't that beautiful?" he said, gesturing to the bright colors on the horizon. "This world is pretty incredible, you know. As scary as it is, as dangerous as it can be, and man, it can be dangerous, sometimes you just have to sit and appreciate what you have. Which, in my case, is a confusing mix of all sorts of things."

Glancing down at his hands, Mark flexed his fingers, watching as they transformed into bone blade and then back into normal flesh.

"You know, sometimes, you get the feeling that you're the protagonist. That everything is going well for you. That the whole world is bent in your direction. And that all of this exists for you. And then other times, usually when you're staring down the business end of a screamer's throat, you realize that you're not really all that much. And that in the blink of an eye, it can all be gone. It's kind of crazy being able to fluctuate between those feelings so quickly. But that's how life goes, right? Ups and downs. Peaks"—Mark gestured over his shoulder with his thumb, then pointed to the land falling away in front—"and valleys."

He fell silent for a long moment and turned to look to the west, in the direction of New Emery. From where he sat, he could see the edge of the mountain that had collapsed, closing the roads.

"It's been three weeks, and I'm starting to sincerely doubt that anyone's coming. We might have to take the trip back to New Emery by ourselves."

Cocking her head to the side, Mime stared at Mark for a second, then shook her head, using her paw to point down at the mountain below them. Mark's forehead furrowed as he tried to puzzle out what Mime was trying to communicate. Seeing that he wasn't getting it, she grabbed his cuff with her teeth and tugged, clearly wanting him to follow.

She jumped down from the rock, padded a few feet away, and then paused and looked at him until he got up. She led him back down the mountain into the base and through the door into the mine. Arriving inside, she continued past the workstations and down into the tunnel. She often disappeared in this direction, but this time, she wanted Mark to come with her.

As he proceeded farther into the darkness, Mark found himself curious. He had assumed that the mine was largely empty, save maybe for the occasional power slug. But as they continued down, following the rails, he realized that his estimation was probably completely wrong. Three times the tunnel split, and each time Mime led him off the main path into a side tunnel. Never once did she hesitate, leading Mark to believe she had been down here a considerable number of times. The tunnels were silent except for Mark's footsteps and quiet breaths, as Mime's paws made no noise on the dirt underfoot.

They walked for nearly half an hour, traveling deep into the center of the mountain, before Mime paused and then gestured with her paw for Mark to go ahead. Feeling oddly hesitant, Mark walked to the end of the passage and peeked around the corner, only to see a patch of light up ahead. Even the rail had stopped a considerable distance above, so seeing the bright glowing light confused Mark. Getting closer, he realized that it was a solitary mana-powered bulb poking out of the dirt wall.

24

Beyond the light, Mark saw a white concrete wall with a heavy metal-and-glass door in the middle. He edged closer—the last thing he had expected to run into this deep in the earth was human construction, but that was obviously what was in front of him. Through the glass, he could see more light, and it was dawning on him that this was where the extra power from the generators was going. Glancing over his shoulder, he saw that Mime had disappeared, but rather than fear, he found himself filled with curiosity.

There didn't seem to be anything else in the passage, but as Mark stepped forward, he heard a clank and stopped. At first, it didn't look as if anything had changed, but then he saw, at the top of the wall, a faint movement. The area was shrouded in darkness, but as he waited patiently, he saw something move again.

There was another clank, and a metal vent opened, flashing as it moved. It covered a small opening for airflow, no more than five inches in diameter, near the ceiling. As Mark watched, a power slug squeezed its way out of the narrow passage and inched down the wall, its tentacles swinging this way and that.

The power slug paused as it reached the ground, its tentacles testing to make sure it was still on a solid surface, and then, with a squelching noise, it continued, its underside rippling as it slowly made its way down the dirt tunnel toward Mark. The power slug seemed oblivious to Mark's presence, though the closer it got, the slower it went. Mark wasn't sure how it sensed what was around it, but still, he backed up, not wanting to tangle with the creature right in front of the glass door, in case there was something on the other side. As he retreated, the power slug moved quicker once again until it had turned the corner.

Wishing he had his suit, Mark jumped forward and struck down, killing the thing in one blow. The spray of ichor its body released as it popped filled the air with a disgusting stench, and not wanting to leave it to rot, Mark gritted his teeth and devoured it. He was fully expecting it to taste disgusting, but to his surprise, his shadow seemed to like it just as much as any of the other Exlian it had consumed, and a moment later, the passage was clean, save for the faint stench in the air.

Waving his hand to try to disperse it, Mark headed back around the corner, watching the vent carefully to see if any other slugs came out. There was no movement for a full five minutes, so he crept down the passage, into the pool of light and then beyond it, to the door. The door was perfectly smooth, save for a slight bump where the metal and glass met, and a keypad was next to it. Mark looked at the keypad but ultimately didn't press anything, as he was afraid entering the wrong code would have an adverse effect.

There didn't seem to be any other way to open the door, and though he tried to cut the metal, it was reinforced, making it impossible for his fingers to slice through. That left peering in through the glass to try to see what was beyond it. The door led to a room with a single desk and a hallway that extended some fifty feet before turning. It looked to Mark like a reception room, and it was quite a mess. Whoever would have sat behind the desk would have been able to see clearly through the door.

Just then, Mime leaped up from behind Mark, springing off his shoulder to reach the vent up above. With one smooth motion, she slipped inside, and a moment later, Mark saw her drop down inside the room. She turned and gave him a smug look through the glass, causing him to roll his eyes.

"Just see if you can get the door open," he said, unsure if she could hear him.

She must have been able to, because she nodded and began to look around as Mark waited as patiently as he could. Eventually, she disappeared behind the desk, and a moment later, there was a click and a hiss as the door slid to the side. Rather surprised that it had worked, Mark stepped through, scanning the room. His initial impression had been accurate. The room, some sort of reception area, was an absolute mess, papers and bits of trash scattered everywhere.

A wastebasket had been knocked over, and a chair lay discarded behind the desk. Someone had clearly left in a hurry, not even taking the time to close the filing cabinets. Trying not to touch anything, Mark scanned the documents. Most of them concerned administrative matters, and as he read through them, a picture began to emerge.

The term *Felwer Testing Facility* came up numerous times, though exactly what was being tested wasn't clear. Additionally, the majority of the staff seemed to be doctors, which was not what Mark would have expected to find in a testing facility buried miles underground in a mine. He did find a few memos addressed to an Emily Coleman, which matched a nameplate under the desk. About halfway through his search, he struck gold in the form of a scribbled note in the margin of one of the documents.

> *Dr. Curtis is requesting a wider variety of animals to test.*
> *Cites Report 2633A—improved mana-absorption rates.*

Letting out a low whistle, Mark shook his head. "Were they testing the effect of mana on animals? That's been illegal for a long time."

Finding nothing else of interest on the desk, Mark turned his attention to the filing cabinets, peeking inside and taking a look at the few files that remained. Most of them were incomprehensible, mixes of numbers and jargon that he couldn't make heads or tails of. Mime didn't rush him, but when he was done looking around, she pointed with her paw down the hallway. Growing more curious by the minute, Mark walked down the passage. There were doors on either side, most of them locked, but through the glass windows he could see more offices. Every single one of them was a wreck. Either this facility had been ransacked, or the people who had inhabited it had left in a tremendous hurry.

Given what Mark knew about the history of Felwer Mine and the base outside it, he imagined it was the latter. The base had been evacuated on short notice to avoid a massive Exlian wave, and he couldn't imagine that the doctors and other researchers in this lab would want to stick around while their security detail hightailed it back to the city.

The passage turned left and then right, then split into three corridors. Pausing at the intersection, Mark looked down at Mime, but she just shrugged, so he decided to take the rightmost passage.

About a hundred feet down the corridor, he came to a set of double doors that hissed open as he approached. Beyond them was a large room full of overturned equipment. Like the rest of the facility, this lab was well lit, though occasionally the lights would flicker, producing an eerie ambience. As he stepped through the door, Mark felt a haze wash over him, and blinking, he realized that he had once again been engulfed in whatever ability Mime used to stay hidden. Glancing back to thank her, he didn't see her behind him, but knowing how she liked to come and go, he shrugged and turned his attention back to the laboratory.

At first, he thought a fight might have taken place, but soon he noticed that much of the damage seemed to have been caused intentionally. Dozens of machines had been turned onto their sides, and their power cords had been torn out. The longer he examined everything, the clearer it became that this was sabotage. All the machines scattered around the room were damaged, and many of them had smashed screens and gaping holes where someone had forcefully removed components.

As he looked around, what struck Mark the most was just how old everything appeared. Almost no one used physical screens anymore, and Mark had never actually seen a computer in real life, only recognizing them from old movies. Everyone these days used virtual consoles, but the laboratory didn't seem to have any.

"Huh, this place is a lot older than I thought . . ."

His voice echoed more loudly than he was comfortable with, so he fell silent, crouching down to examine one of the shattered glass screens. That was when he saw the body—half hidden behind a fallen rack, the skeleton lay stretched out, wearing a decaying lab coat.

Making his way over, Mark saw the skeleton's arms were outstretched, its head tilted back slightly. A faded badge was still clipped to its coat, showing a handsome man with a broad smile and salt-and-pepper hair. Dr. Jonathan Yanos. As Mark's eyes drifted to the skeleton's head, he winced. From this angle, he could see that the entire back of the skull had been blown out, shards of bone scattered across the ground.

At first, Mark thought it was a result of tremendous blunt trauma. Maybe one of the machines had fallen on him. But then he noticed the neat hole in the center of the skeleton's forehead, right above his eyes. It had been a long time since physical projectiles were used with any frequency, but they were still common enough that Mark knew the signs. Guns were typically only effective against the unempowered due to the strengthening effect of empowerment, and with the increased number of empowered that filled society, the only people who used them were law enforcement and members of the military.

Why Dr. Yanos had been killed was a mystery, but as Mark looked around, he was starting to get a sense of what might have happened. Sliding the badge into his pocket, Mark stood up and continued deeper into the laboratory. The farther he went, the more severe the damage became, and eventually he reached a set of double doors that led to a long hall.

This hall, however, was different. Long windows stretched the length of it, each looking in on a different room. Most of the rooms were empty, but in a few Mark saw machines that had presumably been used for whatever the facility was studying. There were even some glass tubes that looked like healing tanks, all of which were broken.

As Mark slowly made his way down the hallway, looking in each window, he could feel his tension growing. Far from the peaceful evacuation he had at first assumed, it was now clear that there had been a fight in the lab. His fingers brushed against the wall, touching a series of holes scattered just under one of the windows. There was a dark stain on the floor, and though he saw no body nearby, Mark was certain that another person had died here.

The hall ended in a small server room that had been trashed just like the other, and after looking around, Mark turned and headed back through the observation hall and the laboratory to check out what the other passages held. Coming out of the lab, he took a right, heading down what would have originally been the passage straight in front of him. It sloped down for a few hundred feet and then turned a corner into another hall filled with observation windows.

Out of habit, Mark had been checking the psychic network, looking for signs of any Exlian, as he was wondering where the power slugs were coming from. As he stepped around the corner, he came up short, noticing a faint psychic flicker in the distance. Slowly, he crouched low, and then, as carefully as he could, he lifted his head to peek through the window.

He was astonished to see a massive room filled with thick vegetation. It was a full jungle, and as Mark watched, there was a hum, and the sprinkler system kicked on, sending down a steady drizzle of rain. There didn't seem to be any Exlian in that room, so Mark carefully made his way to the next. There, he found a massive aquarium filled to the brim with water. Along the floor was sand and rock and a variety of plants swaying with the current, but he didn't see any Exlian inside.

There was one more large window, and as Mark got closer, he realized this was where the Exlian signature was coming from. Peeking around the edge, he saw a rocky, mountainous landscape, clear of all vegetation. A heavy aura hung over the room, and as Mark watched, a massive leech with a spiky shell on its back crawled slowly across the landscape. It was four feet tall and at least three feet wide and left a trail of goo in its wake that crackled with lightning, and as Mark watched, an eyestalk popped out of the creature's body, causing an arc of lightning to jump from its eyeball to its shell.

Mark was astonished by what he was seeing, and he leaned a bit farther in. The movement must have alerted the creature, because one of its eyestalks suddenly swiveled, staring straight at

Mark. He froze and blinked. By the time his eyes were open again, the leech had somehow crossed the distance, leaving a crackling trail of lightning behind that blasted craters in the red earth, and slammed into the window with enough force to send a crack shooting through the glass. Falling back, Mark saw a terrifying mouth filled with sharp teeth that ran the length of the leech's body scraping against the glass as it desperately tried to get to him.

A keening wail rose from the leech, and lightning burst from its body, blasting everything around it with such force the glass trembled and creaked. All around Mark the Exlian network lit up, a dozen bright stars bursting to life. He stumbled backward, then turned and ran. As he did, he saw a massive crab clambering out of the seabed of the aquarium, sand and rocks cascading from its shell as its beady eyes began to look around. In the next room, the entire jungle seemed to have come alive, and as Mark sprinted down the hall, a series of splats echoed as vines slapped against the glass. Just before Mark reached the doorway, a click caused the world to dim, and the wall of the aquarium exploded outward, spilling a massive wave of water into the hall.

25

As fast as Mark was moving, it wasn't fast enough. The wall of water grew by the second, and before he could reach the sloped hallway that led back to the upper levels of the facility, the water slammed into him, nearly knocking him from his feet. Thrown against the wall, Mark let out a grunt, bubbles escaping from his lips as the air was pressed out of him.

The water was flowing fast, filling every available square inch of space. As he oriented himself, Mark knew that he'd be in trouble if he stayed where he was. It was hard to see through the murky water, but he could vaguely make out the shape of a massive claw poking through the hole in the glass, and he wanted no part of it. Since he was close to the passage leading up, he pushed off from the wall, trying to swim in that direction. Though he wasn't fighting directly against the current, it was still flowing strong, and it continually pressed him back against the wall as it ripped by.

He had almost reached the doorway when there was a slight grating noise and another boom. Instinctively, Mark curled, hands covering his ears as he tried to protect himself from the shock wave that tore through the water. The sound waves slammed into him, hurling him back against the wall with tremendous force. He stubbornly gritted his teeth, protecting his head and neck as best he could while ignoring the pain that rolled over his body like a wave cresting on the beach and then swiftly pulling back into the ocean.

The sound seemed to grab Mark and yanked him underwater, and in his disoriented state, he wondered why it was pulling on him. Desperate to get to the exit, he reached out, his fingers scrabbling against the doorframe. The water had suddenly reversed direction and was beginning to rush back down the hall toward the crab.

Mark was so muddled he didn't know which way was up, and worse, he was starting to run out of air. He could feel his lungs burning in his chest, and faint darkness was creeping in at the edges of his vision. He had no idea what was happening behind him and couldn't spare the energy to look, as the water had transformed into a riptide.

Mark felt rather than heard another crack. This one felt more akin to the shattering of glass. It was followed by a sharp shriek that stabbed Mark's ears, nearly causing him to let go of the doorframe. Thankfully, the water had receded enough that there was a slight gap between it and the ceiling, and Mark lunged upward, gasping as his head broke the surface. Yet even as he gulped down air, a strange numbness assaulted his body. Blinking the water from his eyes, Mark looked back and saw a sight he would never forget.

The massive crab, too big to fit in the hall, had reached through and snapped its claws, and the sound had completely shattered the floor of the hallway. It was through this hole in the floor that all the water was now pouring, dragging everything with it. But that was not what dominated Mark's attention.

The weakened window containing the lightning leech had broken as well, and the leech had crawled out of the hole and was now facing down the massive claw. The numbness Mark felt was undoubtedly caused by the arcs of lightning that continually jumped from the leech's body, conducted by the water it was now swimming through.

"Oh no," was all Mark got out before the leech unleashed a bolt of lightning as thick as Mark's waist.

The majority of the lightning targeted the claw accurately, scorching a hole in the thick armor plating that surrounded it. The crab shrieked in pain, pulling its claw back and ripping a giant gouge in the wall in the process.

Though it might have been an optical illusion, Mark felt like he could see electricity racing through the water, a glimmering web of bluish-white energy. He was still holding on tight to the doorframe, head just above the water, kicking against the heavy current dragging him toward the hole the crab had made, and all he could do was pull himself back as best as possible.

It wasn't nearly enough, however, and the web of lightning engulfed him, a million pins and needles erupting in his skin. It felt as if some gigantic hand had grabbed him and shaken him violently, and the darkness that had been creeping into the edges of his vision returned in force, falling like a blanket over his mind.

The lightning was so powerful it knocked Mark out almost instantly, and wisps of smoke rose from his skin as his body burned. His hand relaxed slightly, allowing the swiftly moving water to rip him free of the doorframe. A moment later, Mark's unconscious body hurtled down the hallway, joining the rapidly rushing water as it drained out through the hole under the crab's claw. If the leech or the crab noticed Mark, neither gave an indication. They were too busy attacking one another, and Mark soon slipped by, plunging down into the darkness.

The first thing Mark noticed when he awoke was how wet he was. Everything was wet: the stone under his cheek, his clothing, his hair, even his skin, which seemed to have been covered in a layer of slime that didn't want to come off.

Shuddering, Mark let out a groan and pushed himself to his feet, or at least tried. The passage he was in was small and dark, and as he rose, he whacked his head on a protruding rock. Grumbling, he reached up to feel for the lump on his head, but even as he did so, his regeneration kicked in, and it quickly shrank back down into nothing.

Though he couldn't see very well, there was a faint glimmer of light in the distance, and using his fingers, Mark carefully felt his way in that direction. The passage was angled slightly downward, and a small trickle of water was running down the floor around Mark, which no doubt contributed to his continued wetness.

The last thing he remembered before being washed away was being electrocuted by the leech's lightning attack, and the feeling, along with the memory of the massive crab claw bursting out into the passage, was forever burned into Mark's mind. Just before the crab had appeared, Mark had seen a small sun appear in the psychic network, but as he reflected on it, he realized that it hadn't been the crab. Which meant that another Exlian of overwhelming strength had been hidden near him . . .

He had heard much about the power of terror-ranked Exlian but had never seen one outside a video. One of the great truths about terror-ranked monsters was that encountering them was a sure recipe for death if you weren't at least an A-ranked empowered yourself. Even then, killing terror-ranked Exlian often required half a dozen empowered of the same rank, and Mark was beginning to understand why. In truth, he had absolutely no idea how someone would even go about fighting the giant crab he had just seen.

Shuddering, he refocused on his slow journey down the

passage and soon arrived at a small crack through which the water was trickling. It wasn't quite big enough for his body to fit through, but he could stick his head out to get a good look at the deep cavern that lay beyond.

What he saw completely erased any thoughts of the monsters he had faced above. The cavern was larger than any he had ever seen, at least a mile in length and close to three hundred feet tall. He was about halfway up the wall, and he could see a dense network of catwalks stretching around the edge of the cavern. Numerous rooms with glass windows were positioned among the catwalks, and flickering lights cast the glow that allowed Mark his limited vision.

In the center of the cavern was a glowing pool, so dense with mana that a faint mist rose above it. In the center of the pool was a massive stalagmite thrusting up from the cavern floor a full forty feet. The top looked as if it had been chopped off, forming a flat plateau. Mark could see thick, familiar-looking conduits running up the side of the stalagmite. These were the same cables that pulled power from the generators and kept the base running—this was where power was being siphoned from the generators above.

The conduits ended at a complex-looking device topped with six metal spikes, which released a faint spray of mana. That mana drifted in the air, forming a faint cloud that then settled down around the stalagmite, forming the lake of mana-infused water. Unsure what exactly the function of the machine was, Mark withdrew his head and carefully began to widen the hole, hoping to climb out and onto a catwalk that was only a dozen feet below his opening.

It didn't take him long to make the hole large enough to squeeze his shoulders through, and a few moments later, he dropped down onto the catwalk with a soft thud. The sound, though quiet, echoed in the silent cavern, and Mark felt more than saw the attention of something shifting toward him. Thankfully, Mime's shrouding still seemed to be hiding him, so he hurried along the catwalk on quiet feet, doing his best to distance himself from where he had landed.

At the same time, he looked through the cavern, trying to see what it was that had suddenly looked in his direction. It wasn't until he had gotten closer to the center of the room along one of the catwalks that he saw it, a writhing mass of jellylike flesh that sat atop the flattened stalagmite. As Mark watched, tendrils extended from the black mass, intercepting some of the arcing mana that shot between the six spikes. As it did, the tendrils were destroyed, even as the monstrosity absorbed some of the mana.

At first, Mark wasn't sure exactly what he was looking at, and then he remembered the video he had seen in the training camp showing Ra burning his way through the massive Exlian nest. Mark stopped in place, his heart pounding in his chest. The last thing he had imagined finding, buried deep in Felwer Mine, was a nest, but that was exactly what he was looking at. Even the smallest Exlian were far from harmless, and the nests, though they seemed benign, were among the most terrifying and dangerous Exlian in existence because of their ability to transform mana and biological matter into an endless swarm of monsters. Of course, this was much smaller than the nest he had seen in the video, only a fraction of the size, maybe twelve feet across and four feet deep. That didn't lessen the nervousness Mark felt, however, as he instinctively scanned for it on the psychic network.

To his surprise, he found that it didn't seem to appear at all, though when he concentrated, he could sense a sort of fuzziness in its location. Curious, he'd just leaned forward to get a better look when he heard a loud click echoing through the cavern and one of the walls lower down exploded outward, shrapnel filling the air as the stone rattled off the metal walkways.

Billowing dust emerged from a tunnel Mark hadn't seen below, and a moment later, an enraged giant crab stormed out, its claws waving wildly, its beady eyes darting around. Through the dust, Mark could see faint flashes of lightning from the leech that had chased the crab into the cavern, making the cloud look like a fierce storm. The crab turned this way and that in agitation, its large claws waving through the air. One claw caught a walkway, and immediately the metal crumpled under the force of the strike, collapsing with a screech of shearing metal.

Yet no matter how the crab danced around, swinging its claws, it didn't seem to be able to hit its target. The lightning leech moved in short bursts, traveling so quickly through the air that it looked to Mark like it was teleporting, the powerful bolts of lightning arcing off it, burning through the crab's carapace. The two monsters were engaged in a deadly dance.

As he watched, holding his breath for fear he might attract their attention, Mark thought the lightning leech might have the advantage. Yet no sooner had that thought crossed his mind than the crab suddenly lunged forward, its two massive claws reaching through the air. The leech flashed away, but even as it did, two smaller claws suddenly extended from the crab's shell. As the leech arrived at the crab's side, it met a smaller claw, darting out with incredible speed and snapping shut on the leech's shell.

There was a sharp crack, and a tremendous storm of lightning erupted from the leech, blasting into the crab with such force it nearly flipped it over. As the crab struggled to regain its balance, the leech let out a keening wail and retreated toward the center of the room, leaking lightning bolts. It made it to the edge of the mana-infused water before the lightning started to peter out and its body slowed.

Inching forward at a speed much more in keeping with its leech form, it was just about to enter the glowing water when a tentacle abruptly extended from the pool, wrapping it up and lifting it into the air. What Mark had assumed was a giant rock at the edge of the stalagmite now rose, glowing water cascading off it. It wasn't a rock at all but instead another massive leech. Like the other terror-ranked Exlian, it must have been in some sort of hibernation, because Mark hadn't noticed it in the psychic network at all.

Now its glow completely drowned out the other lightning leech and the large crab. Extending its body from the shell, the leech lifted its wounded brethren into the air and then, opening its massive mouth, tossed the smaller leech into its maw and crunched it up as if chewing on a hard candy.

26

Mark couldn't suppress the shudder that raced through him, and he clearly wasn't the only one who was wary, as the crab had slowly started to back up toward the tunnel it had emerged from. But with a surge of lightning, the massive leech shot out of the pool, swiftly crossing the distance to the crab.

Nearly four times the size of the leech it had just consumed, this leech was at least seventeen feet tall at the back of its shell, easily matching the crab's height. It wielded four long tentacles that crackled with lightning, which it used to whip at the crab. But the crab wasn't helpless, and soon the sharp crack of its snapping claws mixed with the boom of the leech's lightning strikes.

Mark peeled himself from where he had been crouched and began to make his way down the walkway. He had spotted another exit on the other side of the cavern and was hoping that would lead him back up to the main passages. He was entirely out of his league and suitless to boot, and the last thing he wanted was to attract the attention of a terror-ranked Exlian. Much less two.

He had made it halfway across the cavern when he spotted Mime. She was crouched on the walkway in front of him, ready to pounce, her eyes fixed on the nest that still occupied the large stalagmite island.

"What are you doing?" Mark hissed, his voice just about drowned by the loud booms echoing through the cavern.

Mime slowly turned her head to look at him, her eyes gleaming in the dim light.

"We need to go," said Mark.

A faint stubbornness appeared in Mime's eyes. Eyes wide, she sat up slightly, extending a claw down at the nest.

"What about it?" Mark asked, turning to peer through the bars of the walkway.

Opening her mouth, Mime pointed a paw into it, then licked her lips and patted her stomach.

"You want to eat it? Can you even eat something like that?"

As soon as the words came out of Mark's mouth, he realized how foolish they were. His shadow could devour Exlian corpses without trouble. Why would he find it weird that Mime thought she could eat the nest? Shaking his head, Mark looked down at the gelatinous mass. It seemed completely oblivious to the fight happening nearby. Mark was suddenly struck by a strange thought. The nest looked young and underdeveloped, though on closer examination, he thought that maybe *weakened* was a better term. Currently, it appeared desperate to fill itself with as much mana as it possibly could, and with every moment that passed, the feeling it gave off grew incrementally stronger.

It was then Mark noticed the faint hunger in himself. It wasn't the overwhelming hunger he felt when his biofuel was empty but instead a quiet yet insistent drive. Something in the back of his mind was telling him that he needed to devour the nest. By now, Mark had grown accustomed to these sorts of hunger pangs, and he didn't think it strange at all. Rather, he found himself curious as to why he might have such a reaction. His body seemed to know what would benefit it, and Mark was learning to pay attention to these cravings.

From the corner of his eye he caught sight of a massive lightning bolt, followed by a loud shriek as the crab lost half of one of its large claws in the blueish-white onslaught. The sight killed any thought Mark had of trying to sneak closer to the nest. If he got anywhere near the two terror-ranked Exlian fighting below, he'd end up dead in a heartbeat. He needed to leave, and fast. That conviction was reinforced when he saw the nest suddenly pause its frantic mana gathering and tremble.

A moment later, a small lightning leech inched its way out of the dark mass of the nest. Mark had seen a nest producing Exlian in a recording, but being present as a tremendously dangerous creature popped into existence gave him a new appreciation of just how perilous his situation was. The brand-new leech took a moment to orient itself and then started heading down the side of the stalagmite. Its shell glowed with a bluish-white light and rapidly began to absorb the thick clouds of ambient mana, gaining a faint sheen that looked like arcing lightning as it did so.

Abandoning any thought of going down to hunt the nest, Mark picked up Mime, despite her clear protests, and held her close as he hurried along the catwalks, trying to move as silently as possible. The catwalk he was on led to one of the half-dozen observation rooms, and when he arrived, Mark was pleasantly surprised to find the door unlocked. Unlike the fancy sliding doors that filled the upper floors, this was a simple hinged door, and as Mark stepped inside, he was once again struck by just how low tech everything was. There were numerous machines and a few computers still intact, and Mark could hear the faint hum of power feeding into them. Whoever had trashed the upper floors hadn't made it down here.

The console was simple, with a bank of terminals and a few large buttons. The most prominent among them was labeled

Emergency Shutoff and had a metal plate with instructions on it, indicating that there were other buttons elsewhere. A blinking light caught his eye, and walking over to the main terminal in front of the large observation window that looked down on the nest, Mark saw a message asking if the computer should be reset. Though he had never actually used a keyboard, he understood them in concept, and after hunting around for a while, he found the direction keys, which he used to shift the cursor to select *no*.

The blinking light vanished, and the computer's home screen popped up, along with a folder that contained countless files. Scanning through them, Mark found hundreds of observation logs, and while he knew he should leave the cavern as soon as possible, he couldn't help his curiosity.

Though the giant leech was dominating the fight, using its lightning to burn through the crab's armor to put it on the back foot, the crab's healing was rapidly repairing much of the damage, and it was putting up enough of a struggle that the fight wouldn't be over anytime soon. After peering at the two monsters from the window to make sure they were still firmly engaged in their brawl, Mark turned his attention to the logs and began reading through them, starting with the earliest he could find.

Log 115 — Observer: Dr. Moore

Subject shows no sign of growth for the 115th day in a row, though it will respond to outside stimuli, especially anything that could be threatening. It does not otherwise seem aware it is under observation.

Log 116 — Observer: Dr. Hannah

No new movement today.

Log 117 Observer: Dr. Moore

Nothing for the first half of the day. I think we need to find some new ways to stimulate it. The subject has grown increasingly resistant to non-threatening stimuli. In the second half of the day, it vibrated strongly for three minutes but then fell still once more.

Log 118 Observer: Dr. Hannah

Subject shifted around the top of the stalagmite, crawling very slowly from one side to another. We thought it might crawl down, but ultimately it ended up returning to the center of the stalagmite, from which it has not moved. We took the opportunity to measure the subject. It remains less than two feet in diameter.

Whoever had been running this facility had been observing the nest, but Mark could only imagine just how long ago that had been. The logs were not dated, though he guessed the numbers indicated the day since observation had begun. In addition to the bit of text detailing what had taken place that day, there were a few numbers at the bottom of each log, but Mark had no idea what they were supposed to mean. Skipping forward in the logs, he noticed one with a star next to it.

Log 275 Observer: Dr. Armin

At Dr. Moore's suggestion, we have continued the mana-enrichment tests to great effect. The subject responds positively to any mana introduced to it.

It clearly prefers pure mana to mana contained in matter, but it absorbs both with no trouble. We will continue to observe.

Log 276 Observer: Dr. Moore

Tests with inorganic material that has a high mana concentration have elicited a response from the subject, though it only interacts with them for a time before ceasing all movement for the day. Objects the subject absorbs become part of it and seem to be adding to its mass.

Log 277 Observer: Dr. Armin

The subject clearly has a maximum capacity for what it can absorb, but that capacity is growing at a significant rate. We are starting to measure the rate at which the subject can accommodate mana. See below for a simple summary. For the complete daily assessment see file SALPHA.101.3.

As the logs continued, Mark grew increasingly immersed in the fascinating mystery from all those years ago. The scientists, with no idea what sort of fire they were playing with, had discovered the nest's desire for mana and fed it, curious as to what the result would be. And Mark was starting to get a sense of what the attached numbers might mean. They were likely measurements the scientists were taking each day, and Mark found that from that point on, the logs contained an extra measurement that he believed indicated how much mana the nest had absorbed.

Log 291 Observer: Dr. Moore

We got the go-ahead from Dr. Yanos to test with live leeches. The subject responded favorably, pouncing on them as soon as they were dropped on top of the stalagmite. The subject has grown to nearly four feet in diameter and seems to be able to extend appendages, much like an amoeba. After eating all five leeches, it has fallen into an unresponsive state, even when we add more leeches to its platform. Our next test will be to introduce a steadier flow of mana. There have been some concerns that the subject might grow uncontrollable, but based on everything we've seen, I don't think that will be the case.

Pausing, Mark could only shake his head. He, of course, had the benefit of hindsight, but the scale at which these scientists were wrong was sickening. Though the nest wasn't necessarily aggressive in its own right, the monsters it produced were quite another story, and feeding it a steady diet of mana could only have one outcome.

Mark couldn't help but wonder if tests like these had allowed the Exlian to grow into the overwhelming threat they had become. How many places in this world had been studying Exlian like this before the waves that wiped out humanity came? How many nests had the humans inadvertently empowered? There was no doubt in Mark's mind that the leeches Dr. Moore and his peers had fed the nest were the blueprint for the lightning leeches it now produced, and from what he had seen in the observation windows, it was clear that there had been other experiments as well. Flipping through to the last few logs, Mark clicked on one of them.

Log 371 Observer: Dr. Hannah

It is genuinely hard to believe that it has been over a year since the subject was discovered. The changes we've been able to introduce are incredible, and the tests have yielded such fruitful results. Our mana-feeding tests have been going well, and the subject has grown to a healthy fifty feet in diameter. It is almost too big for the stalagmite now. Observation of the creatures that it has created is going well, and I'm excited for the next set of tests to see if we can change the sorts of creatures it creates by adjusting its diet. The work we are doing could change humanity forever.

Log 372 Observer: Dr. Armin

Things are quiet, but it's the quiet before the storm. There have been rumblings of a massive swarm of creatures heading this way. They're calling them ghouls, like some sort of undying monster out of a science fiction or fantasy novel, which is ridiculous. Then again, if those videos that leaked on the web are real, they're certainly dangerous.

Log 373 Observer: Dr. Moore

Orders have come down to close this base, but most of us don't want to leave. The research we are doing is too important. I can feel that we're on the cusp of something incredible. We've been isolating the power anomalies, and I'm almost certain that it's the prime subject that is causing them. Imagine, a creature able to directly interfere with a power system. It would also explain why some of our sensors have been returning gibberish. The readings are consistent with the theory that the subject can adjust the values the sensors send back, but it doesn't understand them well enough to make them coherent. This needs to be studied further!

Log 374 Observer: Dr. Hannah

There are soldiers here, and they're threatening everyone who won't leave with force. They say they are here to evacuate us, but I know they're looking for the Lilith Project (993752)

The last log ended abruptly, leaving Mark with the impression that the soldiers had burst in and dragged Dr. Hannah away. A number was recorded at the end of the log, but Mark had no idea what it might be for.

The mysteries were stacking up. First, what did the scientists believe could change humanity forever? It wasn't readily apparent to Mark how understanding the Exlian nest might help humans, but according to the logs, the scientists had believed it would. The second question was why the nest had shrunk down to its current size. The last few logs indicated that it had once been fifty feet wide, nearly three times the size it was now.

Mark had started to hunt for more information when a tremendous roar reminded him of the two battling behemoths outside. The whole cavern shook as a click rang out, creating a superheated vacuum that threw the lightning leech back, heavy gashes appearing on its leathery skin. Yet a moment later, the leech was back in a burst of lightning, smashing into the crab and trying to bite off its eyestalks.

27

The crab was already in rough shape, missing a couple of its legs and the majority of one of its claws. Still, it battled on and seemed to have set its sights on the pool of mana, no doubt hoping to absorb the tremendous energy it contained to heal itself. The lightning leech was equally determined to keep the crab away from the pool but wasn't having much luck. As they fought, they got ever closer to Mark's position, and he realized that he was playing with fire. As reluctant as he was to go, since he didn't have any way to bring the logs or other files with him, Mark grabbed Mime and headed for the exit nevertheless.

Mime had been sitting on top of the computer, gazing down at the nest intently, and was quite unhappy to be dragged away. Ignoring Mime's silent protest, Mark hurried through the door opposite the one he had entered from and out onto the catwalk beyond. He tried to remain quiet and mostly out of sight, but rather than creeping as he had done before, he half walked, half jogged toward the exit, eager to get away from the fight.

In order to reach the exit, Mark had to climb a set of stairs and cross the room on a thin catwalk. On catwalks below him he could see more observation rooms, and though he wanted to learn more about the experiments on the nest, Mark knew that every moment he stuck around increased the danger he was in. He could still feel Mime's hazy psychic ability covering him, but he had no idea how long it could last, and it would be a disaster if it suddenly fell and the two monsters or the nest noticed him.

At the top of the stairs, hidden by the railing, Mark found a crumpled, face-down skeleton dressed in a ragged lab coat, and he paused for a second to search it. The majority of the skull had been obliterated, and the hole in the back gave a clear indication of why. Just like Dr. Yanos, this doctor had been shot in the head. Attached to the front of the skeleton's coat was an ID card, and with a sinking heart, Mark held it up to the dim light.

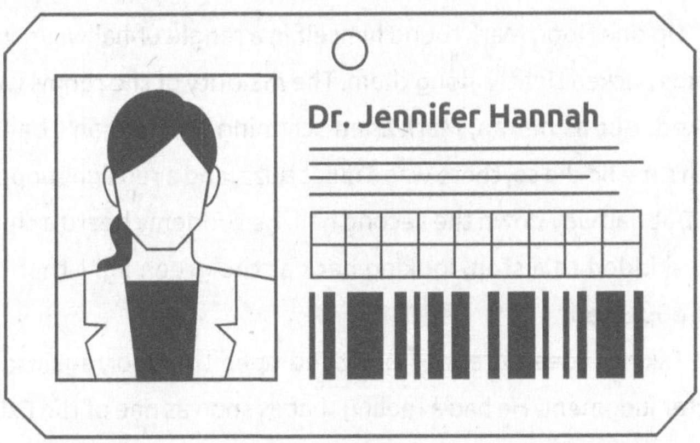

Though Mark didn't know anything about Dr. Hannah, he couldn't help the flash of sadness in his chest. Reading the last log and then seeing her body stretched out on the catwalk added a tragic air to the mystery of what had happened all those years ago. Clearly, nothing was as simple as it seemed. Then again, the fact that there was a secret research facility hidden deep in a mine should have been the first indication that something was wrong.

Still holding the badge, Mark stayed low as he crept along the catwalk. His passage across the cavern was covered by the booms and blasts of the giant leech's lightning and the thunderous clicks of the crab's answering snaps. It wasn't long before Mark had made it to the exit. Praying that it was unlocked, he tried the door, only to find it wouldn't budge. He was just about to despair when he noticed a pad off to the side. Struck by inspiration, he waved Dr. Hannah's badge in front of it. There was a click, and a green light appeared on the pad. Then, with a hiss, the doors parted, allowing him to slip through.

Mark found himself in a well-lit hallway. At the far end, a set of stairs headed back upward. Dispensing with his stealth, Mark took off running, wanting to get as far away from the terror-ranked Exlian as he could. As he ran, he scanned the psychic network, looking for any potential threats. Mercifully, it was empty.

Up one floor, Mark found himself in a tangle of hallways, with rooms packed tightly along them. The majority of the rooms were locked. But as he ran, Mark tried scanning Dr. Hannah's badge. Each time he did so, there was a quiet buzz, and a red light popped up. But halfway down the second hall, he suddenly heard a chime and skidded to a stop, looking back at the green light that had just appeared.

Taking a deep breath, he pushed open the door, against his better judgment. He had a feeling that as soon as one of the Exlian won, especially if it was the leech, this whole complex would become incredibly dangerous. But he couldn't help himself. At the moment, all he had was a name—the Lilith Project—and a number that Dr. Hannah had recorded just before her death.

The door opened into a small bedroom, comprising a desk with a mana lamp, a set of dressers, and a small bed. They were deep underground, so there were no windows, and the room felt closed in and claustrophobic. Nothing looked out of the ordinary, and a quick search didn't reveal anything suspicious. Dozens of books were packed onto a small shelf on the wall. While Mark checked them, Mime jumped up on the bed.

The books were primarily biology and physics related, and Mark found a few papers that he couldn't make heads or tails of sitting on the desk. From how disorganized the desk was, it looked to Mark as if somebody had rifled through it, and he imagined that it had been one of the soldiers, hurriedly searching before they evacuated.

Disappointed, Mark stepped over to the bed to grab Mime so they could continue on their way, but she shook her head and tapped the headboard. Taking a seat on the bed, Mark leaned over. The headboard was composed of a dozen small square panels set at different depths to create a bit of dimension and add some texture to the room. As he examined it more closely, however, Mark realized that one of the panels didn't follow the pattern of the others. At a quick glance, it looked entirely normal, and he hadn't noticed until Mime pointed it out.

There was a slight gap at the back of the panel, and with his fingertips, Mark peeled it away, revealing a small keypad. For a moment, he stared at the keypad, then at Mime, a slow smile appearing on his lips. He held out his hand for a high five, and with a rather smug look, Mime slapped her paw against his palm.

Punching in the code Dr. Hannah had left in her log, Mark heard a faint grinding noise and realized that the entire dresser had popped forward half an inch, revealing a cubby behind it. There was just enough space by the bed to shove the dresser sideways, and Mark did, surprised to find that it slid smoothly along hidden rails.

Inside was a simple shelf with four things laid out neatly. The first was a journal with a lock. Unable to open it, Mark stuck it in his pocket. The second item was a vial, and as soon as Mark picked it up, he felt something in it stir. It was such a strange sensation that he nearly dropped it, but after that first movement, there was nothing else, so though he felt it was a bit strange, he stuck it in his pocket as well.

The third item on the hidden bookshelf was a picture showing a dark-haired woman Mark immediately recognized as Dr. Hannah and a handsome, salt-and-pepper-haired middle-aged man who looked like Dr. Yanos. In the picture, Dr. Yanos was looking straight at the camera, while Dr. Hannah was looking up at him, the infatuation in her eyes clear.

The final item was a small black rectangular device that Mark couldn't identify. It had a port on one side, though one of a configuration he had never seen before. It looked to him like some sort of data-storage device, but he had never run across anything like it, so it, too, went into his pocket. Having cleared everything out, Mark grabbed Mime, and they headed back out into the hallway.

"We really need to get out of here," Mark said, glancing around as they came to yet another T-junction. "This place is a maze."

Mime jumped down from his arms. Hoping that she was leading him out and not back down to the nest to try to devour it, Mark followed as she swiftly padded down the hallway. She seemed to know exactly where she was going, making Mark wonder if the times she had vanished into the mine had actually been spent exploring this space.

Eventually, she led him to a stairwell that rose six stories to the floor where Mark had originally entered. They had left the nest and the battling Exlian far behind and hadn't encountered any enemies on the way out, which Mark was tremendously grateful for.

When they arrived at the facility door, he checked to see if Dr. Hannah's badge would work. He also had Dr. Yanos's badge, and both of them worked fine. Mark was rather startled at just how much relief he felt stepping out into the rough-hewn mine tunnel, but after a moment of reflection, it made sense, as none of the terror-ranked Exlian would fit through the smaller hallways at the top of the facility, making it unlikely they'd be able to leave the lower floors. Mime also seemed completely relaxed, and the farther away he got from the research facility, the more relaxed he felt as well.

When he finally returned to the entrance of the mine, he felt as if he had just been put through a wringer. Mentally exhausted by his ordeal, he lay down to take a nap and quickly fell into a sleep that had him battling screamers all night. He hadn't actually realized that it was so late, and when he woke up the next morning, he just lay on his bed for a while, staring up at the dark stone ceiling, reviewing what he knew.

Given what he had discovered in the research center below, it was incredibly unlikely that the order to reopen the mine was simply about restarting ore production. Mark doubted that the leaders of New Emery weren't aware of the research facility hidden deep in the mountain. Of course, no evidence pointed to New Emery having been involved in the research . . . The mining company that had been primarily responsible for running the mine wasn't technically affiliated with the city, so there was a chance that New Emery was in the dark. Of course, the fact that soldiers had forcefully evacuated the research facility, destroying much of the evidence in the process, pointed to it being an official research site.

Mark knew that some of the larger companies and upper-class families had private armies, but they were mainly composed of empowered, who simply had no need to use ballistic weapons. The fact that he had found two bodies, each executed with a shot to the head, indicated more mundane forces. Of course, if the leadership at New Emery knew about the facility and was planning on reactivating it, it made little sense that Mark and the Black Mountain Battalion had been sent out with next to no support. Clearly, multiple things were going on, and Mark didn't like any of them.

His original plan had been to hang out at the mine until the backup battalions were able to dig their way through the collapsed mountain or at least find a way around. But he was starting to suspect that it was a fool's errand. The mission had been plagued by problems all the way along, and Mark had a sinking feeling that if anyone found out that he knew about the research facility, his life would be in even more danger than it already was.

Sitting up, Mark stared into the darkness and sighed. A glance at his watch told him that it was still early. Four in the morning, to be precise. Part of him wanted to go back to sleep, to ignore the problems piling up on his plate. But he knew that eventually he'd have to get up and face them. Checking his biofuel meter, he saw he was still more than half full. The increase brought about by his growth to the C rank meant that he could last two days longer without hunting. But Mark couldn't shake the antsy feeling that was starting to work its way through his mind.

Walking out of his makeshift bedroom, Mark took a moment to double-check the workstations. Nothing had been disturbed, but that still didn't put him at ease. According to his normal schedule, after his exercise, he would begin working on alchemy, continuing his efforts to create an elixir. But he was too unsettled for that, and instead he headed outside, breathing in the fresh early-morning air as he climbed up the mountain to his favorite vantage spot.

Mime had followed him, and as he sat on the rock, facing east to catch the first rays of the morning sun, she lay down in his lap. The weight on his legs was comforting. And as Mark waited in the darkness, he found himself calming down. The unknown was always frightening, always disheartening. But the more he thought about it, the more he realized he had little to fear.

Sure, there were many things in this world he was too weak

to handle. Like the two terror-ranked Exlian he had run away from the day before. It was entirely possible that they were still fighting down below, tearing each other apart in their quest for dominance. But even though he was still relatively weak, it wasn't as if he had no power.

Just then, Mark saw a faint hint of blue on the horizon. The subtle shift from complete darkness to a flicker of light. Over the next half an hour, he watched as the sun slowly made its way up from the horizon, dyeing the sky with pinks and deep blues as it spread its golden light across the land. The air was crisp, and every breath felt like drinking a sweet nectar, filling Mark with energy. It was almost intoxicating in its potency, and Mark found his worries and fears receding with the darkness.

28

"I think it's time to head back to the city," Mark said.

Mime sat up, her eyes wide as they met his. After a long moment, she nodded, stretched, and jumped down from his lap. He followed her back into the mine, his mind made up. Rather than continuing to hang out, waiting for someone to come rescue him, he was going to make the trip. Though he would have to cross hundreds of miles of hostile wilderness by himself, Mark was confident that as long as he didn't run into any terror-ranked Exlian, he would be able to survive, especially since he had Mime with him.

Getting his suit, Mark gathered a few things to put in a small bag, making sure to take the items he had retrieved from the hidden facility, as well as the manastone and the powdered core. He also brought Lieutenant Kami's and Sergeant Fletcher's identification tags. He hadn't managed to retrieve IDs for either of the Price brothers, but he figured bringing the lieutenant's and sergeant's would be enough.

He had no food, but even if he did, he wouldn't have packed it, as there was simply no need. He intended on hunting Exlian on his way into the city, though how he was going to explain his lack of supplies to anyone he came across, he wasn't quite sure. Mark had never heard of anybody foraging out in the wilderness, as practically everything was poisonous. Still, it was a problem he would worry about later, when he actually managed to find another human.

It didn't take him long to pack, and he set out as soon as he was done closing up the mine behind him. As he walked out, he noticed one of the lights flickering slightly and suddenly stopped, his mind returning to the scene of the nest absorbing mana from the large conduits in the facility below.

The generators were feeding the thing, but they would turn off after a week. So far, he had been keeping them running by performing maintenance, but they would automatically switch off. It was possible, in fact highly probable, that the reason the nest had shrunk in size was that the mana it had been feeding on had dried up when the generators stopped running.

It was rather terrifying that the nest had survived for all these years. Though when Mark thought about how many of the Exlian seemed to be able to hibernate, it didn't seem quite as bad. Still, he decided to head back into the mine and turn off the generators, not wanting to inadvertently help grow the nest even larger.

From what he understood, nests had to use their own mass in order to create new Exlian. So if he could prevent it from growing, that would stymie the number of Exlian it could create. Of course, all his efforts would be out the window if the leech won the fight, as Mark could imagine just how much the nest would grow after devouring the giant crab.

There was nothing he could do about that, however, so after making sure the generators were off, Mark left the ruins of Felwer Mine, heading west along the mountain path back toward New Emery. He moved at a steady jog, maintaining a quick but sustainable pace, and the miles began to vanish behind him. As he ran, he scanned the horizon, looking for any signs of humans. Part of him was hoping he'd hear the loud crash of heavy equipment carving its way through the collapsed mountain to re-form the path. But as the day wore on, there was only the sound of his feet against the hard earth.

Toward evening, Mark caught sight of the beginning of the rockfall. The Black Mountain Battalion had cleared this section of the path on their way to the base, destroying the boulders to allow the command vehicle to roll through. Pausing to examine the ground, Mark did his best to figure out if the command vehicle had been back through the same way. He genuinely couldn't tell, and after staring at the confusing tracks for a little while, he shrugged and continued on.

It had been weeks since the command vehicle carrying Captain Calder and Sergeant Rogers had left, and Mark didn't anticipate catching up to them. Part of him was hoping he'd come across their corpses, but unless they'd run into multiple Exlian that outclassed them by a terrific degree, Mark had a strong feeling that the two of them had survived. That was fine with him as well, as he fully planned on ending their lives himself once he had the strength.

Mark encountered his first Exlian as day turned into night. A swarm of vultures the size of dogs, with sharp taloned feet that extended like lances as they dropped out of the sky to attack Mark. He had been paying attention and caught sight of them just before the first one launched itself toward him. Waiting until the last moment, he dodged to the side and struck, badly injuring one of the Exlian's wings. It crashed into the ground as it struggled to fly away.

Before Mark could pounce on it, the second monster arrived. He met it with an upward swing of his sword. The sharp mana blade tore through the creature's legs, sending blood splashing. With a shriek, the Exlian flapped its wings, trying to rise away from the attack. Its efforts were in vain, however, as dodging put it in the path of one of its companions. The sharp talons of the other bird pierced through its back, driving it to the ground.

As Mark fought off the other Exlian dive-bombing him, a thought struck him. He tried to direct his shadow to devour one of the dead vultures. At first, it felt impossible, like trying to push water uphill. Then suddenly, his mind shivered and split, as if two versions of himself had begun to exist simultaneously. One was busy fighting off the Exlian birds, dodging their attacks while launching counterstrikes to bring them down. As he danced through the swarm, another version of Mark, another set of thoughts, was calm and unmoving, meditative, as it directed his shadow to eat.

At first, Mark didn't understand what was going on, but then he realized it was just his quantum clone ability. Rather than using it outside his body, however, he was using it in his mind, focusing on two completely separate trains of thought simultaneously. Mark's shadow swelled and spread, engulfing one of the corpses. As soon as it did, three crimson eyes opened in it, and the birds that Mark was fighting began to let out shrieks, rising high into the air as if frightened. One even broke off its attack mid-fall, its wings snapping out to slow its descent.

Watching as the vultures retreated, Mark saw that his shadow had finished consuming the corpses. They gave as much energy as drones and didn't affect Mark's stats in the least, which was disappointing. The vultures circled a few more times, then began to fly away, leaving Mark staring after them. As his thoughts snapped back together, unifying into one stream, Mark glanced down at his shadow, which looked relatively normal, if slightly bloated.

"I really need to figure out what this shadow thing is," he muttered as Mime hopped up onto his shoulder. "It's starting to get a bit creepy."

Though he hadn't quite eaten his fill, Mark had chewed up five of the vultures, giving him fifteen biofuel units, enough to last him a few more days even if he did end up fighting. The fact that he could devour Exlian during combat to refill his biofuel gave him even more confidence that he'd be able to make it back to the city in one piece. After all, one of the most dangerous aspects of the Exlian was their ability to swarm, but Mark had found the perfect answer for that. No matter how many came, as long as he could kill them, he could keep fighting.

Additionally, his shadow seemed to have a deterrent effect, and as he continued on his way, Mark worked on leveraging that. When he focused on his desire to devour Exlian, his shadow would ripple, releasing a faint, predatory aura, one that the creatures seemed able to sense from afar. He first saw the effect when a group of four Exlian in the distance switched directions, fleeing from his path to avoid meeting him. This was tremendously useful and allowed Mark to speed up considerably.

Of course, he knew that there was risk involved as well. Though his predatory aura could scare off Exlian that were weaker than him, it would act as bait for those stronger. With that in mind, he tried to use it judiciously, only activating it when he noticed weaker Exlian in his path that he didn't want to concern himself with.

By the second day, Mark had traveled nearly ninety miles. Thanks to the devil hounds and hunters he'd consumed, his speed was much higher than it had been, and with his increased biofuel storage, he could travel without stopping to rest. The next day, however, he only managed twenty miles, as the terrain was much rougher and more treacherous. He was crossing over some of the rock fields created by the avalanche, and twice he was nearly sent tumbling down the mountain by loose rocks. Once, he had to backtrack to avoid another rockslide, and another time, he found himself lost in a maze of boulders that took him almost two hours to climb his way out of.

That night, sitting down on a rock to regain some of his energy, Mark reflected on just how crazy his life had become. Strangely, when he thought about returning to New Emery, he found himself rather ambivalent. Were it not for the lack of people, he wouldn't mind life out in the wilderness all that much. Of course, New Emery was full of conveniences, while the wilderness had next to none. But life in the city had come with other concerns as well. Mark had spent his whole life desperately trying to live up to the expectations of others, but out here, he had no concerns with money or what others thought of him. There was no one to perform for, save the Exlian, and with them, it was win or die.

Mark had never thought of himself as a loner, and occasionally he found himself missing his friends, but he found he quite liked the stillness, as well as the frantic action of life in the wild. As he sat on the side of the mountain, enjoying the peace and the cool breeze, he suddenly heard a faint noise. From how quiet it was, he judged that it was likely miles away, and at first, he wasn't going to bother with it. But as it continued, his curiosity was piqued, and he rose to climb the ridge above him, hoping to get a better vantage point.

The farther up the ridge he got, the clearer the sound became, and Mark soon realized that a battle was taking place around the other side of the mountain. Curious as to whether it was another one of the engineering battalions that were supposed to be heading for the mine, Mark took off, moving with agile grace across a rock field. Rather than heading up to the top of the ridge, he cut around it, keeping his attention on his psychic network the whole time.

He ran for two miles before he found the fight, and a fight it was. Hundreds of Exlian swarmed the hillside, with hundreds more coming from the south, over the peak, and down the mountain. Mark was approaching from the east, and half a mile in front of him fifty soldiers were dug in behind a makeshift fortification, defending themselves against the Exlian swarm. Mark had never seen so many devil hounds in his life, and the sight made him salivate.

The soldiers were fighting back against the swarms of Exlian and managing to hold their own, but the ever-increasing numbers were clearly becoming a problem. About to rush out into the fight, Mark suddenly hesitated, glancing down at his makeshift armored suit. In truth, he looked like an absolute savage at the moment, and it wouldn't be entirely out of the question for the soldiers to mistake him for a strange Exlian.

At the same time, if he were to announce himself to his allies, it would ruin any surprise advantage he would have against the Exlian. Pondering what to do for a moment, Mark suddenly remembered that he was wearing Sergeant Fletcher's watch, and like every military-issued watch, it had a short-range feature that would allow him to ping his location.

Crouching behind some rocks, Mark spent thirty seconds trying to figure out how to activate the function. When he finally did, it took a moment before any of the soldiers reacted. Then one of them stood up. Looking in Mark's direction, he shouted a command. The Rangers, no doubt thinking Mark needed coverage so that he could get into the formation, began focusing on killing the Exlian between them and Mark. Although he didn't need the help, Mark didn't hesitate to take advantage of it. He rushed out from behind cover, wielding his sword with fierce slashes as he hacked his way through the devil hounds' ranks. They were caught completely off guard, and as their fierce death cries echoed through the psychic network, Mark could feel the other devil hounds' attention turning toward him. While Exlian were driven to kill any other living creatures they encountered, they seemed to hate other Exlian the most. A faint thought flickered through Mark's mind as many of the devil hounds abandoned their attack on the soldiers and turning to rush toward Mark, but it was gone as fast as it came under the devil hounds' frenzied attacks.

Forced into a defensive posture, Mark was nearly buried under a dozen bodies. But at the last moment, half a dozen blasts of mana from the soldiers, along with a few mana-charged arrows, killed the wave of Exlian threatening to overrun him. Grateful for the soldiers' assistance, Mark continued to attack with his sword as he cut his way toward where the soldiers were hunkered down.

As he moved through the crowds of devil hounds, he didn't forget to have his shadow sweep the ground behind him, rapidly enveloping and chewing through the Exlian corpses. As soon as his biofuel was full, he made sure to stop the shadow's efforts in order to avoid freaking out the soldiers. By this time, he was only a hundred feet from the fortification, but more and more devil hounds were charging his position, making it increasingly hard for him to move forward.

Spotting an opportunity, one of the soldiers gave a great shout and charged forward, a number of others following behind. Recognizing them as Rangers, Mark saw the officer who had charged first unleashing a storm of gleaming blue blades, using powerful telekinesis to rend the devil hounds apart as he rushed toward Mark's position.

Behind him, another Ranger, darting from side to side so fast his body was little more than a blur, used a long dagger to eliminate devil hounds with precise strikes that targeted their eyes and ears. Two brutes battered their way through the horde a bit farther out, forming the spear tip that was cutting through the enemy. Behind them were the rest of the Rangers, launching attacks from a distance as they advanced behind the lieutenant and the rest of the vanguard. The assault caught the devil hounds off balance, and the Ranger force melted straight through the enemy, arriving in front of Mark only a few moments later. By this point, everything around Mark had been largely cleared, and though his suit had suffered some damage, he was in perfect health.

"Give us a perimeter," the lieutenant yelled, and immediately his team spread out, forming a barrier around them. "Lieutenant Langford, Flying Scorpion Squad of the Cerberus Battalion. Who are you?"

Mark, stabbing his blood-covered mana blade into the ground in front of him, brought his heels together and saluted. "Private Fields, Black Mountain Battalion."

Langford's eyes narrowed for a moment before returning to normal. If he recognized Mark's name, he gave no other indication. "Do you have some ID, Fields? I'm getting a different name on my scanner."

"No, sir," Mark said, holding up his hands. "Not apart from these. My watch was destroyed, and I'm currently using Sergeant Fletcher's."

"And the sergeant?"

"Deceased, sir. Along with Lieutenant Kami and Privates James and Cody Price."

Just then, a familiar voice spoke up from the Rangers surrounding them. "I can provide positive identification, sir."

29

Looking over in considerable surprise, Mark saw Phoenix grinning at him.

"I'm very familiar with Private Fields. We came through the same training camp," she said.

"I see. In that case, let's get this fight cleared, and we'll debrief," Langford said. "Can you still fight, Private?"

"All day, sir."

"Then get to it. You're next to Batten."

Looking around, Mark saw one of the brutes lifting a hand. He grabbed his mana sword from the ground and fell into place beside Batten, who was providing the primary point of defense against the devil hounds. Mark was used to having to watch his flanks and back at all times, using mobility to protect himself. Now, he had melee fighters on either side of him and ranged fighters at his back, and there was no need to shift from his position. Rather, the only thing to do was swing his blade as quickly as he possibly could.

Every so often, Lieutenant Langford would call for them to move, and the entire unit would shift position, driving forward to better engage the remaining devil hounds. The fight lasted another half an hour, and by the time they had cleaned up, Mark estimated there were close to a thousand dead Exlian. This was his first time encountering a swarm of this size, and it should have been a terrifying force. But with how efficiently the Rangers fought, there was no real suspense.

Twice, Mark almost began absorbing the devil hounds in his vicinity. Thankfully, each time he managed to stop himself. He didn't want to draw undue attention, as he was already feeling rather uneasy. He couldn't pinpoint exactly why, but something in the back of his head was warning him to be careful.

As the fight ended, Phoenix rushed over to Mark, practically jumping on him as she wrapped her arms around him. Mark was surprised at how light the hug felt, but then he remembered that he was now C ranked, while Phoenix was a full rank below him. She hadn't even removed her helmet before giving him a hug, and as their faceplates pressed together, he could see a hint of a tear at the corner of her eye.

Pushing him back, she reached up and unclipped her helmet, surreptitiously brushing away her tears as she wiped the sweat from her face. "I can't believe you're alive."

"Some days I can't either," Mark replied with a laugh, taking off his helmet as well.

"What on earth happened?"

Taking a deep breath, Mark shrugged. "It's a long story."

"One that we don't have time for right now, Private," Lieutenant Langford said as he strode over. "We've got to get the battlefield cleaned up and move positions. The last thing we want is to get locked in an endless swarm. We're escorting the Blue River Battalion to Felwer Mine. I assume that's where you've come from?"

"Yes, sir."

"Are you able to lead us back?"

"Of course, sir. Apart from a couple of troublesome spots, it shouldn't be too hard."

Mark had noticed that the soldiers had no heavy equipment, though many of them had Engineering Core mana suits, and a couple were dressed in even larger suits that boasted four massive mechanical arms.

Gesturing for Mark to follow, the lieutenant brought him over and introduced him to Captain Sorn.

"You're with the Black Mountain Battalion?" Captain Sorn asked, his forehead furrowing as he glanced between the lieutenant and Mark. "I thought all of you had died."

"It was a close thing, sir. And to my knowledge, I'm the only one remaining. Captain Calder and Sergeant Rogers are both unaccounted for, sir, but the others are dead."

"I'm sorry to hear that, Private. I'm sure that's hard, but good on you for surviving. It takes a special breed to survive out in the wilderness for any length of time, let alone weeks by yourself. Are you sure you're all right to guide us back to the mine?"

"Of course, sir," Mark said, snapping a crisp salute. "As long as we're not trying to build a road, it shouldn't take much more than three or four days."

"That's what we like to hear. Let's move out right away, Lieutenant."

Saluting, Lieutenant Langford hurried away to get the Ranger escort moving, and soon the battalion was pushing forward. Mark spent a few minutes wandering through the battlefield to surreptitiously chomp down a few more devil hounds. Once his biofuel was full, he checked to see if he could still increase his stats by eating more. Unfortunately, he found his shadow wasn't particularly interested in eating any past what he needed to refill his energy levels. Mark had been afraid that was the case, and it seemed that he had reached the maximum level of improvement to his stats that devil hounds would give him.

Putting the matter out of his head, he began leading the Rangers forward. Phoenix stuck close beside him, along with Lieutenant Langford. As they traveled, Mark began to explain what he had experienced over the last few weeks, beginning with the assault on the compound.

"The attack was primarily ghouls," Mark said, "a whole host of them, close to two hundred, in fact." Noticing Lieutenant Langford's frown, he nodded. "As you can imagine, they weren't alone. They came with multiple hulks, a screamer, and a brain."

"You survived a brain?" Phoenix asked, her voice slightly warped by the comms channel.

Mark was silent for a moment, and then, with a heavy voice, he said, "Only because of Lieutenant Kami and Sergeant Fletcher. The sergeant managed to kill one of the hulks and then took on the brain by himself. Lieutenant Kami and I were fighting it in the entrance to the mine, and Sergeant Fletcher attacked before it killed us. There was an explosion, and the mine caved in, killing both the sergeant and the brain. By the time I dug my way out a few days later, Captain Calder and Sergeant Rogers had left with the command vehicle. The Price brothers fell outside the base, or at least I assume that's what happened, from the pieces of their suits that I found. The Exlian cleared out all the corpses but thankfully didn't bother to dig into the mine. Lieutenant Kami had been wounded in the fight against the screamer, and the brain finished her off. Honestly, it's a miracle that I survived."

Reaching out, Lieutenant Langford placed a hand on Mark's shoulder. "It is a miracle, and your battalion's losses are incredibly unfortunate. You'll be pleased to know that Captain Calder and Sergeant Rogers did make it back to the city. They reported much the same as you, though they were unsure why the mine collapsed. They had a running battle with the remaining Exlian and were forced to abandon the command vehicle some distance away from the city. They arrived a week ago, much the worse for wear."

Keeping his eyes downcast so the lieutenant wouldn't see his murderous glare, Mark didn't say anything.

"What about the next few weeks?" Phoenix asked. "How did you survive?"

"We had moved some supplies into the mine already, just in case," Mark said, taking a deep breath as he tried to stabilize his emotions. "I've been keeping my head low and doing what I could. Thankfully, I've had power from the generators. But once the food started to run out, I decided I was going to have to make a run for it. That's why I was heading into the city."

"When'd you run out of food?" Lieutenant Langford asked, glancing at Mark.

"Earlier today."

It was a bold-faced lie, and Mark could only hope that the lieutenant didn't notice. Given how vigorously he had been fighting, it would no doubt be suspicious if he claimed he hadn't eaten recently. Thankfully, Phoenix came to his rescue without realizing it.

"I've always been jealous of your energy," she said, shaking her head. "Even back in the training camp, you could run forever on next to nothing. It may well have saved your life."

"I genuinely think it did," Mark said.

Noticing Lieutenant Langford's questioning look, Phoenix explained, "Mark here is able to make his meals stretch further than most. He doesn't lose his endurance nearly as fast as the rest of us. Often, during training, when we'd be dying, the trainers would be having him run a dozen extra laps."

"It was completely unfair," Mark grumbled, causing Phoenix to laugh.

Mark kept a close eye on the lieutenant as he and Phoenix talked. Though Langford behaved normally, Mark still had a niggling feeling that there was something dangerous about the situation, some sort of threat hidden from his view.

That night, they camped along the trail, and Mark was introduced to the rest of the team. Lieutenant Langford led the Flying Scorpion Ranger Squad, and Welton, a speedster, and a ranged healer named Kinsey were his two sergeants. The squad also had three corporals. The corporals were Batten, the brute Mark had fought next to; a woman named Esme, who used a bow and acted as their primary scout and pathfinder; and a melee fighter named Sid, who wore a fully blacked-out helmet at all times. The lowest ranked, Phoenix, was the only private attached to the squad, though she proudly informed Mark that she had nearly made corporal and was on track to be promoted after this mission.

Mark was only half listening as she told him of her achievements, detailing all she had been doing in the recent weeks. Though he was looking at Phoenix as she spoke, his attention was really on Sid, the masked fighter. Mark was fairly certain that that was where his feeling of danger was coming from. Partly, it was the way that Sid sat slightly apart, an extra few inches of distance between him and everyone else. And partly, it was because Mark sensed a familiar aura around him . . . though he couldn't pinpoint it exactly.

That night, as everyone settled down to go to sleep, Mark's mind couldn't help but return to the Black Mountain Battalion. The last time he had been out in the wilderness with others, it had ended in catastrophe, and he couldn't shake the feeling that something similar might happen again. Of course, as far as Mark was concerned, the deaths of Fletcher, Kami, and the Price brothers had been the fault of humans, not Exlian. If it hadn't been for Calder and Rogers, they could have survived the fight against the brain and retreated.

The more he thought about it, the angrier Mark grew, yet

the calmer he became, until his heart felt as if a thick layer of ice had enshrouded it. It wasn't until early in the morning that he finally drifted off to sleep. That night, Mark took out his anger on the screamers in his dreams, using pain as a way to vent his intense feelings. There was something he found cathartic about the savage fights. Though he lost as many as he won, by the time morning came, he found himself much calmer.

30

For the next few days, Mark led the engineering battalion toward Felwer Mine. Having just been over the path, he was able to skirt around some of the more dangerous spots, and they made good time, arriving on the morning of the fourth day after pushing through the night before. When they arrived at the ruined base, Phoenix let out a low whistle, shaking her head as she took in the devastation caused by the Exlian attack.

Of particular note was the ruined front gate. There wasn't much purpose in keeping it around, and a member of the engineering battalion, in a massive suit called a dozer, carried away the twisted metal to make it easier for everybody to enter the base. They spread out to begin examining what they could still work with, while Mark took Langford and Captain Sorn, along with a few others, into the mine. When Captain Sorn saw Mark's door and noticed the heavy metal pylons driven deep into the earth to support it, he grinned and gave Mark a thumbs-up. "That's great work. How do you disengage the lock from the outside?"

"It's magnetic, sir," Mark said, pointing to a chunk of metal sitting on the ground. Picking it up, he showed how the latch worked, running the magnet along the metal to pull the latch free.

As the door opened, Captain Sorn laughed. "You fit well in an engineering battalion. When we get back, I'd be happy to have you join ours. We're always looking for tough, resourceful soldiers."

"Thank you, sir," Mark said, genuinely grateful. "Though I'm not quite sure what I'm going to do once I get back."

With a sympathetic look, Captain Sorn patted Mark on the shoulder and then stepped into the mine, the others following after. Phoenix, who was with Lieutenant Langford, reached out and squeezed Mark's arm. In truth, Mark still wasn't sure what he would do when he returned to New Emery. The thought of joining another battalion seemed almost sacrilegious, but if he didn't, his only options would be taking a desk job, which he had no interest in, or leaving the Engineering Corps altogether. Figuring he could think about it later, Mark pushed his troubled thoughts aside and entered the mine. Inside, everyone was examining the workstations.

"What are these?" Lieutenant Langford asked, pointing at the four workstations Mark had moved into the mine.

"They're workstations, sir. Electronics. Alchemy."

"I know what they are, Private. I'm asking you why they're here."

"Safer to use them in here than out in the base, sir. Plus, the comms network is down, so I had to rebuild it."

Seeing Mark pointing at the makeshift comms relay he had built, Langford exchanged a look with Captain Sorn. Unsure how to interpret the strange glances he was getting, Mark showed them the rest of the home he had built, including the generator room.

"I turned them off before I left, just so there wouldn't be any accidents, but they should be ready to fire back up as soon as we need them."

"Let's go ahead and get them started," Captain Sorn said.

For a moment, Mark hesitated, unsure if he should mention

the facility down below and the nest that was siphoning off mana. His experience with Captain Calder had awoken a deep distrust of those above him, and Mark genuinely wasn't sure if he could trust this new captain. He was starting to see how Joe felt . . . Though Mark nodded almost immediately, Captain Sorn was sharp and noticed his moment of hesitation.

"Why don't you show Sergeant Zebe how to prime them," the captain said. "He'll be in charge of keeping them running while we're at the mine."

Realizing that his hesitation had caused suspicion, Mark quickly saluted. "Yes, sir."

The others either watched or walked back out to examine the workstations again as Mark led Sergeant Zebe through the maintenance cycle, explaining how each of the generators worked.

"It's roughly a closed loop. Of course, we're absorbing ambient mana from the ground underneath us and then siphoning off the bit we need, while the rest is pushed from generator to generator to keep them running. Once a week, they cycle off. They do their own maintenance, but we do have to walk through the controls."

Sergeant Zebe, a broad-chested engineer with a thick beard, crossed his arms over his barrel chest and nodded curtly. "A bit old and less efficient than we'd like, but the models run well enough. You said you've been doing maintenance? They look well taken care of."

"Lieutenant Kami taught me how," Mark said. "I've been doing it for the last few weeks, but before that, it was her. And before that, they'd sat idle for who knows how long."

With the generators taken off his plate, Mark headed back out of the mine, and Lieutenant Langford tasked him with showing Esme and Phoenix the lay of the land. Mark first took them up to show them where the lieutenant and sergeant were buried, then gave them a brief tour of the terrain outside the base. He'd spent the vast majority of his time inside the mine itself but had gotten a pretty good sense of the surrounding area during his hunting trips.

Mark hadn't seen Sid since they arrived at the base, which he found suspicious. But that evening, when they gathered to have dinner, the corporal was there, eating along with everybody else. The full black helmet he wore opened just enough at the bottom for him to shovel food into his mouth, though it still covered his chin almost completely. When Phoenix saw Mark shooting surreptitious glances toward Sid, she elbowed him.

"Has something to do with his power. At least that's what they tell me," she said.

"Why would having a mask have anything to do with his ability?" Mark asked. "I thought he had a physical power set."

"More of a weapons master, I guess," Phoenix said with a shrug, scooping some stew from her bowl. "He's really good with a sword, and I've seen him use a spear as well. He's faster and stronger than almost anybody else on the team, except for maybe Batten, and he's great in melee combat. Maybe his power has something to do with weapon control. I'm genuinely not sure, and it's bad form to ask. But he doesn't have a good temper, so you should stop staring."

Acknowledging her words with a grunt, Mark turned his attention back to his stew.

"What's been happening in the city while I've been away?" he asked. "How's everybody doing?"

"Good. As far as I know, Noah has been deployed with the Dark Wolf unit. They're one of Cerberus's other units, and that's kept him busy. Glenn is doing really well in his engineering battalion. At least, that's what he said when I last saw him, though I have my suspicions that he is finding it hard. Danny is genuinely doing very well, but then again, his job consists of walking around the city's walls, and that's about it. Harper had one deployment that she said was fine, and she's waiting for another."

Phoenix hesitated for a moment, and then, squaring her shoulders, she continued, "Sky is in her last few weeks of training camp. We've been keeping an eye on her. She's the only one who doesn't know what happened to you."

His brow furrowing, Mark looked up, meeting Phoenix's gaze.

"I didn't want to worry her," she said, a slightly guilty expression on her face. "Everybody else learned through military contacts, but she's still in the training camp. I didn't want to distract her."

Whatever was going on was entirely too complicated for Mark to understand, so he just nodded. "Thanks."

Brightening up, Phoenix handed him another piece of bread. "You're welcome. I mean, it's fine now that you're okay, right?"

"What about . . ." Mark paused, unsure how to ask the question. "What about the terrorists? Have there been any more attacks?"

Phoenix picked up on what he wanted to ask immediately and shook her head. "No, though there have been an increased number of other incidents."

"What sort of incidents?" Mark asked, his eyes narrowing as he leaned forward.

"Two high-ranking government officials have vanished. The city is in a bit of a tizzy at the moment."

"When you say 'vanished,' what exactly do you mean?"

"I mean that they were having a meeting in one of their homes, surrounded by a sea of security, and then they were just gone. Nobody has any idea what happened to them or where they are."

Leaning back, Mark rubbed his chin. It seemed that New Emery was getting just as dangerous as the wilderness. If Phoenix and his other friends had heard about his predicament, his brother had too. The two of them had no way of connecting, and Mark could only hope his brother would hear that he was fine once he made it back to the city.

Just then, Lieutenant Langford and Captain Sorn called the

Ranger team together. Mark was about to excuse himself, but the lieutenant gestured for him to sit down.

"Until we get back to the city, you're part of our team," Langford said. "I know that you're a member of the Engineering Corps, but Captain Sorn is lending you to us."

Somewhat surprised, Mark looked over at the captain, who gave him an unsmiling nod. Not having any other options, Mark saluted and sat down. As everyone quieted, Lieutenant Langford turned and saluted the captain, who stepped forward, his expression severe.

"We've done an assessment of the damage to the base. It'll take the better part of six months to get everything back online, largely because of the damage to the computer system. Typically, Exlian don't care about the computers, but the console in the command center was completely obliterated and then vandalized."

Seeing the captain shooting a glance in his direction, Mark swallowed.

"Given the state of the computer system before it was vandalized, it's really not that big a deal, but we will need a completely new unit so we can reconnect to the master network. Our team's assessment is that it will take at least four months to fix the road and a couple months beyond that to get all the equipment we'll need out here. In the meantime, we're going to be shoring up the defenses and rebuilding the wall. This location is a high priority, as we need the metal from this mine.

"Two more engineering battalions are being deployed as we speak. Our primary Exlian threats are devil hounds and ghouls, but the Engineering Corps will be taking care of those. Rangers, you have another mission. One I mentioned briefly before we set out. In addition to taking control of the mine, we're also here on a seek-and-destroy mission. Lieutenant Langford has the details."

"Thank you, sir."

The lieutenant stood up, snapping another salute. He turned to the rest of the team, his eyes sweeping over them and coming to rest on Mark for a fraction of a second.

"As the captain said, we're here on a seek-and-destroy mission. Many years ago, a rogue group of scientists established an outpost in the surrounding area, where they were conducting unethical experiments. Though the facility has not been in operation for a long time, command thought this would be an excellent opportunity for us to destroy it once and for all to ensure that any material and information it contains will not be used by nefarious forces to undermine New Emery."

Mark knew that Langford was making a subtle reference to Joe and the Green Line terrorist group. Of course, it would make no sense for terrorists to come five hundred miles outside the city and risk their lives to set up shop in a broken-down research facility when they clearly had bases in New Emery itself. Additionally, what the lieutenant was saying about the research facility and the scientists who worked in it didn't line up with what Mark had discovered.

"We don't have a precise location of the facility. We only know that it was somewhere in this general vicinity. Once we find it, our goal is simple. Bring the entire thing down."

"Is that why we packed all the explosives?" Batten asked in his heavy voice.

The lieutenant nodded sharply. "Thankfully, we have a rough schematic for the facility itself, and the Engineering Corps has designed charges for us, along with precise placements, that will completely destroy the facility without threatening the surrounding area. Our goal is to bury the place and ensure that none of the research ever sees the light of day."

As the lieutenant was speaking, Mark's mind was working furiously. It was clear the lieutenant was talking about the research facility inside the mountain, and equally clear that he had no idea that the best way to get there was through the mine itself. Mark remembered the convoluted and twisting path that Mime had led him through to reach the facility, and it seemed likely that without a guide, the Ranger team could spend forever wandering through the mine and the surrounding countryside without ever once stumbling into the research facility.

He was torn, however. As much as he wanted to let Captain Langford know that he had already been there and knew exactly how to get back, he was afraid that the lieutenant would find it suspicious. Additionally, it would call into question how he knew of the research facility's existence and what else he knew. Mark still had the old data-storage device taken from Dr. Hannah's room, and if the Rangers did a thorough search before blowing the place up, they would undoubtedly realize someone had been there before them.

At the same time, this was an opportunity to eliminate the Exlian nest and the lightning leeches that guarded it. Though they hadn't broken out of the facility yet, Mark knew it was only a matter of time before they began to make their way to the world above. The last thing he wanted was a swarm of lightning leeches tearing its way through the wilderness.

Phoenix must have noticed something was bothering him, because she reached over and gently touched his arm. Meeting her concerned look with a reassuring smile, Mark raised his hand. "Lieutenant?"

"Yes?"

"I have something to report, sir."

"Does it have anything to do with our current subject?"

"Yes, sir."

Sharing an "I told you so" look with Captain Sorn, the lieutenant took a step back and gestured for Mark to go ahead. Mark, who had been thinking about the best way to explain his knowledge, took a deep breath and began to bend the truth as far as he possibly could.

"As you know, the Black Mountain Battalion was deployed to this location for the purposes of opening up the base. However, though I didn't know about it at the time, there was more to it than that. Before she died, Lieutenant Kami taught me a significant number of things, especially about the mine."

Seeing Sid lean forward slightly, Mark coughed into his hand to clear his throat. "The lieutenant was not always on the same page as Captain Calder, and occasionally their interests would be at cross-purposes. I don't presume to know the specifics of the arrangement, but what I do know is that there is a research facility inside the mine that seems to fit your description, sir."

"Have you been there?" Captain Sorn asked. "Can you get there again?"

"Yes, sir. I can absolutely get back there. However, I do think it's worth exercising caution. As I said, Lieutenant Kami entrusted me with quite a bit of information before she passed away."

Pausing to take a breath, Mark plunged past the point of no return. "There's a nest down there, sir, an Exlian nest, so I don't know how easy it's going to be to plant the charges."

Mark's words were followed by a long silence, and then Sergeant Welton swore and put down his bowl on the table with a hard thud. The rest of the team looked just as unhappy, and Lieutenant Langford took a step forward, his eyes narrowing as he stared at Mark. "You're sure about that, Private?"

"I am," Mark said, meeting the lieutenant's gaze squarely. "We went far enough into the facility to spot Exlian of different sizes. The main enemy is a leech that channels lightning and can move as fast as the bolts it fires. Most of them seem small, but there are at least a couple terror-ranked Exlian down there. I'd bet my life on it."

31

Clearly unhappy with what he was hearing, Lieutenant Langford nodded sharply and then swore under his breath. Across the room, Captain Sorn was rubbing his forehead. "We'll need to verify this information, Lieutenant, but if it's as Private Fields says, we can wait for another team."

Chewing on his lip, the lieutenant shook his head. "No, sir, we can't. The protocol with nests is eliminating them as quickly as possible. It will take a week to have another team here, and with nests, every second counts. As long as we can get the charges in place, we should be able to blow the whole place down, which should kill the Exlian nest and any other monsters down there."

"It's up to you, Lieutenant. I agree that that is the best course of action, but I don't have the authority to order you to do it. It's got to be by your own choice."

"I understand, sir," Langford said. Taking a deep breath, he turned back to the squad. "For reasons I cannot disclose, we do not have the option of waiting for another squad. Flying Scorpion Squad, receive your orders."

Immediately, everyone in the squad, Phoenix included, jumped up, saluting. "Yes, sir."

As the collective shout faded from the air, Langford took a deep breath and then pointed toward their feet. "Our mission is simple, though dangerous. Guided by Private Fields, we will head into the mine, assess the research facility for threats, and then eliminate those threats with extreme prejudice."

"Yes, sir!"

To their credit, the Rangers moved into action right away, rushing out of the room to grab their equipment. As they passed, most nodded at Mark, acknowledging him. He would be leading their team, and it was a brave thing, in their minds at least, for an engineer to guide a Ranger team into the heart of enemy territory. Sid even went so far as to reach out and pat Mark on the shoulder.

Langford and Captain Sorn had their heads together, talking, so Mark went to get his own gear. His suit had suffered some damage in the last fight, and there had been no time to repair it, so he couldn't help but feel rather shabby as he stood next to the sleekly kitted Rangers in his homemade mess. In truth, he had gotten a number of compliments on his suit from those in the Engineering Corps, who appreciated the level of precision he had used to construct it. The Rangers, on the other hand, simply looked askance, unsure if it would be helpful.

"Don't you need wrist armor?" Batten asked, peering at Mark's exposed forearms.

Shaking his head, Mark turned his hand over, and in a moment it had transformed into the ivory bone blade. "No, this stuff is even harder than the suit."

"You mind if I touch it?"

"Go ahead."

Reaching out, Batten grabbed Mark's arm and squeezed lightly. When the bone blade didn't shift, Batten's eyes lit up, and he squeezed a bit harder. Still getting no reaction, he was about to crank down when Esme poked him hard in the side. "Give it a rest before you break the kid's arm."

Mark wasn't too worried about it, as even if his arm had been broken, it would have been repaired within a few minutes. Still, he appreciated Esme stepping in, as it saved him a considerable amount of explaining. All the way back in the training camp, Mark had recognized a problem, which was that he kept accumulating abilities at a rate entirely inconsistent with any other empowered. Even paragons didn't gain abilities like Mark did. Once their initial abilities were set, they couldn't be changed. But Mark had new abilities popping up left and right. As much as possible, he wanted to fly under the radar. Additionally, he never knew when having a secret ability might save his life . . .

A couple of minutes after everyone had gathered, the lieutenant came out as well. The first thing he did was hand Mark a watch. "This one's unlocked. You can use it. It's one of our replacements. We can't sync Sergeant Fletcher's watch into our network, so you'll have to use this one."

"Thank you, sir."

"Say thank you after you know what I'm asking you to do."

"Aren't I just going to be bringing you down to the facility, sir?"

"No. I mean, you will be doing that, but that's not all you'll be doing. Everybody gather around. I've been talking to Captain Sorn, and this is what we have in regard to the facility's blueprint. It was built similarly to an existing building that we have back in New Emery. But unfortunately, we don't know what modifications have been made. Fields, take a look and let me know how far in you got. I also need you to tell me if there's anything that's different."

Swallowing, Mark stepped forward as Langford projected a three-dimensional map of the facility they were about to climb down into. It only took Mark a moment to verify that this was indeed the layout of the facility. With a deep breath, he traced his finger along one of the corridors and down into the observation rooms. "We got to here, sir. This is where we saw the Exlian. There was one of those lightning leeches and then a giant crab. The crab was in an aquarium and was about twenty feet tall at the back. It was too big to fit in the passage, but it smashed everything."

For the first time since he had been knocked unconscious by the crab's snap, Mark saw how he had ended up down in the cavern deep below. The passage underneath the crab's aquarium connected to a large staircase that ran down the center of the entire facility. After being knocked unconscious, Mark had been dragged down six flights of stairs by the water. He wasn't 100 percent sure how he had ended up in the small cave, though he imagined he had Mime to thank for it.

The large cavern wasn't visible on the map, and after examining it closely, Mark gestured to where he thought it might be located.

"We saw the Exlian nest there. After exploring this other side, sir," he said, casually reversing the order in which he had actually gone through the facility. "Through a set of double doors here is where we saw the nest. It's located on a giant flat stalagmite in a large cavern that's dug out this way. The cavern was massive, like, easily half a mile long, and we saw a lot of walkways around it, as well as some equipment near the nest itself."

"Hold on, let me understand something. You're what, D ranked?" Sergeant Welton asked. "If you saw terror-ranked Exlian, how are you still alive?"

"Luck, sir. A couple of the Exlian started fighting, the leech and the giant crab specifically. While they were going at it, we hightailed it out of there. The crab was so large it couldn't fit through most of the hallways, and it appeared to be mortal enemies with the leech, so neither of them chased after me."

"That's often how it goes with high-ranked Exlian," Kinsey said, brushing her hair from her face.

She wore a suit that reminded Mark of Lieutenant Kami's, with a similar medical pack on her back. Unlike the lieutenant, however, Sergeant Kinley had ranged healing that would improve the regeneration of a person's body significantly. It made Mark wonder what would happen if she hit him with her power.

"It's true, and if we've got a territory dispute, we might be able to sneak by without too much trouble," Lieutenant Langford said. "All right, we've confirmed that this is our building, with the possible addition of a giant cavern over here. This means we need to figure out how to set off the charges. I'm sending a copy of this to everyone's watch. Go ahead and pull it up."

Mark, not wanting to have the watch destroyed when he engaged in melee combat, had clipped it to his belt. Popping it off, he held it in front of him and activated the 3D model Lieutenant Langford had sent over. There were four blinking red dots spread throughout the model, and it was to these that the lieutenant gestured.

"These are our explosive-charge placements. We're going to be dividing up into teams in order to get this done as efficiently as possible. From the report we've had, it doesn't sound like there are a lot of lower-ranked Exlian. Is that correct, Fields?"

"Yes, sir."

"Good. So the plan will be simple. There are eight of us, and we'll split up into three teams. Phoenix, you, Batten, and Fields will be one team. Sid, Esme, and Welton, you're the second team. Kinsey, you're with me."

"Are we going bug hunting, sir?" Kinsey said, flashing a bloodthirsty smile.

"Yes, we'll be facing off against the terror-ranked Exlian. Me and you will keep them occupied while the other two teams plant the bombs. Each of you will have three charges. The only nonnegotiable is that you get them planted. I don't care how you do it. They're on a linked timer. As soon as all four of them are planted and charged, the timer will start, and we'll have ten minutes to evacuate."

"What happens if we don't evacuate?" Mark whispered to Phoenix, who gave him a grin and flicked her thumb across her throat.

Laughing, Batten patted Mark on the shoulder. "Don't worry. We'll get out."

Thankful that he and Phoenix hadn't been stuck with Sid, Mark took one of the two bombs assigned to their squad and clipped it onto his back the way the others had shown him. The bombs were quite interesting. Completely inert, they couldn't be exploded without first being activated. In fact, they couldn't even burn. But given the right mana injected into their core, they would explode in a blast that would disintegrate everything within two hundred feet. Four of them together would be enough to bring the entire facility down under its own weight.

Once everybody had double-checked their gear and was ready to go, the lieutenant gestured for Mark to lead them into the mine. The last time he had been in the underground facility, it had been without mana armor or a team. Though in truth, he would have much rather had Mime than almost any number of Rangers. He wasn't quite sure where Mime was, though he knew she was close by now. It was a sort of sixth sense he felt like he had developed, and he was fairly confident that he could call her if he needed her. Then again, he was certainly weird enough already, and having a cat along with him would probably push him over the edge. That thought only lasted until they had gotten half a mile into the earth and were walking through one of the dark passages. Phoenix, who was walking next to Batten, behind Mark, reached forward and tapped him on the shoulder.

"Mark, where's Mime?" she asked. Seeing Batten turn to give

her a confused look, Phoenix hurried to explain. "Mime is Mark's cat. She's part of his power."

Unsure what to say, Mark looked around, hoping that she might just pop up. When she didn't, he shrugged. "She's around. I'm not always sure myself. Sometimes she's there and sometimes she's not."

"Are you not able to use your power when she's not around?"

"No, I can use my power just fine," Mark said. "Speaking of which, it might be a good idea for us to get to know each other a little bit better. I've got a few powers that will be applicable here. I've got my bone arms, extra endurance, and a scouting ability. I've also got a sort of sixth sense for where the Exlian are."

"Oh, that's helpful," Batten said. "You've got a nice mix. You sure you're really an engineer? You seem like you're built a lot more like a Ranger."

"The Engineering Corps wasn't my first choice, but I'm glad to have the chance to serve," Mark said, his face impassive.

"Ha, sounds like a story behind that. You'll have to tell me once we're back in New Emery with a cold beer in hand. But anyway, my turn. I've got muscle and muscle and some more muscle."

Thinking Batten was joking, Mark turned and looked back, but the brute was staring at him, entirely serious.

"Wait, you've got a triple-stacked strength power?" Mark asked.

Grinning through his helmet, Batten nodded. "I do. I'm very strong. Naturally high endurance as well. Though that's more of a side effect of my strength than a power in its own right."

"I'm triple stacked as well." Phoenix jumped in. "All mana control—shield, blast, and a couple other tricks. Unlike you two, I do have to rest occasionally, but I've got maybe half an hour of juice before I've got to take a five-minute break and eat something."

"Isn't that a lot?" Mark asked.

Clearly pleased with the question, Phoenix shrugged. "It's okay."

"Okay?" Batten said incredulously. "Langford handpicked you because finding an energy controller with more than five minutes of juice is an achievement. Thirty is close to the biggest we've seen at your rank."

Mark had known Phoenix was strong, but he had never realized she was that impressive. Of course, compared to individuals like Noah, Danny, or even Sky, her ability seemed a bit more mundane at first. What was incredible about it, though, was that not only did she boast one of the strongest offenses and defenses possible, but her power was tremendously versatile as well. Since she could maintain it for up to half an hour before she'd need a break to recharge her energy, she could fit well in any group and fill just about any role. Remembering how dangerous the brain had been, Mark could only imagine what Phoenix would be like when she rose levels and pulled out all the stops.

32

It took the team almost an hour to reach the facility deep underground, in part because Langford kept stopping to make sure they knew the way back. It was a smart idea, one Mark had not considered. He had already traced this path twice with Mime and, thanks to his excellent memory, had no trouble tracing it again. When they finally arrived at the facility's front door, Langford called for them to stop and gestured for Esme to check things out. Scanning the room beyond the door carefully, she walked forward and pulled off her glove, pressing her bare fingers against the glass. As she closed her eyes, her activator flared, and Mark felt a subtle shift in the mana around him. It was so slight that if he hadn't been paying attention, he likely wouldn't have noticed it. Most of the others didn't, though Phoenix looked decidedly uncomfortable for a moment.

Esme let out a breath and took a step back, her eyes darting this way and that. Her gaze was never fixed in one place for long, and it looked an awful lot like she was peering through the earth, her vision cutting beyond the concrete to reach points deep inside the building. Suddenly, she spun, startling Mark as her eyes burned into his.

"Esme, are you okay?" Langford said, stepping forward. With a loud gasp, she came back to herself, her face paling as she looked around, a faint sense of confusion in her eyes.

"Fields was right," she said, giving him a puzzled glance. "There are close to a dozen terror-ranked Exlian. Thankfully, most of them are pretty small. A couple, though, are"—she shuddered—"not even remotely small. I saw the giant crab. It seemed to be hurt, and it's lurking on the fourth level. There was also a massive leech stuck in some kind of cavern. Those were the two that are free and able to move around. There's also a baeloth."

Hearing a sharp intake of breath from everyone around him, Mark looked at Phoenix. "What's a baeloth?" he asked in a whisper.

With a laugh, Kinsey answered, "A baeloth is a sentient jungle, a root system that takes over other plants. It's a sort of mycorrhizal fungus network that co-opts other plants and transforms them into deadly predators. It's incredibly dangerous because it's almost impossible to kill *and* it can parasitize empowered, transforming them into mindless slaves."

Swallowing, Mark remembered the vines banging against the window in the observation room next to where the giant crab had been kept. He had assumed that the plants were regular predators, but hearing that they could dominate his mind sent a shiver down his spine.

"It's a particularly nasty way to go, but you don't have to worry about it too much," Langford said. "As long as you steer clear, it can't do anything to harm you. Just don't go to sleep under a baeloth tree. Or get caught by its paralyzing spines."

"Fair. I'll try to avoid that."

"What else did you see?" Langford asked Esme.

Rubbing her forehead, she didn't answer for a moment, as if trying to sort out the thoughts in her head. "I saw the nest. It's down in the middle of the cavern, just like Fields said."

As she spoke, Esme manipulated the 3D model projected

above her watch, and when she made changes to it, those changes were reflected for everyone else. Seeing symbols representing the leech and crab and baeloth popping up, Mark was fascinated. Esme marked out the nest and then a dozen more leeches.

"Some of these leeches are high-ranked warriors, what we would call B ranked. Others are terrors. I'm not sure exactly how to tell the difference, but that is what I felt."

"Anything else?" Langford asked, scanning over the 3D map once more. Esme hesitated and then finally nodded and added another marker in the tunnel where they stood.

"I don't know where it is, but there's another Exlian. Rank undetermined. It was in a passage like this."

"What do you mean, like this?" Langford asked, glancing around warily.

"I mean, outside the facility. It looked like a mine tunnel with a light like this one."

"All right, it might be somewhere else in the mine. If that's the case, we're not going to worry about it for now," Langford said. "Well done. Let's get ready to move, team. Batten, can you take the door down for us?"

Nodding, Batten flexed his fingers and stepped forward as Esme gave way. Reaching out, he gripped the sides of the door, and just when Mark thought to mention that he had a key card that could get them in, Batten let out a grunt and shoved his hands forward. There was a great crash, and the entire frame of the door bent inward. Slowly putting down the hand he had raised, Mark watched as Batten obliterated what was left of the door with a few well-placed punches.

"Door breached," he said happily as he kicked the mangled mess of broken glass and twisted metal aside.

Gulping, Mark was quite happy he was on Batten's team. The door had been reinforced by mana, making it entirely immune to

Mark's best efforts to cut through it. Yet Batten, who, as far as Mark knew, was also in the C rank, was hardly fazed. Mark had always heard that people who were able to stack the same power multiple times gained the ability to practically skip ranks, and Batten seemed like a clear example. The strength he expressed was what Mark would have expected from somebody at the upper end of the B rank, and Mark was quite impressed as they all moved inside.

Mark had done his part in getting them to the facility, and from here, their teams would split up. Everyone was avoiding the baeloth, and while Langford and Kinsey headed for the crab, Sid, Welton, and Esme would travel through the research side of the facility, while Phoenix, Batten, and Mark went through the personnel side, where the rooms and cafeterias were located.

This was the side of the facility Mark had already climbed through on his way out of the cavern down below. As he led the way forward, scanning the psychic network, he moved quickly. Their journey was smooth, and it wasn't long before they'd made it to the second floor. There, however, they ran into their first challenge.

It started with a faint glimmer in the network, a hint of color that quickly blazed to life like a bright flame. Mark was caught off guard, especially since the Exlian was almost right above them. Freezing, he held up his hand, and the others stopped as well. The three of them stood stock still as Mark stared up at the white ceiling.

"Uh, Mark? Is there something there?" Phoenix asked, not shy about speaking since they were communicating through their suits' comm systems.

"Yes. High-ranked warrior. I just don't know where it is."

Looking around, Batten didn't see anything. He cautiously took a step forward, drawing even with Mark. And then another step forward. As he did, the ceiling exploded, filling the air with dust, and there was a sharp zip. At the last second, Phoenix managed to get a shield up around Batten, barely saving him from the thick lightning bolt that fell from the hole above.

With a loud shout, Batten lunged forward, not backing down one bit as a large leech fell from the ceiling, its maw attempting to close around his metal-clad fist. With a roar, Batten punched as hard as he could, his fist sinking deep into the creature's mouth. The force of the blow radiated through the leech, and the skin on its back exploded, cracking its spiked shell. It writhed in agony, more and more lightning beginning to cascade off its shell.

"Get back, it's going to blow," Phoenix screamed, and thrust both of her hands out, forming a heavy mana shield that covered the lightning-clad leech. Batten's punch had ruptured something inside the creature, because as it twisted, its shell discharged every ounce of lightning it had stored up, cooking the creature alive. It all happened in only a few seconds, and when the storm of lightning finally began to subside and Phoenix felt safe enough to lower her shield, the three of them looked at each other.

"Well, that's kind of terrifying," Mark said, licking his lips as he glanced at the leech's smoking corpse.

"What happened? I mean, it just came out of nowhere," Batten said, his eyes wide.

"I think they're hibernating," Mark said. "It wasn't there one moment, and then all of a sudden, it popped up the next. They don't teleport—at least I don't think they do."

"Let's certainly hope not," Batten said, nudging the thing with his foot. As he did, a faint spark jumped off it, causing him to retreat quickly. "Do you think that it sensed our presence, and that's why it woke up?"

Considering Mark had been through this area before, though with Mime's stealth ability, he found himself genuinely perplexed. Calming his breath, he closed his eyes and began scanning the network again. There was nothing, not a single sign of an Exlian anywhere nearby. That was exactly what he had sensed before the lightning leech appeared.

Mark's brow furrowed as he continued to concentrate, slowing his examination as he swept through. That was when he saw it, the faintest of glimmers. It was so suppressed that at first he took it for nothing, merely a figment of his imagination. But stubbornly, he continued to look until he saw it again. It was the barest hint of connection. Fixing the location in his mind, Mark opened his eyes and tapped Phoenix on the shoulder.

"Can you give me a blast down there," he said, pointing across the room.

They were currently in a large cafeteria, standing between the tables, and as Phoenix peered past the pillar Mark had pointed at, Batten pushed some of the tables aside to make room if they were attacked again. Holding out her hand, Phoenix summoned one of her mana blasts and sent it across the room. It slammed into the pillar, tearing through the solid concrete and metal rebar. Even before it impacted, the glimmer Mark had been watching transformed into a small fire, and Mark felt rather than heard a faint screech. It was only then that he realized the other leech hadn't made a death cry.

In his moment of distraction, the leech arrived, burning a hole through the ceiling as it shot straight toward Phoenix. Mark moved by instinct, intercepting it with a heavy kick that slammed into the side of the leech's shell, sending it tumbling past Phoenix to crash into the ground. Lightning crawled up Mark's leg, and he could feel it cooking his flesh. It was excruciating, and he wanted more than anything to scream, but he gritted his teeth and turned to face the monster as it lifted itself up, revealing its mouth.

Whether it was trying to intimidate Mark or getting ready to rush toward him and bite, he never found out, as a storm of fireballs from Phoenix blasted into the thing, burning massive holes through its body. After throwing three or four more fireballs than she needed to, Phoenix finally stopped, her breath heaving. She had clearly been frightened by the abrupt attack, and Batten, walking over, patted her on the shoulder. "Little buggers are fast, aren't they? We'll have to be on our toes. Speaking of toes, how's your foot? Seems like it cooked you pretty good."

Looking down, Mark could see the spots where lightning had scorched his leg armor.

"Toes are fine," he said, giving his leg a wiggle.

And it was true. Though the lightning had hurt terribly, his regeneration had kicked in as soon as the damage was done, repairing the burns on his leg almost as fast as they had been caused.

Giving Mark an appraising look, Batten nodded. "Huh, you must be tougher than you look."

Mark shrugged and gestured toward the door in the distance. "I think I've figured out what's going on. There are tunnels above us, likely dug by the leeches themselves. These guys hibernate up there, and anytime anything with a mana signature passes close by, they wake up. If we just barge through here, we're in for a nasty fight."

"We'd better tell the others," Batten said.

"About that," Phoenix replied, holding up her wrist to show her watch. "We have no signal."

"What do you mean? Of course we have signal," Batten said, tapping on his helmet. "We have to have signal to talk to each other."

"What I mean is I can't contact the lieutenant, or anyone else for that matter."

"What?" Tapping his watch, Batten tried to send out a message. A moment later, his expression ugly, he began to curse under his breath.

Mark hadn't noticed, but just like the others, when he tried to send a message, he found it simply wouldn't transmit. On a whim, he sent something to Phoenix and saw her glance down at her watch.

"Messages work locally," she said, holding up the digital screen to show him, "but for some reason, they're not leaving the area. Some sort of jamming? I'm not sure."

"Do we keep going or turn around?" Mark asked, looking at Batten.

"We keep going," Batten replied. "Hopefully, there aren't too many more of these lightning leeches. If there are, that's fine; we'll fight our way through them. But you heard the lieutenant—the only nonnegotiable is that we plant the charges. If there's a nest in here, it's got to die."

Mark totally agreed. In fact, he'd been wanting the nest to die for some time. The only difference was that he couldn't help but feel like it would be a complete waste if the nest died in the collapse of the facility. Biting his lip, he nodded and gestured for the others to follow him. "Let's go, then."

33

They moved slowly through the rest of the cafeteria, and Mark paid careful attention to the ceilings, constantly sweeping to see if he could detect a glimmer indicating the presence of one of the leeches. They soon reached the end of the second floor and began making their way down the staircase to the third. They had elected to stay out of the center stairwell, as that was where Langford and Kinsey were going to be fighting against the giant crab, and instead took side staircases. Unfortunately, each one only went down a single floor, and they had to trace their way back across the length of the facility before descending to the floor below.

They only had to face two more leeches, but rather than be happy, Mark found himself growing more and more paranoid. Finally, just before heading down to the fourth floor, he hesitated, curling and uncurling his fingers as he tried to figure out what was bothering him so much.

"Mark, is everything okay? Why did we stop?"

Taking a breath, Mark shook his head. "I'm not sure. I just . . . I'm feeling really uneasy."

"So far, your gut hasn't been wrong," Batten said, slamming his fists together. "What kind of uneasiness are you talking about?"

"Like we're walking into some sort of a trap."

"Hmm, is there another way to get down to the sixth floor? We need to plant the charges there. It might be better to fight our way back up rather than having to fight down and then back up."

"The only other way to the sixth floor is a central staircase," Mark said.

"There are actually some access shafts as well," Phoenix said, pulling up the map and pointing to some vertical shafts that ran up and down the length of the facility.

"Those things are probably crawling with the leeches," Batten said. "That's probably how they're getting to all the different floors."

"It may be, but our only options are the access shafts, the central stairs, or these stairs."

Looking at the stairs Phoenix was gesturing to, Mark took a deep breath. "All right, I'm probably just imagining things. You know, paranoid because we haven't seen more leeches. Isn't it crazy how I'd feel better if there were more leeches?"

"It is sort of funny," Batten replied. "I can take point. This facility is not going to blow itself up, so let's go."

For all his bravado, Batten moved very cautiously down the stairs. They made it to the hall below and began walking toward the other end. According to the map, they would have to turn right, and then they would come to a four-way junction. After turning left, they would find themselves in a long, open hallway. Mark had walked through this area and was familiar with it.

As they stepped around the corner into the wide hallway, his senses went wild, and he jumped forward, lifting his bone blade arms in front of him. There was a sharp crack, and a blast of mana slammed into him, dispersing over the bone blades. Had it hit his or Batten's mana suit, it likely would have punched a hole straight through. As it was, cracks radiated through Mark's arms, accompanied by tremendous pain.

There was a hum as a second blast shot toward them, and this time, Phoenix was ready with a shield. Mark, scrambling to his feet, cradled his left arm, which had fared the worst, his eyes searching for any sign of the attacker. He couldn't see any Exlian in the network, and it was only when Batten let out a yell and pointed that he noticed the strange device that had lowered itself from the ceiling and was pointing at them. It looked a bit like a flashlight taped to a small cask, but as it began to hum and gather mana, Mark realized that he was looking at a rudimentary mana cannon.

"You've got to be kidding me. This place has automated defenses?" Batten groaned as they rapidly retreated around the corner. "How does a facility like this have automated defenses?"

Mark checked his watch to see if there was any way to send messages yet. Seeing that they were still failing, he shook his head. "Something is really wrong with this place. It wasn't like this at all when I was down here. We came through this entire area before, and there was nothing like this."

"We're being jammed, defenses are activated, and we keep getting ambushed by these stupid leeches," Phoenix said, her brow furrowing. "Why does it feel like this whole thing is a trap?"

"Because it likely is," Batten replied, taking a deep breath.

It sounded to Mark like he knew something he wasn't saying, but when he and Phoenix both stared at Batten, the Ranger lifted his hands and shook his head. "Look, I'm not saying I know anything. It's just, you can never underestimate Exlian. Ever."

"I mean, I've heard some of them are as smart as we are," Phoenix said. "But smart enough to activate a centuries-old defense system?"

"I genuinely don't know," Batten said. "They might be. I mean, any of our engineers probably could. So why not a superintelligent Exlian? Regardless, let's hope I'm wrong, because I would like to get out of here alive."

"Well, what's the plan?" Mark asked. "Because we've gotta get a move on."

"We've got a couple options," Batten said, lifting two fingers. "First, Phoenix, can your shield stand up to another shot?"

"It can, but only one, so I'll be hard pressed to keep us covered for very long."

"So our options are, we try to smash the defense system, or we find another way around."

Seeing that Phoenix was glancing at Mark's arms, Mark held them out to show her there weren't any problems.

"I think it must have glanced off," he said, shrugging.

The bone blades had healed just as quickly as the rest of his body, though Mark noticed that they had taken significantly more biofuel to do so.

"I vote we make a run for it," Phoenix said. "Let's see if we can block them."

"All right, I'll bait the first one."

Before the others could protest, Batten stepped out from around the corner. Almost immediately, there was a hum and a blast, and in the same moment, he jumped back, barely getting clear as the mana ball ripped past him, carving a deep furrow in the floor where it landed.

"Let's go!"

Following close behind Batten, Mark ran in front of Phoenix to help give her a layer of protection and allow her to maximize the use of her shield. Mark could see the mana cannon in the distance, but even as he focused on it, it suddenly angled straight down and then slipped back up into the ceiling, which closed up behind it, leaving the three of them dumbfounded.

"Over there," Phoenix yelled, her shield rising at the last moment as another mana cannon in a different part of the room lowered and took a shot.

As the mana ball hit the shield Phoenix had summoned, the shield cracked and broke apart, causing Phoenix to stumble. Mark spun, slipping his arm around her and pulling her forward as another mana ball tore through the place her head had just been. Batten, gauging the distance between them and the door, called for a retreat, and rather ungracefully, the three of them piled around the corner again. Mark ended up half on top of Batten, and Phoenix on top of him. With a groan, Mark rolled over and got back to his feet, peeking around the corner at the now-empty room.

"How many of these stupid things are there?" he asked, to no one in particular.

"I just want to know where they're getting their mana from," Batten snapped. "It's insane how fast these things are charging."

Freezing, Mark looked up. The others followed his gaze but didn't see anything except for the ceiling. With a groan, Mark pointed. "It's the generators. There are six generators at the entrance of the mine. We've been keeping them running. While we only use a fraction of the power, we thought the rest of the power was going into making sure they maintain their active state. But it's not. It must be coming down here."

Putting a hand against the wall to steady himself, Batten stared incredulously at Mark. "Are you telling me we've been feeding this facility mana for the last fifty years?"

"Not that long, no," Mark said. "Only since the Black Mountain Battalion arrived."

"That's better, but not by much. Tell me, have you seen any large sluglike creatures? Not the leeches, much smaller."

"You mean power slugs? Yes, why?"

Growling, Batten turned and slammed his fist against the wall, leaving a massive hole. "Power slugs are like remote batteries. They suck up mana from the grid and transfer it back to the nest. You haven't just been feeding this facility. You've been feeding the nest."

Biting his lip, Mark decided it was better to hold his tongue than tell Batten about the six-pronged mana conduit that was currently drip feeding mana directly into the nest. Clearly, that would not go over well.

"Nests grow at an unbelievable rate," Batten said, taking a deep breath and glancing around the corner. "We absolutely cannot afford to let it grow any more. We'll have to pick a different path. With the generators running and feeding them mana, the cannons will keep firing forever. Come on."

Tracing their way back through the halls, they were about to ascend the stairs when Mark sensed an Exlian up ahead. It didn't burn nearly as brightly as the leeches, but after the first one appeared, a second, a third, and then half a dozen more materialized in rapid succession.

"We've got enemies ahead," Mark said, his eyes narrowing.

Unfortunately, through the network, he couldn't discern what type of Exlian he was facing, though he did get a good sense of their power level from the brightness of their mind glow in the network. Gritting his teeth, Batten ascended the stairs first, only to let out a shout and jump right back down, nearly knocking Mark over in his haste.

"Get down," he whispered. Mark, who had been monitoring the Exlian milling about, sensed them turning and coming toward the stairs.

"Too late."

When the first Exlian poked its head into the stairwell and peered down at them, Mark was confused. It wasn't an Exlian at all but something that rather looked like a human skeleton. It was only then that he noticed the thick vines woven through the bones. They squirmed like worms, twisting and shifting to control the bones, which gave them some structure. Phoenix's mana bolt hit a moment later, smashing through the skeleton's head, shattering shards of bone everywhere.

"You have to burn the vines. Otherwise it won't die," Batten said as the skeleton ignored its broken head and took a step closer.

Mark stared at the creature, trying to understand what he was looking at. "Wait, is that the baeloth?"

"Part of it, yes. That's what they call a necroseed," Batten said, taking another step back as the skeleton stepped forward.

In the center of its chest, protected by its rib cage, was a pulsing pod, from which the vines extended in every direction. It carried a sinister air, and Mark felt as if the pod were staring straight at him. Unable to help himself, he drew his sword and jumped forward, managing to ascend the staircase in two rapid leaps. With a shout, he brought his sword down, slashing straight through the skeleton and cutting the pod in half, even as the vines erupted from it, all reaching for him. The pod let out a grating psychic shriek, and the other necroseeds began to charge.

Mark let out a roar and ran to meet them, even as Batten and Phoenix raced to the top of the stairs. Grumbling under his breath, Batten pulled a mace from his back and, brandishing it, rushed into battle. Though he couldn't cut the necroseeds in half, every swing shattered bone and sent the plant creatures reeling.

Mark, hacking and slashing his way through the enemy, was nearly surrounded, but Phoenix soon came to his rescue, sending out blasts of mana that crushed the skeletons into dust. Though the necroseeds lost their bone rides, that didn't stop them from charging toward Mark and trying to climb onto him. He could feel the ends of their vines worming their way into his armor, trying to pierce through the layers of synthetic muscle to get to his flesh beneath. Soon, so many of them had gathered around Mark that Phoenix clearly found herself at a loss. She couldn't very well start throwing massive blasts of mana straight at him, as they would deal as much damage to him as they would to the monsters.

Though Mark was waving his sword frantically, he wasn't in that much of a rush to break free from the increasingly tight grasp of the baeloth necroseeds. When he had first seen them, his overwhelming instinct hadn't been revulsion but instead a powerful hunger that drove him toward them. One of the necroseeds tore a chunk of armor from the waist of his suit, but just before it could stick its vines through his stomach, Mark's mind split, and he commanded his shadow to devour it. As if facing their greatest foe, the necroseeds froze in place, not moving an inch, as Mark's shadow rippled and pounced on his attacker.

His body flashed with darkness, and suddenly, the other necroseeds were crawling away as fast as they possibly could. The ones that hadn't been sliced in half, smashed with Batten's mace, or burned to a crisp with a mana bolt were now desperately trying to flee from Mark, but before Phoenix or Batten could register what had happened, they were all gone. Mark spun around, his sword waving wildly, before slowly coming to a stop, seemingly as baffled as his teammates.

"What was that?" Phoenix asked, taking a step toward Mark.

About to answer, Mark heard a furious roar. It started above them and echoed through the entire facility. It was so loud the walls shook, and it lasted for a full thirty seconds before slowly subsiding. His mouth still open, the words long since having fled, Mark turned to look up.

"No, what was that?" Batten whispered.

Mark had a sinking feeling that he knew. A presence so large that it caused the psychic network to activate, even though it was multiple floors away, was beginning to stir.

"I think the baeloth just woke up," he said, his eyes still on the ceiling.

He could feel his psychic network expanding, its edges growing ever outward, as the shadow finished processing the necroseeds. At first, he didn't understand what was happening, and then he realized that with each one he had consumed, his will had grown considerably. It made sense, as there was next to nothing to the necroseeds besides will.

Unfortunately, because the baeloth was one giant network, every bit of will Mark carved off by consuming a necroseed was taken directly from the baeloth itself. Mark could only imagine just how angry he would be if someone started devouring his flesh. The only saving grace was that the baeloth was a plant, so it didn't move quickly at all. Of course, that didn't apply to the necroseeds or the creatures they took over. Mark could feel the baeloth heading in their direction, and he didn't need to be able to tell the future to know that this floor would soon be swarmed with the creatures.

34

"We need to go, *now*," Mark said, looking around. "It's either down the main staircase or through that access chute. It's up to you, but we need to pick one."

"The access chute, then," Batten said, nodding.

Mark led the way at a run, the others pounding along behind him. Once Phoenix had pointed them out, Mark had spotted the entrances to the access tunnels, and when he arrived at the nearest one, he only paused for a moment before smashing the grate that closed it up.

With a clang, the metal grate fell down through the tunnel. It slammed into the cement wall and pinwheeled away, causing sparks to fly. There was a sharp screech, and half a dozen lightning leeches woke up, their shells beginning to charge as their eyestalks extended to peer around, clearly looking for whoever had disturbed their slumber. Pausing for just a moment, Mark was about to jump down when a sixth sense prompted him to look up. Immediately, he began to back up, running into Batten, who stumbled backward.

"What are you doing?"

"Access chute is not an option," Mark yelled, continuing to retreat. After staring at Mark's white face for half a second, Batten turned and bolted, Phoenix right next to him, as a mass of vines suddenly burst from the open hole in the wall, stretching toward them. With a shriek, Phoenix spun, her hands thrusting out as she summoned a heavy-duty mana shield to block the opening. As it manifested, it tore through a dozen of the vines, causing sap to spurt like blood and leaving wriggling strands littering the hallway. They looked like snakes, but thankfully, once they were cut off from the baeloth's main body, they quickly stilled, removed from the network. There was a loud shriek, as if a dozen angry witches cried out at the same time, then a boom as flames erupted. The force of the blast shattered her barrier, causing her to stumble and nearly collapse to the ground as the backlash washed over her.

At first, Mark had no idea what was happening. Then he realized that the vines were catching on fire as lightning crashed against them. The leeches, having spotted the baeloth, had gone to war. Holding up his hands for the others to stop, Mark paused for a moment, blinking as he tried to understand the flashing war happening in the access tunnels.

The baeloth had stretched its vines down into the tunnels, slowly engulfing the facility, and the leeches didn't seem to have noticed. After all, for all intents and purposes, the baeloth looked no different from a regular plant. Until, of course, it grew angry. Then the plants under its control gathered mana and began to move. That alerted the lightning leeches, who, seeing a challenger entering their territory, attacked.

"No access tunnels," Batten stated. "What about the central staircase?"

"Let's try it."

They made their way out through the hallways and to the main staircase that ran down the center of the facility. Though significant chunks of that were missing and faint sounds of fighting drifted up it, there didn't seem to be any immediate danger.

With as much caution as they could muster, Batten, Phoenix, and Mark began to descend the steps. By the time they got to the fourth floor, they could hear the battle happening below. Peering over the railing, Mark saw the massive crab desperately trying to close its claws around Langford. A storm of blue shurikens, controlled by the lieutenant's telekinesis, was tearing through the crab armor, laying waste to the flesh underneath.

Though he couldn't see where exactly she was, Mark could tell that Kinsey was casting her healing ability constantly, because every time the giant crab managed to land a hit on Langford, he would bounce back up, his flesh and bones knitting back together. It was an insane way to fight, though Mark knew just how effective it was from personal experience. Sharing a glance with the others, he swallowed and pointed toward the stairs down. "Should we plant the bomb on the sixth floor or the fourth floor first?"

"Well, considering that we'd have to walk through that"—Batten pointed at the brawl below—"if we want to plant the sixth-floor bomb, why don't we try the fourth floor first?"

Mark agreed, and when he turned to Phoenix, she clearly did as well. But as soon as they stepped onto the fourth floor, Mark could only groan. The leeches, once spread out and hidden, had now begun to clump together, and one such clump was standing directly in their way, around a corner.

He was just about to alert the others when Batten accidentally brushed against a chair, which slid across the hard floor with a sharp squeak. Immediately, an eyestalk popped around the corner, staring at them. As they looked, a dozen more eyestalks appeared as well, all looking straight at them.

"Oh, come on," Phoenix said as shrieks began to erupt and lightning began to dance.

The first leech to come around the corner slammed into the wall so hard it shook, but the creature didn't mind one bit, fixing itself onto the wall as its eyestalks waved. The others made the turn a bit more gracefully, and then, with the sound of a hundred zippers being pulled up, the seven lightning leeches pounced.

Mark, who was still holding his sword, met the first one with a slash. The monster was moving so quickly he nearly missed it, but at the last moment, he managed to adjust the angle, catching the leech right in the head. He could feel lightning surging up his metal blade, but he gritted his teeth and powered through the strike, cutting deep into its head. As it began to writhe, Mark lunged forward, kicking it across the room.

Next to him, Batten blocked another leech's charge and then crushed its head with his fist. As more leeches shot toward them, Phoenix summoned a wall of mana, but instead of placing it straight in their path, she formed a large curve, deflecting them to the side. Even as they hit the wall, it began to break, but Phoenix poured more power into it, holding it together through sheer force of will as she prevented the leeches from slamming into them.

As the last ones landed, she let out a shout, and the wall began to collapse, transforming into half a dozen shards that shot toward the leeches, carving great gouges in their skin and cracking their shells. Clearly overdrawn by the experience, she took a deep breath and began firing mana bolts as fast as she could. Each one left a gaping hole in the leeches' shells, causing the lightning they wielded to go wild.

It was incredibly hard to fight the leeches in close combat, so Mark and Batten spent most of their energy blocking them from reaching Phoenix as she continually pummeled them. The first leech to go down caught a mana bolt as it opened its mouth to try to swallow Mark's head. The bolt burned through the back of its mouth and emerged from the other side, where it shattered the leech's shell. With a wretched cry, the creature fell to the ground.

Once again, Mark was surprised to find it left no echo in the psychic network. He had assumed that every Exlian would behave the same way, but it seemed that there was significantly more variety among them than he had first realized. The fight went on for a furious fifteen minutes, and by the time they had finally managed to kill all seven of the lightning leeches, Phoenix was exhausted and ready to collapse.

"Do you need to rest?" Batten asked, brushing some ash from his gauntlets.

"No, I can keep going," Phoenix said through her gasps.

That was clearly a lie, but in truth, they couldn't afford to slow down.

"Come on, we're close to where we're supposed to plant the bomb," Batten said.

Mark, who had walked over to one of the creatures and crouched down to examine it, gave him a thumbs-up. "I'll follow in just a sec," he said. "I just want to check something."

Supporting Phoenix, Batten led her around the corner as Mark's shadow rippled. Less than a minute later, he joined them, jogging to catch up. Seeing Batten's sharp look, Mark grinned and held up a piece of broken leech shell.

"This thing conducts lightning like nothing else I've ever seen. I'm an alchemist, or at least training to be one, so I thought it'd be worth taking back and testing."

Staring at the shell and then up at Mark, Batten sighed and shook his head. Since Phoenix needed a moment, Mark took the bomb she carried on her back, and while she sat with Batten, he set it against a large pillar and activated it. This was one of the main structural supports of the facility, and blasting it into smithereens would cause the floors above to sag. Taking out pillars below as well would cause the entire thing to destabilize and fall in on itself, hopefully crushing everything inside in the process.

Of course, everyone on the team knew that they were playing with fire. After all, they only had ten minutes to escape once all the bombs were set. If when Mark and the others set the bomb on the sixth floor, the other team had already set their bombs, there was next to no way that they were going to be able to get out alive, unless they managed to make it up the central staircase without being attacked, which was highly unlikely. Still, there wasn't much choice.

Of course, Mark was quite confident that nothing was going to go according to plan. After all, nothing had so far, and he had no reason to believe the bombs would be any different. With the first bomb activated, they huddled together and opened up their 3D maps to try to plot a route down to the sixth floor that wouldn't take them through the access tunnels or the central staircase.

"If you give me a couple more minutes, we can go kill some more of those leeches," Phoenix said.

"The real problem," Batten replied, "is here. There's a staircase that'll take us to the fifth floor and another that'll take us down to the sixth nearby. The problem is, the staircases are guarded, and unless we can figure out a way to make it through the automated defenses, we're hosed."

"I wish we could tell how the others are doing," Mark said, unbuckling his helmet and wiping at the sweat on his forehead.

Quietly, they stared at their maps, each trying to come up with a viable plan. Finally, Mark, unable to see another way, let out a sigh and opened his mouth to let the others know about his null field. Using it, he'd be able to shut down the automated defenses, clearing their way to get to the second bomb position. But Batten beat him to the punch.

"This is a dumb idea," he said, standing up, "but it's better than jumping into the middle of a war with a terror-ranked Exlian. Come on."

Phoenix and Mark stood up and followed after Batten as he jogged toward the stairs down to the fifth floor. As they got close, Mark heard the familiar hum, and a mana cannon popped out of the ceiling. Before it could fire, Batten let out a loud roar and slammed his fist into the ground so hard that the entire room shook.

The mana cannon, waving wildly, let off a blast that carved through the ceiling as Batten, completely ignoring it, lifted his other hand high into the air and brought it down in a pounding blow. His first punch had left a crater in the cement floor. His second caused a deep crack to run through it. The mana cannon was recharging, but Batten simply punched again, causing it to shake wildly on its mounts.

With each punch, the crater widened, and suddenly a large chunk of the floor near the stairs gave way with a cracking sound, and Mark, Phoenix, and Batten all fell through. Batten, leaning forward because of his punch, slammed into the ground with a groan, while Phoenix spread her hands below her just before she landed, causing her body to slow and hover right above the floor.

Releasing her mana control, she dropped the last few inches as Mark hit the ground beside her, doing his best to cushion the fall by bending his knees. Batten sat up with a groan, but before he could say anything, there was another whir, and a mana cannon popped out of the ceiling directly above them.

"Oh, you've got to be kidding me," Batten groaned.

As he tried to roll over, Mark helped him along with a light kick, sending Batten tumbling across the room, while Phoenix unleashed two mana bolts directly at the cannon. Unfortunately, it was made of a metal that allowed it to resist mana, and the bolts did nothing.

Mark grabbed Phoenix around the waist and leaped out of the way as the mana blast hit the ground where they had been standing. There was an explosion of stone and dust, and as Mark and Phoenix got up, they saw that the powerful blast had just melted another hole in the floor.

Batten had finally stabilized himself, and though he was a bit woozy as he got to his feet, he managed to make his way over, and the three of them just stared at the hole that had been blasted to the sixth floor below. Unable to see them because of the dust in the air, the mana cannon buzzed for a moment, then retracted back up into the ceiling.

"Huh, that worked way better than I thought," Batten said, sounding quite pleased with himself.

Resisting the urge to roll his eyes, Mark pointed at the hole down to the sixth floor. "Are you sure that's where we want to go?"

"What do you mean? It's the sixth floor, isn't it?"

"Sure, but it's currently covered in water." To illustrate his point, Mark kicked a small rock, which tumbled down into the hole and splashed in the water below. "I don't know about you, but I certainly don't fancy jumping into a lake and then getting in a fight with a bunch of lightning leeches."

About to retort, Batten's face turned ugly.

"Yeah, that sounds like a really bad time," Phoenix said, shaking her head. "Maybe we can see if there's another way to get this bomb planted."

35

Looking at the map, Mark gestured for them to follow. "Actually, let's try to go through here. I think there's a spot where we can get to our planting location. It shouldn't be filled with water."

"Wouldn't the whole sixth floor be filled with water?"

"No," Mark said, pointing at the 3D map above his wrist. "You can see that part of the sixth floor is lower here. That's what's filled with water. Or at least I think that's what is filled with water."

In fact, Mark was positive. All the water from the massive aquarium had drained down the central staircase, carrying Mark along with it. While Mark had somehow ended up in a small crack in the earth, the water had continued the journey down until it filled the bottom of the sixth floor. The two wings of that floor were higher, built to join up with the catwalks that surrounded the nest, and it was through these that Mark had retreated.

"How are you feeling?" he asked Phoenix as they jogged along.

"A bit tired, but I'm fine," she said.

"Well, we have another fight coming up. Maybe a couple," Mark said, slowing to a walk and pointing ahead. "So if you want to take a moment to rest and eat, now is the time."

"Honestly, I could use some food. Punching through three feet of solid concrete takes its toll," Batten said.

With a nod, Phoenix stopped beside him. Mark, who had absorbed seven leeches on the fourth floor, was feeling fine and fit as a fiddle, but the other two were clearly starting to lag, so as they broke out their energy bars, Mark did a bit of scouting. By the time they had finished eating and were ready to go again, he had mapped out their path forward.

"There are two groups of leeches," he said. "The first is a group of three that I think we can get the drop on. The next one is a group of four, and they'll probably have heard us coming, so we'll need to end the fight as soon as we possibly can."

"I can do that," Phoenix said, flexing her fingers and rolling her shoulders.

"Leave one to me," Batten said, cracking his neck.

Looking between the two of them, Mark shrugged. "Honestly, I'm pretty much no help against these things," he said with a grin, "so I'll have to count on the two of you."

Rolling her eyes, Phoenix cracked her fingers and gave a sharp nod. "Let's do this."

Bursting around the corner, she clapped her hands together, a ball of mana forming between them. At the same time, Batten let out a roar and shot forward, his legs pumping powerfully to propel him across the room in a flash. Mark followed close behind, chasing after Batten, who had already reached the leeches. He wasn't faster than a fully charged leech, but they had noticed that it took the leeches some time to build up the lightning charge that allowed them to move so quickly.

As lightning was beginning to arc around their shells, Batten reached the first leech, his fist slamming out with such force the air itself rattled. It was like a cyclone had slammed into the leech as a solid wall of force generated by his fist splattered it across the wall.

The other two leeches, sent tumbling back, righted themselves, their mouths wide open as they shrieked. Phoenix, her face white and her eyes blazing, filled their mouths with half a dozen small mana darts that swarmed through the air like piranhas. The darts burrowed into the leeches' flesh and then one by one detonated in fiery explosions, killing the two creatures almost instantly. The attack was tremendously powerful, and watching Phoenix execute it, Mark genuinely didn't know how he would block something like that if it were thrown in his direction.

Even as the shrieking leeches fell silent, there was a powerful ripping sound. A leech from the second group, alerted by the commotion, arrived in front of Batten. Its mouth was wide open as it tried to bite down on his shoulder. Instead, Mark's palm tore through the side of its neck, causing its head to snap to the side as slimy green blood poured out of the wound.

Smoke was rising from Mark's armor, and he could feel his flesh cooking as the thick lightning that shrouded the leech raced over him. But with a growl, he spun his hand, tearing through the rest of the monster's neck, decapitating it. As he fell back, he tore his armor from his body before it could fuse to his skin. The lightning had caused the metal to grow so hot that it began to melt the synthetic muscles. Mark had no desire to have the same thing happen to his skin. He wasn't sure if regeneration would be able to handle that, and it certainly wasn't worth the risk.

The other three leeches were already attacking, but Batten and Phoenix met them with lethal force. Batten's fists hurled the leeches back without even touching them as he created shock waves in the air to keep them away from Phoenix. This bought her enough time to use her more powerful swarming mana darts. By the time Mark was free of his armor, two of the leeches were dead, and a third was about to follow.

Their first fights against the leeches had been brutally hard as they adjusted to the creatures' strengths and weaknesses. But the more they fought against them, the easier it was to defeat them.

Tossing the last piece of his armor to the ground, Mark looked at it regretfully and sighed. "I was really proud of that," he said, "but I guess next time I'll build in conductivity."

"You can never build a suit that is perfect for everything," Batten replied, patting out a small fire that had started on the arm of his mana suit. "Of course, if you join the Rangers, you'll get access to the best suits."

Mark held up his hands. "I have a fair feeling that the veterans of the other branches would take umbrage with that."

"Okay, first of all, I don't know what 'umbrage' even means. And second of all, they can try to take whatever they want, because I'm right," Batten replied, laughing.

Phoenix went over to Mark's suit and picked up his helmet. "You should at least bring this," she said. "That's where your comm is located, and it'll be annoying to talk to you without it."

"Good point," Mark said, slipping the helmet back on his head. Without the chest piece to stabilize it, it wobbled a little bit, but it was better than nothing. Scavenging what he could, he picked up the bomb that had been strapped to his back and slung it over his shoulder. "The way is clear, so we should be able to plant the bomb."

As they made their way forward, Mark was amused to see both Phoenix and Batten walking on either side of him, clearly intending to protect him in case they ran into any more enemies. In truth, out of all of them, Mark was probably in the best shape. His energy levels were still relatively high, his regeneration could heal practically anything that didn't kill him immediately, and every enemy he killed could be used to replenish his energy reserves. On the other hand, both Batten and Phoenix were starting to slow down. As they walked, they stuffed energy bars in their mouth, clearly trying to keep their energy up. But energy bars could only do so much. Without something like Mark's biofuel storage, it took too long for them to turn the energy bars into fuel for their abilities.

The spot Lieutenant Langford had picked on the sixth floor was near an office. As they combed through it, Mark kept an eye out for anything interesting on the desks. Unfortunately, there wasn't time to hunt through them. Since he didn't have a back-plate to clip his bomb to, he set it under one of the desks in the office the lieutenant had marked. Looking at the others, he took a deep breath and activated it.

This was the moment of truth, the moment when they learned whether the others had managed to set their bombs already, giving them only ten minutes to escape, or if the others hadn't managed to set their bombs at all. Watching the bomb, Mark saw one light blink.

"Shouldn't there be at least two?" Phoenix asked, staring at the single blinking light.

With a groan, Mark nodded. "It's the jamming," he said. "Whatever is jamming the facility is blocking the signal. Just like we can't communicate with each other, the bombs can't either. They can only communicate with things close by."

"Wait, doesn't that mean that none of the bombs can activate?"

"Yes," Mark said, putting his head in his hands.

This was what he had been afraid of but hadn't wanted to bring up just in case he jinxed it. As it turned out, it didn't matter whether he brought it up or not.

"We need to destroy whatever's jamming everything."

"And how on earth are we supposed to do that?" Phoenix asked. "We don't even know what is causing the problem."

"We don't, but I have a pretty good idea," Mark said, gritting his teeth. "Let's head toward the nest."

In truth, Mark had had a growing suspicion ever since they entered the facility. While the complete lack of defenses he'd encountered when he first entered the facility could be partially explained by Mime's stealth skill, Mark was realizing that it couldn't explain away everything. After all, once the enemy Exlian knew to look for him, they had found him immediately. Yet the entire time he had been down in the cavern, the nest hadn't noticed him even once. Furthermore, it was clear that the automated defenses were acting under someone's direction. After all, why else would they retreat and reposition themselves after every attack?

Having spent time with Lieutenant Kami getting the base's defenses back online, Mark knew the mana cannons couldn't do that sort of thing on their own. There had to be some sort of intelligence behind them, and there was only one intelligence in the facility that had both the access to and ability to manipulate mana at that scale. The nest.

Back when he had been trying to understand how to establish a communication network using the nexus crystal, Mark had read in one of the manuals that high-volume mana flow played havoc with the communication network. So long as there was a lot of moving mana, it would naturally block signals. In fact, it was one of the only things that could block the nexus crystal's signals.

If Mark was right, then currently, the nest was channeling mana throughout the entire facility. And whether it intended to or not, a side effect was that the Rangers' communication devices and the bombs simply didn't work. Even more terrifyingly, the nest was clearly controlling the facility's systems through the mana that it had spread out, which indicated a degree of intelligence beyond anything humanity thought possible. If it could control the facility's defenses, then what could it do if unleashed in a place like New Emery?

Of course, knowing what the problem was didn't automatically solve it.

The best thing to do, of course, would be to kill the mana flow, destroying the nest's ability to distribute the mana through the rest of the facility. That would require heading all the way back to the entrance to the mine. And without a way to alert the others to that plan, it could very well result in all the Rangers who stayed behind getting buried along with the Exlian.

But if they could kill the nest, that would accomplish the same purpose. Of course, Mark was under no illusion that they'd actually be able to. He and Batten were C ranked, though both could fight above their weight class in certain ways. But Phoenix was only D ranked. And furthermore, mana control was clearly what this nest specialized in.

Arriving at the hallway outside the cavern, Mark stopped the others and pointed to the doors ahead. "That's the cavern," he said. "The nest is out there, beyond it. I saw something the last time I was here, and it makes me think that that might be what's cutting off the communications. Unfortunately, to shut it down, we'll probably have to fight the nest."

Taking a deep breath, Batten shook his head. "Look, I'm as willing as the next Ranger to lay down my life for glory. But fighting a nest, with the three of us? That's just suicide."

Closing his eyes, Mark thought for a moment and then shook his head. "Not necessarily. There's a possibility we might be able to turn everything off, as long as we can distract it. As far as we know, the others are all fighting. We don't have time to gather everybody. Remember, there's still a baeloth up there. And once it's killed the leeches, it's coming for us."

Nodding, Phoenix reached out and put her hand on Mark's shoulder. "Sounds to me like we don't have many other options. What's your plan?"

"It's simple, really. We sneak into the cavern, and one of us will try and hide from the nest while the other two make their way to the observation rooms. There are built-in shutoffs for the mana flow that is being fed directly to the nest. As long as we—"

Holding up his hand to stop Mark, Batten interrupted him. "I'm sorry, what did you just say? Did you say there is a mana flow being fed directly to the nest?"

"Look, I didn't design or work in this facility. And I certainly didn't make the choice to set up a facility to study Exlian. Regardless, we are here now, and we need to do something about it. As I was saying, as long as we have two people in the observation rooms and they hit the button at the same time, the mana will shut off. It's an emergency protocol built into the system."

Already on edge, Batten narrowed his eyes and leaned forward slightly. "And you know this how?"

"Does it even matter?" Phoenix asked bluntly, staring at Batten. "As Mark says, this is our opportunity. Are we doing it, or are we going to join the fight against the crab?"

Holding up his hands, Mark tried to speak as lightly as he could. "Look, when we get out of here, I'll buy you that beer and explain everything. But knowing how I know won't help you. Just trust me—it will work. The only challenge is that both people have to press and hold for ten seconds. And I doubt the nest will just sit back and watch as we turn off its pipeline."

After taking a quick turn about the hall, Batten stopped in front of Mark, his jaw set and his lips closed tight in a grim line. "Fine. We will try it. But you'd better have a *really* good excuse once we are out of here."

36

The cavern was dark, at least compared to the brightly lit hallways. However, the lights in each of the observation posts were burning bright, casting a soft glow through the gloom. In the center of the cavern, Mark could still see the thick clouds of glowing mana. If anything, they appeared to have gotten thicker. Though it had only been a week since Mark was last in the cavern, he could swear the nest had grown exponentially in size. Originally, he had assumed that its small size was simply a function of its inability to consume mana rapidly. Now, he was beginning to wonder if it had been mass-producing the leeches to avoid getting bigger.

Next to him, Batten ground his teeth audibly. Looking over, Mark saw the brute was staring at the power conduits that plugged into the mana-extrusion device. It was impossible not to see that the nest was being fed intentionally. If Mark's new suspicion was right and the nest had been manipulating its size to ensure that the researchers didn't notice anything, it would mean the nest was much smarter and more terrifying than Mark had originally assumed. It was one thing if the nest was just operating on instinct, but to understand it was being observed and adjust its behavior accordingly took a level of intelligence that spelled disaster for humans. Humanity didn't know much about the more powerful Exlian, but Mark's short time in the wilderness and his encounter with the strange, humanoid Exlian were starting to make him think that there was a lot more to the monsters than met the eye.

"Where should I head?" Phoenix asked, her voice a whisper in Mark's ear.

Mark pointed up at one of the observation posts. "You'll head up there. The buttons are big, bright red, and labeled 'Emergency Shutoff.' You really can't miss them. Remember, though, you'll need to hold them for ten seconds before they'll activate, and two of them have to be pressed at the same time. Once you get up there, go ahead and shut the mana off as soon as possible."

"Do you think the nest will interfere? If they send a lightning leech after us, we're gonna be in trouble."

"I know," Mark said, his eyes searching the mist-covered mana lake, "and there's a terror-ranked leech lurking in the water. I'll do my best to distract them, and we'll just have to pray that they don't notice you for those ten seconds. In fact, try to stay as low as possible and avoid being seen. If we can cut the mana flow off, that'll do a lot to help us."

Licking his lips, Batten nodded. "You know, I still think we should have gathered everybody else, but we're here, so let's do this."

The three of them split up, Mark beginning to make his way down to the cavern floor while the other two crept along the catwalks, staying low as they approached the observation posts. Phoenix was heading for a post just above ground level, while Batten was heading for one higher up. Both of them would take at least a few minutes to arrive, which gave Mark time to work his way closer.

As he reached the bottom of the stairs and began scanning the cavern, looking for places to hide, he felt something shift behind him. Glancing back, he saw Mime crouched in his shadow. Her eyes were gleaming, and her pink tongue slid across her lips as she stared past Mark toward the nest.

"I know you want to eat it," Mark said, "but that might not be an option. Please don't do anything crazy."

Giving him an offended look, Mime swished her tail and began to creep forward, staying low. As she wove her way toward a pile of discarded pipes, Mark followed her, crawling on his stomach to try to avoid being spotted. About halfway to the pipes, he froze in place as he caught sight of a large shell looming in the glowing mist.

Moving much slower than Mark expected, the giant Exlian leech crept by. Its eyestalks drooped, and it had a listless aura. As it continued past, making a loop around the stalagmite, Mark saw a large section of its shell had been crushed, undoubtedly by the crab's claw. Mark was surprised to see such a terrible wound, as he had assumed that the leech had the upper hand. It appeared the crab's vitality was not to be underestimated. As the leech finished its path around the stalagmite and vanished into the mist, Mark offered up a quiet prayer for Lieutenant Langford and Sergeant Kinsey.

With the giant threat having passed, he continued forward until he made it to the pile of pipes. From there, he could see a faint path made of scattered stones that crossed the pool of mana-infused water, as well as the rough outline of steps leading up the side of the stalagmite to the top. From what he understood, nests were horrifically dangerous and would try to absorb anything that got close. Yet that didn't coincide with what Mark had read in the research facility's observation logs. The scientists had been able to interact with the nest without any trouble whatsoever. That got Mark wondering—if nests were intelligent, would it be possible to communicate with them? Was there a chance that humanity was actually going about this all wrong? No sooner had the thought occurred to him than he felt Mime's paw whack him in the head. The blow was sudden and hard enough that Mark's head bobbed, smacking against the ground.

"Ow," he hissed, glaring at Mime. "What was that for?"

Mime, her expression serious, shook her head, pointed a claw at the nest, and then pointed the same claw toward her open mouth. Watching as Mime patted her stomach and licked her lips, Mark held up his hand in defeat. "Okay, I get it. They're food, not friends."

With a firm nod, Mime turned her attention back to the stalagmite and the rippling black mass atop it. From where he was crouched, Mark couldn't see either Batten or Phoenix. But it wasn't long before his comm crackled to life and he heard Phoenix's whisper.

"I'm in position. I see the button, and I'm ready to push on your command."

"It'll take me another two or three minutes," came Batten's reply.

In truth, Mark didn't mind the waiting, as the cavern was quiet and peaceful. None of the fierce fighting engulfing the rest of the facility had made it down into the cavern, though Mark imagined it would only be a matter of time. Nests were a prime target for Exlian they hadn't produced, and considering multiple incredibly powerful Exlian from different sources were roaming the facility, it was a sure bet that they would eventually clash, just as the giant crab and the lightning leech had.

Mark was especially curious about how the baeloth would fight. Given its nature, it wasn't nearly as strong in direct combat. But it had its advantages too. Since it was composed of plants, it never had to rest, and though its combat power was relatively weak, it used swarm tactics to great effect.

Thinking about the baeloth got Mark thinking about the necroseeds, and he couldn't help but lick his lips as he remembered how eating them had improved his will stat. Part of Mark wondered if it would be better not to destroy the facility but instead to use it to farm stats. He hadn't eaten enough leeches yet to know what stats they would give him, but he could imagine that they would focus on speed. Between the baeloth and the nest, there was a good chance he could produce an endless number of them. If he focused on culling their numbers, keeping them manageable, he could eat as many as he wanted, and who knew how high his stats could rise. Then there was the crab. Mark was quite confident that killing it and eating it would produce a drastic increase in his strength. After all, a single snap of the monster's claws was enough to shatter concrete with the sound blast alone . . . Lost in his daydream, Mark almost missed Batten's signal.

"Three, two, one."

As both of the emergency-shutoff buttons were punched at the same time, Mark realized he hadn't yet figured out how he was going to distract the nest. As he hesitated, a siren suddenly began to wail, shattering the peace that filled the cavern. A red light began to flash, casting a strobe effect that dyed the surrounding mist a deep crimson. The nest reacted immediately, surging upward and pulling its bulk together as it began sweeping this way and that, searching for the source of the sound. From its reaction, Mark imagined that it might have experienced this situation before. He wouldn't be surprised if, when the soldiers had shut down the facility, they had attempted to kill the nest as well. After all, if they were eliminating the program, it would have made sense to eliminate the primary subject too.

Mark could feel the nest's anger pulsing, and lightning began to erupt from the pool around it. The massive leech let out a keening wail that mixed with the harsh siren. Seeing the nest shifting toward the observation booth where Phoenix was currently crouched under the window, Mark knew he had to act, *fast*. He let out a loud shout, which was drowned out by the blaring sounds, and jumped from his hiding place to sprint toward the pool. He had no idea what he would do when he got there, but he knew that surges in mana were the most effective path to attracting the nest's attention. Though he lacked a flashy, mana-heavy move like Phoenix, he still knew how to move mana around. As he ran, he did his best to pull as much mana from his surroundings as possible. His only goal was to create as big a disturbance as he could, and by the time he plunged into the thick cloud of mana that surrounded the stalagmite, he could feel it beginning to swirl around him.

Mark had never been in an environment so rich in mana, and he nearly faltered as it poured into his body. As he charged toward the nest, the tall black pillar of quivering flesh shifted toward him, sensing his arrival through the disturbance he caused. The nest wasn't the only thing that spotted Mark. The terror-ranked leech's eyestalks twisted around, fixing its gaze on him. With lightning cascading off its shell, the leech rotated its bulk surprisingly quickly and charged toward Mark like a speeding freight train, throwing up sheets of charged water.

Thankfully, the leeches could only travel quickly in a straight line, or Mark would have been crushed. He noticed its attention a moment before it attacked, and instinctively dove to the side. Only six seconds had passed since the alarm had sounded, leaving four more until the mana conduits were shut off. Though that was hardly enough time to think, to Mark, each second felt like an eternity. He felt his shoulder slamming into the ground as he dove out of the massive lightning leech's path. Borrowing the rebounding force, Mark bounced up just as another large leech, its shell sending out massive arcs of lightning, charged toward him.

Though he managed to dodge its snapping teeth, the edge of its shell brushed against his ribs. The contact burned his flesh as lightning danced across him, sending him tumbling to the side.

It took him a second to control his muscles, which were vibrating violently as the powerful electricity tore through them, and before he could regain his balance, the massive leech unleashed a thick bolt of lightning toward his chest. Mark got his arms up just in time, covering his head and neck, but as it struck his arms, the bolt spread out and splashed around them, drenching Mark in millions of volts.

Blasted backward, Mark could feel his entire body cooking. There was a strange pop, and it was only after he hit the ground that he realized one of his eyeballs had burst. The lightning was so intense that Mark's brain didn't catch up to the pain until another second had passed. When it did, a terrible scream was wrenched from Mark's lips. At the same time, the blaring alarm cut off, and with a dying hum, the mana conduit rapidly dried up. The air shook as the nest let out a silent scream, its body vibrating at a tremendous rate that seemed to match the horrific pain raging through Mark's body.

37

Hearing Mark's scream, Phoenix jumped to her feet, peering down at the cavern below. Before she could spot him, however, the nest spotted her, and all its rage fixed on her. Phoenix knew they were both in trouble . . . Even as she summoned her shields to try to defend against whatever it would throw, she found the mana that normally readily obeyed her call began to rebel.

She had never experienced anything like it in her life, and it left her frozen in fear as the nest forcefully took control of all the mana surrounding her, locking her in a bubble of pure force and waving a long tendril up into the air. The mana around Phoenix began to boil. With a shriek, Phoenix was pulled straight through the glass-and-steel front of the observation room, the mana in front of her melting away everything that obstructed her. She felt suffocated and found herself entirely paralyzed as she was dragged out into the open.

The nest, clearly furious, lifted a second tendril, then another, until four waving arms extended from the top of the black mass. One of them controlled Phoenix as the others began to sweep through the area, seeming to look for any way to turn the mana flow back on. Down on the ground, Mark's body lay twitching, lightning still occasionally jumping between his limbs and his torso.

Watching all of this from the observation room above, Batten crouched, trembling, with no idea what to do. Seeing how easily Phoenix had been shut down, he was genuinely at a loss. Though he had tremendous strength, what good would that do against a monster who could control mana so freely?

Still, he had to do something. Summoning his courage, he burst out of the door and hopped over the railing, falling fifteen feet to the catwalk below. He landed with enough force to warp it but didn't stop as he jumped down again to the catwalk just above the cavern floor. The nest had already noticed him, but it simply waved one of its tendrils in his direction, causing the smaller leeches to shriek and throw themselves toward him.

With a roar, Batten met the leeches, his fists flying and his teeth gritted as he tried to fight through the storm of lightning to reach Phoenix. She was still hanging in the air, fighting with all her might to break free from the nest's control. No matter how she struggled, however, it was like smashing herself against a concrete wall. The nest used little to no finesse, simply brute force, overwhelming control, and a tremendous flow of mana to completely oppress Phoenix, trapping her in her own power.

The tendril controlling the mana around Phoenix shifted, and she began to slowly float toward the black mass on the stalagmite. Just as she was starting to truly despair, she caught sight of a hint of movement. Though she couldn't turn her head to see what was happening, it was clear that the nest had noticed the movement as well, and it shifted its attention. The orb of pure mana around her froze, and she hung suspended in the air like an insect trapped in a drop of amber.

There was a loud crash, and the wall caved in. Then a deafening click echoed through the cavern, and two figures tumbled into the room. Supported by Kinsey, Lieutenant Langford was in rough shape, but despite his wounds, he shrugged off Kinsey's grip and took a staggering step forward.

With a sharp cry, a massive, battle-scarred crab shoved its way into the room, its wide body bashing into the edges of the hole it had created as it forced its way into the cavern. Though it was missing half a claw and covered in wounds, the giant crab was undeterred. It glared down at Langford and Kinsey, but just as it was about to launch an attack, a thick bolt of lightning slammed into it, sending it reeling. A moment later the giant leech was on top of it, resuming their apocalyptic battle. Pure fury erupted from the crab, and it spun around, using the jagged edges of its shell to tear against the giant leech's body. Between the leech's sharp teeth and the jagged blade edge of the crab's carapace, it was as if two saws had met, sending sparks flying.

Langford and Kinsey, shocked by the sudden development, looked around, finally realizing where they had stumbled. Catching sight of Phoenix hanging in the air and Batten fighting desperately against a horde of lightning leeches, the two Ranger officers sprang into action. Langford headed for the nest with no hesitation, while Kinsey raced around the stalagmite to get Batten into view. Skidding to a stop, she extended her right hand, gripping her wrist with her left. A green glow lit up her palm, and a similar glow erupted around Batten, covering his body and rapidly healing the wounds he had suffered.

While she was supporting Batten, Langford had gotten close to the nest. Like most empowered who fought with telekinesis, he used mana-charged blades, creating a storm of rapid attacks that could shred just about anything. Unfortunately, as he charged toward the nest, his blades completely failed him. They shot forward, only to grind to a halt, as if stuck in the very air itself. The blue mana that shrouded them began to shift and warp, and then, one by one, the blades were extinguished, falling with plops into the water below.

Stunned, Langford stumbled as his connection with the shurikens was cut off, but before he could retreat, one of the nest's waving arms pointed down at him, and a torrent of mana coalesced from the thick mist above the mana lake and blasted into him, sending him tumbling across the floor. Gritting his teeth, Langford jumped up. Though the blow had been hard, he was an A-ranked empowered. With an angry roar, he charged back into battle, determined to kill the nest if it was the last thing he did.

The leech and the crab, resuming their epic feud, slammed their bodies together, biting, clawing, and bashing with relentless force. Thankfully, with the intensity of their fight, they had no time to spare for the Rangers. But currently, it didn't seem to matter, as the nest continued to fight everyone. Still locked up by the mana, Phoenix was finding it harder and harder to breathe as the orb around her began to constrict, while across the cavern, Batten's fight against the leeches had finally stabilized. Yet it was impossible for him to break through, as every time he would try to smash one of them, two more would attack him from the back.

The leeches seemed to have an instinctive understanding of how to work together, and rather than just attacking in a disorganized mess as most Exlian did, they coordinated their attacks, rotating to cover each other's recharge periods. Kinsey was desperately trying to keep Batten healthy while also sparing the occasional spell for Langford. Unfortunately, she had already been fighting for almost an hour without stopping, and her energy was starting to run low.

Just then, she saw Mark roll over onto his side. Originally, she had assumed that he was dead, nothing but a scorched corpse, a view reinforced by the wisps of smoke rising from his flesh. Now, seeing him move, she gritted her teeth and forced out a bit more power, sending a surge of healing energy toward him.

Power surged through him like spring rain soaking the dried earth, and Mark's scorched flesh returned to a perfect state. His burst eyeball rapidly re-formed, and a minute later, he blinked, his vision restored. The pain that had shaken his body faded to a memory, and Mark sat up with a jerk. Nobody saw him, however, as at the same moment, a portion of the cavern's ceiling fell in with a crash, burying half of the catwalks in a massive wave of stone and dirt. A writhing sea of vines appeared through the dust, and for a brief moment, everyone in the cavern froze as the baeloth's main body made its entrance.

"I don't think they're supposed to get that big. They're not supposed to get that big, are they?" Kinsey said in horror, pointing at the forty-foot-high wall of vegetation that was creeping toward the center of the cavern.

"No," Langford said, "they're certainly not, but they're also not supposed to have an unlimited supply of mana."

Recognizing the new threat, the nest waved one of its arms, and the leeches that had been fighting against Batten rapidly abandoned their struggle, turning their attention to this new foe. At the same time, the massive lightning leech disengaged with the crab, turning and becoming a blur as it shot across the cavern to smash into the approaching wall of vines.

Absolutely enraged, the crab lifted its good claw and let out a bloodthirsty cry, yet even as it turned its attention to the nest, a slithering sound behind it caused it to turn as more vines began to pour out of the hole it had created in the cavern wall. Recognizing the baeloth as a new threat against the nest, the crab screeched in anger and threw itself into battle, tearing through the vines with relentless sweeps of its claw.

38

The cavern was an absolute mess, and Mark hardly knew where to look. The leeches were waging a war against the main body of the baeloth, while on the other side of the cavern, the crab was defending against the baeloth's flank attack. At the same time, the nest was beginning to produce more leeches to send into battle, disregarding the Rangers. Sensing their opportunity, Langford, Kinsey, and Batten launched renewed attacks on the nest, which it warded off with one of its tendrils, using the thick mana that filled the cavern to try to crush them.

Phoenix was unconscious, blood beginning to drip from her nostrils and ears as the tremendous pressure squeezed the life out of her. Knowing that he had to act, and act quickly, Mark hauled himself to his feet. While healed, his body was terribly weak, and a screaming hunger had replaced the pain that had racked his flesh moments earlier.

Biofuel 1/30

He was almost completely out of juice, and he couldn't imagine how bad it would be if he ran out completely. But he didn't have a choice. Rushing toward Phoenix, who was still suspended nearly twenty feet off the ground, Mark gathered what strength he had left and leaped, flying through the air toward her. As his body approached the thick orb of mana, he could feel the danger it posed. Striking it would melt through his flesh in an instant. So just before he reached it, he activated his null field.

There was a ripple, and then the thick globe began unraveling as the mana rapidly fled. The closer Mark got, the faster it dissipated, and he reached her just as the last bit released its hold and she began to fall toward the ground.

Grabbing her in his arms, Mark dropped back to the earth, landing with a heavy thud as he tried to cushion their fall. Phoenix was unresponsive, her head lolling back, as he put her on the ground and checked her vitals. Her heart was still beating, but she wasn't breathing, which sent Mark into a panic. Canceling the null field, he grabbed for her belt, opening up the small emergency pack every Ranger carried and pulling one of the health potions out of it. Worried that it wouldn't be effective enough, Mark popped the cap off and, with a flick of his fingers, cut through his palm. Blood welled up, forming a thick crimson droplet, which he carefully dripped into the potion. Recorking it, he shook it even as the wound on his palm vanished.

As his blood mixed with the potion, the color began to change, shifting to a brilliant red that carried a hint of black. Mark didn't have time to worry about what was happening to the potion, and once it was sufficiently shaken, he poured it down Phoenix's throat. Almost immediately, her body spasmed, and Mark quickly grabbed her neck, holding it stable as her body thrashed. He was just beginning to worry when she calmed down, and though she didn't wake up, her breathing restarted, color flooding back into her face.

Glancing at her wrist again, Mark saw her vitals were back where they should be, yet she still didn't stir, no matter how he tried to wake her. Unsure what was going on, he gathered her up in his arms and quickly retreated.

The fight in the cavern wasn't going well. The baeloth was continuing to gain ground, sending out swarms of necroseeds to attack the leeches and the giant crab. Though they fared poorly against the lightning-clad leeches, they were beginning to win in the fight against the crab, worming their way into its existing wounds, their vines piercing deep into its body. In the meantime, Langford, Kinsey, and Batten were doing their best to kill the nest, as it remained their primary target. Yet even though it was currently fighting battles with multiple people, they didn't seem to be able to do any real damage to it. As he tucked Phoenix out of the way behind some rocks, Mark looked around the battlefield, trying to figure out where he would be best suited to engage.

Slowly, the ambient mana in the room was beginning to drop as it was used up without being replenished. Though it didn't seem as if it had done any good, in truth, Batten and Phoenix having shut off the flow of mana into the room was tremendously important, and Mark could only hope that the Rangers would be able to hang on long enough for the effects to truly come into play. Of course, the real threat was the baeloth. He could see the vines creeping ever closer, and he was genuinely unsure how they were ever going to fight such a monster. Suddenly, a sharp pain struck him, and he doubled over with a gasp.

Mark had been forcefully ignoring the hunger growing in him, but with every bit of biofuel he used up, it grew stronger and more insistent. And now, as his biofuel meter hit zero, it became impossible to ignore. As his mind began to blank, Mark's body shook, and his shadow rippled, creeping toward Phoenix, who lay unconscious beside him. He was out of sight behind one of the rocks, and no one noticed the change that was slowly coming over him.

As thin fingers of shadow began to rise, reaching for Phoenix's exposed neck, Mark growled, a deep and guttural sound that caused his shadow to freeze in place. Crimson eyes slowly opened, glaring up at him. He met their gaze, a crazed look matching their intensity, and another low growl escaped from his lips. With a shudder, his shadow quickly retreated and the eyes lost their ferocity, taking on a begging expression.

Mark's body was trembling, his fists clenched so tightly that his nails dug into his palms, causing drops of blood to well up and slide down to the earth. Desperately, his eyes began to rove, searching for something, anything, that he could consume. When he caught sight of a vine worming its way along the cavern wall, Mark sprang to his feet, and his shadow surged behind him.

In a flash, Mark was sprinting as fast as he could, straight for the massive wall of vegetation fighting against the leeches. One of them, seeing Mark coming and recognizing the threat he posed, turned, unleashing a blast of lightning. But just before it struck, his body shifted, moving smoothly to the side, as the lightning brushed past.

A moment later, he hit the leech, his fingers sinking deep into its flesh, even as its teeth locked around his leg. With a growl, he tore its head apart, his fingers ripping through its body like a pair of scissors rapidly cutting snips of paper. He completely ignored the damage to his leg and the lightning burning him as he forcefully drove the leech back. Chunks of flesh that fell to the ground were rapidly gobbled up by his shadow, and Mark was past the dead monster, rushing toward the baeloth.

39

Lieutenant Langford was all the way across the room, fighting desperately against the nest, when he caught sight of Mark just before he vanished into the sentient jungle of the baeloth's body. Swearing, the lieutenant stretched out his hands, lifting a discarded piece of pipe and using it to hammer down on the nest's body. The pipe was met with a blast of mana that blew it apart, transforming it into thousands of pieces of shrapnel. Without missing a beat, Langford took control of the pieces and transformed them into a whirling storm that he threw at the nest. Because it wasn't inherently mana charged like his blades, the shrapnel couldn't be controlled by the nest, and he succeeded in carving out a chunk of its flesh. Enraged, the nest began firing blast after blast at him, forcing the lieutenant to flee as fast as he possibly could.

Batten was in even worse shape, as every attempt he made to get close to the nest was met with a wave of force that sent him tumbling across the room. The best he could do was try to predict where the waves would come from and unleash heavy punches in that direction, hoping to break up the mana before it slammed into him.

The only reason he was still on his feet was Kinsey's relentless healing, and she was on the last dregs of her power and running out of good options. Her healing abilities were tremendous, but even they couldn't stand up to hours of constant fighting, especially against Exlian of this rank. Desperately in need of rest, she finally staggered backward, her ability failing to activate as she came up dry.

"I need a break," she gasped, and Langford gritted his teeth.

"Retreat to the rocks," he said. "I'll cover Batten."

As the two men rotated to try to join up, Kinsey half stumbled and half ran to the rocks where Phoenix's body was lying. Surprised to find her there, Kinsey dropped down next to Phoenix, gasping desperately as she unbuckled her helmet, and grabbed a tube of nutrient paste to try to replenish some of her energy. Afraid that Phoenix might be hurt, she reached out to check her vitals and was surprised to see that Phoenix was practically bursting with vitality. So much so it was almost concerning. Holding the tube of paste in her mouth, Kinsey started checking Phoenix over, trying to determine whether there were any hidden dangers. Thankfully, it seemed that Phoenix's body had forcefully induced a coma to prevent the surging vitality from adversely affecting her. What the effect would be, Kinsey didn't know, but it was clear that something astounding was happening to Phoenix's body.

As the fight continued to rage, Mark was buried deep in the heart of a writhing jungle. With every step, he was attacked relentlessly from hundreds of angles. His flesh was pierced by thorns, his limbs bashed by heavy branches. Vines constantly tried to worm their way into his mouth, ears, and eyes or crawl up his nose. But even as he was assaulted, Mark gave as good as he got. His shadow formed a writhing cloak, protecting his back even as it gobbled up everything it could touch.

Tearing vines from his throat and swatting a piercing thorn from his ear, Mark pushed forward. His mind was in a strange daze, a shifting, cloudy state that made it impossible for him to think clearly. Had he been able to, he would have fled with all his might, trying desperately to get out of the death trap he had just thrown himself into. Instead, his body operated almost independently, as a single overriding thought was fixed in his mind. Somewhere in the center of this jungle was something delicious he simply had to devour, so he pressed forward, his mind locked onto a silvery light that stood out in the psychic network. It seemed tantalizingly close, yet as he pushed forward, his speed began to slow.

The deeper he went, the fiercer the baeloth's attacks became. Though his body was riddled with wounds, they healed just as fast as they appeared. His consumption of biofuel was so rapid that the shadow trailing him could barely keep up, even though it was swallowing massive chunks of vegetation down as fast as possible. A thread of fear appeared in Mark's mind, cutting through the haze. Yet before it could blossom and bring clarity, it was ruthlessly squashed. Mark, biting through a vine that tried to wrap itself around his head, surged forward, his eyes fixed straight ahead.

Outside the jungle, Kinsey had just finished checking over Phoenix when she heard a faint hum and a beep that sent a thrill racing through her. Unable to believe her eyes, she double-checked her watch and then activated her comm, calling Langford and Batten. "The bombs! They're active! In ten minutes, this whole place is going to blow."

Langford was so surprised he missed a block and was forced to rapidly retreat, pulling Batten with him, to avoid being crushed by one of the nest's waving appendages. Glancing down at his watch, he saw the timer starting to tick down, and making a quick judgment, he called for a full retreat. "The fastest way out is through the central stairs. Let's go."

"What about Fields?" Batten yelled, looking around, as he saw Kinsey emerging, carrying Phoenix's limp body.

"He's gone," Langford said, clenching his jaw. "We have to go, now."

As they disengaged from the nest, Langford caught sight of the crab skittering this way and that. Its body shook as hundreds of necroseeds covered it, their vines linking together and piercing through its carapace, forming a fungus-like mass. Realizing that the giant crab was on the cusp of being absorbed into the baeloth, Langford knew they couldn't hesitate any longer. Gathering everybody together, he let out a roar, his power flaring, as he forcefully seized control of all of them.

"Clear the way," he yelled as he lifted himself and the other three Rangers into the air.

Batten, his face pale, nodded and clenched his fists, gathering as much strength as he could as they began to fly forward, carried by Langford's powerful telekinesis. When they hit the thick wall of vines that covered the exit, Batten threw his fist forward, unleashing his most powerful strike. Pure force rippled out from his punch, tearing apart the vines and causing the baeloth to shake in anger.

Its attention wavered, allowing the crab a hint of freedom, and with a defiant screech, the massive monster reached out and snapped its claw, producing a blast that tore the vines apart even further. The edge of the blast caught Langford and the others, sending them tumbling through the air even faster than they had been flying. With a desperate roar, Langford barely held them together, and then, as the force of the shock wave petered out, they shot forward once more, back under his control. After flying out into the central staircase, they rose through the air rapidly, managing to climb the six stories in less than a minute.

Deep in the sentient jungle, Mark was locked in a desperate struggle against the baeloth. Though he was moving forward, his progress was slow, impeded by a thick wall of endless vines. The shadow, despite eating as quickly as it could, began to falter, unable to keep up with the sea of vegetation crashing down on them.

Mark's regeneration seemed on the verge of faltering as well, and as he stubbornly pushed forward, his mind grew increasingly cloudy. Suddenly, the glimmer of silver drew closer, and through the vines, a massive silver necroseed appeared. A crimson slit ran down it, and the pulpy flesh peeled back to stare at Mark. As its gaze washed over him, the cloud of confusion retreated, and Mark found himself locked in place, unable to move even an inch as the thick vines pressed around him.

Vaguely, he felt that something was wrong, that something was impeding him. Not physically but mentally. It felt as if some part of him was struggling to hold him back from reaching out and grabbing what he desired. The eye of the baeloth peered at Mark with deep greed, and a large vine tipped with a sharp thorn shot out, piercing deep into Mark's chest. Before he could react, the thorn pierced through his heart, and Mark's body shook violently as blood began to gush out of the wound. The vines around him drank it up as rapidly as it appeared, trembling with excitement, and more and more thorns began to appear, piercing deep into Mark's body as the baeloth attempted to drain him dry.

So commenced a fierce struggle as his shadow desperately bit apart the vines, chewing them up and transforming them into biofuel, which Mark rapidly expended to replace the blood that he was losing. At the same time, the baeloth, its thorns stuck deep in Mark's body, absorbed his blood, using it to regenerate its vines, wrapping Mark ever tighter in a cocoon of verdant death.

In all of it, Mark found himself strangely detached, as if he were separate, observing everything dispassionately. On the one hand, he had a screaming fear, a feeling of desperation, begging him to escape, to flee from his looming death. On the other, Mark had a fierce hunger, a desire to press in, to give himself completely to what was happening.

Both clamored for Mark's attention, and as his body was locked in this strange cycle of withering and replenishment, he knew that he had to choose. Something in him kept him from making a decision. Both voices were beginning to grow overwhelming, but Mark found that when he concentrated, there was a third voice. A voice that was intimately familiar, though he couldn't place where he had heard it before.

"You could be more. *Much more . . .*"

The words weren't loud, yet they still drowned out the two screaming desires and brought a measure of calm to Mark's fuzzy mind. The words carried a promise, one Mark found irresistible after years of striving to be good enough, to be better, to be *more*. His entire life had been focused on this very goal, on reaching the same heights as his parents, as his brother. And now, the chance to not only achieve that goal but surpass it was within easy grasp.

All he had to do was reach out and take it.

The baeloth's eye, which had gotten close to Mark, was the first to sense the change, and as Mark's body twitched, the baeloth rapidly pulled back, increasing the suction force on Mark's body.

Though his chest was laid open and blood gushed from his heart, Mark's expression calmed. Slowly, his lips curled back, revealing his teeth in a wide smile. His pupils glowed with a deep-crimson light, and a thin curved line appeared on his cheekbone under his left eye. There was a faint tearing noise, and a third eye blinked open. As soon as the third eye looked at the baeloth, the monstrous plant froze. For a brief moment the two eyes gazed at each other, and then, with a fierce rustle, the baeloth tried to retreat even faster.

Mark's shadow let out a shriek and rapidly spread, growing larger and larger as it took on a feline appearance. Thousands of claws and hundreds of mouths erupted from it as his body surged with power. The vines piercing him were forced out as his flesh rapidly healed, and every new wound that was created was gone a moment later as he lunged forward, relentlessly chasing after the baeloth. Furious with fear, it expanded, intending to crush Mark into paste. But before its vines could land on his body, he stepped to the right and the left at the same time, his body splitting. In a single breath he transformed into a dozen copies that each moved in a different direction, rapidly getting lost in the undergrowth. The baeloth shifted to look at one of the bodies, and with a popping sound, it vanished. Yet elsewhere, two of Mark's bodies split apart, re-forming the destroyed clone in an instant.

He appeared to be everywhere at once, his body continually splitting as copies darted in different directions. What was truly terrifying, however, was how every clone carried the shadow with it, drastically increasing its devouring power. With a shriek, the baeloth shook its vines, trying to smash the clones apart.

Having sent his clones to distract the baeloth, Mark pulled his shadow close, shrouding his body with it, as he lunged toward the monster's central eye. As a last line of defense, the baeloth summoned its overwhelming mental power and tried to obliterate Mark, but it was too late. As it gathered its power to strike, Mark's shadow transformed into a massive cat that pounced. Fangs of pure darkness pierced through the necroseed's shell, rapidly absorbing everything inside. The baeloth's attack faltered and moments later faded.

A faint crunching sound rang out, and then, with a shiver, Mark came back to himself. He was standing in the midst of a thick jungle, and his head ached terribly, as if his mind had been split into a dozen tiny threads, making it impossible for him to hold a concrete thought. Suddenly nauseous, he backed up, nearly tripping over a thick vine that lay against the ground, and doubled over as his mind snapped back together. There was nothing in his stomach to throw up, save for bile, but he felt better after puking it all over the leaves.

The thick vegetation around him didn't react, and still rather disoriented, Mark began to stumble through the brush, trying to make sense of what was happening. He had a vague recollection of the last five minutes, though much of it was little more than a blur in his mind. What became crystal clear, as he reached the edge of the now-inert jungle, was that he was now the center of the nest's attention.

40

In the distance, he could see the giant crab half collapsed on its side, feebly waving one of its claws, as it struggled against the hundreds of necroseeds slowly parasitizing its body. Langford and the other Rangers were gone, and Mark had a good guess as to why. If the other bombs had been planted, then the countdown timer was almost certainly also on, since the mana source had been turned off. Unfortunately, Mark had no idea how long he had left, and there was one very angry nest between him and the exit.

Retreating into the jungle wasn't an option, and though the nest had used up the majority of the ambient mana in the room, it still had more than enough to crush someone like Mark a dozen times. Yet curiously, Mark didn't feel even an ounce of fear. Instead, he looked upon the nest and saw power that was his for the taking. He blinked, a small smile gracing his lips as he realized that his powers were actually an almost perfect counter to the nest.

Taking a deep breath to try to clear his head, Mark slowly walked forward. Part of him expected the nest to respond with anger. Instead, as he blinked his three eyes, it shivered in fear. It only took Mark a few hops to cross the now-dull water that surrounded the stalagmite, and with quick steps, he bounded up the stone staircase and arrived on the top.

Finding the nest's reaction curious—he had fully expected it to attack—he took a step forward and watched as it shrank backward, its body curving in as it tried to stay away from him. He knew it needed to die; that much was clear. A nest could not be allowed to grow in the wilderness, as the mindless creatures it produced would eventually become a problem for humanity. But still, Mark didn't attack, despite being completely confident that he could kill it.

What he found most curious was that the nest seemed to understand its weakness as well. It had an unbelievable level of mana control, a level so high that it could actually manipulate all the mana running through the entire facility, as well as forcefully seize the mana wielded by others. Against almost anyone, such a power was unbeatable. Against Mark's null field, it was worthless.

Mark knew he was running out of time, and with every moment he delayed, there was a higher chance that the entire facility would come crashing down around him. Though he would have loved to stay and study the nest further, he no longer had that option. Reaching his hand out, he got ready to activate his null field, but before he could, the nest shook desperately, and its body began to rapidly condense.

Unsure what it was doing but feeling no threat from its actions, Mark paused. Within thirty seconds, the thick mana that made up the nest's gelatinous form had compressed down into a small marble that could easily fit in his palm. Hopping down from his shoulder, Mime trotted over and sat on her haunches next to the marble. She looked at Mark and glanced down at it before using her paw to nudge it toward him, as if asking if he wanted it. Mark crouched down and looked at the marble. He couldn't feel the presence of the nest anymore but assumed that it was contained within the incredibly small but superdense ball of mana he was staring at.

"Is this edible?"

Mime gave an emphatic nod. Though Mark had just consumed the better part of the baeloth, as well as countless other Exlian, he wasn't sure that he could handle knowingly swallowing the nest, despite the attraction that it held for him. Hesitating slightly, he shook his head, and Mime shrugged and swallowed the marble with a single gulp.

"We need to get out of here," Mark said, standing up.

His body was bursting with energy, and he could feel himself growing stronger. His vague memories of his fight with the baeloth were starting to grow clearer, and Mark could sense that the energy he felt coursing through his body was thanks to the seed he had consumed. It was slow, and it seemed that it would take a long time to digest the baeloth's seed, but Mark could only imagine how strong his own will would be after its power had become his. Ignoring the blinking notifications on his wrist, Mark focused on leaving. Jumping down from the nest's perch, he raced for the gap in the cavern wall that led out to the central staircase. As he passed the crab covered in necroseeds, Mark paused. It appeared that one of the main reasons that the baeloth was almost impossible to kill was that each necroseed it produced was an independent creature, though they shared a sort of collective hive mind that was ruled by the strongest seed.

Mark had just consumed their main mind, but the remaining necroseeds were still active, and eventually, the strongest of them would reemerge as the new baeloth. Currently, they were locked in a fierce battle with the crab, and they would continue to attempt to control it until they succeeded or it died. As happy as Mark would have been if the crab died, he couldn't bear to see any necroseeds survive. He commanded his shadow to move, and with considerable glee, it pounced on the closest necroseed. Moving swiftly, it spread over the crab's body, forcefully extracting the necroseeds before they could flee and crunching them down. Mark considered trying to eat the crab as well, but despite the incredible damage it had suffered, the core of its vitality still burned strong, and he was worried it would take too long.

"You know, I heard somewhere once that crabs are essentially immortal," Mark said, staring up at the massive crab, which was too weak to even snap its claw.

Through its single remaining hazy eye, it stared down at him as his shadow retreated to his side, its thoughts impossible to determine.

"You look like you're on your last legs, but who knows—maybe it'll be true for you."

With a wave, Mark turned and left, racing through the massive hole in the wall and rushing out into the central staircase. He was six floors below, and running all the way up would take too long. With a shake of his hands, he transformed them into bone blades and leaped, gripping one of the pillars that supported the staircase. His fingers bit into the concrete, and he jumped again, propelling himself farther up. He had to be careful to ensure that he didn't accidentally throw himself backward, but he was able to maintain his momentum well and soon had climbed more than halfway up.

Mark had no idea how close he was to death, as he had no means of tracking the timer on the bombs, but he knew that every second was precious. After taking a few moments to catch his breath, he leaped again, continuing his ascent. It took him almost two minutes to reach the top of the stairs, and the whole time he was anticipating an explosion, so it was with some relief that he jumped from the pillar onto the steps. Racing toward the hall that would lead him out onto the first floor, Mark could feel a premonition of danger pressing around him.

Though he didn't know how he could sense it, he knew the bombs were about to go off half a second before the blast rang out. It was as if a massive earthquake had struck, causing everything to tremble violently. The floor began to creak as it wobbled, rising and falling feet at a time as the ripples of force spread out. Yet strangely, they only seemed to be coming from one direction, and as the floor began to collapse, it started with the left.

Mark scrambled away, jumping to safety, even as chunks of the ceiling crashed down around him. It took a few minutes, but eventually everything settled down, and looking around at the devastation, Mark found himself confused. To his inexperienced eye, it seemed as if only half of the facility had collapsed, but if that was the case, then how had the bombs gone off? After all, a total of four bombs had to be planted before they would trigger, yet it was abundantly clear that only the bombs Mark and his team had set had actually exploded.

Unsure what to make of it but exceedingly thankful he had not gotten caught in the blast, Mark carefully made his way across the shaky floor toward the exit. The entrance to the facility, as it wasn't directly over the six floors, had been badly shaken by the blast but was still intact. As Mark jogged through the halls, he sensed people up ahead.

Taking a moment to pause, Mark rubbed his face, trying to make sure his third eye wasn't still visible. He knew he should be concerned at its appearance, but he felt surprisingly at peace with himself. Of course, that didn't mean that he wasn't going to have some introspection to do later. After all, he wasn't sure he liked the idea of turning into a monster . . . but he reassured himself that no one got to choose how their power manifested.

Once he felt like he was in order, Mark walked forward and stepped into the large cafeteria. Beyond was the hallway that led to the reception area and the facility's front door, but standing in his way was Sid. Next to him, lying on one of the tables, was Esme, her body crumpled up and blood leaking from a wound on her head.

"She wouldn't shut up," Sid said by way of explanation, shrugging one shoulder. "She was forever prattling on about this and that, wanting to flee. She said some sort of terrifying monster had awoken down below when I had her scan for you, and she wouldn't stop screaming. I told her the charges would take care of it, but she was too crazed to understand reason."

Seeing Mark's gaze drift to the opposite side, Sid let out a laugh and leaned over to pick up Welton's head from the table it was resting on, leaving behind a bloody smear. "He got lippy too, which I didn't appreciate."

"You killed him?" Mark asked, surprised at how calm his voice sounded in his ears.

"Yes, I did," Sid said. "After all, I can't have any witnesses, now can I?"

"That depends. What did you do?"

Chuckling, Sid unbuckled his helmet and pulled it off, revealing Sergeant Rogers. Shock ran through Mark, and he took a quick step back, his hands coming up defensively. The sergeant flashed a nasty smile and tossed Welton's head to the floor. "Made a bit of an executive decision. The boss doesn't like witnesses, so I chose a different place to plant the bombs."

Seeing Mark's narrowed eyes, he waved his hand. "Huh, I thought you would be more surprised. Look, I'm not some monologuing villain who's going to explain my plan to you. Instead, I'm just going to end this. I'm sick and tired of being out here in the wilderness."

Lifting his hand, Rogers snapped his fingers, and Mark felt mana beginning to coalesce around him. Lunging forward, he was brought up short, and when he tried to retreat, he found himself slamming against another barrier. Grinning, Rogers twisted his fingers as if drawing lines in the air, and Mark felt thick barriers forming all around him. Striking out with as much force as he could muster, Mark saw his fingers cutting into the thick barriers, but as soon as they passed, the mana sealed back up, keeping him from being able to break through.

Sergeant Rogers picked up Welton's head again and regarded it for a moment before tossing it aside. "You know, the funny thing is that normally speedsters are some of the most dangerous empowered around. After all, very few things can beat raw speed. Not that you're a speedster, of course. Compared to any true powerhouse, like me for instance, you move slow as molasses."

Mark was only half listening to Rogers's words as he pressed all around himself, trying to find a weak spot in the cage the sergeant had just trapped him in.

"Of course, the problem is that speedsters are only truly dangerous when they can go fast. And it's really hard to go fast if you're stuck in a box barely bigger than you are. Truthfully, the same is true for just about everyone. Even brutes need some time to wind up. As long as you wrap them up nice and tight, they are fish in a barrel. In truth, the world is divided into two groups of people. Predators and prey. I'm the former, and you are the latter."

As he finished speaking, Rogers flicked his finger, and Mark's hand shot up, his fingers slashing apart the razor-thin barrier that manifested in front of Mark's neck. The barrier shattered, peppering his skin with shards of mana that cut open a dozen gashes. A few drops of blood squeezed out of the stinging wounds, but then Mark's regeneration kicked in, and the wounds sealed back up.

Seeing how rapidly Mark healed, Sergeant Rogers's eyes went wide. "So that's it. You know, I had wondered how you had survived. After all, you should have been crushed under a mountain of stone. But if you have a strong regeneration power, that would explain it. Your threat detection seems really high as well. Bone blades, regeneration, threat detection. You know, you're awfully strong for someone of such a low rank."

Stepping forward, the sergeant peered at Mark, watching with interest as Mark tried to break through the mana barrier in front of him with a Cutting Palm slash. His fingers ripped at the wall of mana, but the barrier repaired itself almost instantly, making it impossible for Mark to truly pierce through.

"I'm afraid you're just not strong enough," Sergeant Rogers said with a nasty grin. "After all, the gap between us is pretty big, and an A-ranked barrier isn't something a D-ranked empowered can cut through. Still, you did more damage to it than poor Welton there. Of course, doing damage and actually managing to get rid of it—two completely different things. Like I said, predator and prey."

Mark had already suspected that Rogers was hiding his powers, so the revelation that he was A ranked didn't come as any surprise. The suspicion had formed when Mark saw the ease with which Rogers had killed the B-ranked screamer that nearly eliminated Lieutenant Kami, and now, testing how firm the barriers were, he confirmed it.

"I know I masquerade as a weakling like you guys. As prey," Rogers said with a shrug. "It certainly helps with my hunts. Everything is more fun when you can catch people off guard."

He glanced down at his watch and chuckled. "It seems that Langford and the others have made it back. Hopefully, they'll enjoy what remains of the base. Now, it's about time we close up here. I'm not looking forward to the journey back to the city, and I'd rather get it over with as fast as possible. So do me a favor and die."

41

Stepping forward, Rogers placed his hand on the barrier, and it quickly began to thicken, growing inward toward Mark. Mark felt the space around him beginning to compress, and he reached out to touch the barrier, as if trying to press back against it. Slowly, the space between his hand and Rogers's began to widen, until, with a suddenness that left Rogers gawking, the barrier simply evaporated as Mark activated his null field. One moment the thick mana was there, an impenetrable barrier between the two men, and the next it was gone.

Mark's hand, already within an inch of the sergeant's, flashed out, wrapping around Rogers's wrist in a tight grip, and Mark's body surged forward. As shocked as he was, Sergeant Rogers was still an A-ranked empowered, and his reaction was instantaneous. He threw another barrier straight at Mark's chest, or at least he tried to. Instead of being blasted backward, Mark casually brushed Rogers's hand aside and stabbed his fingers deep into the sergeant's chest, cutting straight through his mana suit and piercing the flesh underneath.

With a scream, Rogers tried to tear himself free and retreat, but the mana he had summoned to empower his suit fizzled away into nothingness, leaving him trapped in place. Letting go of Rogers's wrist, Mark maintained his grip on the sergeant's chest, and his other hand rose, tearing the sergeant's helmet from his head. Though physically stronger and faster than Mark, the sergeant had to fight against his suit in order to move, and Mark's fingers closed in on his throat before he could struggle free.

Even as he lifted his hands to shove Mark away, Mark's fingers wrapped around his neck, pressing down with enough force that it made the sergeant hesitate. Had he shoved Mark backward, his throat would have been ripped out in the process, leaving him with no chance of survival. Hoping the barrier's failure had been a fluke, he desperately summoned another, trying to protect his neck, but no matter what he did, the mana simply failed to materialize.

Mark didn't squeeze immediately, instead gazing dispassionately at the sergeant as his null field vibrated around him. Part of him wondered, rather idly, who was behind the sergeant. After all, it was clear somebody higher up had issued the command. Another part of Mark simply didn't care. He already had a lead through Captain Calder, and he had a sneaking suspicion that if he made it back to the city alive, whoever it was would reveal themselves eventually.

Though Mark wasn't exactly sure what had shifted in him, he knew one thing for certain: His heart had grown firm, carrying a confidence that told him he would be able to handle anything thrown at him.

The sergeant must have recognized death in Mark's eyes, because he quickly began to babble. "Don't kill me! There's a lot I know! I can tell you who hired me. They wanted to target you specifically. I can tell you all about—!"

"I'll take your words to heart," Mark said, and his fingers squeezed, destroying Sergeant Rogers's heart and throat at the same time.

Power fled from the sergeant's limbs, and his words turned into a bloody gurgle as air escaped through the heavy gash in his throat. As he collapsed to the ground, Mark flicked his fingers, shedding the blood from them. Standing over Sergeant Rogers's body, Mark didn't feel as good as he had thought he would. In fact, he didn't feel much of anything at all. The anger he had at Captain Calder and the sergeant for abandoning him seemed to have vanished, as if it simply wasn't worth worrying about. Feeling a strange disconnect, Mark allowed the null field to fade, and suddenly his emotions came rushing back to the forefront, hitting him like a ton of bricks. Anger, frustration, and all the feelings he had been bottling up came out in a loud breath, and Mark felt his chest lighten. He still had another enemy to kill, but eliminating Rogers was a good start.

Crouching, Mark began to strip Rogers's suit away, checking for anything of value. There wasn't much, though he did find a small booklet and a credit stick in addition to Rogers's survival kit and identification. Putting everything away to examine later, Mark touched his fingers to Sergeant Rogers's bloody cheek, preparing to absorb. He was curious about the barrier power after seeing Rogers use it to great effect. Yet just before the power began to flow into him, he heard a gasp, and looking up, he saw Esme staring at him.

"Private Fields?"

Her voice was shaky and her gaze even shakier. Abandoning his absorption, Mark slowly stood up and walked over. "I'm glad to see you survived."

His voice was calm, but that only seemed to freak Esme out further, and she quickly scrambled off the table, getting down on the opposite side of him. As soon as she touched the ground, her leg gave out, and she sagged, nearly crumpling to the floor. She had a nasty wound on her forehead from where Rogers seemed to have struck her, and her eyes were unfocused.

Grabbing one of the health potions from Rogers's survival kit, Mark placed it on the table and took a couple of steps back. "You should drink that. You're wounded."

It took Esme a second to work up the courage, and whenever her gaze got close to Mark, she hurried to look away. He had no idea why particularly, but it was clear that she was absolutely terrified of him. Seeing that she wasn't reaching for the potion, Mark frowned and pointed at it. "Drink the potion."

Like she had been struck with a switch, Esme jolted and then grabbed the potion and quickly popped open the lid. Gulping it down, she choked. As she indulged in a coughing fit, Mark rubbed his forehead and turned back to look at Sergeant Rogers's body. He was a bit disappointed that he couldn't absorb the sergeant's barrier power, but it wasn't the end of the world. As useful as being able to create barriers was, Mark was perfectly content with his current power set, and absorbing the corpse's vitality in front of Esme would only frighten her even more.

It took a few minutes for the potion to kick in, and as Esme grew less shaky, Mark gestured toward Welton's head. "Do you know what's going on there?" he asked. "The sergeant attacked me as soon as I got here."

Staring rather incredulously at the sergeant's dead body and then at Mark, who looked entirely unharmed, Esme took a breath and shook her head. "I'm not sure. He attacked us as well and killed Welton before striking me. That's all I remember." She still didn't want to meet Mark's gaze, but at least she was talking to him.

"Any idea why he would do that?"

"I think he wanted to plant the bombs in the camp," she said, "to destroy the base. He was a lot stronger than even Welton."

"Hmm." With a noncommittal nod, Mark rubbed his forehead, trying to figure out what to do next. There was a very real likelihood that the path leading out of the mine was completely sealed, though Mark didn't imagine that Rogers had been planning on digging his way out, which meant that the tunnel probably hadn't been targeted. Of course, the only way to find out was to head in that direction. Leaving Rogers's body and Welton's head where they lay, Mark gestured for Esme to follow him. "Let's head back to the camp and see what the damage is."

Giving Rogers's body one last frightened look, Esme nodded, and they left the cafeteria, heading into the hallway that led to the reception area and the front door. They had just stepped out when Sergeant Langford stepped around the corner, fury blazing in his eyes. When he saw Esme, his expression hardened further.

"Where's Welton and Sid?" he asked, his eyes narrowing.

Much less frightened of Langford than of Mark, Esme rushed past him, squeezing to the side so she didn't have to get near him. After she passed him, she seemed to feel a great sense of relief in getting close to Langford, and she offered a messy salute.

"They're back through there," she said. "Both of them are dead."

Mark could hear Langford's teeth grinding, and after stabilizing his emotions, the lieutenant placed a hand on Esme's shoulder, as much to calm himself down as her. "You want to tell me what happened?"

"It was Sid. He turned on us shortly after we separated. He made us carry the bombs back to the surface. Along the way, Welton tried to fight him but got killed. I . . . I should have fought him too," she said, shaking her head.

Langford squeezed Esme's shoulder. "If he could kill Welton, then he could have killed you easily. You said he's still in the facility. Can you lead me to him?"

Esme nodded and then hesitated, looking at Mark. Stepping forward, Mark snapped a salute. "He's dead, sir," he said simply. "Additionally, the corporal you called Sid was actually a sergeant assigned to the Black Mountain Battalion. He was an A-ranked empowered who was assigned to guard Captain Calder. Last name Rogers."

Langford and Esme both stared at Mark in disbelief. Then the lieutenant, suddenly looking tired, rubbed his face. "Are you telling me that the person who was assigned to our unit a week ago is actually one of two survivors who left the base?"

"One of three, but yes, sir."

"And you said he's dead?"

"Yes, sir."

"Why do I feel like this is out of my pay grade?" the lieutenant muttered. "Can you take me to see his body?"

"Of course, sir."

Leading the way back into the facility, Mark brought Lieutenant Langford to where Rogers's body lay. He was doubly glad that he hadn't absorbed it, as it would have been much harder to explain a wrinkled mummy.

When Langford saw the wounds, his eyes immediately darted to Mark's hands. "And he died how, Private?"

"That'd be me, sir," Mark said calmly. "I managed to catch him by surprise, and my fingers can be pretty sharp."

"I can see that."

Langford crouched down by the corpse and pressed on Rogers's neck. His gaze then drifted down to the corpse's chest, where a large gash had been cut in the mana suit that covered it and the corpse's heart had been dug out. "'Sharp' seems to be an understatement, Private. You're telling me you can pierce through an empowered mana suit and an A-ranked empowered's flesh?"

"His flesh wasn't as strong as you're thinking, sir. He was masquerading as a brute, but he was actually a barrier user. I used that information to my advantage when I fought him. Plus, I'm something of a close-combat expert, sir."

Though the lieutenant didn't buy it, Esme had still been

unconscious, only waking up just as Mark was about to absorb Rogers's powers, so she hadn't seen the fight either, and Langford couldn't press the issue.

"This is going to be an absolute headache," Langford said, rubbing his forehead. "The camp is in shambles, but thankfully, most of the corps wasn't on the base when the explosion went off. Regardless, we need to salvage what we can and get back to the city. There's no point in staying here now, and the blast will undoubtedly have drawn the attention of the nearby Exlian. Do you have his badge?"

Pulling Sergeant Rogers's identification from his pocket, Mark handed it over, and when he saw the name on it, Captain Langford cursed again. "Let's go."

Taking Welton's head with them, they left Sergeant Rogers lying where he had fallen, and in silence they made their way back through the tunnels up toward the surface. The entrance to the mine was a hive of activity, packed with angry-looking soldiers and an absolutely furious Captain Sorn. When he saw the lieutenant and then the head the lieutenant held, his eyes blazed even hotter.

"Do you have an answer for me?" the captain asked, and with his jaw clenched, Langford saluted.

"Yes, sir. Our team had been infiltrated."

Without providing any more details, he handed over Sergeant Rogers's ID, and when the captain saw it, his expression turned ugly. "You mean he never . . ."

He didn't finish his sentence but lifted his eyes to search Langford's face. The lieutenant looked uncomfortable, and he just shrugged, clearly not wanting to speak where others could hear him. Captain Sorn glanced at Esme and Mark in turn.

"At least tell me the nest is dead," he said.

As Lieutenant Langford hesitated, Mark stepped forward and gave the captain a smart salute.

"I can confirm it, sir. I saw the collapse with my own eyes. I didn't quite make it out in time, but because some of the bombs weren't placed, I had a path I could climb out afterward. But I can confirm that the nest is gone."

"You're sure about that, Private? You're saying you saw it with your own eyes?"

"Yes, sir."

Though he wanted to believe Mark, Captain Sorn clearly didn't know what to do with him. And in truth, Lieutenant Langford didn't either. He had seen Mark vanish into the midst of the baeloth. And yet here was Mark, completely unharmed. Of course, this wasn't the first time Mark had defied guaranteed death, since he had managed to make it multiple weeks alone in the wilderness after surviving the total collapse of the mine entrance.

"We can send a team down to confirm," Mark said. "I'd be happy to lead them."

With a heavy nod, Captain Sorn patted Mark on the shoulder. "I think that's a good idea, Private. Lieutenant, organize a team to go down. I'll send some men with you to assess the damage."

"Yes, sir."

The captain hurried off to continue organizing his men, and Mark, following the lieutenant, stepped outside the mine into the bright morning sun. The majority of the base had been utterly flattened by the blast, and all that was left was a smoking crater.

Seeing Mark's astonished gaze, Langford nodded grimly. "We're lucky that the captain had ordered his men out of the perimeter to establish an outer wall, since they were intending on expanding the size of the base to accommodate the other battalions. All but six people were working on it when the blast went off. None of them survived."

"What happened to the other bomb?" Mark asked. "Weren't there supposed to be four?"

"We're not sure. Our best guess is that Sid, I mean Rogers, stacked two of the bombs together, thinking it would increase the size of the blast. It's not how they work, thankfully. Otherwise, the entire battalion would have been lost, along with the entrance to the mine."

Sergeant Kinsey was just stepping out of the battered-looking infirmary when the lieutenant and Mark arrived.

"How are you alive?" Kinsey said, staring at Mark in astonishment. "Didn't you . . ."

Langford held up his hand, stopping her words. "I'm bringing Fields in for an examination," he said, keeping his tone calm, "just to double-check that there are no issues."

Blinking, Mark suddenly realized why Langford kept looking at him askance. He had jumped into the middle of the baeloth, a creature known for taking control of the minds of others. Adding the mystery of how he'd survived the explosion and collapse of the facility, Mark could admit that it was reasonable for Langford to think he might have picked up a baeloth parasite.

42

Sergeant Kinsey led Mark into the infirmary. There were several beds, each separated by a partition. At the far end of the room, Mark spotted Phoenix lying down. Noticing Mark's gaze, Kinsey gestured for him to sit.

"Phoenix is fine," she assured him. "She's just sleeping off an overly potent dose of potion."

Feeling slightly stricken, Mark took his seat.

"You wouldn't know anything about that, would you?" Kinsey asked.

After a moment's hesitation, Mark nodded. "I may have gotten a little overzealous. She looked like she was in pretty bad shape."

Kinsey chuckled, flashing a sly smile. "Better overzealous than under—more potion never hurt anybody. She'll be fine. Right now, we need to focus on making sure you're fine. Do me a favor and relax. This shouldn't take very long. First, I'm going to need to draw some blood. Can you help me with that?"

Nodding, Mark transformed his hand and sliced his finger, letting a few drops splash onto the plate Kinsey held out. Before she could notice his finger healing, he stuck his finger in his mouth.

"That's gross. Entirely unsanitary. Don't do that," Kinsey snapped, putting the plate down. "Give me your finger."

Slightly sheepish, Mark pulled his finger out, but the cut was nowhere to be seen. For a moment, Kinsey just looked at his completely smooth skin, then up at Mark, her eyes starting to rove his body. "Hold on. Do you have a regeneration power?"

Though he wanted to deny it, it would make whatever happened next rather awkward. So, hesitantly, Mark nodded.

Kinsey, grabbing Mark's file, scanned through it. "I don't see a regeneration power listed. Did it only manifest recently?"

Deciding he could be liberal in his understanding of the word *recently*, Mark shook his head.

"Unreported power. Got it."

Making a note, Kinsey took the plate with the drops of blood and slid it into the analysis machine, clicking it on to allow it to run as she came back over to Mark. "All right, let's check the rest of your vitals."

Taking his wrist, she turned it over, then frowned. "Where's your watch?"

"I haven't had a watch for a while, and my spare watch wouldn't fit in my suit, since it was pretty hacked together. Then, when we were down in the facility, my suit got melted, and I had to take it off."

Again, Kinsey blinked, staring at Mark in considerable disbelief. Suddenly, it struck her. Mark had had no suit on when she saw him in the cavern, which meant that he had gone headfirst into a baeloth jungle with absolutely no protection.

"No wonder the lieutenant wants you checked," she said.

Mark nodded meekly.

"All right, we'll need to get you a new watch and a new suit. It's too dangerous for you to be running around in the wild without support." Her words sort of trailed off at the end as she looked down at Mark's bone blade arm. "Then again, if anyone could be safe in the wilderness without a suit, it's someone whose skin is harder than metal and who has regeneration as quick as yours. Actually, while we're waiting for the blood samples to come back, do you mind if we test that?"

"Feel free."

Mark held up his palm, and Kinsey grabbed a scalpel. "Let me administer anesthesia," she said. "Otherwise, this might hurt a lot."

Blinking, Mark realized she was right. He seemed to be getting so used to pain coming and going that he hadn't even thought of it. Grabbing a syringe gun, Sergeant Kinsey loaded in an ampoule and held the gun against Mark's skin before clicking the trigger. The injection was so quick and painless that Mark practically didn't feel it. And after she had injected four more times, Mark felt his hand starting to grow numb.

She pricked his palm with the tip of the scalpel, studying his face to see if he'd react. When he didn't, she made a small incision. Unfortunately, it was so small that by the time she had finished, it had already healed, and it appeared as if she hadn't cut him at all.

Mark chuckled, and Sergeant Kinsey smiled. This time, she was more aggressive, cutting a crimson slash across Mark's palm. And together, they watched as the skin rapidly knit back together. The sergeant made some notes and then cut again, varying the length and depth of the cut. For almost fifteen minutes, Mark watched as she sliced his hand to pieces. The only interesting moment was when she asked if she could cut a bit deeper and slice through one of his tendons. A wound like this would normally require a potion and at least a few days of not using the injured hand to heal. Mark was able to use his fingers perfectly within less than five seconds.

When she made her final note, Sergeant Kinsey sterilized the knife and put it away. "I cannot believe that you hid what is probably an A-ranked recovery ability. Do you understand how valuable regeneration on this level is? It makes you practically indestructible."

Thinking quickly, Mark shrugged and rubbed his palm. "I'm afraid of pain."

The sergeant didn't believe it for an instant. She rolled her eyes as she walked over to the machine running the analysis on Mark's blood. The infirmary was silent as she read over the report. When she was done, her brow furrowed, and she looked at Mark for a long minute and then back at the report.

Mark had found that not much frightened him anymore, and things that would have made him frantic with worry before now hardly stirred him. Previously, he would have worried that she might find information about his powers or discover the strange abilities his blood had. Now, however, the thought didn't bother him. If she did, Mark would act as the situation called for. Even if he ended up having to run, Mark was fully confident in his ability to survive, so long as there were Exlian around. And considering how widespread they were, Mark was sure he'd be fine.

"It must be a function of your regeneration," Sergeant Kinsey said, walking over and handing the report to Mark.

He glanced at it and saw all sorts of phrases that meant absolutely nothing to him. Blinking at the report, he looked up at Kinsey and saw her laughing.

"Sorry, I find the face people make when they see these reports hilarious. Sorry. Anyway, as I was saying, most of the time, your blood will pick up trace toxins. Nothing terrible, not enough even to poison you. But through general life, the things you eat, the air you breathe, substances you interact with, your body should be picking up trace amounts of impurities. You have none of that. It's like your blood is completely fresh and new. Actually, do you mind if I check you again? The anesthesia I just injected into you should leave some trace, so I'll be curious to see if it does."

One of Mark's worst nightmares was that the city, in finding out that his powers were abnormal, would begin running experiments on him. And seeing the fascination in Sergeant Kinsey's gaze, Mark had a sneaking suspicion that if he wasn't careful, he might find himself suffering that exact fate. Thinking about it for a moment, he nodded.

"Sure, I can do that. But I want your guarantee that you won't tell anybody what you found. The lieutenant is worried I might have a parasite. Rightly so. But I'd like it if you could keep my medical information confidential. I'm pretty sure I don't have a parasite. But then again, if I had one, I probably wouldn't be able to tell."

"I'm pretty confident you don't either," the sergeant said, shaking the report. "If you did, the toxins in your blood would be off the charts. In fact, you're probably the healthiest person I've ever examined. I'm just interested to see if your regeneration is actively working in your blood to filter out toxins."

As she spoke, she held out the plate again, and Mark complied, dripping another drop of crimson blood down onto the sheet. This time, he didn't stick his finger in his mouth and instead made as if to wipe it on a piece of gauze the sergeant handed him. As she inserted the plate back into the testing machine, Mark licked his finger quickly and then wiped it on the gauze. The last thing he needed was for somebody to dig through the trash and pull out his blood for testing. Hopping up, he tossed the piece of gauze into the trash as Sergeant Kinsey turned around.

"What else do we need to do for the examination?" he asked, wanting to move things along.

"We'll need to do a physical examination, and then we'll run a series of cognitive tests. For the physical examination, you can just strip down. We're checking for burrowers."

"Sounds terrible," Mark said, pulling off his shirt.

Although Sergeant Kinsey was accustomed to working with the empowered, who all had fabulous-looking physiques, she couldn't help but comment on Mark's. "Your muscle definition is pretty incredible, which would track with the stats I got on your metabolism. You burn energy quickly, it seems."

"Sort of," Mark replied. "It might be part of my regeneration, but I seem to have a lot of control over how quickly I burn through surplus."

"What do you mean?"

"Well," Mark began, scratching his shoulder, "if I am in a fight, I can drag it out, using minute amounts of energy to maintain peak performance longer. On the other hand, I can also expend it more quickly, allowing me to engage in slightly above-peak performance for a short burst of time."

"Huh. That sounds a lot like Captain Fields's . . ."

Sergeant Kinsey's voice trailed off. She was currently behind Mark, examining his back. There was a long silence. Mark had no idea what she was thinking, and as she walked around to face him, her eyes searched his face.

"I feel kind of dumb," she admitted, "but you're Joe's little brother, aren't you?"

Mark nodded, seeing a complex mix of emotions surge in Kinsey's eyes.

"We all owe your brother a lot. I was going to say, what you're describing sounds a lot like the theories Joe established, the ones the Rangers use actively. In fact, it's the first thing any new Ranger is taught. What happened to your brother?" She sighed and shook her head.

"It's okay," Mark reassured her. "He was proud to serve, and there's no guarantee that serving will end well."

Giving Mark a searching look, Sergeant Kinsey gestured for him to put his clothes back on.

"I think it's hard for those who aren't in the battalion to understand just how important Joe was," she said. "I've been serving in active duty with the Cerberus Battalion for the last seven years, and last year the Flying Scorpion Squad was in the vanguard. We were there when the battalion got swarmed. Sixty percent casualties within minutes. It would have been a hundred percent casualties if your brother hadn't shown up."

Pulling over a stool, the sergeant sat down as the machine analyzing Mark's blood began to spit out a paper. "He was like an avenging angel or some sort of phoenix, falling out of the sky and obliterating the Exlian horde. You should have seen him. He was like a god. One moment, death was inevitable, and in the next, salvation came on fiery wings. Your brother is a genuine hero, no matter what the city says. Though we can't speak of it, we all know if Joe is doing something, it's something that needs to be done."

As he listened, Mark could feel his body tensing, his expression hardening. He could hear the sincerity in the sergeant's voice, but he couldn't help the stab of pain that lanced through his heart when he thought about his brother.

With a soft smile, Sergeant Kinsey grabbed the report and, without even looking at it, patted Mark on the shoulder and walked out. Before the door shut, he could hear her speaking to Lieutenant Langford. "He's completely clean, healthier than all of us. I mean, look at these blood scores. It's like he's never—"

The rest of her words were cut off, and for a moment, Mark sat in silence. His heart was steady, despite the pangs he was experiencing. And he found, maybe for the first time in his life, that he was able to critically examine the situation with Joe without emotion overwhelming him.

43

Hearing the whisper of cloth and then the soft sound of feet heading in his direction, he peeked over his shoulder as Phoenix stuck her head around the partition, her eyes twinkling. She saw Mark, and then her expression fell. "Aw, darn, I heard there was somebody naked over here."

"I can take my shirt off again if you want," Mark deadpanned.

With a delighted laugh, Phoenix walked over and sat down on the bed next to him, close enough that their shoulders leaned against each other. "Once we're back in the city, I might just hold you to that. I've heard it's quite the sight."

Unsure just how much of his conversation with Kinsey Phoenix had heard, Mark didn't know what to say. Phoenix was something of a mystery to him, a consummate professional of incredible skill and tremendous potential. She occasionally let another side, a more playful, sweet side, peek out from her normal, no-nonsense exterior.

"What happened?" she asked after a moment of silence. "I mean, down below. The last thing I remember is getting torn out of the observation box."

Her forehead wrinkled, and Mark didn't answer right away,

giving her space to process whatever it was that she was remembering.

"It was incredible," she said finally, her voice catching. "I don't even know how to describe it, but the nest's control over mana was absolute. It crushed my control in a heartbeat and was well on its way to crushing me as well, but I don't think it was even trying. It was like it had commanded the mana to solidify, and so that's exactly what the mana was doing. It was solidifying and was crushing me in the process. But then, all of a sudden, well, it was gone."

Realizing that much of Phoenix's confusion stemmed from his use of the null field, Mark watched her carefully.

"Is there anything else you remember?" he asked, genuinely curious.

"No. No, there isn't. I remember the mana being there and then all of the mana being gone. That's the last thing I remember before waking up here. Considering we're in the infirmary, we must have been rescued or at least made it out safely. You know, it's hard to describe how comforting it was to hear your voice right after waking up. I know you didn't come in here for me, but still, thanks."

Mark knew exactly what she meant. More than once he'd experienced being knocked out or falling unconscious for some reason and then waking up in a completely different place. The disorientation it produced was tremendous. Hearing something familiar, something that could ground you, was undoubtedly a wonderful comfort.

"Well, after the nest grabbed you, things got a bit crazy. The wall blew in, and the lieutenant, along with Sergeant Kinsey, crashed the party. They brought their giant crab friend with them, which was fine, because it ended up getting into a fight with the terror-ranked leech."

"That must have been some sight."

"Oh, it was. They were going at it hammer and tongs, which freed up the lieutenant, Kinsey, and Batten to fight against the nest. Along the way, Kinsey lent a hand to heal me, because I had taken a lightning bolt to the face. Somewhere around there, the nest dropped you, and I was able to grab you and pull you to safety. I got a little bit excited, since you weren't breathing, and I fed you a few too many mana potions, which certainly helped you get healthy but also put you into a catatonic state. So, sorry about that. The reason you were knocked out was, well, because of me."

Smiling, Phoenix bumped him with her shoulder. "All is forgiven. Believe me, being unconscious for a few hours and waking up in a bed is much better than having my brain juiced and squeezed out my ears."

Returning Phoenix's smile, Mark continued. "About that time, the baeloth decided to make an entrance. And it was some entrance. Broke in through the ceiling and filled up half of the cavern with a giant jungle in about two minutes flat. It was pretty insane, actually. The thing spread so fast I can see why everybody was scared of it. Thankfully, the nest recognized the baeloth was a threat and sent a few dozen leeches straight toward it. They got locked up in a big fight, which the baeloth won in short order. I got swept up by the jungle, and from what I understand, Sergeant Kinsey grabbed you when the bomb timers started to go off.

"This is all secondhand, but I think Lieutenant Langford used his telekinesis to pull you, Batten, and Sergeant Kinsey out of the facility. I was still stuck in the middle of the jungle, which was quite unpleasant, if I'm honest. But then the bomb went off. And the next thing you know, bang, bang, bang. Stone coming down everywhere," Mark said, freely skipping major portions of the fight that he hadn't mentioned to Langford either. "However, unbeknownst to us, Sid was actually Sergeant Rogers, who was one of the other two survivors, apart from myself, of the Black Mountain Battalion. He had intended to sabotage the efforts to open the mine and moved some of the bombs into the camp, killing Sergeant Welton in the process. He still had Esme with him, and I happened to encounter him as I was crawling my way out of the half-collapsed facility."

"Wait, he was a traitor?" Phoenix asked, enthralled by the unexpected twist.

"Yeah, he was. Not only a traitor but actually pretty highly ranked too. You know how we thought he was a brute? In reality, he was a barrier user. It's actually kind of impressive how he was able to fake it."

"Okay, so you encounter him on your way out. What happened?"

"He miscalculated," Mark said with a shrug. "He revealed who he was before we fought, which means he didn't have a chance of catching me off guard, since I knew him from the battalion. That allowed me to anticipate his moves, and I managed to land a lucky hit or two. Anyway, after he died—"

"Hold on right there," Phoenix said, glaring at Mark. "You can't just say 'I managed to land a lucky hit' and then skip right over the fight."

"Eh, it wasn't that interesting," Mark said. "It was actually over really fast. You know I practice the Cutting Palm, right? Well, the thing is, it's pretty lethal."

To demonstrate his point, Mark hopped up from the bed, his hand transforming into a bone blade. With a casual swipe of his fingers, he cut the metal edge of the table clean off and caught it before it hit the ground. Holding up the piece of metal, he showed the perfectly smooth edge to Phoenix. "Imagine that was his throat."

Her eyes wide, Phoenix took the edge of the table, brushing her fingers against his. "Okay, maybe, but still, it seems like an achievement to take down somebody who's ranked above you."

Not wanting to dwell on the fight, since it involved more than one of his secrets, Mark leaned against the table. "Anyway, like I was saying, after he died, we met with Captain Langford and found out that a bomb had been planted here in the camp. When the bombs went off, the majority of the camp and six engineers went down with it. We talked to Captain Sorn, and we're going to be mounting an expedition back into the facility, just to make sure the nest is dead. Most of the cavern came down, and I saw the nest collapse with my own eyes, so I'm confident it's not a threat anymore. Still, it'd be a good idea to double-check."

Still holding the edge of the steel table, Phoenix stood up, her eyes bright. For a brief moment, she stared at Mark, and he found himself slightly disconcerted. Her lips parted, but whatever she was going to say died with the moment as the door opened and Lieutenant Langford walked in.

"Hello, Phoenix. Glad to see you're up and around. Fields, Sergeant Kinsey tells me that you are healthy as a horse, which is good, because we've got our orders. First thing tomorrow morning, we're going back in to make sure that the nest is gone and that no more nests can use the facility as a breeding ground. With that in mind, we'll be setting two more bombs, making sure we can take down the rest of the facility. However, in order to do that, we've got to make sure that you have a suit. You seem to go through these things fast. We also need to get you another watch. Seriously, I'm going to need to ask for an increase in budget just for watches. The engineers found you an extra one. They also have a suit that might work. We didn't bring any extra. Phoenix, do you think you're feeling well enough to accompany us?"

"Yes, sir," Phoenix said, snapping a sharp salute. "I don't think I've ever felt better in my life."

"Hmm, I can see that. You're practically bursting with spirit."

For some reason, Phoenix blushed, and Lieutenant Langford

cracked a grin. Even Sergeant Kinsey, who was standing behind the lieutenant, was smiling. But if he was honest, Mark didn't understand what was going on at all.

"Well, just to be safe, let's have Kinsey check you out. Mark, come with me. We'll get you that suit."

Following the lieutenant out of the infirmary, Mark walked with him up to the mine. The door he had put on had been removed, and the engineers were busy digging out the passage. Other engineers were rebuilding the original door, getting ready to weld it into place as soon as the frame had been installed.

Seeing Mark, Sergeant Zebe, who was working on the frame, waved. "Sorry we had to take your door apart, but the captain's orders are to use the mine as our primary base, so we'll be needing better access in and out."

"Oh, I don't mind," Mark said. "I would have built big doors if I had been able to, so I think this is great."

Inside the mine, the captain led Mark into one of the smaller storage rooms, which had been co-opted into a makeshift mana-suit workshop. Two engineers were at work, tinkering with a heavy-duty buster suit. Thinking that the suit was for him, Mark raised his eyebrows and glanced back at the lieutenant. "Sir, there's no way this is going to fit into the mine, or the facility for that matter."

"Oh, I'm aware," the lieutenant said, "but that's not your suit."

One of the engineers, pausing what she was doing, looked Mark up and down for a moment and then introduced herself. "The name's Sergeant Calypso. You can call me Cali or Sarge."

Straightening up, Mark returned the salute. "Private Fields, Black Mountain Battalion."

"I'm familiar with who you are, Fields. Practically everybody's familiar with you at this point. I heard your suit melted. Bit of a shame. It looked like you had proper heat resistance. What happened?"

"Lightning."

Both Cali and the other engineer grimaced, their faces matching Mark's. "Ah, yeah, that's a tricky one. Your normal heat sinks aren't going to work there. Let me guess—it started to bond?"

Mark didn't know anything about the jargon around building mana suits, but he could imagine, so he nodded. "I got out of it just before it started fusing to my skin," he said, causing Cali to chuckle.

"That's a rough one. Glad you came out in one piece, or at least enough of a piece that the potions could get you fixed up. Well, at the captain's request, we've got a suit for you. It's nothing fancy, but it's probably a step up from what you used before. No offense."

"None taken," Mark said, shaking his head. "I know some people can get a little bit touchy about the things they make, but in my opinion, it's always better to have something better, whoever makes it."

"Well, let me show you how this suit is set up. This is the NG-2.3, or the NG-Lite, also referred to as the Light Pack. It's built on the Storm Wind 5 chassis and has titanium-infused steel plating with a standard set of resistances, including, I'm sure you'll be pleased to hear, a rating-six conductivity system. Completely shockproof. Of course, if the shock is sustained long enough, it'll fry your parts, welding your joints together and making it impossible to move. So in short, don't stand in the lightning. It's also got a peak warrior-ranked mana-dispersion coating, which will help against blasts."

Surprised, Mark looked over at Cali, who laughed and patted him on the shoulder. "We heard you encountered a brain as well. Unfortunately, not much I can do about the screamers. The only thing that helps against them is pure padding."

Cali pointed at the buster suit they had been working on. "Unless you're in one of these bad boys, screamers will go right through you. Still, the Light Pack is highly mobile, which I heard is a requirement. You're a melee martial artist, right?"

"Yes."

"Then you shouldn't have any trouble. The Storm Wind is built for mobility, specifically in the legs and waist. You might have to make some adjustments to the upper torso. So if you don't have any questions, let's get you in it, and I'll put you through your paces."

At some point during the introduction of the suit, Lieutenant Langford had disappeared. And figuring he didn't have anywhere else to be, Mark spent a very enjoyable four hours getting his suit dialed in and chatting with Cali and Corporal Rowe, the other suit engineer.

The suit they had assigned him was, without question, the nicest suit Mark had ever worn. When he asked Cali about it, she laughed and waved him off. But with a sly grin, Corporal Rowe told him that the suit cost a cool twenty million credits, and that was *before* the modifications. The price made Mark freeze in place, not daring to move in case he accidentally broke something.

Half smiling, half scowling, Cali glared at Corporal Rowe. "And this is why we don't tell people how much suits cost. Listen, Private. Suits are designed to be used, and so I fully expect to see this one coming back all beat up. After all, that's going to tell me that you have been killing Exlian. And that is our goal. But in all seriousness, this is one of the captain's extra suits. He's only loaning it to you. He's not giving it to you. When you get back to the city, you'll have to turn it in. But until then, it's yours to use and abuse."

After thanking the two engineers, Mark headed back out to see what was happening with the camp. Currently, the ground was being filled in, and the remainder of the interior wall was being demolished. Progress on the outer wall was quick, and from what one of the corporals said, the plan was to be done with it within two days. Mark had been issued a new watch along with the suit, and after heading to the small shed where Lieutenant Langford and the other Rangers had set up shop, Mark activated it and connected with their squad.

"All right, let's get some food and then turn in," the lieutenant said. "We're not going to be on watch tonight, since we're heading down into the facility tomorrow morning. The team will be me, Kinsey, Batten, Phoenix, and Mark."

Slightly surprised to hear the lieutenant using his first name, Mark suddenly felt as if he was actually part of the team. That feeling was reinforced as Batten gave him a thumbs-up.

"Esme's already done a scan, and we're pretty sure the entire facility is clear," Langford went on.

Slightly pale, Esme nodded. "There was nothing above the warrior rank."

"She's going to stay up here to assist Captain Sorn and the Blue River Battalion in scanning for threats. We're going to be taking an engineer in her place, Corporal Ford. Our goal will be to double-check that the nest is actually dead, and then, once we've determined that the threat is gone, we'll plant bombs and detonate the other side of the facility. This time, there won't be any mistakes."

"Famous last words," Batten said in his heavy voice.

Cracking a grin, Langford patted him on the shoulder. "You better hope they're not. The last run was rough enough. We don't need another one like it."

"That's for sure," Sergeant Kinsey said.

To Mark, it felt as if it had been an age since he had last eaten a proper meal or slept. He stretched out on his cot and immediately fell into a deep sleep, not stirring until he woke, refreshed, the next morning. His dream battles had seemed like a cakewalk after his frantic experience fighting against terror-ranked Exlian, and when Mark and the others gathered, he found himself energized and ready to go.

44

Mark's suit, though quite advanced, had been painted to match the rest of the engineering suits so didn't stand out particularly. Corporal Ford, a no-nonsense, mustached man who looked rather like a brick and talked about as much, showed up in a heavy engineering suit that had clearly been modified. He carried a large case on his back and no visible weapons. Mark assumed that the lieutenant knew what he was doing, so he didn't say anything. And besides, Esme had scanned the facility the day before and assured them that there were no powerful Exlian.

Climbing through the broken door into the facility's reception area, Mark found it exactly as they had left it. The power running into the facility flickered, as the shifting of the earth had made the cables running down from the generator rather unstable. Flicking on their flashlights, the team navigated the half-collapsed passages as they made their way toward the central stairs. There wasn't much need to explore the rest of the facility, as half of it was buried and the other half was going to be buried soon. Occasionally, as they were tromping along, more stone and dirt was dislodged and came crashing down.

In each case, they had ample warning and were able to get out of the way.

Thankfully, there were no major cave-ins, and when they arrived at the stairs, the empty central area was largely free of debris. Mark had been curious about how they were going to get down, but before he could ask, Corporal Ford took the large box off his back, opened a section of it, and removed some familiar-looking devices. One he hurled down to the ground at the bottom of the broken-up stairwell. There was a distant thud as a pin drove deep into the earth, anchoring it in place. After securing another spike on their floor, Ford kicked out a broken piece of the railing, forming a clear path between the two spikes, and then deployed a rope that homed in on the end of the rod down below, affixing itself firmly.

Getting out a series of handgrips, he passed them out, one to each person, and demonstrated how to clip them onto the rope. After looking around to make sure everybody had seen what he'd done, he jumped off the staircase and zipped straight down. It was close to a free fall, but just before he reached the end, the handgrip slowed, and with a flick of his wrist, he disengaged it and landed heavily.

Langford, who didn't need the zip line, dropped down with Kinsey, and Phoenix, Batten, and Mark headed down after. Dropping straight down six stories was an incredible feeling, and Mark was moving fast by the time he reached the bottom. Thankfully, then Mark's suit slowed, and he landed with a light thud. The others had already begun clearing the path into the cavern, which mostly consisted of cutting through some thick vegetation that had grown there. There were no signs that any of the vegetation was sentient, and in fact, Mark couldn't sense any Exlian in the network as they stepped inside, their flashlights illuminating everything.

The cavern was only half the size that it had been before. A third of it had been taken up by the baeloth's sentient jungle, and all of that space, plus a bit more, was now gone, buried under a thousand tons of dirt and stone. Even if the baeloth had still been alive, there was almost no chance that it would have been able to survive the crushing pressure of the collapsed earth.

More important to Mark, however, was that the crab was gone. There were no signs that it had been here, apart, of course, from the utter devastation it had caused. Mark also noticed that more than a few of the leech corpses that should have been lying around were mysteriously missing, and he guessed that his crustacean friend was responsible. Where the crab might have disappeared to, Mark wasn't sure, but he had a strong suspicion that it was still alive and well. He had never seen a hardier creature, and part of him wondered if he might have been able to steal its constitution, had he consumed it. That reminded him that he still hadn't checked his status, but unfortunately, now wasn't the time. After thoroughly searching the cavern and surreptitiously devouring a few more dead leeches when no one was looking, Mark met back up with the others.

"That's where the nest was, and there's no sign of it," Lieutenant Langford said, "which means it's dead." His expression didn't look great, prompting Phoenix to raise her hand.

"Sir, could it have moved somewhere else?"

"No," Kinsey said. "Nests are not able to move from where they spawn. At least, we've never observed a mobile nest before. This nest was a bit peculiar, especially in its control of mana, but the reason it didn't roll off the stalagmite and attack us is because it couldn't."

"Sergeant Kinsey is right," the lieutenant said. "Nests grow and die in one place, but the bigger they get, the more area they can dominate and the faster they can produce Exlian of all different ranks."

"Shouldn't there be a corpse?" Batten asked, staring at the completely empty platform.

It took everything in Mark not to look around for Mime, since he knew that wherever she was, the nest was as well, or at least what remained of it after her digestive system had a chance to work.

Again, the lieutenant shook his head, but Sergeant Kinsey was the one who answered. "Nests are made of pure mana. They don't leave a corpse. Instead, they melt into the soil."

"Then should we test the ground for high mana concentration?" Corporal Ford asked.

"Actually, that's a great idea," the lieutenant replied, nodding.

Snapping a salute, Corporal Ford carried his case up onto the platform where the nest had lived. Flipping open the end, he pulled out a smaller case and opened it up, revealing a series of spikes, which he pulled out and stuck into the ground. Mark glanced inside the case and saw a readout popping up every time he inserted one of the spikes. Though he didn't know how to read it, he could tell that the numbers kept increasing every time Ford added a new spike. After a moment, the corporal nodded and began pulling the spikes out to put them away. "Significantly higher mana content, sir."

Letting out an audible sigh of relief, Lieutenant Langford thanked the corporal, and they headed off for the second part of their mission.

Planting the explosives went smoothly, and after taking a ride back up the zip line, the team set the final charge and strolled out of the facility. They stayed near the door, waiting the ten minutes until the earth shook, and then, after waiting a further half hour for everything to settle, they went back inside to double-check that everything was closed off. Just as intended, the main passage leading into the facility had been crushed, transforming it into a solid wall of earth and stone, ensuring the research facility could never be used again.

They were on their way back to the surface when the lieutenant's watch buzzed, and glancing at the message, he barked out an order for everybody to speed up. As they ran, he sent out the alert that he had just received from Esme. She had detected a large force of Exlian, including powerful warriors, heading toward the base.

"No terror ranked yet, but it's always best to be careful," Langford said. "As soon as we get outside, we're deploying to the wall. It's our job to figure out how many are coming and where they're coming from. We'll need to do a scan of the area."

"Sir?"

Hearing Mark call out, Langford glanced back at him. "What is it?"

"I have a pretty good sense of the land surrounding the base, sir. If Esme has any details about where she saw them, I might be able to pinpoint their source."

By that point, they had already arrived at the mine, and Lieutenant Langford ordered Mark and the others to go meet with Esme as he went to alert Captain Sorn of the coming danger. Finding Esme sitting at a desk in the shed where the Rangers had established themselves, Mark saw a sheet of paper in front of her. She had sketched out what she had seen, and almost immediately, he was able to identify it.

"This looks like the valley that's south of here. It runs east and west, and it's full of these kinds of trees. It's about a two-hour trip to this hill, but I'd expect the Exlian will be able to cover it in an hour, especially the hunters. They're pretty quick."

"What are those?" Phoenix asked, pointing at a six-legged monster Esme had sketched out.

"Screamers," Mark said. "They're nasty, and you don't want to stand in front of them."

"It's true. Their scream will liquefy metal. Your insides too," Batten said, patting Phoenix on the shoulder encouragingly.

"Don't listen to him," Sergeant Kinsey said. "But also, don't get hit, because nothing short of a miracle will be able to save you."

"Don't stand in front of a screamer. Check."

Not long after, the lieutenant arrived, and the team shared what they knew. Chewing on his lip as he looked down at the drawings, Langford nodded. "Batten, I want you, Esme, and Kinsey to meet up with Captain Sorn. He's going to give you your orders to support the defense team. Phoenix, Mark, you two are with me. We're going to do some advanced reconnaissance. I want eyes on the horde, just to make sure we're not missing anything."

"Yes, sir." Mark's and Phoenix's voices overlapped as they both saluted.

Splitting up, the team headed in two different directions. No more than five minutes later, Mark and Phoenix followed the lieutenant out of the base. The wall, though not finished, was more than ten feet high already, and engineers were still dutifully working on it, even as their companions set up defenses around them.

Langford led the way quickly, his suit practically skimming across the landscape. Phoenix and Mark both had to sprint to keep up. But sprinting downhill was rather treacherous, and more than once, Phoenix had to use her slow-fall ability to keep herself from face-planting. Mark found it troublesome as well, but thankfully, his suit performed much better than he anticipated, and its internal gyroscopic sensors did a good job compensating. With that and his increased agility, he managed to make it down the hill safely, and soon they were all on the valley floor.

Once there, Lieutenant Langford made the hand motion for stealth mode, and the three began to proceed cautiously. Mark had been finding his access to the Exlian psychic network was growing at a tremendous rate. Although things were fuzzier the farther from him they were, he managed to spot the horde of Exlian when they were still almost a mile away. Their team had just paused in a small copse of trees, and Mark, knowing the enemy was in the distance, squinted and pointed. Of course, he couldn't actually see the Exlian, but he pretended he could. "Sir, I think I just saw some movement out that direction."

Giving Mark a sharp look, Lieutenant Langford reached up and tapped his visor, scanning the hill that Mark had been pointing to. A grim smile flashed across his face. "I see them. Good eyes, soldier."

Even Phoenix looked impressed, and Mark mumbled something under his breath about the suit. The lieutenant completely ignored him, totally focused on the approaching Exlian.

"We're going to skirmish our way back," he said. "Mark, you're responsible for keeping them off Phoenix. Phoenix, we'll split targets. You take the hunters. I'll take the hulks and screamers."

The closer the Exlian horde came, the easier it was for Mark to identify their various strengths. He even found that as he concentrated, he was able to zoom in, getting a granular sense of their numbers and respective levels.

"Mark, are you listening?"

Snapping out of his hyperfocused state, Mark quickly saluted. "I'm sorry, sir. I'm unsure how to explain myself."

"Mark, just stop talking. Now's not the time to be zoning out. Pay attention, please. I said that we'll want to be careful. Hordes this size typically have a terror-ranked Exlian behind them. That doesn't mean that they're here. It might be a nest, hidden somewhere out there. And this might just be one of the armies it's sending out to try and kill us, because we're on its territory. But seriously, no more zoning out. It can be deadly on the battlefield."

"Yes, sir, it won't happen again. Sir."

As Langford turned away, Phoenix nudged Mark. "Are you okay? The captain spoke to you like two or three times."

"I'm totally fine," Mark said. "I was just getting a count of the enemy."

"What do you mean, a count?"

"There are six hulks, three screamers, and about a hundred seventy hunters intermingled. There's also a separate group of fifty hunters with one hulk on our flanks."

When she looked in the two directions Mark pointed, Phoenix didn't see anything. But that didn't stop her from believing him. She nudged Mark again, but he shook his head slightly, so she stepped forward. "Lieutenant."

Adjusting his gauntlets, Langford glanced back at her. "What is it, Private?"

"Is it possible that we're being flanked right now?"

The lieutenant shook his head, and then he caught sight of Mark and hesitated. "Maintain position."

His words hung in the air as he stomped his foot and shot up into the sky, moving almost too fast for an eye to follow. Almost immediately, the Exlian in the distance caught sight of him, and shrieks and howls rang out as they began to charge in Mark and Phoenix's direction. A moment later, Langford swooped back down, his eyes bright. Mark felt a tremendous force lock around him, and suddenly he was in the air too. With Phoenix floating on one side and Mark on the other, Langford took off, zipping up the side of the mountain, casually weaving between trees as branches slapped Mark's head and shoulders.

45

Cradling his head in his arms, Mark felt the world shift again, and he found himself standing just outside the newly built wall of the base. Patting Mark on the shoulder as he regained his balance, the lieutenant turned to Phoenix. "Thank you for saying something, Private. We were being surrounded. And more than that, there were at least two other forces further out. We're facing nearly twice as many enemies as we originally thought. I won't have time to both fight and help you two. Report to Sergeant Kinsey."

"Where are you going, sir?"

Jumping into the air, Langford spun around to face Mark. As he hung there, a dozen blue-coated shurikens launched from his suit, floating in a circle around him. "To run some delaying action, of course. Tell Captain Sorn I'll be escorting the enemy to the base."

There was a whoosh of wind, and Langford was gone, little more than a distant speck on the horizon.

"I genuinely can't wait till I can do something that cool," Phoenix said. Mark could only agree. Hopping over the wall, they went to find Sergeant Kinsey, who assigned them to the southeastern corner, where the fighting would be heaviest.

"The engineers fight differently than we do," she said, pausing to scratch her head and stare at Mark. "I mean, technically you're an engineer, but you really fight a lot more like a Ranger. Well, that's not true either. Rangers typically don't want to get hit. This is really strange. You're an engineer, you fight like a member of the Defense Force, but your tool kit is that of a Ranger. I don't know anymore. Regardless, the point is that when you're on the wall, pay attention to what the engineers say. If you end up dead because you're not listening, it's no one's fault but your own. We don't accept fratricide, but it's not fratricide if you step in front of a mana cannon that's about to blast. That's just idiocy. All right, get yourselves on the wall and listen to what the officer on point tells you to do."

At the southeastern wall, they found Corporal Ford and a number of other engineers, along with Lieutenant Ellos, who was in charge of the entire southern stretch.

"Who are the two of you?" she asked as Mark and Phoenix saluted.

"Private Mark Fields, ma'am, reporting for duty."

"Oh, that's right. You're the Black Mountain Battalion kid."

"Private Phoenix Borner."

Phoenix's last name earned her a raised eyebrow, and Lieutenant Ellis looked her up and down. "Surprised to see you're in a standard-issue Ranger suit."

"The family doesn't believe in playing favorites, ma'am."

"Ha. Well, neither do I. The two of you have been assigned to my stretch of the wall, which means you'll fight alongside everybody else. What are your specialties?"

"Ranged energy controller, ma'am."

"Close-range melee combat, ma'am."

"Isn't all melee close combat?"

Shaking his head, Mark held up his hands for Lieutenant Ellis to see. "Hand-to-hand combat, ma'am."

"Your funeral, but whatever. Since you've worked with Ford before, hang out with him. Corporal, head up to the southeast corner, Y-76. There will be no breaches. Do you understand? Absolutely none. The honor of our battalion rests on it."

"Yes, ma'am." Corporal Ford snapped a salute and led Mark and Phoenix to the marked location on the wall.

As they waited, Mark watched the soldiers setting up their defenses. Mobile mana cannons and a variety of other devices were deployed. In front of the walls, triangular devices were set up and lines of sticks were stabbed into the ground. Mark recognized them as the fences used to deter Exlian, but he was quite curious what they were going to be used for on a battlefield.

When he asked, Corporal Ford spat over the edge of the wall and pointed at them. "See how they're being set up in triangles? It's to funnel the enemy into a choke point. Doesn't work for the big ones. But low-ranked warriors or drones? Works like a charm. It'll force them into these kill zones, which gives us the maximum coverage with the mana cannons. The main problem is always the powerful enemy, since most of our static defenses are worthless against them."

As he spoke, the corporal's watch beeped, and glancing down at it, he unclipped his large case from his back and set it down with a heavy thud. Putting it parallel to the wall, he set it up on its edge and tapped a key combination into the end of the box. There was a hiss, and six sections of the box slid aside, rods curved at one end extending from them. They looked like old pistols, but Mark had never seen anything like them.

"Let's get ready. They're less than five minutes out."

Standing to the side with Phoenix beyond him, Mark stared out over the rugged landscape. He could sense the Exlian on the edge of his perception, and soon they began to stream in. He sensed them before he saw them, a nearly overwhelming mass of glittering gold that rushed toward him in a wave.

He heard a loud boom and, gazing down the mountain, saw a storm of stone raging through the Exlian ranks. A screamer gave a loud shriek, but Lieutenant Langford shot back up into the air before the blast could hit him. Instead it rolled through the ranks of the Exlian, decimating half a dozen of them in an instant.

The screamer didn't care one bit and leaped to try to snatch the floating lieutenant. Thrusting his hand down, Langford sent his blades to swoop in from all angles, stabbing into the unprotected screamer's neck, chest, and back. The blades tore chunks of flesh from the monster, but the attack wasn't enough to kill it, and Langford was forced to retreat as the screamer snapped at him. It fell back to the ground, crushing another two hunters, and while its sound blast recharged, Langford shot down toward it again, continuing his harassment.

Originally, there had only been six of the hulks in the main force, but it appeared that the other forces had all come together, and Mark counted an astonishing thirteen of the massive Exlian ghouls stomping their way toward the wall.

"Fire at will, targeting primaries. Let's go, folks, we haven't got all day."

Despite the order, Ford didn't move. His arms were crossed over his chest as he stood above his box with the six curved handles protruding from it. Another engineer, not so reticent, lifted a massive pipelike object to his shoulder. His suit's arms had been modified to hold it in place, and Mark saw him sight it in, aiming at one of the large hulks.

Holding the huge tube steady, the engineer flipped a switch and slowly depressed a button with his thumb. There was a click, and a small point appeared at the front of the tube, barely poking out past the end. For a moment, nothing happened, and then Mark felt a jolt as the button was pressed all the way. With a crack of thunder, lightning jumped from the back of the tube as a heavy metal rod, sharpened to a razor point on one end, was hurled through the air. It landed squarely on the right side of the targeted hulk's chest, tearing a hole straight through it and continuing to fly into the ranks beyond.

The hulk was spun around by the force of the shot, screaming in pain as it collapsed to the ground. Despite the incredible damage it suffered, it started to struggle back to its feet. But before it could lift itself up, a beam of mana slammed into its head, punching through its eye socket and blowing out the back of its brain.

Across the battlefield, two more of the thirteen hulks had been taken down, leaving only ten behind. There was a loud roar, and the Exlian force, some three hundred strong, began to charge.

Phoenix had already activated her power and held a glowing ball of mana in her hand. As the enemy drew close, she began to release little flickers of mana that transformed into whizzing darts. Each dart drew a peculiar twisting pattern through the air before landing with absolute accuracy on the enemy. The darts burrowed into flesh and then exploded, slowing and crippling hunter after hunter. Some were even struck in the throat or head, and the explosions killed them instantly. Though she had already produced a dozen darts, the ball of mana Phoenix held didn't get any smaller, and Mark realized that she was channeling more mana into it all the time.

When the hunters arrived at the fifty-foot mark, Ford finally moved. Uncrossing his arms, he reached for two of the handles, pulling out long, strange-looking rods that he pointed at the enemy. Lining up shots, he fired, releasing two fist-size balls of mana that detonated in the midst of the hunters' lines. Thrusting the two sticks back into the box, where they swiftly began to recharge, he pulled out two more, unleashing another explosive blast. By the time his third set of shots had fired, his first rods had already recharged.

From the wall, Mark prepared to attack. Despite the absolute horde of hunters charging straight for them, not a single one made it within ten feet of the wall. A few jumped from farther out, but before Mark could move to intercept, Phoenix's twisting darts blew their heads off or tore holes through their chests big enough for Mark to stick his fist through. The larger Exlian weren't faring any better. A barrage of powerful mana bolts from the mana cannons and specialty weapons the engineers had set up on the walls absolutely eviscerated them.

One hulk managed to get within arm's length of the wall. But before he could unleash his punch, Lieutenant Ellis pointed two fingers at him and made a firing motion. From out of the wall itself came a blast of mana, angled slightly upward to send the hulk tumbling head over heels. Now close to fifty feet from the wall, the hulk struggled up and was met with a devastating wave of firepower that left nothing but a single twitching finger behind.

The screamers, of which there were far fewer, fell just as fast, as the barrage of attacks was too relentless for them to block with their scream. Mark, somewhat nonplussed, stood at the edge of the wall, watching glumly as not a single one of the Exlian made it to him. The engineers weren't even worried and spent the majority of their time between attacks chatting. Many of them seemed to be trying new weapons, and there was a lively discussion going about the effectiveness of each of them.

Even Lieutenant Ellis got in on the conversation, pointing out that the launch charges she had installed in the wall were working exactly as intended. That led to further discussion on the effectiveness of nonlethal weapons for controlling the battlefield, and by the time the last of the Exlian forces had fallen, Mark felt like he had just wasted an hour and a half of his life.

Noticing his expression, Ford cracked a rare smile and punched him lightly in the shoulder. "Be thankful, kid. Exlian fights are easy, until they're not. And when they're not, well, that's when people end up dead. All of the weapons you see here, they're things we're testing to see if they're effective enough to use on the wall during the next wave. Behind all of the joking are people trying to solve a deadly serious problem. A problem that, if not solved, will result in the death of millions of citizens. We do this so they can live normal lives."

Properly chastised, Mark took a deep breath and nodded. "You're right," he said. "I shouldn't treat this like a game. I mean, joking around is fine. But it's better that we resolve it easily than struggle."

That night, Mark volunteered for patrol and spent close to six hours making slow loops around the base. The majority of the Exlian had been burned on the battlefield, and those that hadn't had been carried into the base to be cut open and used for supplies before their remains were burned.

Trying to calm the restlessness in his soul, Mark took a moment to sit at his favorite vantage point. The stars were out in full force, and as he gazed into the distance, he contemplated his life. Since he'd set foot outside the city, it had been full of twists and turns. But he had a feeling that his time in the wild was starting to wind down, producing a faint sadness in his heart. It wasn't true sadness but rather a sense of infinitesimal loss. He would miss this place. He would miss the wide-open spaces and the ability to see for miles and miles.

The mountains had a rugged beauty, and Mark found he genuinely enjoyed life out here. He had no idea what he was going to do after returning to the city. He could always apply to be transferred to one of the other branches or step into a new battalion. But part of Mark wondered if there was a chance to find an obscure deployment far outside the city . . .

It wasn't that he wanted a peaceful life. On the contrary, Mark had an almost overwhelming desire to hunt and slay. Thankfully, that desire seemed entirely focused on Exlian. It was just that while he could hunt Exlian from New Emery, the city felt so closed in. Out here, with a single breath, he felt like he could expand, filling the horizon.

Chuckling, Mark shook his head. He knew he was being silly, but that didn't change how he felt. As he turned to look down toward the camp, a flicker of movement in the far distance caught his eye. It was a tiny thing, the subtlest of shifts in the shape of the horizon. Mark's eyes immediately jumped to it. Something was sitting on a far ridge, staring at him. It was so far away he couldn't actually see it. And even if the sun had been shining bright, it still would have been beyond his range. And yet he knew. Slowly standing up, Mark felt a weight on his shoulder and reached up to scratch Mime's chin.

"Shall we go check it out?" he asked.

Mime, her eyes fixed in the same place as his, nodded. Mark double-checked the area, scanning to ensure that no Exlian were around. Then, because he didn't want to leave his post unattended, he tapped out a quick message on his watch. A few minutes later, there was an answering buzz, and he began to make his way down toward the wall, where he met Phoenix, still rubbing sleep from her eyes.

46

"What's going on?"

"I need to do something," Mark said. "I'll be right back. Do you mind grabbing the rest of my shift for me?"

Her eyes sharpening, Phoenix carefully buckled on her helmet. "Mark, the rest of your shift is an hour and a half. Why would I need to hang out for the rest of it if you're going to be right back?"

"This is why smart friends are annoying," Mark said with an easy grin, poking Phoenix in the shoulder.

"Just don't get yourself killed," she said, waving his hand away. "Call me if you need something."

"It's fine. I'm just gonna go check out something interesting I saw. I really will be right back."

Mark took off into the darkness, Mime riding on his shoulder. His suit gave him tremendous speed once it got going, and he crossed the two miles between the ridges in only a couple of minutes. Slowing down about halfway up the ridge, Mark checked his biofuel. He had no idea what he was in for tonight, but he wanted to be prepared. Flexing his fingers, he jogged the rest of the way up the ridge and arrived at the top a few moments later. He didn't bother checking the psychic network, as he already knew who, or rather what, was waiting for him.

There, perched among the rocks, its head tilted to the side, was the lean humanoid Exlian Mark had seen those weeks ago during the first attack on the base. The creature didn't move, save for its tail lashing back and forth. As Mark stopped fifty feet away, the creature straightened, its smooth, carapace-covered face dipping slightly as if greeting him.

Just as before, Mark felt no real threat from the creature, only a deep curiosity. And at the same time, he knew that if he showed even an ounce of weakness, it would strike. Mime, hopping down from his shoulder, advanced toward the creature, and Mark followed a few steps behind. It didn't react until Mime stepped within twenty-five feet. And then, in a blur, the strange Exlian retreated, leaping from its position among the rocks to the top of one, maintaining almost exactly twenty-five feet between it and Mime. Mime's lips curled in what looked to Mark like a smirk, and she sat down, turning to look at Mark as if to say, *Look how scary I am.*

"Yes, very nice. Good job, Mime."

Walking up next to the strange cat, Mark once again faced off against the Exlian. For a long moment, they simply stared at each other. At least Mark assumed that was what the creature was doing. It didn't have any eyes or even a mouth that he could see. In fact, its body seemed abnormally smooth, though it looked rather muscular. It was completely devoid of hair, but when he looked closely, Mark could see tiny scales covering the entirety of its body. And then, of course, there was the tail, which had a small ridge of spikes extending from it. The creature's fingers ended in sharp talons, as did its toes. Mark identified them as bone blade immediately. On a whim, he carefully unbuckled his gauntlets and took them off, placing them next to Mime.

"Make sure those don't get lost or broken," he said to the cat.

Then, straightening back up to face the humanoid Exlian, he flexed his fingers, transforming his arms into bone blades. As soon as his mana activated, the creature drew back again, this time shifting so there was thirty feet between them. It watched Mark's arms warily. Once again, Mark was at a loss to explain how he could tell where the creature was staring, and yet he seemed to be able to tell just fine.

After another minute or two of silence, Mark started to feel foolish. He wasn't actually planning on fighting but had just wanted to show off to the creature that he had bone blades as well. Glancing down at Mime from the corner of his eye, he could see the cat was snickering, her paw covering her mouth and nose in a very humanlike gesture.

Just as he was considering putting his gauntlets back on to save himself from further embarrassment, the creature took a step forward, and Mark felt a heavy presence entering his mind. It carried a sound that wasn't a sound, an image that wasn't an image, and a garbled string of symbols that looked like nothing Mark had ever seen before. They landed in his mind like a boulder, causing him to sag in place until the suit kicked in, keeping him upright.

The creature tilted its head, and another boulder of information rumbled toward Mark. He knew it was impossible to dodge. It was coming from the creature's mind, but Mark had no idea how to interpret the symbols, images, or sounds he was receiving.

There was a sharp hiss, and Mime stalked forward, her shadow beginning to wave wildly. That was when Mark noticed that his shadow was shifting and dancing as well, clearly ready for a fight. Immediately, the creature retreated, its head bobbing twice. Realizing it was about to leave, Mark tried to say something, but all that came out was a groan as he struggled with the mental boulders.

When he blinked, the creature was gone, and Mime slowly relaxed, the fur on her back smoothing out. It took almost ten minutes for the heavy mental weight to dissipate, and after it had, Mark found that he could barely remember what he had seen. Despite the burden it had caused on his mind, Mark knew he had been able to see all of it clearly, though he couldn't understand even a bit of it. Yet now, his memory failed him, as if the strain of remembering whatever the Exlian had tried to communicate was simply too much.

His body was incredibly tense, and Mark slowly relaxed as he put his gauntlets back on and headed back to the base. Phoenix didn't ask what he had been up to, and Mark didn't volunteer the information, genuinely unsure how to explain that he had gone out to visit a humanoid Exlian, who'd then nearly split his head in half trying to communicate with him. Mark couldn't even believe it himself, and he could imagine that the first thing Phoenix would do after hearing the story was recommend a psychiatrist.

He found himself rather distracted for the next few days, but after a week had passed, another team of Rangers and two battalions of engineers arrived. They were going to begin working on the road, starting from the base and pushing back toward the city, while another two battalions did the same in the opposite direction. It was clear to Mark that he had drastically underestimated how valuable the resources in the mine were, which made it all the stranger that the Black Mountain Battalion had been deployed in the first place.

Lieutenant Langford called the team together and informed them all that they were heading back to New Emery, Mark included. The trip was expected to take a week, but because they were traveling light, Lieutenant Langford took them across the original path, braving the rockslides, since his telekinesis could lock everything in place and create temporary bridges for everyone to walk across. They made good time, and by the second day, they were within striking distance of the city. Despite the fact that they could make it to the city before noon if they pushed it,

Lieutenant Langford slowed them down and set a moderate pace, just in case they were ambushed along the way.

They were met at the gate by one of the administrative staff for the Cerberus Battalion, who, apart from glancing at Mark a few times, simply acknowledged their return and sent them to rest. The lieutenant told everybody to take the next day off and meet up the following day at the command center. As everyone else split up, Langford called for Mark to come over.

"I just wanted to say thank you," the lieutenant said, patting Mark on the shoulder. "You really pulled your weight out there. More than that, in fact. I know that your future is uncertain at the moment, but if you're looking for a home in the Rangers, I'd be honored to work with you. I know Phoenix would love it too, and the others as well."

"I'm not sure," Mark said, chuckling. "I'm pretty sure Esme is still afraid of me."

"Yeah, I don't know what that's about," Langford said, shrugging, "but I'm sure she'll get over it. No pressure, of course, but genuinely, it would be great to have you on the team."

"Thank you, Lieutenant. I appreciate it more than you know."

The lieutenant saluted, and Mark, clicking his heels together, returned the salute. He found Phoenix waiting for him outside. She had already shed her suit and waited as Mark did the same. He had a small bag he had submitted for scanning, and after collecting it, he and Phoenix headed out of the gate compound and stepped out onto the street.

Reaching for his watch to order a taxi, Mark remembered that he didn't have a watch anymore. His watch had been destroyed, and the one he had been using was on loan. He had returned it with his suit. Though he had plenty of money, it was all in the bank, and he wasn't quite sure how he was going to get a taxi home. With a laugh, Phoenix came to the rescue and ordered him a taxi.

"Look, it's going to take me a couple of days to get settled," she said. "Tomorrow, I don't think I'm going to do anything except sleep, and the next day, we'll be debriefing. You're probably going to get called for debrief as well, maybe a couple given everything that's happened to you, and I'm sure your captain will want to meet up with you. But after that, maybe in a few days, the end of the week or something, do you want to hang out?"

"You mean with the gang?" Mark asked.

Phoenix stiffened slightly, and too late, Mark realized she had been asking him on a date. He had never been the most astute when it came to emotions, but recently, it felt like he was even denser than normal. To his surprise, though he had never thought of Phoenix romantically before, he didn't hate the idea of dating her and in fact was quite interested. The only person he had ever dated was Sky, if the time they'd spent together could even be called dates, but their conversations had never progressed past the friend stage.

Phoenix flashed an easy smile and began to turn away, clearly intending to drop the subject, but Mark reached out and grabbed her arm. "I'm sorry, my brain isn't working very well right now. I'd really love to hang out with you, maybe just the two of us. I'll have a watch by then, so I can take you to dinner."

The words tumbled out of his mouth, and slowly, her shoulders relaxed.

"That would be really nice," she said. "Just send me a message once you pick a place, and we'll figure out a good time."

"Deal."

He was still touching her arm lightly, and she stepped closer, slipping her arms under his and around his chest. She squeezed him for a moment, and he returned the hug, letting her go as she shifted her weight back.

"Thank you, Mark. You know, for saving me, for being my friend, for just all of it."

"I'm the one who should be saying thank you," Mark said with a laugh. "It'd take me hours to get home from here if I was walking."

Just then, their taxis pulled up, and with a wave, Phoenix was gone. Mark watched her car's taillights until they vanished, then climbed in his taxi.

"So where do you want to go, bud?"

Looking forward, Mark met the taxi driver's amused gaze in the mirror, and suddenly it struck him. He was back, actually back, in New Emery. There were more than a few times in the last two and a half months when he had assumed he'd never see the city again. And yet here he was, sitting on a comfortable seat, no mana suits in sight, or Exlian for that matter. Taking a deep breath, he gave the driver his address and leaned back as the car took off.

"Your lady friend's pretty," the driver said. "Are you in the same unit?"

"She is pretty, but she's not in the same unit. Though who knows? We'll have to wait and see what the future holds."

The ride was quiet after that, as if the driver could sense Mark didn't really want to talk. He was dropped off in front of Abrams's warehouse, and walking up to the door, he punched in the code and stepped inside. The cold air hit his lungs, and Mark felt a weight fall from him. He looked around, but Abrams was nowhere to be seen. He headed upstairs. Sky wasn't there either. Mark went into his room and settled down, tossing his bag onto his desk and lying down on his bed. He put his arms underneath his head and stared up at the ceiling as Mime settled down on his chest.

For a few minutes, he remained there, not really thinking of anything. He hadn't realized just how much tension he was carrying during his time in the wilderness, but now that he was back, it was starting to bleed away. It was a rather disorienting feeling, not having to constantly be on the lookout.

Mark had scanned the Exlian psychic network almost a dozen times while in the taxi and had to forcefully stop himself from continuing to do so once he got back to the warehouse. He needed something to distract himself. Mark flexed his fingers and activated his status. He had been ignoring the blinking notifications he had gotten after he devoured the baeloth, waiting for a time when he wasn't near other people to check them.

He wasn't sure what made him so hesitant, as nobody else could see his status unless he showed it to them. Still, he hesitated again before taking a look, and suddenly he realized what the problem was. Mark knew that something in him was changing, shifting away from who he had been his entire life, and in truth, it scared him.

What person could dive headfirst into a baeloth jungle and then do exactly what the monster was trying to do? He had devoured a terror-ranked Exlian, and his only thought afterward was whether he should eat the nest too. His thinking was diverging further and further from that of a human. Mark found himself hesitant to look at the proof of it, as if somehow it would prevent him from ever going back.

Of course, he had already come too far, and even if he wanted to retrace his steps, to reclaim his humanity, he wasn't sure that there was a chance.

He decided to embrace the change, giving in to neither the fear of his human mind nor the mindless bloodlust of the Exlian spirit. Instead, he would walk the path between, using reason to guide his bloodlust and power to curb his fear.

47

Resolutely, Mark shifted his gaze from the ceiling and looked down at his status.

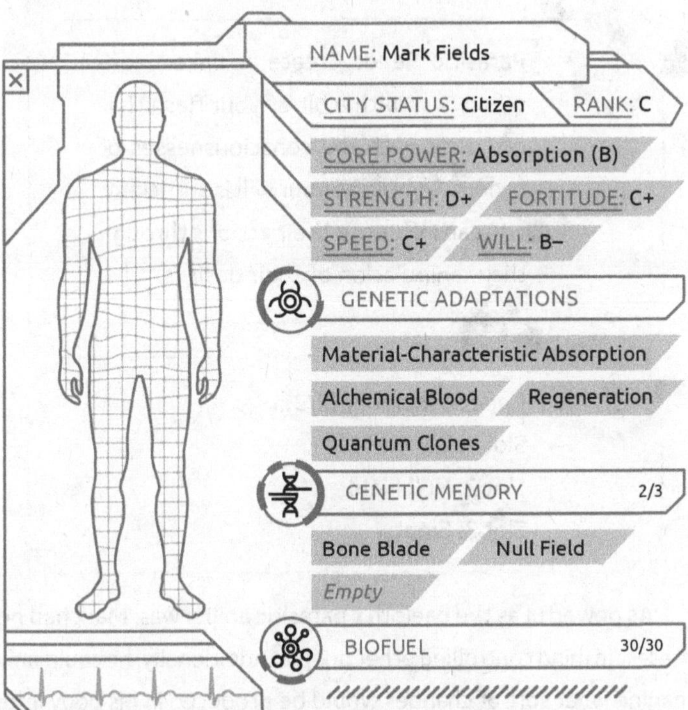

There was a whole pile of notifications that Mark had been ignoring, and after glancing at his status, he looked them over.

Your fortitude has increased from C to C+.
Your will has increased from C+ to B–.

Sufficient specialized genetic material acquired. Would you like to remember Parasitic Seed?

Mark had been wondering if he would get an ability from the baeloth, and sure enough, he had unlocked its parasitic seed ability. Since he had an extra slot for genetic memory, Mark figured it was worth taking a look and opened up the ability description.

Parasitic Seed: Create a linked consciousness with a bit of your flesh that can meld with the consciousnesses of others. So long as your will is sufficient, you can influence their actions through the manipulation of their desires.

Genetic Memory (2/3):
Slot 1: Bone Blade
Slot 2: Null Field
Slot 3: Empty

As powerful as the baeloth's parasitic ability was, Mark had no interest in mind controlling other people. Additionally, he could only imagine what sort of changes would be produced in his body if he accepted it. The idea of having to use his own flesh to create the seeds was so off-putting that he immediately selected *no*, causing the window to vanish. Mark realized that he was starting to come to a better sense of how he wanted to proceed with the changes in his body.

As much as he didn't want to think about it, Mark knew that as he grew stronger, he was becoming less and less human. Not only did his power allow him to absorb the characteristics of objects he touched, but it allowed him to assimilate other beings' genetic structures as well, binding their powers into his body. The cost of these powers was that he became more like the beings they came from, which in turn meant that with each Exlian power he gained, he was becoming more like an Exlian. This explained why the facility's automatic defenses had turned to track him and why Exlian often tried to target him first.

Mark was coming to accept that the price of power, at least as far as he was concerned, was becoming less human, but regardless of how powerful he became, he needed—wanted—to be able to pass for human. And he had a growing concern that the Exlian sensors in New Emery would start picking him up if he absorbed too much of their genetic code. In fact, reflecting on Esme's fear of him, Mark was fairly certain that Esme had seen his true nature more than once. Whether she was noticing Mime or Mark, he wasn't quite sure, but she had clearly sensed that there was a powerful Exlian lurking nearby, and Mark seemed the most likely candidate.

If Mark ended up turning himself into a target in New Emery, it would be a major problem. It was one thing to escape into the wilderness while on the base. It was another entirely to try to escape from New Emery. The last thing Mark needed was to transform himself into some sort of monstrosity while inside the city walls.

That didn't mean he wouldn't be on the lookout for powerful new abilities, just that he would be choosy with what he selected. The bone blade fit perfectly with his absorption ability. After all, it was easy enough for him to say that he had implanted a shard of it somewhere on his body, giving himself access all the time. And the null field was simply too strong of an ability for him to pass up. He would rather leave the third slot open, just in case he came across something of similar value. It wasn't as if he hadn't gained something from absorbing the baeloth. His will had shot up, and he could tell that though it was currently constrained by his other stats, it would continue to rise explosively as he ranked up everything else.

Feeling a good bit better about his situation, Mark got out of bed and headed to his desk, only to remember that in order to use the virtual screen, he needed a watch. With a sigh, he went back to bed. There was a lot that he wanted to do now that he was back. He needed a new watch, had friends to spend time with, and was excited to get back to training with Master Abrams. He was also looking forward to getting back to studying elixir creation, which he had been forced to put on pause after his initial, unsuccessful attempts. However, it was late in the evening and nothing was open, and since Abrams and Sky weren't home, he had nothing to do but go to sleep, which was exactly what he did.

The next morning, he awoke, his stomach rumbling, and smelled something delicious wafting up from downstairs. Getting up, he stretched and took a quick shower. His hair was still wet as he walked down the stairs into the freezing cold, and it frosted quickly, making him look rather ridiculous. He had completely forgotten just how chilly the warehouse was.

When he got to the bottom of the steps, he saw a box sitting on the desk. In it was a hot breakfast from Jason's restaurant, where Mark had worked as a dishwasher, and a note in Abrams's scrawled handwriting.

I'm going to be away for a while. Don't look for me, and keep your head down until I get back.

The note had an ominous tone to it, and though Mark was no expert in handwriting, it looked like Abrams had been quite agitated when he wrote it.

The dichotomy between the warmth of the hot breakfast and the dire tone of the note struck Mark, and for a long moment, he stood there, staring at them alternately. Then he balled up the note, stuck it in his mouth, and chewed. Picking up one of the warm pastries, he took a bite out of it and swallowed. He wasn't sure why he'd suddenly decided to destroy the note, but at that moment, there was a loud rapping on the door, and Mark, his gaze growing hard, ignored it. He finished the pastry, picked up the egg wrap, and walked to the door. On the way there, the knocking sounded again, this time louder. Mark was dressed in a tank top and sweatpants, and his hair was slicked back from his forehead, the tips white with actual frost. He imagined he presented quite a picture as he opened the door just before an angry officer could knock again. As soon as the door started to open, the officer tried to shove it farther, but Mark had a grip on it, and it didn't move even an inch. Going red in the face, the officer was about to say something, but Mark cut him off.

"Hello, Officer. Bit early to be trying to break down people's doors. What can I do for you?"

"Do you mind if we come in?"

The man who spoke was a captain, according to the rank on his uniform. All four of the people currently standing outside the warehouse door were members of the Defense Force, and as Mark looked them over, he could sense half a dozen other people loitering around the warehouse's other exits. The captain's smile didn't reach his eyes, and his stare reminded Mark of a snake's gaze. Thinking for a moment, Mark took a bite of his egg wrap and slowly chewed it. With every second that passed, the captain's smile grew more brittle, and the officer who had tried to shove his way in grew redder in the face. Just before both of them reached their breaking point, Mark swallowed and shook his head.

"Sorry, you can't come in. I do mind. There's a lot of valuable stuff in here, and I'm not going to be the one responsible if you accidentally break it."

"Is there? That makes me quite curious. I'd always heard Abrams's warehouse was full of frozen corpses. They don't seem very fragile to me."

Ignoring the captain's sarcasm, Mark gave him an earnest nod. "Exactly. Do you know how valuable those corpses are? Some of those Exlian are literally priceless, the only ones in the world, and it's almost impossible to tell which are which. Master Abrams is incredibly picky. Even putting your hand on one of them wrong could ruin the integrity of the ingredients inside. What am I supposed to do if you come in, start poking around, and all of a sudden owe hundreds of thousands of credits? If he loses millions of credits because you guys are wandering around touching things, are you going to give him that money? When he's out hundreds of millions of credits because one of you accidentally leaned against something you shouldn't have, do you think the Defense Force is going to want to take that bill on? When the four of you come in and accidentally fall down the stairs and break your heads open, tainting the warehouse with blood, and he's out billions of credits, is the city going to cover it?"

Realizing that Mark was just going to keep going, the captain interrupted him. "Enough. We understand. Can you call Master Abrams out?"

"Nope. I'm sorry, I can't."

"Is Master Abrams here?"

"It's a great question. I don't think so."

"Boss, what are we waiting for? Just grab him and drag him in."

Hearing his subordinate's suggestion, the captain nodded. "It's clear you don't want to cooperate. Maybe some time in prison will help with your memory."

Mark simply smiled and remained in place, hiding the growing worry in his heart as he finished off the wrap in a few bites. Seeing his complete lack of response, the captain's eyes narrowed, and he took a step forward, a faint pressure extending out from him. Mark judged that he was at least in the B rank, and likely high B as well. The pressure the captain exuded didn't bother Mark at all, but he memorized the man's face and then slowly turned to look at the others, committing their faces to memory as well.

"Maybe you don't think that I can make good on my threat," the captain said, "but we have a warrant for Master Abrams's arrest, and if you obstruct us in any way, we can drag you in as well."

"Oh, I believe you," Mark said. "Are you going to do it? I mean, I'm not just going to come with you because you threatened me. If you want me to come, you have to actually arrest me."

Stepping onto the already crowded porch, with no regard for the captain's personal space, Mark pulled the door shut behind him. The other soldiers had been forced to back down the steps so the captain could take a step back, and with a smile, Mark held out his wrists. "I can't call Master Abrams out because I have no idea where he is. You can't go in the warehouse, because nobody is allowed in the warehouse without his permission. If you have a warrant that says otherwise, you're welcome to show it to me, and we can get a lawyer to take a look at it. If neither of those options suit you, you can either arrest me or walk away."

Mark's tone was practically flippant, a far cry from how he

really felt, and a flash of anger raced through the captain's eyes. Mark saw his fist balling and got ready to dodge, but before anything could go down, Jason strolled out of the alleyway. The restaurant owner was wearing an apron and a pair of sandals, along with a ratty T-shirt, but as he stopped at the mouth of the alley, the captain forcefully restrained himself.

"Everything okay, Mark?" Jason asked.

Lowering his outstretched wrists, Mark gave him a wave. "Hey, yeah, it's all good. These gentlemen are looking for Abrams and can't find him. They want to take me in, since I don't know where he is."

"They want to take you in? Why would you know where he is? You just got back yesterday."

Shrugging, Mark looked back at the captain. "As Jason says, I've only just gotten back. You can check at the gate. I was deployed with the Black Mountain Battalion into the wilderness and have been gone for almost a month and a half. During that time, I've had no communication with Abrams whatsoever."

Taking a step back, the captain shot a glance at Jason and then gestured for his men to cuff Mark. "Bring him in. We'll see if he's telling the truth."

Eyes narrowing, Jason started forward, but Mark shook his head. One of the officers stepped forward and slapped cuffs on Mark's wrists. They were heavy and metal, and as soon as they touched his skin, Mark could feel the mana draining from his body. These were cuffs designed for restraining dangerous criminals, intended to prevent powers from being activated, and seemed like complete overkill for someone who was willingly cooperating.

They led him to a Defense Force vehicle parked nearby. The entire time, Jason stood in the alleyway, watching them with a hard gaze. One of the officers, clearly unnerved, wanted to say something, but the captain hushed him. They put Mark in the back of the vehicle, and one of the officers got in with him. As the doors shut, the man flashed a not-so-nice smile at Mark. "You're in the belly of the beast now, kid. Just remember you got in willingly, so you can't blame us for what happens."

Smiling slightly, Mark reached up and scratched his nose. "You know, there's a kind of Exlian called a widow worm that Master Abrams once had me take apart. The widow worm is fascinating. It masquerades as something harmless, and then, once swallowed by another creature, it consumes their intestines, cutting off access to the creature's stomach. From then on, anything the monster puts into its mouth to try and feed itself goes straight to the widow worm, allowing it to grow until it's large enough to consume the host from the inside out."

The officer stared at Mark, completely disgusted, as Mark laughed lightly.

"I only bring it up because it's an interesting example. One should be very careful what they try to swallow. Some things give you a stomachache. Others can kill you."

"Quiet back there."

With a shrug, Mark complied, sitting in silence for the rest of the ride, until they arrived at a large building made from heavy gray stone on the outskirts of the city. It was a massive fortress, imposing in every sense of the word. The building was close to ten stories high and twice as long as it was tall. Heavy parapets surrounded the guard towers, and though Mark had never been inside, he knew that those who stepped into the building rarely ever emerged.

He had assumed that he'd be taken downtown for questioning, that this wasn't a big deal, but when the officer said he'd stepped into the belly of the beast, he wasn't joking. This was Gray Rock, the maximum-security prison for violent and dangerous empowered criminals. Tenure at Gray Rock was permanent, and Mark's heart plunged as they pulled in.

The officer across from him leered, and Mark ignored him, looking out the window as they pulled up in the yard. When the door opened and the officer got out, he waved for Mark to come out as well. "Get out here, or we'll drag you."

His arms were still shackled together, so it was a bit awkward, but he managed to scoot out of the car, and soon he was standing on the hard gravel courtyard just inside the gate. If anything, Gray Rock was more imposing from the inside. The windows were tiny and double barred. Mark could even see faint sparks jumping between the bars and realized that they had been electrified.

The captain led Mark inside and had him stand in the middle of the hall while he spoke to one of the desk attendants. Mark detected a hint of pity in the gaze sent his way, and the bad feeling in his heart intensified. For a brief moment, he thought about making a run for it, but he curbed that feeling, trusting that he'd be able to deal with any situation that came.

48

After he was checked in at the front desk, Mark was processed, much like he imagined a regular prisoner would be. First, he was searched, which was easy enough considering what he was wearing, and then he was given a physical examination and a power assessment. Finally, they brought him into a room, pulled up his profile, and began asking him questions.

Most of the questions revolved around Abrams, where his master might be, what his master had been up to in the last month, and so on. Mark patiently explained, repeatedly, that he hadn't been in the city for the last month.

Two men and a woman were interrogating him: the captain who had had him arrested, a man who looked like he worked in the prison, and a woman who neither looked at Mark nor spoke. She was dressed in a simple but elegant black skirt suit, and her hair was neat rather than stylish. She wore no jewelry save for a stylized bracelet with a small watch in the center, and a heavy signet ring on her left pinkie finger. She sat in the corner of the room, her legs crossed, and occasionally, as they asked questions, the captain looked in her direction. She either nodded or shook her head slightly. Whenever she nodded, he continued with his questions. Whenever she shook her head, he changed their direction. Mark found the whole situation mildly fascinating, but he was quickly growing tired of it.

When a soft chime sounded, the woman glanced at her watch and stood up. She walked over to the table, and the captain cut off mid-sentence. Her gaze was cold, as cold as any predator Mark had ever seen. She looked at him as if he were nothing, or rather, less than nothing. "I'm Special Officer Elma Vory, and I have some concerns that I hope you can help me with. First, however, there are a few things we need to clarify. You claim that you're a member of the Black Mountain Battalion of the Engineering Corps. Is that correct?"

"Yes."

"And you claim that you were deployed a month and a half ago. Is that correct?"

"Yes."

"Furthermore, according to witnesses, you appeared in front of the Blue River Battalion of the Engineering Corps, over a hundred miles away from Felwer Mine, in a nonstandard mana suit, claiming that the rest of your battalion had been wiped out in an Exlian attack."

Mark could sense he was walking into a trap, but there was no way to avoid it. He nodded, and Elma continued.

"There's also a report that you participated with the Flying Scorpion Squad of the Cerberus Battalion of the Ranger Corps, the battalion your brother was involved with."

"I was ordered to assist them, yes."

A faint smirk crossed Elma's lips, though it was gone as fast as it had appeared. "After participating with them in their mission, you agree that you came back to the city with Lieutenant Langford and the surviving members of the Flying Scorpion Squad."

"I did."

"In that case, I have everything I need. Thank you. Warden, you may lock him up."

Without another word, Special Officer Vory spun on her heels and walked out of the room. The captain glanced at Mark and then raced after her, asking something in a low voice. Mark wasn't sure what he had asked or if she answered, because as soon as they left, two burly guards entered the room, and the warden gestured for him to come out. "Come along, kid. You're going to be our guest for the foreseeable future."

"Am I allowed to know why?"

As soon as the words were spoken, one of the big guards slammed a fist into Mark's solar plexus, knocking the breath from his lungs. Mark's recovery was almost instantaneous, but he remained hunched over, his shoulders shaking as if he were trying to get his breath back. The guards hauled him to his feet and dragged him along the passage as the warden continued on his way, as if Mark had never said a thing. They brought him down two flights of stairs, close to the ground floor, and tossed him into a cell.

There was a hard wooden bed and nothing else, and after the door clanged shut, Mark frowned and took a seat, his mind churning. He had a sneaking suspicion that looking for Abrams might have only been an excuse. He hadn't forgotten that Sergeant Rogers had been sent back out into the wilderness specifically to make sure he died, and whoever was behind him had likely known that Mark was back in the city for the entire day.

The next day Mark remained locked in the cell. No one came to visit him, and there was no food or water. Of course, to Mark, whose biofuel meter was full, this didn't matter one bit. With thirty biofuel units and no physical activity, he estimated he could probably last close to sixty days. Even his dream fights didn't consume much biofuel as long as he was careful with them and kept his activity low.

On the morning of the third day, he heard footsteps that stopped in front of his door, and with a clang, it opened. He was still sitting on the wooden bed, as if he hadn't moved an inch, when the warden stepped into the room. He looked at Mark for a moment and then, with a smirk, walked out. "You have five minutes, but that's it."

"It'll be enough."

As soon as he heard the voice, Mark felt his heart tighten. And then Andre Javesi, Noah's father, walked into his cell, Special Officer Elma Vory following behind him. Once again, for a brief moment, Mark considered striking. He was confident that he could get out of the cuffs, confident that he could shove his fingers through Andre's throat before he had time to scream. He had no idea how powerful Special Officer Elma Vory was, but he was sure he could at least kill Noah's dad. And then he squashed the murderous impulse.

Whether Andre noticed the shift in his emotions, Mark wasn't sure. The city councilman gestured for Special Officer Vory, and she stepped forward and handed a paper to Mark before returning to her position and beginning to speak.

"You have been accused, tried, and found guilty of the murder of one Sergeant John Rogers. Not only is murder a heavy crime in New Emery, but fratricide is an even heavier one. As a member of the Black Mountain Battalion, you are responsible for upholding the honor and glory of humanity. And yet you raised your hand against a brother in arms. Normally, these cases would be tried by a jury of your peers. However, considering that we have multiple testimonies that you proudly confessed to this crime, the military tribunal has ordered you stripped of your rank and imprisoned for the remainder of your life in Gray Rock."

The sheet Mark was looking at was a list of all the crimes he had been accused of. It was extensive, and fratricide, or the murder of Sergeant Rogers, was only the first. Each additional charge, all of which Mark had been judged undeniably guilty of, added to his sentence. And the total was close to three hundred years, which was significantly longer than he expected to be alive. At the bottom was a stamp that read *Not Parole Eligible*.

As she finished speaking, the cell fell into silence. Mark read over the list of charges and then put it down on the wooden bed next to him and turned his eyes to Councilman Javesi. For a long moment, they just stared at each other. Mark, mostly out of pettiness, refused to be the first to speak, and finally, Andre broke the silence.

"It's a long and damning list"—he pointed at the paper—"and no possibility of parole either. I'm afraid there isn't much that can be done. Of course, in light of your friendship with my son, I would be willing to make some calls, to see what I could do."

Mark smirked. "With strings attached."

Andre responded with a smirk of his own. "There are always strings attached, young man, to everything in life."

"Like baiting my master by arresting me. I sure hope you know what you're doing by pulling on that string. I recommend sleeping with one eye open at night. Maybe two."

Andre's expression hardened, and he gave Mark a curt nod. "Clearly, we won't reach an agreement. But who knows—maybe in a couple years you'll be more amenable. Warden, we're done here."

Andre left the room first, and as Special Officer Vory turned toward the door, Mark called out to her. "Officer Vory, a moment."

Pausing, she turned and looked at Mark, her face impassive.

"I would like to sincerely request, for your sake, that you think hard about what you're doing. The special office is a branch of the military tribunal, which is itself part of the military. The code of the military is, and will forever be, 'For glory, for humanity.' Be sure that that is the code you operate by. Because if it is not, there will come a day when those words will be carved into your bones."

The special officer's expression tightened, and though it was subtle, Mark saw her fist clench. Without a word, she turned and stalked out, and the warden and two large guards came in.

"You're awfully young to have committed all those crimes. But there they are, black and white," the warden said. "We'll escort you to your new home, but first we've got to get you fitted. After all, we can't have you down there slinging your abilities around."

Taking Mark from the cell, they dragged him to a laboratory, and after they ran a number of tests, pairs of custom-made bracelets and anklets were fastened around Mark's limbs. Each had a sharp needle that pierced into Mark's body, continually pulling mana from him, which caused the mana in his body to move erratically. This was intended to prevent his abilities from being activated, making it easier to keep him contained. As soon as the first needle slid into his skin, he felt a sharp weakness filling his body, and his thoughts began to grow muddled.

Pulling him out of the room, the two guards half carried him down a long flight of stairs, then took an elevator even farther down. By this time, Mark was completely disoriented by the chaotic mana flowing through his body. He had a vague impression of loud shouts and the rattling of bars as they hauled him down a dark passage and threw him into an empty cell. As the door banged shut behind him, Mark groaned and tried to roll over. His thoughts were chaotic, a jumbled mess, and he seemed unable to hold anything in mind for more than a few seconds. Before he could gather himself, the faint light squeezing into the cell winked out, and Mark's mind went with it, plunging into an abyss of endless darkness.

To be continued . . .